Eliza

Best wishes

Jak Lore

M000304486

THE LAST DEMON HUNTER

Jak Lore

Published by Mythic Legends Publishing Inc.
2014

Copyright © 2013 by Jak Lore

All rights reserved. This book or any portion thereof may not be reproduced or used in any manner whatsoever without the express written permission of the publisher except for the use of brief quotations in a book review or scholarly journal.

First Printing: 2013

ISBN 978-0-692-26941-1

Mythic Legends Publishing Inc.
Elmwood Park, IL 60707

www.mythiclegends.com

This book is a work of fiction. The characters, incidents and dialogues are products of the author's imagination and are not to be construed as real. Any resemblance to places or real people, living or dead, is coincidental or used in a fictitious way.

Cover Art by Manthos Lappas and Shir Dahan

All rights reserved.

Acknowledgements

I would like to dedicate this page to those that have helped me and stuck with me throughout the writing process. From simply being patient while this book was written and edited into what it is, encouraging me and keeping me motivated, and helping me with various fact checks. To you who helped me and helped keep me on track, I thank you; my parents, Eufemio, Derek, Rubi, and the various members of the CPD that were patient enough to answer my questions. To all of you, I thank you.

I would also like to thank the cover artist, Shir Dahan, as she worked hard and helped me get the cover just right. Her help was invaluable in the creation of this cover and I thank her deeply for her patience and help.

PROLOGUE

A legion of armed angels whisked across the sacred ground. Wicked barbed chains, each equipped with a different vicious head, ripped through the legion, darkening the sacred ground with their blood. The many chains pulled back and danced around the dark and slick body of jagged metal before lashing out again. Serrated and metallic, his body a living weapon towering over the host of angels. This was War.

The ground shook beneath the massive girth of the second. Fire and lightning bounced off his bloated form. He opened his toothy maw and inhaled, uprooting trees and stone. The legions of angels before him were powerless against the powerful suction. Ripped from the ground and pulled from the sky, they were swallowed whole as if they were small bits of chocolate. A powerful belch knocked down an advancing battalion of angels. The ground shook as he advanced. This was Famine.

A black, unstable form washed over legions of angels, wrecking them with crippling disease and pain. Their skin cracked and their pours bled. They cried out as from the being's crimson maw spewed vomit that burned like acid, stripping away the angels' skin and destroying their armors. This was Pestilence.

A form cloaked in darkness slowly advanced amidst the chaos of battle. All around him the army of Heaven battled his brethren. Bleach washed bone peered from the tattered cloak. Each step of his boned foot saw to the death and decay of the grass and flowers underfoot. Angel after angel rushed forward, weapons drawn and elements raging, but all fell to his malignant aura. Not a bony finger was laid upon them. No attack harmed him. Neither fire nor ice slowed his advance. None may deny the Fourth his presence. All around him fell to ruin and decay. This was Death.

Death stood before the Pearly Gates. Before him were seven angels; the Great Archangels. Each baring their weapons and draped in their armor of war. They were prepared to release all their unbridled fury upon this trespasser. If need be, they were prepared to lay down their lives. A scythe wielding red-head wearing red armor led the charge. Her gleaming white scythe struck true, but each strike merely passed harmlessly though the skulled shadow. Upon its head her final strike landed, but Death remained unmoving. Nary a hint of harm lain upon his form. The angel's eyes filled with dread as Death's mouth slowly opened.

A flash of light saw to the archangels' defeat. Their forms laid smoking and singed at Death's feet. All the Heavenly Legions lay defeated. The four destructive forces stood before the gates of golden bars and pearl hinges. The chains of War ripped from his body and wrapped around the heavenly bars. With a grunt of exertion, he pulled the proud and pure gates from their hinges. Like refuse, they were tossed aside. Beyond the rising smoke a lone figure advanced. Gleaming scimitar grasped in his right hand and dagger in his left. The destructive forces towered over the young man that stood in their path. He was small compared to them. His short dark hair flowed in the turbulent breeze. His brown eyes stared back at them unafraid. A brown leather trench coat was draped over his powerful body and fluttered in the air. In a firm voice, holding his weapons tightly, he shouted, "You shall not pass!"

***

An alarm sounded, rousing Rebecca from her sleep in a start. Sweat covered her body and her breathing was deep and short. Never had she seen such horrifying creatures. They were the Four Horsemen of the Apocalypse, of that she was certain. The man that stood before them; just who was he? Why were they all at Heaven's Gates?

CHAPTER I

The bitter cold January winds bit at Rebecca as she stood on the school bus corner. Though she was a high school senior, she didn't have a car like most other seniors in her class. Her parents didn't believe that just because she turned sixteen and earned her driver's license that she deserved to be bought a car of any type. That was fine with Rebecca. If she needed it and it was available, her parents let her use their car as much as she liked, so it wasn't that bad in her opinion. Her peers disagreed, but she didn't care. It just meant getting a ride or taking the bus. Today she was stuck on the bus because she couldn't get a ride from anyone and she decided it was far too cold to walk.

Rebecca was by no means tall, barely reaching five foot four. She accepted herself at five foot three. Locks of her golden blonde hair peeked out of the hood of her heavy purple winter coat. Pink earmuffs helped protect her ears from the bitter cold and green mittens helped keep her hands warm. Forced to wear a skirt as part of the school uniform, even in winter, her legs were always getting the worst part of the cold winds. Her blue snow boots didn't help too much either, even though they rose to her shins. There wasn't even any snow on the ground, though the forecast called for a blizzard. She never believed what the weatherman said, though. There wasn't a cloud in the sky. Yes, it was a typical Chicago January, cold with no snow. She knew when the blizzard finally did hit the city would most likely be buried. That's the way it was every year.

Rebecca closed her deep blue eyes as the wind picked up and nipped at her face. Only when the wind blew did she notice the cold. Her body may have been standing on a cold corner, but her mind was stuck elsewhere, wrapped around fear. She couldn't stop thinking about that dream. She had had nightmares before, but never like that. She had never dreamed about those four massive, destructive forces before, but somehow she knew them.

They terrified her. Rebecca couldn't help but think that they were only showing a fraction of their power and even then, Heaven's angels could not stand against them. Then there was the man with the scimitar. He, Rebecca knew, almost intimately. Who he was, she didn't know. Even though Rebecca had been dreaming about him since she was a little girl, she didn't know his name. In the dreams, there was just never a need to exchange it. She knew him, trusted him. That's all that mattered.

The roar of War echoed in Rebecca's head. She flinched and her stomach dropped. She shook her head. "Snap out of it girl," she said to herself. "It was only a dream; a horrifyingly scary nightmare, but still just a dream." She unzipped her coat a little, revealing an old golden cross draped around her neck. She touched it and it soothed her. She recited the hymn, "The bearer of this cross is protected by an angel's love." It was usually enough to soothe her fears and worries. It was incredibly old, passed down through generations, along with the hymn. It was the only heirloom her family kept. Unfortunately, it did little to chase away the nightmarish figures.

The roar of the approaching bus helped to draw Rebecca back to the present, something she was thankful for. She didn't want to continue thinking about the nightmare. She zipped her coat back up.

"Stuck on the bus today, eh?" the bus driver stated as Rebecca boarded.

"Yeah," Rebecca replied. "All this week it looks like."

Rebecca walked towards the back of the empty bus. Being the first stop of the driver's rounds gave her first choice of seats. She sat all the way in the back and stared out the window, trying consciously to not think about her dream. Instead, she tried to focus on the day. Normally, Rebecca didn't like taking the bus to school, but she knew this week wouldn't be so bad. Her boyfriend, Michael, would take it too, as well as two of her closest friends, Heather and Monica. Neither Heather nor Monica had a car to drive. Monica's parents held the same beliefs as Rebecca's, that becoming sixteen did not entitle her to a car. Heather's parents promised her a car as a graduation gift, which meant another year of walking and bus riding. Heather and Monica were only juniors after all.

THE LAST DEMON HUNTER

Michael was what Rebecca's parents would have called pampered. He had always received a healthy allowance, spent two of his four years on the football team as captain, given a brand-new car when he received his driver's license, was bought the best clothes and gadgets, and even dated a cheerleader. Even Rebecca thought he was stuck up when they first met. Michael, however, was smitten with Rebecca and worked hard to change her mind about him. Once she showed interest, Michael promptly dumped his cheerleader girlfriend, much to her angst, so he would be available for Rebecca and she would have no excuse not to give him at least lunch. Rebecca found herself very thankful for that lunch almost two years ago. Michael found himself on the bus because his car was at the mechanic's so they could take care of a knocking it was making. He could find a ride, but not one that would take Rebecca as well. Not wanting to be without her at his side, he promised to ride the bus with her until his car was fixed. Then they could ride together again.

As the bus approached the second stop, Rebecca looked out the window. As usual, no one was there. Usually, almost always, that stop was empty. In her four years of high school people were seldom at that stop, but every once in a great while someone would be standing there, waiting. As the bus pulled away Rebecca smiled and lightly laughed as she remembered the time the driver left someone there. He was so used to nobody ever being there that he didn't even bother stopping, not noticing that somebody was waiting. It was a couple of days before the principal found out and it almost cost the driver a week's suspension. Even the student that was left behind said it was an honest mistake and he wasn't angry about it. As the bus turned the next corner to continue its rounds, Rebecca saw a young man standing off the corner staring at the bus. He stood a few inches less than six feet and looked strong. A black shirt hugged his muscled body and a pair of black jeans covered his legs. The only protection from the cold he had was an old dirty brown trench coat hung open, whipping about in the wind. His hair was dark and cut short and his brown eyes were haunting. But more than that, Rebecca knew him. She had seen him many times in the past, more times than she could count. This was the man with the scimitar.

Rebecca's heart began to race and she began to sweat. Her stomach knotted and her lips trembled. As the man turned to walk away, she could see the sheathed sword strapped to his back. She knew what she was seeing was impossible, yet there he was. The very man from her dreams, sword and all. She rubbed her frightened eyes to take a second look, but the man was already out of view. She sat back into her seat when her breath had completely fogged up the window. Gripped with terror, her breathing was deep and shallow.

"Calm down," Rebecca whispered to herself. "Just calm down. There has to be a reasonable explanation for this, right? Of course there is. Coincidence, that's all. He just looks like that guy. That's all it is, a coincidence. It's coincidence that he's carrying a sword too, right? No, that was probably just my imagination. Who in their right mind would walk around with a sword?"

"Are you okay back there?" the driver called back. "You look like you saw a ghost."

"N-No, I'm fine. Thank you, but I'm okay."

"Are you sure?"

"Yeah, I'm fine. Don't worry."

"Well, if you say so."

Rebecca caressed the old cross and managed to calm herself down some by the time the bus made it to the next stop. She had to be by that stop, her friends and Michael boarded there. She didn't want them to know that something was wrong or that she was scared out of her mind. About seven or eight people, besides her friends, boarded at that stop. Monica boarded first, followed by Heather. Michael took up the rear of the group and the three moved towards the back of the bus.

Rebecca was the shortest of her group of friends, but it wasn't by much. Michael was only a few inches taller than she was, while Monica and Heather stood somewhere between the two of them. Michael had dark brown hair that, at Rebecca's behest, he kept cut short—she hated how he was always pulling it out of his warm coffee brown eyes. He wore his Letterman jacket almost religiously since he had gotten it. He wore his patches proudly from both football and track, which were etched in large letters on the back. He almost never wore boots, but without snow that really didn't make a difference. He never wore gloves either and when he thought Rebecca wasn't looking, he buried his hands in his pockets for warmth. She thought it was cute, but she wished he didn't always try to act so tough. If he was cold, he was cold.

Monica had long, thick black hair which she kept down. Her eyes were a deep black. She wore a thick brown winter coat that came down to her ankles to help shield her legs from the cold winds. Even in high snow she didn't wear snow boots and always wore her favorite style of sneakers. Currently that was a black low-top with a tan stripe on either side. Heather had short light brown hair, about shoulder length, with matching eyes. She kept her hair pulled back in a simple ponytail. Her coat was similar to Monica's but was light blue. She wore the same brand of snow boots and mittens as Rebecca, each matching her coat, but in slightly darker hues.

Monica and Heather found their seats across from Rebecca, but someone had beaten Michael to his seat beside her. The screech of music could be heard from the boy's two piece headset. Michael pulled one free and said, "Uh-uh. Move."

The boy, probably only a sophomore by his looks, stared back up at Michael. "There are plenty of other seats," he said.

"That's my seat. Move or I move you."

The boy looked angrily at Michael, then at Rebecca. She gave him a look and shrug that said move. Reluctantly, he moved. Michael sat beside Rebecca with a smile. "Sorry about that," he said.

Rebecca smiled back. "It's okay. He didn't know."

Michael kissed her cheek. "I missed you at the match Saturday," he said.

"I'm sorry Mikey," Rebecca cooed, trying to hide her fear. Talking to him always seemed to help calm her down, especially when her cross failed. "You know how Leonato is. No late work. I had to finish that essay or fail English. I procrastinated too much. I'm sorry. I'll make it up to you, I promise."

"I knew you had a good reason. It's okay." He kissed her again. Rebecca knew his world revolved around her. He was always so patient and forgiving with her. She found this so very endearing, especially the fact that only she was allowed to call him Mikey, a nickname, until she had spoken it, he had always hated.

"Did you win?" Rebecca asked.

"I placed third. You know that one move I've been practicing? I almost lost the staff. It didn't end up being too bad, but I was forced to change the routine to recover. I'm not sure how much it cost me. I guess I needed more practice."

Rebecca smiled and gave him a peck on the lips, something she did rarely in public. They had only French kissed a handful of times before. Such kisses were treats Michael savored. "You'll do better next time."

Rebecca turned to address her friends. She hoped that they would have some information that could calm her beating heart. "Hey, Monica?"

"Yeah?" Monica answered.

"Um, do you know if anyone new moved into the neighborhood?"

"I have no idea. Why?"

That wasn't the answer Rebecca was looking for and she continued without thinking. "Well, I saw someone at the last stop. I've never seen him before, so I thought maybe he was a new student or something."

"The driver missed a passenger huh?" Monica laughed. "Sorry, I don't keep track of things like that." She slightly giggled at a thought. "But I bet Melissa would know. It's kind of like her hobby, after all. That little information broker; I'm sure she'd cut you a pretty good deal."

Heather and Michael laughed with Monica. Rebecca tried to laugh with them, but her laugh was weak. For her, this was serious. She just wanted some assurance that what she saw wasn't what she saw. Michael noticed her weak laughter, but assumed it was from embarrassment. He decided to tease her a little about it.

"I didn't know you were a member of the welcome wagon," Michael teased. "Are you going to bake cookies that spell out, 'WELCOME'? Can I help?"

They laughed while Rebecca began to blush red. Her urge to defend herself was overwhelming and she didn't think. "No, it's just that he kind of creeped me out." Rebecca knew immediately that the statement was a mistake. Michael bit his lip in embarrassment and regret. Heather looked away to hide her surprised and concerned face. Monica just stared at Rebecca for a moment.

"Well," Monica finally said, "Melissa can probably find out anything that you need to know about him."

Michael saw Rebecca's hand go to where her cross would lay beneath her jacket. He knew then that something was bothering her. She only played with her cross when something weighed heavy on her mind. He took her hand into his own. "Hey, I'm sorry. I didn't know there was something weird with the guy."

"What was wrong with him?" Heather asked.

"Yeah," Michael added. "What was so creepy about him? Did he do something? Are you okay?"

Rebecca knew she had cornered herself, but she also knew she couldn't tell them what was really wrong. She was still struggling with the fact that she had seen what she believed she had seen. Telling her friends that she had witnessed a man she had been dreaming about since she was a child was simply unacceptable. How would Michael take that? Still, she had to tell them something. "Well," Rebecca began, embarrassed about what she was about to say. She could not tell them about the sword, could she? No, that may get Jason's father involved. She wasn't even sure she actually saw it and that it wasn't just her imagination. "He was just standing there in the cold, with his jacket wide open like it was the middle of spring." Though this was true, it wasn't her real concern. She decided this half-truth would suffice for now.

"That's it?" Heather asked in disbelief.

"Yeah," Michael added. "That does seem weird, but not enough to be freaked out by. Maybe he likes the cold."

Rebecca was silent in embarrassment at lying so blatantly to her friends before finally saying, "It was just...so...unnatural. Something about him just worries me—I guess."

"Well," Monica began. "Melissa will let you know if you should be worried about this guy."

Rebecca nodded. "Yeah, I guess you're right." She did not want this conversation to continue. "It's not really that big of a deal though, you know? How about we change the subject?"

Monica curled her lips into a half grin. "Sure, why not?" Though her response was sarcastic, much to Rebecca's relief the subject was changed and they chatted about more normal things during the rest of the trip to school. Upon arriving they waved their good-byes to each other and went their own separate ways. They each had their own responsibilities to attend to before the first bell. It was their first day back from Christmas Break. Michael stole a kiss from Rebecca before heading to his locker. "Hey," he said. "Don't worry about it. I'm sure it's nothing, but—if there's something wrong, please tell me."

Rebecca smiled at him. "There's nothing wrong, but if something does happen, you'll be the first to know."

"Alright. Don't forget, I'm always there for you. Don't hesitate to call me."

"I won't." She kissed him once more, on the cheek since they were in public, before heading on her way.

Michael slipped his key into the lock on his locker. He always had trouble remembering the combination to a combination lock, so instead he kept a key lock on his locker. Gym had always been interesting. He was worried as he opened the door and slipped his bag off his shoulder. Rebecca only touched her cross when something was really bothering her. He could never understand how a person could put so much faith in a symbol, or anything for that matter. He knew how old the cross was though and usually lent it to the fact that so many hands had touched it. He supposed that if he had something that old and important, it would lend him comfort too. As he put his jacket away and prepared for his first class his friend Jason rounded the corner and called out to him. Jason was about the same size and height as Michael, but had a little more bulk to his body. He had short blonde hair, which contrasted greatly with his dark eyes. He was trying to grow a mustache, but wasn't having much luck as he only had peach fuzz as a senior. It didn't help the fact that what hair he did have on his face was barely visible because of its light color. He was wearing his old football jersey from earlier in the year. He usually got to school early and spent anywhere from half an hour to an hour in the school weight room before school began. Like everyone else, he hated the uniform rule and used his weight training as an excuse to walk around school during the early morning out of uniform. It helped that his first class was gym too. The jersey was red and blue, the schools' home colors, with the phrase CRAGOFF across the back of his shoulders and the number 73 centered in large font on the back.

"Hey Jas," Michael greeted as he traded books between his backpack and locker. "What's up?"

"Not much," Jason replied. "Just finished working out. You?"

Michael chuckled. Jason was training to be a cop after graduating. Maybe he could shine some light on the subject or at the very least poke enough fun at it to ease his mind. "Funny thing happened, actually. Some guy managed to freak Rebecca out. She saw him while she was on the bus. It sounded like he was just walking down the street, minding his own business."

"He freaked her out, huh? Must've been some butt ugly dude."

The two friends laughed. "I guess so. I didn't think about that. I don't know though."

"What else could it be? I mean, the only person that hates her is Sarah."

Michael laughed. "Yeah, that's true. She's her only enemy isn't she? By the way, how's the mustache coming?"

Jason rubbed his upper lip. "Not too good. I'm thinking about quitting. It's just refusing to come in."

Michael closed his locker door and swung his backpack over his shoulder. "You do know you have to shave so the hair will grow in thicker, right?"

"Uh…yeah, I knew that."

"Sure you did," Michael laughed.

"Yeah, I think I'll shave tonight then."

"Unless you like looking goofy."

"What, you mean like you?" Jason ruffled Michael's hair. "You loved that goofy hair of yours until Rebecca made you cut it."

"Yeah, whatever. Hey, you decided if you're going to college or the army to get into the force?"

"Not sure. My dad is saying try the army. We're not at war or anything. I have time to decide. I can't even take the test until I'm twenty-one anyway."

"Must be nice to know where your future leads."

"It just takes some planning. We graduate this year. What are you planning on doing?"

"I never really thought about it. My padre's want me to go to college, so I guess I'll give that a try. Won't be hard to get a scholarship; I'm a good quarterback."

Jason looked at the clock jutting out of the wall. "Bell will ring soon. I should get going. Later Riviera."

Monica walked into the cafeteria and surveyed the room. She was pretty sure she could find Melissa somewhere in that noise filled room. Rebecca didn't really ask her to have Melissa find out anything. Rebecca wanted to drop the subject, but Monica's curiosity was lit. Besides, it seemed to bother Rebecca so at the very least Melissa would say that there was nothing to worry about and that she was being childish. Also, it was a good excuse to hunt down a friend she hadn't seen in awhile.

Monica thought Melissa always liked to hang out in the cafeteria before school because that's where everyone conjugated before the first bell. Between a place to have breakfast and do last minute homework, it was full of gossip; though Monica never knew how Melissa was able to hear anything in the tangled mass of words and laughter. Still, she guessed it was the perfect place to gather information on the goings on in the school and the lives of the students.

After a few minutes Monica finally spotted Melissa alone off to the side with a book in hand and munching on a bag of chips. Melissa was about Monica's size, but with a toner physique. Her auburn hair was shoulder length and tied in a short braid. Her backpack was resting on the table. Though her green eyes were focused on the book in front of her, Monica was sure her ears and attention were focused elsewhere. Monica joined Melissa at her table, drawing her friend's attention as she did so.

Melissa smiled as she put her book down. "My! A visitor! To what do I owe the honor?"

"Hi, Melissa," Monica replied.

"Monica, I don't think I've seen you since the summer. How are you?"

"Has it been that long? We don't have any of the same classes this year, do we?"

Melissa shook her head before lifting her can of pop to her lips for a drink. "No, we don't. I was so busy during the start of the year that you all stopped inviting me out too." She held out her bag of potato chips. "Chips?"

"No thanks. I don't care for sour cream and onions."

Melissa shrugged. "Suit yourself. So, something tells me you didn't come by just to say hi."

Monica blushed. "I guess I seem kind of callous now, but yeah."

"So what's up?"

"You're pretty good at finding things out about people, right?"

"So they tell me," Melissa replied nonchalantly as she popped a chip in her mouth. "Who do you need to know about?"

"Would you be able to find out if someone new is in town?"

"People move in and out all the time. You got a name?"

"No. Rebecca saw someone today on the way to school. I guess he freaked her out. No idea why. I don't really know the whole story."

Melissa laughed. "Wait, wait! Back up one second. Someone freaked Rebecca out? Little Miss Doesn't Surprise? The only one that ever managed to do that was Michael. And that was only after dumping Miss Perfect Cheerleader."

Monica had to keep from bursting out laughing. "Oh yeah, I remember that. Sarah was so mad."

"Are you kidding? The slut is still mad. Sarah would put out for Michael, but Rebecca won't and she keeps throwing that in Michael's face trying to get him back. From my standpoint, that little difference makes all the difference to him."

"Michael doesn't complain about it. He must really like her."

"You know what I think personally?"

"What do you think?"

"Seriously, this is just between you and me. Don't tell anyone else, especially Rebecca."

Monica leaned in closer with a smile. "Am I about to hear some juicy gossip?"

"Just my opinion and only between us."

"Okay, I promise. My lips are sealed."

"I think Michael's big thing is Rebecca is different. She's not like what he's used to. Rebecca doesn't do half of the things Sarah did and what little Michael can get out of her he has to work for. It's not just, 'Let's make out.' and then they make out for three or four hours."

"It's not like they've never done that. Rebecca's admitted they've made out before."

"It took Michael almost a year to get to first base. Most guys would have called it quits after a couple weeks. I don't think they do it very often and I doubt Michael is anywhere near second base. And that doesn't seem to bother him. With Rebecca, all of that means something to him. It's not just a given. You have to admit, the boy is spoiled, which you can't tell when he's with her. She made him a straight arrow, like her." Melissa laughed. "I really wouldn't be surprised if in a couple years we get invitations to their wedding."

"You think it'll be that serious? Are you sure? Michael's been around the block a few times, right? He's all Rebecca has ever known."

"And when you have something good you don't let it go. But who knows, right? What about this other guy she saw? I mean do you know anything about him?"

"He likes the cold? I really don't know anything else."

"That is definitely not much to go on, but this could be fun. Just give me a couple of days and if there's someone new in town, I'll find out. Like you said, it's what I'm good at."

Monica laughed. "Thanks Melissa. You should hang out with us this weekend, if you're not too busy. It's been awhile. We can all catch up."

"Yeah, that sounds like a plan. Oh and one more thing. If you tell anyone what I said, I'll let everyone know you still wet the bed."

Monica's eyes widened in shock. "How do you know that?"

Melissa just smiled in response as she popped another chip into her mouth.

Heather walked down the hall on the second floor of the school. The halls weren't empty, but they weren't full enough to warrant weaving around a crowd. There were about fifteen rooms on each side of the hall, beginning with room 201 and zigzagging up the hallway, odds on the right side, evens on the left. Heather was heading for room 209, her biology class, to see her teacher, Samuel Santano. She peeked through the glass window of the classroom to see him sitting at his desk, which was full of several piles of paper. Santano measured in at six feet, perhaps slightly over, with a large frame that nearly made him menacing when he stood. He had a thin beard and mustache that was graying with age, as was the brown hair on his head. His brown eyes had grown very pale, even for a man nearing fifty. Santano often wore some kind of suit to school that varied from day-to-day. Today's was grey.

"Mr. Santano?" Heather asked as she knocked on the door and came into the room.

Santano stopped what he was doing, looked up from his desk, smiled and said, "Ms. Lusha, what can I do for you?"

"I was absent the Thursday before vacation, when you gave the Chapter Thirteen test. You weren't here on Friday and I never had a chance to make it up. I'd like to know when I can."

"Well, let's see. As you can see by these piles of paper on my desk, I got behind on grading over break, so I was just going to spend the day grading these papers, most of which happen to be the test. If at all possible, today would be a great day to make up the test."

Heather smiled. It seemed fate smiled down on her. "Yes! I was really hoping to take it today. I studied over break, just in case."

"That was very good planning. You're always prepared Heather, that's a good trait."

"Okay, fourth period today."

"Correct. I'll have a copy of the test ready for you."

"Thank you, Mr. Santano."

"My pleasure. If you could, please close the door on your way out. The hall noise distracts me."

"Sure. I'll see you fourth period."

Heather closed the door behind her. Santano glanced down at the paper he was grading when he clenched his chest. It hurt. "Not again," he moaned. He rifled through his pocket for a small vial. Nitro. He tapped on the bottle until a tiny pill fell out and placed it under his tongue. Hopefully one would be enough to calm his chest pain.

The bell rang as Rebecca walked out of the library with a book in hand. She needed the book for her history project. She thought she could find some good information inside of it, but as she headed to her history class she began to wonder exactly what she thought she could find on the economy of Feudal Japan from a book entitled The Tale of the Samurai.

When Rebecca arrived in class everyone had already broken into their groups. On the board was written,

WORK ON PROJECT

WITH YOUR GROUP

Rebecca's friend, Glenda, noticed her first and waved her over. Glenda was a couple inches taller than Rebecca. Whenever asked, Glenda would proudly proclaim that she was five foot six inches even, which was tall for a Mexican woman. Her mother was only about five foot one. Her long raven hair was pulled back into a ponytail which sharply exposed her exotic face. With both of her parents hailing from Mexico she was one hundred percent and proud of that fact. Despite being born and raised in Chicago she spoke both English and Spanish fluently, which Rebecca could find aggravating at times. Glenda had a habit of switching languages without warning mid-sentence. Having known each other since the seventh grade, when Glenda moved into the district, Rebecca had managed to learn some basic Spanish. Strangely, Glenda only had a Spanish accent when she spoke Spanish.

Rebecca took her seat beside Glenda and Austin and laid the book on the desk. Austin was barely taller than Rebecca. His dull blonde hair was cut incredibly short and his blue eyes were a light shade. Though not fat, he was a little on the heavier side.

"What ya got?" Brian asked as he reached for Rebecca's book. He was the tallest of the group, but only by a few inches. He worked out regularly and his body showed that fact. His dark hair was short, but not as short as Austin's. His light brown eyes skimmed through the book. "Uh, Rebecca?" Brian said. "Weren't you supposed to research the economy?"

"Yeah, sorry," Rebecca said. "I —"

"No problem!" Austin gleamed. "Military was mine and well..."

"You didn't get anything, did ya?" Glenda asked.

"No, but I can do the currency since she got the military."

"But won't you just forget to research that too?" Brian asked. "Besides, it's not just currency; it's the whole economic system of the time."

"Well, that's just it…I, uh…have all that information…at home; the currency too."

"You have all the economy information?" Rebecca asked. "Why didn't you tell us?"

"When Ms. Dale assigned the project points, I was going to ask you to trade, but I never got the chance. She did it last minute, you know?"

"How did you come into all the information?"

"Yeah, that's a funny story actually."

Brian drummed his fingers on his desk. "Well, we're listening."

"Well, you see, the thing is, I've always had a fascination with Feudal Japan. My dad was in the Navy and when I was a kid he talked about Japan a lot. He was always going on and on about its culture, its architecture, and its food. He really likes Japanese food. My mom had to learn how to make it." Austin laughed.

"What's your point?"

"Well, he still goes there for a week or two about once a year. Sometimes my mom goes too, but she doesn't really like it there. I've been there a couple times too and I think it's fun."

"What do your vacations have to do with our project?"

"When I was about six or seven, we went sightseeing in Japan. I found a koban."

"What's a koban?"

"It's Feudal Japan currency from the Edo era. The thing was huge. Been fascinated by the stuff ever since and I've managed to build a huge collection."

"Espera," Glenda started, motioning stop with her hands. "¿Quieres decirnos that because of your hobby you have this project already almost done? Tengo razón?"

Austin nodded sheepishly.

"I understood the important part," Brian said. "You have the project half done. So, were you just going to keep that to yourself? While we ran around trying to get all this information, you just sat at home and laughed at us, didn't you?"

"Eso es. Brian, hit him for me, ¿Por fa?"

Brian popped his knuckles with a grin. "This should be fun."

"Hey, I'm sorry," Austin defended. "My cousins would always tease me about the 'chunks of metal' I collected. So I just never bother talking about it."

Glenda threw her hands up as she sank back into her chair. "¡Dios mio!" She exclaimed. "¡Este muchacho es un idiota!"

"I'm not sure what you just said, but the idiot part sounds about right," Brian said.

"Austin, you should have told us," Rebecca said. "We're your friends. You should have known we wouldn't have laughed at you. It would have actually saved us a lot of time."

"Yeah, I know," Austin said. "Like I said though, I was going to try to trade with you. I thought that would just be easier."

"Maybe, but it would have been better if you just said from the start—"

"Hold on a second Rebecca," Glenda started with a sly smile. "Let's not forget about your stunt our little blue-eyed blonde friend."

Rebecca turned to Glenda. "What do you mean, 'my stunt'?"

"Like most girls with that golden hair, I guess numbers are just a little too difficult for you, so you looked up the macho man of the era. And here I thought you were different."

Catching the joke, Brian and Austin started to laugh. Rebecca flushed red in embarrassment and frustration. Because they were usually blonde jokes, she did not like being the butt of any joke.

"That is not why I got that book," Rebecca defended.

"Then why?" Glenda asked with a grin.

"I have a lot on my mind today, okay? I just grabbed the wrong book."

"I bet you did," Brian said as he leafed through the book a second time. "I think it was the rippling muscles and long hair."

Austin grabbed the book. "Dude, look at these guys. They're huge."

"Oh Mr. Samurai," Glenda taunted in her best damsel in distress mock, "I am but a poor helpless maiden. Will you please protect me?"

The three burst out laughing, but Rebecca crossed her arms and pouted. "I hate blonde jokes. They are so not funny."

Between gasps Glenda managed to say, "Claro que sí ellos son, if you're not blonde."

Rebecca sat nearly fuming. Suddenly, a sharp pain ripped through her head. It forced a sudden yelp from her lips as she clutched her head. The instant she closed her eyes she saw the man from her dream, the same man from that morning, waving back and forth as he laughed maniacally. However, his skin was gray and his hair ghostly white. His eyes were almost as deep a blue as hers. Around him everything was ablaze. Her heart sank and she nearly jumped out of her seat.

"What's wrong?" Brian asked. "You look like you saw a ghost."

"What?" Rebecca asked, still trying to regain her senses and calm her racing heart. "No, just—just a slight headache."

"What a convenient time," Glenda said. "Ah, it's just as well. Tenemos que empezar working on the project anyway. Bueno, let's see what that samurai book has in it, besides the manly pictures of course."

Brian and Austin joined in Glenda's laugh, but Rebecca only gave a weak, halfhearted smile. The day had begun so strangely, and unfortunately, it was only becoming stranger by the minute. Rebecca had managed to calm herself, but she was unable to keep herself focused. For the most part Glenda, Brian, and Austin didn't notice. Rebecca was thankful when the bell finally rang. The sound of murmured discussions was quickly replaced with the screeching of desks as they were moved back into place as quickly as students could manage so they could get to their next class.

"I'll see you guys tomorrow," Rebecca said to her friends as they left the class.

"Yeah," Brian said. "Don't day dream too much about those samurai."

Austin and Glenda laughed. "Alright, I'll see you guys tomorrow," Austin said. "Sorry about all this Rebecca."

"It's alright," Rebecca responded. "Why don't you bring one of those 'koban' things tomorrow?"

"Will do!" Austin said as he made his way to his next class.

"Well, Becky, I should get to biology," Glenda said.

"I told you not to call me that. You know I hate it."

"Which is why it's so easy to poke fun at you." Glenda laughed. "Lighten up, Becca. I'll see you tomorrow." Glenda waved as she headed off to class.

Rebecca waved back as she made her way to English. She wasn't in a terrible rush to beat the bell. Her next class was only a few rooms away and across the hall. Really, it took no time at all to transverse the distance. As she entered the room she laid her essay paper on Leonato's desk as she and the other students had done since the beginning of the year. That was just his routine. "Come in and drop off your work," he would say. "If it's done, I shouldn't have to collect it from you." Leonato was of average build and in his thirty's. His hair was a chocolate brown with eyes to match behind thin silver rimmed glasses. Unrestricted by the students' dress code, Leonato dressed casually, as usual. Most of the students thought it was just to spite them and were happy that the dress code was not going to be in effect next year. Rebecca could relate.

Rebecca entered high school during the dress code test, which for the most part had failed. To say she was unhappy when she found out she would have to wear a school uniform would be an understatement. All throughout grade school she and other students had been able to wear whatever they pleased. Though she did not participate in the protests throughout the years, which usually ended with the students being suspended, she and many others wrote to the school board to get the uniform requirement lifted. Now, being a senior, she didn't really care anymore. Her high school career was spent in a uniform, but she was still pleased that her voice was heard and the requirement was ultimately lifted. To Rebecca, it proved that the system worked and her opinions had meaning. With that in mind, she decided it was all worth it.

Leonato was leaning against the front of his desk when the tardy bell rang. He said nothing as the students spoke amongst themselves, only looking periodically to the clock. Leonato was a strict teacher, but he had his own sets of rules. He never thought five minutes was enough time for every student to get to class, only most. After all, some students came all the way from the other side of the school. Without trying to kill themselves and running, they wouldn't make such a trip. So in order to compensate, Leonato gave every student an additional three minutes to get to his class. Of course, this did not apply for his first class of the day, only to the proceeding. After three minutes had passed, Leonato began to gather up a pile of papers. "No need to wait for the lingerers on this one," Leonato said as he handed out a bundle to the beginning of each row. "I will start grading your papers today. In the meantime, you can start working on this packet. It's extra credit, so it's not mandatory. I'll be accepting these until Friday. After that, you're out of luck. Make sure you tell any lingerers that come in, because I'm not repeating myself." Someone in the back of the room raised her hand and without missing a beat Leonato added, "No, you don't get any bonus points for making any lingerers think its mandatory and getting them to turn it in by tomorrow. Nice try though." The class broke out in laughter. It had become commonplace for the class, and Leonato, to poke fun at the students that, for whatever reason, required more than eight minutes to get to class. They were given a couple extra minutes before they were marked tardy, but the cost was some social chastising. The students were given the term "the lingerers" by one of Leonato's classes at the beginning of his teaching career. The term stuck.

The boy behind Rebecca leaned forward and whispered, "Looks like Leonato's in a good mood today, doesn't it?" Sitting, it was hard to tell that he was slightly taller than Rebecca, about five foot six or so, and was thin, but not the scrawny or wiry kind. His dark hair was short and straight, and his eyes were a dark brown. Unfortunately for him, since their sophomore year, he had been known as a male chauvinist pig. As time went on, the title bothered him little, if any at all. It was a well accepted fact by the students that any virgin dates he had were not so by the end, usually through force. Though it was only a rumor, and no one had ever admitted to dating him, it was a powerful one that had kept most of the girls away from him. Why he wasn't in jail, nobody knew and no one would ever talk about it. Rebecca didn't follow the story too much, but took Melissa's advice at the time and stayed away from him. Her advice was usually correct.

"What do you want, Nicholas?" Rebecca asked in a harsh whisper. She was almost always annoyed when he spoke to her because it was almost always to hit on her. She had only ever told Michael once. He had gone looking for Nicholas and threw him into a locker, threatening him to back off. It was during the beginning of their relationship, and though Rebecca didn't think Michael would do it again; he had changed a lot since then, she didn't want to risk them fighting over what she thought was nothing. Nicholas hit on almost all the girls.

"Can't a guy say hi?" Nicholas asked?

"Your 'hi's' always have something attached."

"Oh, don't be like that."

"I have a boyfriend, Nicholas."

"Come on, you know I don't mean anything serious. I'm not trying to steal you away or anything. I just like to talk is all, and when it's with a pretty girl I get flirty."

"Well, it makes me uncomfortable, and you know why. That's why Michael went after you. Don't make me pull him off you again."

"Man, that's not my fault. It's not true, I keep saying that. Nobody believes me and how can I prove it's not true when no one trusts me? I mean, I'm here aren't I? Doesn't that count for something? Rapists go to jail and I'm not in jail."

"That's true, but…What is it you want Nicholas? I already told you I don't want you flirting with me. I don't like it."

"Alright, fine. I want to talk to you about something serious anyway."

"Like what?"

"I need some help. I'm failing and need some tutoring."

"What does that have to do with me? I'm not a teacher."

"But you're good at math, right? I suck at it. I need someone to help me on the weekends."

"Why on the weekend?"

"I work just about every day after school. I don't really have the time during the week. I just need someone to come over for a few hours on the weekend to help me."

"I can't do something like that. Ask someone else."

"It's my rep, isn't it? Look, I already told you it's not true. Someone got mad at me and tried to make me look bad, that's all. I didn't hurt anyone. Besides, since that all calmed down, you really haven't heard anything, have you?"

"Well…no, I haven't."

"Look, you know Stacy and Marcy, right?"

"Not well. I know they don't really like you, but what does that have to do with anything?"

"Well, Stacy has been helping me in biology; I'm not doing well in there either, and Marcy has been over plenty of times to work on our history project."

"Just the two of you? The project was supposed to be at least three people."

"We have three people, but the other guy is never around. That's beside the point. There has been two girls hanging around me for a few weeks now and you haven't heard anything bad, have you?"

"No, I haven't, but you should know I can find out."

"Yeah, you know some gossipy people, don't you?"

"If you're done, will you please leave me alone?"

"At least hear me out."

"I have. I'm not interested. Please, find somebody else."

"Will you at least think about it? Please, give me a chance. I'm asking you for help here."

Rebecca was silent for a moment. "Yeah, I guess I can think about it."

"Cool! Here's my number. Let me know when you make up your mind."

Rebecca took the piece of paper Nicholas handed to her. Agreeing to think about it was a quick way to get him to shut up, but she had no plans on 'thinking about it'. She was just going to tell him she couldn't the next time he asked. She began working on the extra credit packet, though she had no need for the extra credit. Her friend Rene reached over and poked Rebecca with her pen. The brunette with streaked hair and a puffy face smiled, showing thin braces on her teeth.

"He bothering you again?" Rene asked.

"Doesn't he always?" Rebecca leaned towards her and replied. She wasn't sure if Nicholas could hear her or not. He probably could, but it didn't bother her. It's not like she bad mouthed him, though most people did.

"Why don't you just ask to be moved? I'm sure Leonato would move you?"

"The only open seat is by the AC vent. It's cold over there, even in winter. I like not wearing my coat in class."

Rene looked over to the edge of class. Most of the students either wore thick sweaters or their coats. "That thing is never off, is it? Why doesn't the school fix that stupid thing?"

"I don't know. Why don't they fix anything?"

"So the superintendent can pocket that money. That's why they don't do anything, that crook."

They laughed. Even Nicholas chortled a little. The rest of the class period was spent mainly talking to Rene, or rather, listening to Rene complain about Leonato moving Samantha to another seat for the two of them always disrupting the class. Rebecca never mentioned it, but that was exactly how Nicholas ended up in the seat behind her. Rene knew though, because every now and then she would apologize whenever she repeated her complaint.

The bell rang and the class dispersed. Rebecca and Rene waited for Samantha. Unlike Rebecca and Rene, Samantha needed the extra credit and worked tirelessly on it during class, not even realizing that the period was over. Standing, both were about half a head taller than Rebecca. Most of her friends were taller and it made her feel like a shrimp. Most everyone in her family was taller than her, so Rebecca thought she just received that elusive short gene. Samantha's strawberry blonde hair was curly and wrapped around her oval face like a wiry frame. It centered her bright green eyes nicely and brought attention away from a slightly crooked nose. After having it broken a few years ago by a softball, it didn't heal right and had a slight slant to it. Samantha hated it and wanted nose surgery to fix it, but unless someone really looked, it really wasn't noticeable. Rebecca thought she just over exaggerates the whole thing. After the bandage came off, she got more attention from boys. Apparently, and Rebecca had pointed that out to her a few times, guys liked her new nose.

Rebecca walked with them until her locker. She stopped to change books for her next class. Samantha and Rene stayed with her, talking about their winter vacation and Christmas until Rebecca had her books changed out. They parted ways from there. Samantha and Rene went to have lunch while Rebecca went to math class. As Nicholas had said, Rebecca was good at math. She was good at everything. Except for the occasional 'B', she was a straight A student. Of all the subjects she had taken in high school, math had always been her least favorite. At least she had friends to talk to in it; Adam and Nicole.

When Rebecca entered the class, it was already about half full. Adam and Nicole were sitting beside each other when she came in. They usually were, but it was Rebecca's desk that Adam usually sat in. He didn't notice Rebecca walk up to them, even when Nicole's eyes diverted and she waved. Rebecca tapped his shoulder.

"Can I have my seat, please?" Rebecca asked.

"Oh, sure," Adam replied. He left her seat and allowed her to sit before squatting on the floor between them, resting his arms on Nicole's desk. The cycle was repeating, almost customary, day in and day out. Rebecca would come in to find Adam in her seat, he would move to allow her to sit then squat between them waiting for class to begin before taking his seat; unless their teacher, Mr. Spencer, said otherwise.

When standing, both Adam and Nicole stood about the same height, about an inch or so above Rebecca, but that was as far as their similarities went. Adam had short brown hair and light brown eyes, a serene, yet intimidating face, especially when he needed it. At times, he could be very intimidating, but would never hurt a fly. Nicole, on the other hand, had long, black, silky hair and eyes almost as dark. Her skin was fair and her face seemed to belong to a girl younger than she really was. If she was pushed, she had no problem pushing back. Adam liked hard rock and heavy metal, Nicole preferred the softer melody of country and jazz. Adam liked to play his video games and tabletop games. Nicole preferred to be outside. Adam more childish, Nicole more mature. They were as different as night and day, and when Rebecca introduced them about a year ago, she had never thought they would fall for each other, or when they did that it would last, but the two had been almost inseparable.

The bell rang and Adam made his way to his seat. The couple, unfortunately, sat at opposite ends of the room. Their teacher, Mr. Spencer, spent half the class in lecture, calling on various students to solve the equations that he was teaching. Whenever he couldn't get a correct answer, he would call upon Rebecca, who almost always had the right answer. Picking up the formulas came easy to her. What she didn't like was being the fall back, the book of answers that Spencer would open when he was frustrated with everyone else's answer, or if he just wanted to move on quickly. It was seldom that Rebecca volunteered to answer anything. If she did, it was only because her patience ran out before Spencer's. After the assignment had been given Spencer left the students to work alone. He allowed talking to 'discuss the work' but only if it didn't get out of hand. Rebecca glanced at Adam. He was literally scratching his head as he stared down at the text book problems.

"He's always a little slow on the pickup, isn't he?" Nicole asked.

"I guess," Rebecca answered, turning her attention to her friend. "But he gets good grades, right?"

"Yeah, I guess. I'm just surprised how much trouble he has sometimes. Some of the games he plays, like all of them, are math heavy."

Rebecca giggled. "He gets you to play them a lot?"

"I play a few games of cards with him, he goes skating with me." Nicole shrugged. "They're fun, I guess. I actually like the game where you get to paint the models. Well, not actually the game itself. I like painting the models. That's fun."

"So things are going good with Adam?"

"They're going great. I'm so glad you introduced us."

"I really didn't think you two would click like you did. How long have you been going out anyway? Almost a year now, right?"

"It'll be a year tomorrow."

"Wow, tomorrow? So then, we've known each other for about three years then, haven't we?"

"Yep, sure have. Time flies, doesn't it?"

"Yeah, it does." Suddenly, Rebecca's stomach dropped and her heart skipped a beat. A sense of foreboding dread that she couldn't explain filled her being.

"Hey, you okay? You just shook."

"I did? Sorry, just a chill, I guess." Rebecca looked down at her text book. "Yeah, I think I'm going to try and finish this before the end of class."

"Yeah, me too. No sense bringing it home if we don't have to."

Rebecca smiled at her friend, thankful that she agreed, but in truth she just wanted to wrap her mind around something to ease away the unwanted feeling. She figured something to focus on would do that. Not having to do it at home was only a bonus.

Four bells later, the fourth period lunch bell rang. Third period was always longest because it coincided with four alternating thirty minute lunch periods. By the time the final lunch period began, Rebecca was starving, especially if she skipped breakfast like she did that morning. Afterwards, there would only be one class left to finish off the day; but first, lunch.

Adam and Nicole never appeared in a hurry to go from place to place. They usually left class last. Even with Rebecca stopping at her locker to put her books away, she was always astonished that Adam and Nicole always beat her to the lunch room. Her locker was on the way to the lunch room, theirs was not, but they were always there and in line before her. It was something that she could not explain and never bothered to ask about. They always let her cut in if they could, so Rebecca never wanted to bring up the fact that they were able to cover almost twice the distance that she could in less time. For Rebecca, it was just plain embarrassing.

Adam and Nicole hadn't gotten to the counter yet and urged Rebecca over. Despite complaints from people behind them, Rebecca cut in. Nicole would just cast a glance backwards and the complaints would cease. On the few occasions that it didn't, Adam would turn around as well. Together, the couple appeared very intimidating, despite their friendly looks. Rebecca tried to join in their conversation, but the unpleasant feeling still lingered, making it difficult to focus. They each bought their lunch and waited for one another before heading to their table. Rebecca bought her lunch, French fries with a side of ketchup, a slice of sausage pizza, a can of Coke, and a chocolate chip cookie. It may not have been the best lunch, but it would tide her over until she got home.

Rebecca walked with her friends to their usual table, furthest from the entrance by the windows. On nice days she could bask in the sunshine and admire the view of the sports fields. If she was cold and the sun was out, she would sit with her back facing the window and let the amplified heat from the glass warm her. Her childhood friend, Peter, was already saving their seats. Everyone knew they sat together, so why he had to constantly shoo people away was beyond Rebecca.

Peter was Rebecca's oldest friend. They had started as neighbors when they were five. When they were ten, he moved away, only to move back a year later. Rebecca was ecstatic to have her best friend back. Being an only child, Rebecca looked towards Peter as a brother. The only person who may have known her better than Michael, excluding her own parents, would have been Peter. They had been around the same size until seventh grade, when he suddenly went through a growth spurt. Rebecca had barely grown at all that year and hadn't grown since. Peter was tall, reaching nearly six feet in height. His body was well toned and Rebecca knew he had some power in it. He had no trouble hitting a homerun if he had a mind to when he was up at bat during baseball season. His pitches were also hard to hit, he had such a powerful arm. He had already been offered a college scholarship to play baseball. His eyes had a violet hue to them and he had his dark hair dyed blonde since sophomore year. It was beginning to fade.

Rebecca popped the can open and took a drink. She gave a silent sigh as she dipped one of her fries into the cup of ketchup. She let it sit there, unmoving. She didn't even realize that she was staring blankly at her food. Her mind was elsewhere, but she couldn't grasp what her mind was swirling around. Though Nicole was sitting next to her, she didn't notice something was on her friend's mind. She was too busy teasing Adam, rubbing her foot against his. Peter, however, noticed something was on Rebecca's mind.

"What's on your mind, Becca?" Peter asked.

Rebecca didn't answer. She didn't even acknowledge that he said anything at all.

"Hey, Becca, what's wrong?"

Still, she gave no reply.

Peter reached out and grasped her hand, pulling it to finally get her attention. "What's the matter?"

"Nothing," Rebecca said before finally eating her fry. "I was just thinking."

"About?"

She wasn't even sure what she was thinking about, but when Peter asked, Nicholas did come to mind. "Nothing really."

"If it was nothing, then how come you were in your own little world?"

Rebecca averted her eyes from his. Was it Nicholas she was thinking about? Was she really considering what he had said?

"You can't hide things from me, I know you too well. Something's wrong. What is it?"

Adam and Nicole stopped playing and looked at each other for a short moment. Nicole placed her hand on Rebecca's shoulder. "Hey, tell us what's wrong, Becca," she urged.

Finally, Rebecca sighed. "I guess its Nicholas."

"Say the word," Peter said as he struck his palm with his fist. "Michael and I'll pound him; or just me. Mike might kill him this time."

"Hey!" Adam broke in. "Don't forget about me. She's my friend too, you know."

"You can have what's left. You know, this could be fun."

"I appreciate it," Rebecca said, "but he wasn't hitting on me this time. He was asking me for help."

"So tell him to buzz off," Nicole said. "He's not worth your time or the risk."

"Yeah, but…what if he's telling the truth? What if nothing happened?" Adam scratched his head. "I don't get it. What did I miss?"

"So, what; you're considering helping him?" Nicole asked. "Well, I guess if it's at school, it's not that big of a deal."

"He wants help on the weekend," Rebecca added. "I guess…I'm thinking about it?"

"No offense Becca," Peter said. "Are you stupid? Being around him is trouble. It's a bad idea."

"Yeah," Nicole said. "Do you want to get it on with him or something?"

"No!" Rebecca defended.

"That's what everyone will think. Hell, it's probably what he'll tell everyone."

"I don't know. What if the rumors are just rumors? I mean, have any of you heard anything about him lately?" Rebecca couldn't believe she was actually defending him. "Besides, if they were true, wouldn't he be in jail?"

"Okay, this is stupid," Peter said as he rubbed the center of his brow. "The best case scenario is this; the rumors are just rumors and no one was raped or anything of the sort. Maybe it was just a one night stand that got a little out of hand because they wanted two different things. Kind of like what he says. Worst case scenario; it's all true and you get the distinct pleasure of dragging his sorry butt to court. That's the bad news. You get to drag him to court."

"I didn't say it was a perfect plan," Rebecca defended.

"What plan? There is no plan. All that's going to happen is you're going to regret it, big time. Nicholas will end up in the hospital and Michael will probably end up in jail because he'll put Nicholas in the hospital. And that's if I don't get to him first. Still considering?"

Rebecca sighed, not in frustration, but gratitude. She was smiling. "You're right, it is stupid. I have no idea what I was thinking. It's a bad idea and I'm not going to even consider it anymore. I don't know why I was in the first place."

"Don't take too much offense to it," Nicole said. "We're just concerned about you, that's all. Nicholas is a sleazebag, pure and simple."

"I know and I'm grateful. I've just been a little off today, that's all."

Rebecca decided that it was Nicholas causing the sense of foreboding and general unpleasantness. She wouldn't think about it anymore and would tell Nicholas where to go when he brought it up again. She forced her mind to relax and enjoyed the rest of her lunch with her friends. She was so very thankful the day was finally almost over. She couldn't wait to get home and take a nice hot bath and wash this strange day away. She thought maybe she would even add some bubbles. Yes, that's a good idea.

The bell rang and lunch was over. Much too soon in Rebecca's opinion, but it meant the rest of the day would only last about another hour. As each of her friends trailed off to their own classes Rebecca waved good-bye to them. By the time she reached her locker, only she was left. Rebecca rummaged through her locker for her biology book and notebooks. Suddenly a pair of arms wrapped around her and pulled her back into a hard body. She yelped in surprise as Michael growled, "Gotcha!"

"Michael!" Rebecca playfully chastised.

"Missed lunch," he said, still growling playfully. "Smell so good. Could eat you up."

Rebecca giggled. "Are you sure? I'll kick all the way down."

"Mm. Even better." Michael laughed and took Rebecca's books from her hands. "You eat good?"

"As good as the school provides." She pulled away and closed her locker. "Let's go," she said as she offered her hand.

Michael readjusted his backpack and held her books in one hand while holding Rebecca's hand in the other. Hand-in-hand, they walked to class. A few at a time students wondered in. Santano was sitting at his desk going over the piles of paper before him and picking at his lunch that was hidden behind the piles, paying little attention to his students as they came in.

Michael walked with Rebecca to her desk and leaned against an empty one next to her. They talked and laughed, waiting for the class to begin. Rebecca thought about telling him about Nicholas, but decided against it. Michael might overreact and have a 'talk' with Nicholas before she had a chance to tell him off first. He really didn't like Nicholas.

Monica and Heather walked in shortly before the tardy bell rang and took their seats. Michael and several other students followed suit. Santano sat patiently behind his desk finishing up the remains of his lunch as his class found their seats. Even after they had found their seats, the room was still full of chatter. Santano wolfed down the remains as he did a quick mental headcount of his students. He marked a check next to everyone's name that was present for that day. He cleared his throat and made a purposely loud noise as he scooted his seat back to stand. The chatter ceased and all eyes went to Santano. He walked to the front of his desk, his chest stinging. It wasn't as bad as earlier, but it was distracting. He stood before his desk and addressed his class. "It looks like everyone's here today. Good." He rubbed his forehead as he continued to speak, trying to focus on something other than the pain. "I hope everyone had a good holiday. Since I'm still catching up on your grading, today is going to be a make-up day. You can do homework, make up any missed assignments, or move into small groups and talk quietly."

That was all the invitation the class needed before the room roared to life with noise as desks were shuffled across the floor. Monica pushed her desk closer to Rebecca as Michael carried his over. Heather did not join the group. She went to speak with Santano.

"Heather's not joining us?" Rebecca asked as she watched Heather converse with Santano.

"When she makes up her test," Monica said as she came to rest in her seat.

"Oh yeah, she missed the test before break, didn't she?" Michael asked.

"Yeah; dentist appointment or something." Heather received her test and went back to her seat, waving to her friends and pointing at the test. "I gotta do this first," Heather said, barely audible over the noisy classroom.

"Good luck!" Monica shouted across the class and above the noise.

"It's easy!" Rebecca added. "You'll be done in no time!"

Heather smiled and waved a thank you from her seat.

"Think she'll do okay?" Michael asked. "I've already forgotten most of that stuff."

"Heather does her homework Mr. Procrastinator," Rebecca said. "She'll be fine."

"Yeah, like you and last weekend, right?"

Rebecca blushed, having forgotten about that. "Hey, I said I was sorry."

"No problem Ms. Procrastinator."

"One time."

"For two weeks." Michael smiled.

"You're talking yourself out of that make-up date."

"Shutting up now."

Monica laughed. "Oh, Becca, I talked to Melissa," Monica said.

"You did?" Rebecca asked. "About what? How is she doing anyway? I haven't seen her in awhile."

"Yeah, she was busy a lot. So she said. She wants to hang out this weekend."

"That's great. I'd like to know what she's been up to."

"You asked about that guy, didn't you?" Michael asked, not at all pleased.

"Oh, lighten up," Monica said. "And yes, I did."

"Why?" Rebecca asked. "I said to forget it."

Monica grinned and wagged a finger. "No you didn't. You said it's not a big deal and change the subject. You never said don't go ask her. Besides, you made me curious."

"You had set your mind to asking her, didn't you?"

Monica smiled and nodded her head.

"I could have never talked you out of it then anyway. You never change your mind."

"But you're a girl," Michael teased. "Aren't you supposed to change your mind, like, every five minutes?"

"I do," Monica said without missing a beat. "Right back to the decision I made."

"Well, what did she say about him?" Rebecca asked.

"Yeah," Michael added. "What about this weirdo guy? It's one thing knowing about everything that goes on here, but about some perfect stranger? That's entering stalker territory, isn't it?"

Monica shrugged. "She said defiantly though; it would be fun. Though I'm not sure how much fun stalking somebody could be."

It drew a laugh, but Michael's was only half-hearted.

Michael sighed. "Rebecca," he said, "I got to ask. What's the deal with this guy anyway? He's probably just moved into the area or something."

"I know," Rebecca said, disappointed that the whole conversation was brought up. She was hoping to avoid the topic altogether. She didn't want to keep thinking about it or keep lying about it. "It's just something about him bothers me. I can't explain it. I was just curious to know who he was. I guess I wanted to know why he bothered me so much." It was a lie; Rebecca already knew why he bothered her. She knew him.

Michael groaned. "Alright. It's weird, I gotta say, but if something about him bothers you, I'll support you in this little crusade."

Rebecca smiled, thankful for his understanding. "Thanks Mikey."

"Don't worry, Michael," Monica said. "I'm sure this crusade will be over by tomorrow. Rebecca either completely forgets about it or Melissa lets her know that there is absolutely nothing wrong with this guy." She leaned towards Michael, shielded her mouth with one hand and circled her finger around her head with the other. "She's crazy, you know?"

Michael laughed. "Yeah, I know. Uh, not about the crazy part!" he quickly amended.

Rebecca huffed. Until Monica brought it back up, she had forgotten about it, though that was probably because of Nicholas.

"But understand, Becca, I'm your boyfriend and here you are obsessing about some other guy. Yeah it's because you find him creepy, but you are still obsessing."

Michael's comment hit her hard. Rebecca was so frightened by the fact that the man she saw looked like the man from her dreams that she didn't realize she was appearing to be obsessed with him and what it was doing to Michael. Perhaps she was just obsessed. "You're right," Rebecca smiled as she took his hand. "I didn't even think about how you would feel about this. I know it's stupid and there's no reason to pursue this. I don't know what I was thinking even bringing it up. Monica, you can tell Melissa to forget about it. I don't care who he is."

Monica shrugged. "Eh, let her have her fun. Besides, I'm curious. Maybe he's single? Was he handsome?"

They laughed. The mood had finally lightened. As strangely as the day began and as strange as it went, at least it looked like it would end on a good note. The conversation quickly changed to other, more pleasant things. Though the bad feelings had lightened, they still lingered. Rebecca had made lots of mistakes today and worried her friends. The things she had considered and pursued were not even things she would normally consider, even on a bad day. She tried hard to push them from her mind. Even after Heather had finished her test and joined them, Rebecca had trouble focusing, but was glad the only thing mentioned to Heather was that Melissa would meet with them over the weekend. Rebecca didn't want to go through the whole conversation again.

After what seemed like an eternity to Rebecca, the final bell rang. The desks were quickly shuffled back into place and the students left through the door with vigor that they would never show during the day. School was over and all anyone wanted to do was go home. Santano watched his students as they left as he had done in years past. However, his gaze was solemn and tired. He sighed and left shortly thereafter to make his own way home.

The four friends boarded the bus and waited for it to pull out for the ride home. Rebecca laid her head on Michael's shoulder and hugged his arm. Her sigh caught his attention.

"Hey, Becca, is everything okay?"

"Yeah," Rebecca lied. "I just want to hold you for awhile."

Michael smiled and laid his head against hers. Rebecca couldn't explain it, but she almost felt sick to her stomach. The feeling had gotten worse throughout the day. Something very bad was going to happen.

JAK LORE

CHAPTER II

Santano walked slowly through the halls with a heavy heart as he watched the students gather their things and make mad dashes for the exits. His steps were slow through the hall. A dark shadow seemed to loom over him. No one paid him any mind. It was as if he wasn't even there. As if he didn't even exist. The pain in his chest was growing. It had been for the last hour. If his doctor had known, Santano would have been scolded. He didn't want to take another pill, but he wanted to see if he could get a reaction from the passing students. He fumbled in his jacket pocket for the small bottle and tapped it until another of the small pills fell into his waiting hand. He closed the bottle and placed it back in his pocket. He placed the pill under his tongue and watched. One pill was never enough to quell the pain; it usually took two, but he would have to wait fifteen minutes before he could take the second one.

Santano's gait continued slowly to his car. He stared at his reflection in the station wagon window. He looked old, tired, and alone. No one had noticed him. Glances lasted no more than a few seconds. No one cared. Santano unlocked his car and got in. He sat behind the wheel for a few minutes, watching the students pass by; living out their lives without a concern for tomorrow.

Snot-nosed little brats, Santano thought angrily as he turned the ignition key. *I bet none of them will even notice when I'm gone. Why would they? They look at me as little more than a jailor.* He pulled out of the faculty parking lot and began his trip home. *Why do I even continue to bother? What did I do to deserve this?*

Even in the afternoon traffic, his ride home took less than an hour. During the drive, Santano had taken the other two allotted pills before his chest pains had finally dulled. He questioned his reasons for continuing to teach. Why was he still doing it? His doctors had told him he had about a year left to live. Why was he spending that with kids that barely even acknowledged his existence?

The nitro pills would eventually stop working. Chemotherapy wouldn't help; they said it wasn't cancer. Surgery was almost suicidal; his heart was too weak. Prayer didn't work. Santano was not ready to die. He had but one hope left. He needed it. He would give anything for it. Anything that was asked he would gladly give up in return for his continued existence. He had seen some of the best doctors in the country and none could find a reason that his heart was failing. Everything that they had tried had done nothing to strengthen his failing heart. Santano was unwilling to accept that the powers that be had simply decided that it was time for such a healthy man to die; to cheat him of life by plaguing him with an incurable, indeed an un-diagnosable, heart disease.

Santano pulled into his driveway and walked the path to his front door with slow, heavy steps. He unlocked his door with no enthusiasm. The plain outside of his house betrayed the dark and dismal inside, showing just how truly lonely a man Santano had become. He laid his workload on the nearby end table and put his jacket into the closet, taking the bottle of nitro from it and slipping it into his pants pocket. He hated how he had to carry that little vial around just to make it through the day. Without it he was as good as dead.

Santano leafed through the day's mail; bills he had no intention of paying. What was the point, if he wouldn't be around much longer? He descended into his basement, its dark dismalness matching the rest of his home. Or perhaps it was his home that matched the darkness of the basement? He had pushed everything he stored down there against the walls to make room in the center. There he had painstakingly painted a large pentagram on the floor in a deep red paint. The pentagram rested inside a dual circle, which housed archaic symbols. At each point of the pentagram rested large black candles sitting inside glass candle saucers. Each point was encircled with smaller dual circles with smaller archaic symbols within. In the center sat an even larger candle of the same color, but resting on an elevated holder. Its encrypted circle was larger than the circles of the five points.

Santano sighed as he looked at it. It had taken him three days to make it so perfect. Three long days of loving care, desperate care. Santano spied his work bench and approached it. Resting on it were a hammer and a cross. He stared down at that cross for a long moment. Anger, fear and sorrow grew in a mix inside him. "You are supposed to do miracles," Santano whispered. "You are supposed to save people. Why won't you save me?" He cried out. "Why won't you give me my miracle?! Why did you give me this disease?!" He grabbed the hammer. "Why did you forsake me?! What did I ever do?!" Crying he struck the cross repeatedly with the hammer; stopping only when the cross lay in pieces. Santano stood there crying like a baby for long minutes. When he finally gained control of his emotions again, he wiped his tears away. "Screw you too."

Santano rummaged through the drawers of the work bench. He found a switchblade knife and butane lighter. He flicked the lighter's hammer a few times to make sure it still had fluid in it. In another drawer was a small black book with several bookmarks protruding from it. Santano leafed through the book and read the passages, approaching the pentagram as he did so. Contained within its pages were instructions on summoning and binding a demon for bargaining. Depending on what was to be bargained determined what demon or devil needed to be conjured. The extension of life required the assistance of some of the most powerful of devils.

"God will not help me," Santano said as he compared the diagram in the book with his finished work. "Maybe the legions of Hell will."

Santano was satisfied that his pentagram was the same as the one in the book; the characters of summoning and binding were all correct and in place. All was prepared as it should be to begin the Ritual of Summoning; to bargain with his eternal soul. Santano read over the incantation prayer, memorizing it for the ritual. It was a simple prayer. "Call out the name of the devil you beseech and cry your conviction. Beg to be graced by their presence and state that which you wish to bargain. Call you the devil's name again followed by your own." The ritual itself was as simple. Let his own blood as an offering. If his conviction was strong enough, a sign would be given that the prayer would be heard. If his conviction was strong…

He believed it to be strong enough.

It was strong enough.

Meticulously, Santano began to light the five point candles. With the main candles of the ritual lit, Santano traded the lighter for the knife and kneeled before the center candle. The center candle, the Candle of Summoning, would not be lit by fire, but by the offering. He took a few deep, cleansing breaths. A little pain. It would be nothing compared to what he felt every day. It would be nothing compared to the pain of death. Santano made a fist with his left hand and held it above the unlit candle. He flexed his fist in fear and anticipation as he switched open the switchblade. He placed the sharp edge against his palm. A blood offering was required. His blood must be offered to the flame. Santano would not be afraid. He could not be afraid. After a few quick breaths, he pulled the blade across his hand, slicing it open and dripping blood.

Santano held his hand over the unlit candle as the blood flowed freely from the wound. It gathered around his wrist and dripped onto the candle. The book only said that the offering must be made to an unlit candle and nothing more. Santano hoped he was doing it right.

The drops fell quickly and heavily onto the candle, drowning the wick and staining the black candle red. As the blood ran down the candle and pooled inside the glass saucer, Santano could feel heat beginning to burn his hand; heat that seemed to be coming from the drenched wick. He prayed and begged that the darkness would answer him. Suddenly, a flame burst to life. Santano's eyes widened as a small grin crossed his lips. It had worked. He would be heard!

Santano started searching around him for a bandage, but realized that he had forgotten about his own first aid. Using the switchblade, Santano cut a length of fabric from his clothes and used that to bandage his bleeding palm. Santano, in his gaiety, had forgotten the hand positions for the ritual. Quickly he leafed through his bookmarks to find the page concerning the prayer. The flame flickered violently in anticipation. Upon finding the page he sought Santano wasted no time continuing.

Santano clasped his hands together, as in normal prayer, but brought his index and pinky figures out, as well as his thumbs, creating three points in his clasped hands. The opening prayer was spoken in Latin, the phrase taking Santano the better part of a month to perfect. He didn't even know what it was he was saying, but he didn't care. He eyed only the end result.

"Sterilis lux deserit anima. Lux deserit sterilis anima. Abyssum invocat in anima. Recipere oblatio. Exaudi orationem perditi profunda inferi. Exaudi orationem meam, ad clamorem dolorem. Aeterna regna spiritus tenebrarum, exáudi oratiónem meam."

As the prayer was brought to a close the large candle's flame flickered and turned from a red flame to black, and then back again. Santano hesitated only for a moment, gathering his thoughts and desire. The conclusion of the ritual would be easier. Only the opening prayer, according to the book, had to be in Latin. The bargaining itself could be in the conjurer's native tongue. "Great Demonic Lord of Darkness!" Santano bellowed. "I beckon thee! Grace your loyal servant with your divine presence! Grace him and grant him his wish of continued life! Of eternal life in your glorious name! Satan! Great Lord of Gehenna! Grace me, Samuel Santano!"

The flame became black again and flickered violently, as if a strong wind was trying to smother it, but the air in the basement was stale. Then the flame began to grow in size, slowly at first, consuming the center circle. When it touched the first of the dual rings in the center and across the archaic symbols, the flame returned to its normal color. When the slowly growing flame reached the second ring it suddenly sprang to life. Santano jumped back as the flame consumed the floor, at once surprised and delighted that the ritual he performed had actually worked. From within the flames a pair of large eyes formed. They opened, red and bloodshot, and stared at the human almost quivering in front of them.

"Samuel Santano, I presume?" The voice of the greatest of the fallen angels echoed throughout the room.

A smile crossed Santano's face as he realized that he had indeed contacted not only a devil of Hell, but the greatest of all devils and stuttered, "Yes."

The eyes looked around at the pentagram around them. "Your Circle of Binding is impressive, but surely you do not think that it can contain me?"

The flame began to grow out, pushing against an invisible field that shook the room as Satan's power fought against it. The fires reached out for Santano, taking the form of a hand. Standing outside the pentagram, Santano quivered but did not move as the fiery hand reached out for him. The book said a devil could not reach out of the inner circle, so Santano was much surprised when the hand stopped short of his neck. Santano could feel the flames licking at his skin. A chuckle could be heard coming from the flames before the hand was retracted.

"Very well," Satan said. "I have heard your wish human, but you know not what you do. You are a novice, not even a true follower. You seek only to extend your own life."

"Please don't deny me!" Santano pleaded. "I'll do anything. I'll give you anything you want!"

Satan laughed. "So they all say. So they all willingly give, until I come to collect. What makes you so different, Samuel Santano? You did not even use the right ritual. You drew the wrong circle. Your prayer was mediocre at best."

"I did everything that the book said!"

"A book you could barely understand. Your wish is for your life to continue, so you drew a Circle of Binding that you thought could help you achieve that goal. Then you call out to me, but your circle was to summon and bind Demon or one of his cohorts. You do not realize that this is a Circle of Awakening."

"A Circle of Awakening?"

"By summoning Demon, or one of his lieutenants, you beseech to have your own demons unleashed upon you. We call this the Unleashing of an Inner Demon. It is quite the spectacle. Most cannot overcome their demons."

Santano fell to his knees and raised his hands pleadingly. "Please don't forsake me too. I have given you your offering. I am willing to do anything to be cured of this disease."

"Then you certainly seek help in the wrong place. I do not deal in miracles."

Santano began to cry. "I don't want to die. Don't let me die. Don't let me be forgotten."

"Health and fame. Is that what you seek, Samuel Santano? Yes, I could extend your life a number of years. I could slow the disease, but I cannot cure it. I can give you fame so that you will not be soon forgotten. I could give you anything your heart desires, in exchange for your soul."

"I don't care about fame and fortune. I just want to be free of death."

The eyes seemed to smile. "Now we are getting somewhere. To escape Death's cold grip. That is a different wish. That is a wish I can fulfill. And it just so happens that I can use this circle to do that."

"You—You can?"

"If you are willing to pay the price, I can fulfill that wish. Your wish is to control Death itself. Yes, this I can do."

"Then please, do it."

"Are you willing to pay the price I ask?"

"Anything. Just tell me what I have to give."

"Your humanity. Give me that and I can grant your wish."

Santano stared at the eyes within the flames for a moment, a look of confusion on his face. "How do I do that?"

"Send unto me the souls of innocents. Commit to me these blood sacrifices and I will grant you that which you seek."

"You want me to kill people?"

"Is that a problem? What better way to sacrifice your humanity to me than by sacrificing the lives of the pure?"

"How would I do that?"

"It is a simple task. Would you be willing, no matter the lives that I ask?"

The pain in Santano's chest began to throb and grow. It was all the incentive he needed. Santano rose to his feet. "Yes. Anything that you ask."

"Your enthusiasm is lackluster, but I can sense your conviction. I will lay out the terms of our contract. Then I will ask you to sign."

Santano nodded.

"Let it be known that I, Satan, Lord of Gehenna, accept you, Samuel Santano's, Offering of Awakening. Your desire of an extension of your life is duly noted. In exchange for your eternal servitude I offer you the power of Death itself. In exchange for ten innocent souls I will make you Death, the Fourth Horseman."

"A Horseman?" Santano asked, bewildered. "You mean of the Apocalypse?"

"You will be my Horseman, the most feared of all. As a Horseman your life will be extended indefinitely. As Death, it is life that you will have dominion over. As you offer your ten souls unto me your power will be increased respectively. These souls must be innocent and in some way connected to you, the avatar. Samuel Santano, if you accept to becoming my avatar, state your profession."

"I'm a high school biology teacher."

"Then the ten innocent souls will come from the students you keep in your care. As an avatar, you will gain privileged access to the Blood Weapons. Using the Blood Weapons you will sacrifice your chosen, allowing me to obtain their innocent souls and keep the Heavenly Angels from interfering. Upon accepting these terms, your soul is hereby forfeited to me. Samuel Santano, as an avatar, do you accept these terms?"

"I care nothing for those brats. I accept!"

Blood began to pour from the flames as did two strands of fire. The leaking blood from Santano's hand began to waft from his wound, as well as the small pool on the floor. All the strands of blood rose to hover before him. The strands of flame began to envelope the blood as it pooled together into a pulsing ball.

"Very well," Satan said. "By your blood I will summon forth the Blood Dagger."

The flames consumed the pooled blood as Santano's freshly fallen blood continued to pour into the flames. His blood soaked bandage was drying as all the blood it had collected was pulled out of it. Santano removed the bandage to see that his slashed hand was healing quickly. As the flames collected and boiled Santano's blood, the flaming sphere grew in size. When finally Santano's wound was closed and no more blood could be drawn, the sphere had grown to the size of a basketball. Santano could smell the iron of his blood as it boiled within. The heat from the flaming sphere intensified as it started to condense. Santano was forced to take a few steps back because of the intense heat. The sphere condensed to the size of a baseball before it exploded. The flames landed harmlessly around the room, amazingly not lighting anything ablaze. Santano's eyes followed a blood red dagger that was left behind as it fell, blade first, into the floor.

The entirety of the dagger was the color of crimson blood. The dagger's blade, which measured slightly longer than Santano's hand, was one edged with a flared tip. Along either side of the dagger's blade ten white spots gleamed in stark contrast. The handle was etched as flames and the hilt was forged of dragon heads with opal eyes. In the hilt's center rested a large gleaming opal. Santano approached the dagger and the eyes of the dragons started to glow. As he reached for the handle, the dragons roared to life. Instinctively, Santano jumped back.

"Do not be afraid," Satan said. "That is the Blood Dagger, forged of your own blood. It is one of the Blood Weapons of which I spoke. Accepting this gift will signify your signature on the contract."

Santano pulled the dagger free, a red wave quickly spreading from the dagger and over his body. Santano did not notice, or he did not care. "I accept. I'll get you your ten souls."

"Slay your victims with this blade. As I stated before, it will prevent any angels from interfering in your affairs. Understand that for its powers to work, you must have your chosen victim etched in your mind. This blade will only accept the souls of your students, no one else, and will only consume one soul a day. Do you understand my avatar?"

"I understand. As long as Heaven can't get in my way, I doubt anyone else can."

Santano left the basement, almost running up the stairs so giddy with excitement. Satan's eyes watched as Santano left. "Make haste," the fallen angel said. "Time is short. The demon hunter, Angel, draws near."

Santano tore open his closet door and donned his jacket. Knowing that he would have to hide his identity if he was going to go on a killing spree, he rummaged through the closet for something to hide his face. Finding a black ski mask he decided that it was a good thing that it was cold out. Now, he just had to figure out who to kill. He was in such a hurry that he had forgotten about that part until he gripped the door handle on the front door. Where was he going to go? Who was going to be the first? Any of his students were good choices, but which one? He hadn't thought this through. He needed to make a decision quickly.

Adam Segulis. It just popped into Santano's head. He had nothing against the kid, but he certainly seemed like a prime target. Santano knew his parents worked late, it had been brought up before. That meant that Adam would be alone, except for perhaps his girlfriend, Nicole Amnesty. What luck would it be to have two victims to sacrifice instead of one? Satan's words returned to Santano. "The Blood Weapons will consume but one soul a day." Santano looked at the pulsating dagger in his hand. It was hungry for blood; he could almost feel it. If both Adam and Nicole were there, what would happen if he killed them both? Could he risk leaving one alive to come back for later? No, he couldn't do that. The risk was too great. He had to kill everyone, but the dagger would only take one soul. Isn't that why Adam came to him? He would be alone.

Nicole stole a kiss from Adam as she left the school. "I have to go take care of something for my parents today," she said. "They're away right now and can't do it themselves."

"Aw, Nicole," Adam almost groaned. "I was hoping you could spend the day with me."

Nicole kissed him again. "I will. I'll call you when I get home, then we can make plans. Maybe you can come to my house." She gave a sly wink. "No one has to know that we'll be alone."

Santano blinked. It had come out of nowhere and was fast and fleeting. What was that; the knowledge Satan had spoke of? Santano grinned. Adam would be alone. Santano decided that Adam would be the first sacrifice. He needed to know where Adam lived. Santano wracked his brain, but no information came to him. Perhaps the knowledge was limited? Perhaps he was given only knowledge he wouldn't normally have access to? Santano raced into his living room and turned on his computer. He didn't want to waste any more time. While the hefty machine warmed up Santano switched the phone line from his telephone to his computer. He only had one line and when he wanted to search for anything online he had to switch the cord.

After several minutes the machine was finally primed and online. Santano accessed the high school's offsite mainframe and began to log on. He wasn't a good typist and pecked the keyboard, entering his username letter by letter. S A M S A N T A N O. He did the same for his password, taking extra care since the letters were replaced with asterisks, the letters never appearing onscreen. C O O L T E A C H 1. The site took a moment to register, but then Santano was inside. It took him a few minutes to find and pull up Adam's profile information. Cropped into the page was Adam's school ID photo from his freshman year, or perhaps eighth grade. The picture was at least three years old, but Adam hadn't changed much. Except for Adam's photo, the page was basic, containing a few lines of information and links. Looking at the link, Schedule, Santano couldn't help but wonder if it was up to date or not. Soon, it wouldn't matter. They would have one less student.

Santano scrolled down the page. The information it had was rather basic and not accurate. For age, it stated Adam as fifteen. Santano chuckled. Whoever was in charge of the site was doing a poor job. Adam was seventeen, or would be soon. Santano hoped that what mattered was at least accurate. A person's address doesn't change year to year as one's age does. Santano wrote the address on a torn piece of paper from his computer desk. Below the emergency contact information—which of course was Adam's parents—was a commented note. As Santano had thought, Adam's parents could only be reached via cellular phone before seven p.m. That gave Santano almost four hours to deal with Adam.

Santano logged off and exited the browser. He couldn't be bothered with shutting the computer down; it was too time consuming. He left it on and made haste out the front door, ready to offer the first of his ten sacrifices.

Snow had started to fall during the short drive. Even in the light snowfall, the streets were fairly lax, so Santano didn't encounter much traffic or potential problems on his way to his first victim. As Santano pulled onto Adam's block he was delighted to find a large parking spot right in front of Adam's house. He parked in the middle of it so no one could park around him and ruin a quick getaway. He turned the car off and sat there for a moment. Fifty feet away. His first sacrifice was only fifty feet away. If he had wanted to, could he turn back? Could he change his mind? The dagger pulsed in his hand, drawing his attention to it. No, he had already signed the contract. This dagger, forged of his own blood, was his signature. Why would he want to turn back? Why should he care about those that don't care about him? Why should he care about a person that forgets he even exists as soon as he leaves class? Santano sighed and looked around. The streets were, for the most part, empty. The few people that were out were focusing more on keeping themselves warm and arriving at their destination as soon as possible than anything Santano was doing. No one was paying him any attention. Why would they? He was no one and for once that was just the way he wanted it. Santano found it fortuitous that the snow had begun to fall with increasing ferocity. It was the perfect time for the storm they had been predicting to hit. Santano looked around one last time before donning his ski mask and exiting his car. He walked with vigor to Adam's front door.

Santano first tried the door handle, hoping it was unlocked. It wasn't. Santano hoped, since Adam was expecting Nicole, that he would leave it open for her. A dangerous prospect, as Santano was proving, but kids never take something as simple as a locked door seriously. It was usually, as most things, taken for granted. Santano hadn't anticipated this. He hadn't thought any of this through. How would he get in now? Break the door down? Even if he had the strength to do that, it would certainly draw attention to him.

Santano looked at the Blood Dagger. The red metal gleamed in the light of day. The blade began to glow red hot. Black smoke began to waif from the dragon mouths as they emitted a low roar. Santano could feel the heat emanating from the dagger's blade against the cold winds at his back. He touched it to the metal of the dead bolt and it began to burn and melt. The smell of hot metal filled his nostrils as the dead bolt melted into slag and ran down the face of the door, burning marks deep into it. Santano did the same to the handle. It was quick and when it was done the metal of the blade cooled. The dragons quieted and the smoking ceased. Santano easily and effortlessly pushed the door open. There was no longer anything keeping it secure. With the obstacle gone, Santano entered the house with a smile. With the power of the dagger, the sacrifices should be easy.

Santano entered into the living room. The walls were lined with bright wallpaper and pictures of Adam and his parents. Steel frame shelves and cabinets housed a whicker bowl with several pieces of mail, more pictures, one or two depicting Nicole alongside Adam during some outing, and various knickknacks that Santano had no interest in. The lights were out but the home was not dark, not like Santano's home. Judging from the pictures, Santano guessed that Adam was an only child. He was the only child that appeared in every family photo Santano saw. He found himself looking at a photograph of Adam and Nicole posing with Santa Clause. It was dated Christmas of ninety-nine, this past Christmas. Both had an arm around Santa and smiled at the camera. Nicole poised bunny ears over the fake bearded man's head.

Santano jumped when he heard a sound above him, almost dropping the picture. It must have been Adam in a room upstairs. Santano laid the picture back down. He spied a carpeted staircase at the other end of the living room. Santano tiptoed across the hardwood floor and climbed the stairs slowly, trying not to make them creak as he advanced. Adam could not know he was there. As Santano ascended slowly up the steps he could make out the faint sounds of heavy music. As he came closer to the landing, the music became louder and clearer. He wasn't sure of the band, but from the sounds of it, it wasn't rap, which most teenagers seemed to be taking a liking to. Santano had nothing but distaste for it. It was defiantly heavy music, but Santano wasn't sure what kind. He didn't listen to music anymore, but the music would help hide his advance.

At the top of the staircase Santano could see the illumination of light. The upstairs hall was small and short. Three doors were upstairs, two average sized and one smaller. The door to his right, staggered beyond a closed door on the left, was left ajar. The smaller door was at the end of the hall, stuck in the center. Santano guessed the smaller door was a closet. He tipped toed to the first door and tried the handle. It creaked open into an empty room. Santano was thankful that the loud music masked the door's noise. A twin sized bed rested in the center of the almost barren room. The windows had their white curtains pulled closed and there was a dresser and mirror against one wall. A folding door closed off what could only be a closet. Santano mused it must have been a guest room.

Santano closed the door and looked at the smaller door at the end of the hall. It was almost definitely a closet. The pain in Santano's chest began to return and he grimaced under it. He did not need to deal with the last room. It was just a closet. Whoever was home was in the second room, where the music was coming from. It had to be Adam. Santano peeked through the opening to find Adam typing something into his computer. Santano nearly grunted in frustration at the computer Adam was working on. It was newer than his. Any reservations Santano had about killing the poor boy left him upon seeing the expensive computer that he seemed to have all to himself. The growing chest pains only added to that incentive. It was too soon to even think about taking another Nitro. Under normal circumstances, Santano would be considering a hospital visit, not murder. No. Not murder; a sacrifice.

Santano's aching heart began to race as he crept into the room. Adam was right in front of him and alone. There was not another soul in the room. Santano advanced slowly, raising the Blood Dagger higher as he came closer to Adam, trying not to startle his young victim. The fiery effigy of the handle began to pulse, not a throb as before, but as if veins ran through it. It was different this time. The pulsating started slowly at first but quickly kept pace with Santano's own rapidly beating heart. It was almost as if the two beats were one. The opals in both the hilt and dragons eyes began to glow. Numerous images of how to kill the boy flashed through Santano's mind. He saw himself bringing down the blade repeatedly into the teen's back, blood soaking his shirt and Adam crying out in anguish. He saw himself thrust the dagger quickly into the back of Adam's neck and then again, but the second vision ended with the blade in the boy's skull. So many images danced in front of Santano's mind. Each vision felt like he had killed the boy each time and each time his stomached knotted and twisted in disgust less and less. Santano's eyes were growing cold. His chest was stinging in pain and the pulsating in his hand quickened with his own heartbeat. He was almost upon the boy when the loud song playing ended and the floor creaked. Adam's head shot up and he saw Santano's shadow fall onto the computer screen. Adam jumped and turned in his chair. Santano almost panicked and closed the short distance between them quickly. He reached around Adam with the Blood Dagger and quickly slid the blade across Adam's throat. His flesh was sliced open effortlessly and his life giving blood spurt out of his neck and onto the desk and computer.

Santano leaped back as Adam grasped at his neck. The spray became a waterfall of blood between his fingers as it trailed down his body and onto the floor. Adam flew from his seat in panic and fell to the floor. He convulsed on the floor as his bloody hands grasped at his throat. Strands of Adam's blood flowed from his body and to Santano's crimson colored blade. Santano took panicked steps back. His breathing was fast and deep in shock and disbelief at what he had done. He had ended a life; a life of someone he was supposed to protect and guide. Santano wasn't sure if he wanted to smile or cry.

Santano watched as the strands of blood broke away from Adam's body and swirled around the dagger's blade. He watched the blood swirl around one of the white spots on the blade. It was being drawn within. As Adam's spasms slowed, the swirling blood darkened the spot red, slowly matching the stark white to the rest of the crimson blade. The minutes dragged on and Adam's movements finally ceased. The spot that his blood had swirled around was filled and matched the rest of the blade. Life finally left the boy and his immortal soul had been drawn into the very depths of Hell by the power of the Blood Dagger. Santano finally found his smile.

Adam lay lifeless on the floor. One hand clutched weakly at his neck while the other was drawn out and drenched in blood. In a panic, he had tried to crawl away. Santano took a step back as the pool of blood around Adam slowly grew around him. Watching him flop around like a fish out of water, it wasn't hard for Santano to look at the remains as less than a human being and more as a means to an end. Santano stared at the lifeless body for a long moment, the racing of his heart quelling alongside that of the dagger's pulse. It was done. The first sacrifice had been made, but Santano didn't feel any different.

The glow of the opals had faded and an eerie silence filled the room. Santano could hear a heartbeat. Was it his heartbeat? It was slow and steady. The pain in Santano's chest was slowly subsiding. He looked at the blade in his hand, the weapon that had ended his student's life. Standing alone in the room with the dead body, Santano could not help but wonder if it was all real. The last hour, was it all real? Did he really sell his soul? Was this life the price he had to pay? Or was he simply imagining the whole thing; or worse, parts of it? In the blade Santano spied an instant reflection of himself. The reflection revealed his face beneath the ski mask. His eyes. There was something different with his eyes, but it was too quick for Santano to see. He looked from the blade to his former student, lying on the ground in a growing pool of blood. The flame etched handle began to pulse in rhythm with the sound of the heartbeat. Santano no longer had a reason to stay. It was time to go.

Santano raced down the stairs and out the door. He entered his car and started the engine. He shifted the car into gear and was about to tear out of the lot. "Calm down," a voice said into his head. "Pull away slowly. Remove your mask. Now." Santano listened to the voice of Satan and removed his mask. He took a deep breath and checked his mirror. A police car drove by. Santano stared after it. If he had taken off in his panic, he would have been spotted. The events were no dream. It was all true. Calmly, he pulled out of the spot and made his way towards home. His mind drifted back to Adam. How long would it be before his body was discovered? Santano looked at himself in the mirror. His eyes had a dark glow that disappeared when he blinked. He couldn't help but smile. "Thank you Adam," Santano said. His quest for power had begun. His mind was already reeling with who to sacrifice next. He had a day to decide.

***

Rebecca tested the flowing water with her hand. It was hot, but not too hot. She plugged the drain in the tub to let it fill. It had been a long day and she couldn't wait to let it all soak away. From under the sink she grabbed a bottle of bubble bath and poured some of the fluid in. Her chores were done and she didn't have much homework to worry about. Dinner wouldn't be for awhile yet, so she had some time to spare and enjoy herself. Hopefully this would help loosen the tightness in her stomach.

As the tub filled with bubbly water, Rebecca went to her room to retrieve a small portable radio. She closed the covered toilet lid and placed the radio on top of the flower decoration. She plugged it into the wall outlet by the light switch and adjusted the volume. She tuned it to the local classical station. She thought such calming music, with such a calming bath, would help calm her much agitated nerves. She made sure the door was locked before she started stripping off her clothes, letting each piece fall to the floor. She pushed the heap against the wall with her bare foot.

Gingerly, Rebecca tested the waters with her toes, letting her skin get used to the heat of the water before setting an entire foot in. The water ended up being a little hotter than she meant, so she lowered herself in slowly as to not shock and burn her skin. Once submerged, she stretched out beneath the bubbles and sighed. "This feels good," she mused. She pinched her nose and went under for a moment. Coming back up, she brushed her golden hair back and wiped the water away from her face. "That's much better." She turned off the water and leaned back, content. She closed her eyes and listened to the music. As she relaxed she drifted to sleep.

Explosions rocked the war-torn fields. Bullets fell like rain as soldiers ran for cover. Tanks tore the grass and soil as they crossed the landscape. "They know not what they do," a woman's voice said. "The power is too unstable for them to control." The scene shifted to another land. White trucks with red crosses drove through a small town. People ran for the trucks which had workers handing out packages of food. "They have upset the balance," the woman continued. "The plans of the Fallen cannot come to pass." The scene shifted yet again, this time to a hospital. It was overcrowded and the medical personnel overworked. They tried their best to comfort the sick and dying. "He can no longer hold back their forces," the woman said. As she spoke, she began to appear as she walked forward. She was tall, though Rebecca was unsure how tall, and had a curvaceous build. Her legs were long and toned, her calves held taunt by the black heels she wore, which added several inches to her already tall height. Her tight black leather pants glistened in the light. The black leather halter top she wore tucked into her pants. Around her waist was wrapped a black leather belt with a white buckle. It was the only thing on her that wasn't black. The halter top circled her neck, almost as if she wore a choker. Her long dark hair was left down and flowed as she walked; her skin a dark tanned tone. Her features were almost Amazonian. "It has already begun. He cannot stop this one alone. Giver of Life, you must rise up and destroy them. Destroy them all." Suddenly, a dark form with red eyes appeared before the woman and lashed out. Its cry was sickening.

Rebecca jumped awake in the tub, water splashing onto the floor. Her heart was racing and fear mercilessly gripped her, refusing to let go. She tried to catch her breath, but it was hard. A word echoed in her head. One phrase, which for reasons she couldn't explain, she knew the meaning of all too well; Pestilence. Rebecca curled her legs up and cried.

***

Night had fallen and a light sheen of snow coated the ground. The falling snow had lightened back into a flurry and coated the ground with less than an inch. The snow crunched beneath his feet. The street was bathed in flashing red and white lights. He stood away from the crowds, watching the scene before him in sorrow. He knew what had happened.

The woman had a blanket over her shoulders and she was crying into the arms of her husband. From across the street, the young man could hear their cries. The woman cried and begged. Her son was dead. The young man's brown eyes locked with the paramedics as they brought a covered body from the house. The woman's cries as her son was carried away drew his attention back to her. Her husband held her back as she begged the paramedics not to take her son away.

The man touched a silver cross about his neck as his dirty brown trench coat fluttered in the cold wind. Tears rolled down his face. It was never easy. "Forgive me," he whispered. "I had no choice. Lord, you know the hopes of the helpless. Surely you will hear their cries and comfort them." He watched as the paramedics hoisted the body into the back of the ambulance and closed the doors behind it. The woman cried fervently for her son, Adam. The young man swallowed hard. "I will save him," he whispered. He made the sign of the cross towards them and prayed, "O God, you do not willingly grieve or afflict your children. Look with pity on the suffering of this family in their loss. Sustain them in their anguish and into the darkness of their grief. Bring the light of your love. Hear my prayer. Amen."

On slow steps, he turned and began to walk away. He turned only momentarily as the ambulance drove away. "It will be some time yet, before another is chosen." The man placed his hand on a dagger hidden at his side. "Quickstep." His form momentarily became blurred and he was gone.

CHAPTER III

After her bath, Rebecca was quiet the rest of the night. She skipped dinner, stating to her parents that she didn't feel well, and went to bed early. She did not sleep well that night. The dream of the Four Horsemen returned again. This time, however, they were not at the Gates of Heaven. They were chasing her. They laughed and jeered as they chased after her. The dark shadow of Death spurred them on. War's barbed chains lashed out at her, trying to ensnare her, but only managed to cut her flesh. They could not get a grip on her. "I will slice every inch of your body," War decreed. "I will crush every bone and rip every organ out from within you." The ground shook as Famine leaped ahead of War. "I will devour you," Famine slurped, drool falling from his massive toothy maw. "Piece by piece, joint by joint, enjoying the taste of your succulent flesh." Pestilence screeched as his form vaulted over the previous two. "Let me touch you!" he wailed. "Just once; it's all I need. I'll shut down each of your organs one by one. I'll make you vomit until you vomit the very flesh of your esophagus. Until your teeth fall out! I will rot your skin and shrivel your tongue. Let me touch you!"

"No!" Rebecca screamed. "Get away!" She ran and ran; as fast as she could. The Horsemen only closed the gap, little by little. They were not tiring, but she was. Her legs ached and her throat was rasped and dry. "Help me! Somebody!" A young red-headed girl ran up beside her, keeping in stride with Rebecca's panicked pace effortlessly. She was a little wisp of a thing that didn't look older than fourteen. She wore sandals and cut-off jean shorts. Her plaid shirt was tied in a knot at her midriff and buttoned the rest of the way. Freckles dotted her face. Her short, frizzled hair brought out her bright green eyes. "You can't run forever sugar drop," the young girl said in an Irish accent. "If you keep running like that, they'll catch you. Don't be afraid." Rebecca tripped and the four were upon her.

Rebecca woke up screaming. Her mother burst into her room in a pink fur-laced nightgown. Mother's instinct drew her to embrace Rebecca and rock her in her arms. "It's okay," she said. "It's okay." Rebecca's mother was a few inches taller than she, with duller and shorter blonde hair, which was a tangled mess at the moment. Rebecca's father could be heard calling from down the hall. "What happened, Jeanine? Is Rebecca alright?"

"I don't know!" Jeanine called back, caressing her daughter's head and trying to soothe her fears. "It's okay Rebecca. Calm down. What happened?"

Rebecca held her mother tight. "They—They were chasing me!" she cried. "And they—! And they—!" Rebecca couldn't finish as she continued to sob.

"Who was chasing you? Where?"

In his pajama's, Rebecca's father finally rolled his wheelchair hastily into the room. He would have been tall, if he could stand. "What's going on?" he asked. "What happened? Why were you screaming?"

"She said someone was chasing her," Jeanine said.

"Who? Where?" Her father began looking around the room and rolled over to the window. His green eyes looked outside, trying to find anyone or anything that moved.

"No, wait," Rebecca said as she calmed. "I think—Sorry, I was dreaming."

"You were dreaming?" Her father said as he rolled over to her bed.

"Yes, it was just a bad dream." Rebecca wiped her eyes of their tears and tried to control her sobs.

Her father ran his hands over his face and through his lightly brown hair. "Wow. You haven't had a nightmare that bad since you were a little girl. Almost made my legs start working again."

Rebecca laughed through her sobs. "Thanks Daddy, I needed that."

He smiled and kissed his daughter on the forehead. "It's almost five. Get back to sleep, okay?"

"I'll try."

"That's my girl."

"Honey," Jeanine said, "do you need anything before we go?"

"No Mom, I'm fine. Thank you."

Jeanine smiled. "I guess I'll just head to work a little early. No point in trying to get another ten minutes of sleep in."

Rebecca laughed. "Sorry Mom."

"It's okay. Come on, Eric. Let's let Rebecca get back to sleep. Lucky girl still has another hour."

Rebecca's parents left the room laughing. Once the door was closed, however, Rebecca's laugher faded. Yes, it was a dream, but it terrified her. It seemed so real. The terror still gripped her stomach, even as she lay in bed and tried to go back to sleep. She couldn't though, she was just too afraid. She was afraid the Four Horsemen would be waiting for her. She just hoped tonight her dreams would be free of those monsters.

Snow crunched beneath Rebecca's boots as she walked to the bus stop. The snow had finally stopped falling and left a few inches on the ground. The cold air against her face helped to finally shake her awake. She never could go back to sleep. She had decided to get up early and cook herself and her father breakfast. Eric knew the dream was bothering her, but when she didn't want to talk about it, he didn't press the issue. The cold winds bit at her face and forced her to lower her head to shield it. It was colder now. The temperature must have dropped overnight. Most of the snow hadn't been shoveled yet and its brightness hurt her eyes.

As Rebecca stood on the corner waiting for the bus, the blowing wind swirled the loose top layer of snow around her, wrapping her in a vortex of glistening white. She let out a breath to watch it turn to vapor before her. It made her smile. It was amazing how something so simple could make her smile. She needed it. Her chest was tight and her stomach in knots. She was afraid, but she wasn't sure of what. The words of the red-headed girl came back and echoed in her mind. "Stop running. Don't be afraid."

"I'm not running," Rebecca said softly to herself. "There's nothing to run from; nothing to be afraid of."

"Yes there is," the girl said. "You just don't know it yet."

Rebecca turned around and saw the girl standing a few yards away, still wearing her knotted shirt and cut-off shorts. Rebecca gaped at the young girl. "No way," Rebecca said. She rubbed her eyes and the girl was gone.

"Great. Now I'm seeing things." The roar of the bus as it pulled up turned her around. Rebecca climbed aboard. "Morning," the driver said. Rebecca returned in kind, trying to quell and hide her fear. She moved to the back and sat down. Holding onto the old cross about her neck, she refused to look out the window this time. Her mind had played enough tricks on her for one day. As the bus pulled up to its second stop, Rebecca looked away. She didn't want to see any more strange things. She especially didn't want to see any more things from her dreams. Her cross was doing little to quell her fears. She wanted Michael. She wanted to hold him. That would make her feel better, just being close to him. One more stop; that is all she had to wait.

At the next stop, Heather and Monica boarded, Michael taking the rear again. No one tried to take his seat from him this time. "Hey you," Michael said as he sat down. He moved to kiss her cheek and she moved her head to let him kiss her lips. His lips lingered, but when he moved away Rebecca wanted more. She reached her hand behind him and held his head still while her lips trailed after his, locking them together. Heather and Monica stared at them with surprised smiles. Michael was even more pleasantly surprised when Rebecca's tongue invaded his mouth, something he couldn't recall her ever having done so publicly. He held her in kind and kissed her back until she stopped and let out a satisfied sigh.

"Wow, what was that for?" Michael asked with a smile.

"I've just been having a really bad day," Rebecca responded. "I just needed you." She wrapped her arms around his and laid her head on his shoulder.

"You see that guy again or something?"

"No, just some nightmares. I guess they've been getting to me."

"Did you forget you were on the bus or something girl?" Heather teased. "Since when do you kiss like that in front of other people?"

Rebecca peeked around Michael. "I don't. So I hope you enjoyed the show because you won't be seeing it again!" She then promptly stuck her tongue out at them.

The four friends laughed and Rebecca finally felt better. She thought maybe now she could forget about the dreams; about the nightmares. She was a little disappointed when Monica spoke up. "Speaking of your strange dreams, Melissa called me this morning. She found something on that dream guy of yours. Guess he's real."

"Great," Rebecca answered, less than enthusiastic.

"Already?" Michael asked. "That was fast. Remind me never to try and keep a secret."

They laughed and Rebecca pinched his arm through his jacket.

"Anyway," Monica continued, "she said to meet her in the cafeteria before class,"

"Alright," Rebecca said. "It'll be nice to see her anyway."

Michael and Rebecca stayed in their own quiet world, lost in each other's embrace. Rebecca was finally content, though she knew it was only fleeting. Heather and Monica talked amongst each other, leaving the couple to themselves. Rebecca looked forward to seeing her friend again. So what if she found out that this guy existed? It probably wasn't even the right guy. So what? A dream was only a dream, she had to remember that. As frightening as they may be, they were still just dreams.

Rebecca and Michael held hands as they walked through the hall. Heather and Monica followed staggered behind them. They saw Nicole talking to Melissa at the cafeteria entrance. Melissa laughed at some joke Nicole made before she noticed the group of friends approaching. She waved at Rebecca and called out, "Hey love birds! How ya been?"

"Melissa!" Rebecca called as she waved back. "Where did you disappear to?"

"Busy with this and that. Nice to know you didn't forget about me."

"Hey Nicole," Heather greeted. "I'm surprised you're not with Adam. Is he sick or something?"

"I'm not sure." Nicole answered. "We were supposed to hang out yesterday, but he never answered my phone calls. I thought maybe he got caught up in one of his games but no one's seen him today. I'm a little worried."

"I'm sure it's nothing."

"I hope so. So what's going on? Mel tells me Becca is looking for a new guy?"

"Geez, I hope not," Michael said. "I'd have to put him in the hospital."

The group of friends laughed.

"Well," Melissa said as she dug through her backpack, "before I say anything, is this him?"

Melissa pulled from her backpack a brown business folder and handed it to Rebecca. She opened it and rifled through the several photos within. The photos looked like they were taken from a security camera and showed the young man from several different angles. The man in the photos was indeed the man Rebecca saw yesterday. It looked like he was in a hunting or gun supply store. Rebecca wasn't sure which.

"This is him!" Rebecca exclaimed as her stomach dropped. He was real. "This is the guy."

"I think his name is Angel," Melissa said.

"You think?" Michael asked as he viewed one of the pictures. "You mean you're not sure? Gotta say though, I am impressed you found this guy."

"It wasn't too hard, given the little information I had. I just cross referenced anyone that wasn't here after Christmas. That was only like two weeks ago. This guy was seen in various shops over the last few days. Finding him was the easy part; finding out who he is proved to be a little harder than I expected."

"He's cute," Monica said.

"I wouldn't get too attached. Something doesn't add up about this guy. It's almost like he doesn't exist. This shop sells guns and knives. He was there trying to buy something, knives I guess. The clerk wouldn't sell because this guy wouldn't produce any ID. Normally they turn the other way, but they had just been stung."

"Especially since he's carrying that huge sword on his back," Rebecca said. "How are the cops not stopping him?" Her friends looked at her strangely. They took a glance at the pictures in her hands before returning their confused gaze to her. "What?"

"There's no sword in that picture," Heather said.

"No one said anything about him carrying a sword either," Melissa said. "That would freak people out."

"But its right there," Rebecca insisted. "It's strapped to his back. Kind of hard to miss."

"Becca," Michael said as he took the picture from her. "There is no sword in this picture. None whatsoever."

"Seriously, this isn't funny."

"Are you okay? You've been acting strange lately."

They can't see it? Rebecca thought. *Why can't they see it?* "Never mind."

"Focus Blondie. My advice for you is to be content with this and drop it. There is something weird with this guy. I think he's trouble and I'm usually right about these things."

"Nicole?" Peter interrupted. He and Jason were approaching the group with sorrowful looks. Michael knew something was up. Jason was in his uniform and not his workout clothes. He didn't hit the weights.

"What is it?" Nicole asked. "What's wrong? Why do you two look so upset?"

"Let's go outside," Peter said. "We have to talk, but not here. It's important."

"O—Okay." Nicole followed Peter as he led the way out of the building. She looked back to her friends with worry on her face.

"Hey Jas," Michael asked. "What's going on?"

Jason rubbed his hands over his face. "I'm not quite sure how to say this. Um...You've heard that Adam isn't here today, right?"

"Nicole said she couldn't get a hold of him yesterday," Monica replied.

"Yeah, there's a reason for that."

"Jason, what happened to Adam?" Michael asked.

"My dad was one of the first responders. Adam's dead."

"What?" Michael exclaimed in unison with the girls' gasps. It was then that they heard Nicole scream. Melissa, Monica and Heather ran to her. Rebecca stayed put, in shock and unable to move. "What do you mean he's dead?" Michael pressed.

"My dad told me this morning. I wanted you guys to hear it from me before the Principal. I ran into Peter and we both came looking for you guys. Peter said to tell Nicole outside."

"Are you saying Adam committed suicide? Why would he do that?"

Jason shook his head. "No. They're treating it like a homicide."

"They're pretty sure someone killed him? Do they have any ideas?"

"They've been dusting the house for prints since last night. Don't repeat this, but the locks on the front door were gone."

"Gone? What do you mean gone?"

"I mean gone. Removed. Not there."

"Why the hell would someone force open his front door and then remove the locks?"

"It wasn't forced open. The locked were melted."

"Melted? Wouldn't you need like a blowtorch or something for that?"

Rebecca thought about what the girl had told her. It ran through her head again and again. "There is something to fear," Rebecca whispered.

"What?" Michael asked. "What did you say Becca?"

"Nothing," she replied as she started to move past him. "I—I have to get to class!" She ran away from them. Michael started to follow, but Jason stopped him.

"Let her be man," Jason said. "She'll come to you when she's ready."

Michael stared after Rebecca as she ran. He wanted to go to her, but thought his friend was right. He sighed in frustration. "What about Nicole?" Michael asked.

"You heard her. Pray. It's all you can do. She's going to need support now. She's going to need her friends. I wouldn't expect to see her again today."

"Yeah. What does your dad think? Is he working the case?"

"Yeah, until they pull him off. I didn't know Adam that well, so it's not much of a conflict of interest for him. As for what he thinks, he won't say. They're still gathering evidence. They're going to come today to check his locker between classes, then if they allow, his parents will bring what's inside of it home."

"Damn, this isn't good."

"I know." Jason looked at the clock. "I'm going to get going. Classes are starting soon."

"Who else knows?"

"The Principal. He's going to make an announcement during first period."

Jason left, leaving Michael alone in the hall. He wasn't sure what to do. Rebecca had been acting weird all day and hearing that Adam was murdered didn't help. He wasn't sure if Rebecca was even still in the school. He certainly doubted Nicole was. Not after that scream. In silence, he walked to his locker. Jason was right. He had to wait for Rebecca to come to him. Trying to force it out of her would just make her close up more. She was freaking out enough.

Michael rummaged through his locker looking for his papers and books when a pair of hands covered his eyes. A sweet voice mewed in his ear, "Guess who?"

"Sarah," Michael said as he pulled her hands off his eyes. "I'm really not in the mood for this crap."

"It's not crap Mikey." Sarah leaned against the locker next to Michael's. She was a bit shorter than him. She was a senior, like Michael. She kept her light brown hair down around her oval face; she thought it accented her looks. Her green eyes looked Michael up and down like he was a tasty treat before looking at his face. "Aren't you satisfied with your little joyride yet?"

"How many times do we have to go through this? And don't call me Mikey."

"As many times as it take; and why not? She does. Come on," she said as she played with a lose button on her uniform's blouse, "I know you miss this. If you want, I'll let you taste it for a little bit." She pulled the unbuttoned top down, revealing her cleavage.

"You know what," Michael said as his anger rose. "Normally I can deal with your bull—" He slammed his locker shut. "But one of my friends just died!"

Sarah stared at him unmoving with her blouse pulled out enough for a view down it. She wasn't wearing a bra. Michael couldn't recount when she did. He stood there, waiting for her to react, but she remained motionless with a seductive grin on her face. Michael realized it was quiet and looked around. Everyone was immobile, almost like they were frozen in place.

"What the heck?" Michael asked. He waved his hand in front of Sarah's face, but she didn't even twitch.

"Do you love her?" an Irish girl's voice asked.

Michael turned to see a red-headed freckled face girl wearing a knotted shirt and cut-off shorts. "Who are you? Why are you dressed like that? It's freezing outside."

The girl smiled. "It doesn't bother me. Well, do you love her?"

"Who, this bimbo?" Michael pointed to Sarah behind him.

The girl shook her head. "The other one."

"Rebecca? Of course I do. I tell her all the time. Who are you?"

"If you love her, then believe her. Cherish every moment you have with her. She is going to lose you."

"No she's not. Where would I go?"

The girl shook her head with a frown. "I'm sorry. You are to die by fire."

"Wait a minute!" Michael reached for her, but she vanished. The halls filled with noise again. He looked around dumbfounded.

"Hey!" Sarah called. "Don't turn your back to me!"

"Not now!" Michael said as he walked away.

"What does she have that I don't?!"

"Class!"

Rebecca shuffled into her history class like a zombie. She hung her jacket around the back of her seat and sat down. She stared at the folder she received from Melissa blankly. She couldn't believe what she was told. She didn't want to believe that Adam was dead. She would never see him again. No one would. Dozens of questions filled her mind. Who killed him? Why did they kill him? Will they kill anyone else? She found herself looking at the photos of Angel. "He's going to try, but he's going to fail," a voice said. Rebecca knew the voice and turned her head. The red-headed girl was standing next to her. She leaned over Rebecca's desk to look at the pictures. "He tries so hard, but he's so old. He's so tired." She looked at Rebecca. "If you look hard enough, you can see the years in his eyes. He's so weary. You'll try to save him, but you can't."

"Who are you?" Rebecca asked in a sorrowful whisper.

"I am all that hungers. I was the second to fall."

Fingers snapped in front of Rebecca's face. "Hey, snap out of it," Glenda said.

Rebecca looked at her. "What?"

"You're staring off into space."

"I was?" She looked beside her, but the red-headed girl was gone. "I guess."

"Running late today, huh? Who's this?" Glenda asked as she turned one of the photos to look at it.

"No one." Rebecca took the picture from her and closed the folder. "It's not anybody important."

Glenda sat down in the desk next to her. "Are you still upset about yesterday? When did your sense of humor die?"

Rebecca shut her eyes tightly when she heard the word "die".

"Hey, that's my desk," one of the students said.

Glenda looked at the boy and said, "Class hasn't started yet. Via."

The boy groaned and said, "Fine. Then I'm taking your seat."

"Bueno." Glenda waved him off.

"It's not about yesterday," Rebecca said silently.

"No? Then what? You're acting like someone died."

Rebecca swallowed and the bell rang. She was fighting back her tears.

"Come on, lighten up! Espera un minuto, are you crying?"

The built in loudspeaker kicked on and the Principal's voice echoed through the static filled filters. "Good morning students," he said. His voice was not as cheery as it usually was.

"The old windbag," Glenda said. "He sounds upset. Maybe his salary got slashed." Glenda laughed as Rebecca silently listened. She knew what was going to be said. Adam was gone. He would never be coming back.

"Today I have some grievous news to share," the Principal continued. "There is a student that will forever be missing from class."

Glenda furrowed her brow in confusion.

"At seven-thirty last night, Adam Segulis was found dead in his home."

The class came alive with shock. Rebecca could no longer hold back her tears as Glenda's eyes widened. She turned her head and stared at Rebecca. "Dios, someone did die. Rebecca, I'm so sorry. I didn't know."

"I know," Rebecca answered through her sobs. "It's okay. I know you were just trying to make a joke and cheer me up."

"No more jokes. I promise."

The commotion continued, even through the continuation of the Principal's voice. From the back of the class someone shouted, "Shut up! Show some respect!"

"The local authorities are working on the case," the Principal continued. "As yet, there are so suspects, but they are hard at work searching for whoever may have committed this atrocious crime. Please, if you believe you have any information that may be of help, speak to your dean who will contact the police department for you. Social workers are available to those students who need help dealing with this loss. Now, please observe a moment of silence for our dear departed friend."

Rebecca looked at the back of the class. Two rows away the boy that shouted at the class sat at the end of the row. He rested his head against the wall with his eyes closed. He opened his eyes and noticed Rebecca looking at him from over her shoulder. She mouthed thank you. He nodded his head solemnly at her and leaned his head back against the wall, returning to his silent observance. Rebecca had recognized his voice but realized she didn't know his name. "Alright," Ms. Dale said. "I know this is hard for everyone, especially people that knew Adam. If you need to see a social worker, you can get up and go. If not, please get into your groups. I obviously don't expect you to get much done today, but please try. It may help take your minds off this."

The class stood and moved, noise of moving desks filling the silent room. A few students left. Glenda motioned Brian and Austin over, waving off the group that usually sat there. "No el dia de hoy muchachos," she told them. "Leave Rebecca alone. Don't make her move."

"It's okay Glenda," Rebecca said.

"Que no. It's not okay. ¡Por Dios! You just lost a friend. And you just found out. Nobody should be expecting much from you right now. Just…do what you need to do, okay?"

Rebecca gave a weak smile. "Thank you."

"Yeah," Brian said. "We'll handle this today."

"It's okay. I need something else to focus on right now."

"If you're sure."

"I am."

The class for the most part was quiet. Rebecca did her best to focus on her assignment, trying to keep her mind distracted. It was difficult and occasionally she had to wipe away fresh tears. She had put the folder with Angel's pictures in them in her backpack. Seeking him out suddenly seemed trivial. After class she approached the boy that shouted at the class earlier.

"Hi," she said. "I wanted to say thank you for earlier."

"Don't mention it," he replied. He was big, football big, but he didn't play. She had been to enough of Michael's games to know he was not on the roster.

"Did you know Adam?"

"I have no idea who he is. It's just that I thought it was disrespectful. The guy just died and they were just chatting away."

"I know. I appreciate what you did for him. It's a little embarrassing for me, but I don't know your name."

He chuckled. "'Cept for my friends, not many people do. Friends call me Brooklyn, where I'm from, but the name's Xander."

Rebecca laughed. "I'm—"

"Rebecca," he interrupted. "I know. Not many people don't know who you are."

"I didn't realize I was that popular." Rebecca blushed and pushed her hair out of her face.

"Well, let's put it this way. Sarah thinks she's going to be prom queen, but that's not a sure thing. She may be the top cheerleader, but she's also a slutty bitch. You're kind and caring; not a slut. People know and like that. You really changed Michael too. Hey, I got to get going. Next class starts soon. Nice talking to you."

"You too."

Rebecca followed him out of class and then they went their separate ways. She took her seat in Leonato's class and sighed. Nicholas leaned forward and said, "Are you alright? I know you two were friends."

"Not today, Nicholas. Please?" Rebecca pleaded.

"Right," Nicholas said. "Sorry. You've probably had enough of that already."

The bell rang and Leonato addressed his class. "I'm not going to bother with attendance today. I can guess that there are going to be a few students absent, and with good reason. We were going to start reading a book today. Well, a play really. Othello by Shakespeare. I'm still going to pass it out, but we're not going to do any in class reading today. I encourage you to start reading it, but you are free to do whatever you like today. You can get into small groups if you want. Tomorrow, though, it will be business as usual I'm afraid."

Leonato passed out the books to his class before allowing them to break into groups. Rene touched Rebecca's hand, drawing her out of the book.

"Come on," she said. "Let's go sit with Samantha."

"Thanks," Rebecca said, "but I really don't feel like talking right now."

"That's fine. Come sit with us anyway. Get away from you-know-who."

Rebecca sighed. "Alright, but I really do just want to read. Get my mind off all of this."

"I understand. Just come sit with us. We'll let you read."

Rebecca followed her friend to where Samantha had gathered a set of three desks for them. Nicholas stayed where he was. He had few friends in class, or school for that matter. He had gotten used to being a loner. His fingers gripped his book tightly as Rebecca left her seat. He focused his eye on the words on the page and let everything pass. Someone had died.

Rebecca greeted Samantha as she sat down.

"Are you okay?" Samantha asked.

"I guess," Rebecca answered. "I just—don't want to deal with anyone right now." Rebecca clasped her head. "Jeez, I ran away from Michael when I found out."

"We understand. Just let us know if you need anything."

"I will, but I just want to read right now."

"Yeah, okay. That's probably a good idea."

Rebecca opened her book and began to read it. Rene and Samantha talked briefly before reading their own copies. It was just too hard to enjoy a good conversation, provided they had the wills to have one. Rebecca just wanted to immerse herself in the play, but she found it difficult. Her mind kept thinking about the red-head and what she said. "I am all that hungers," Rebecca whispered. "What does that mean?" Hearing that Rebecca had said something, her friends looked at her. When she didn't respond to them, they let her be.

The minutes seemed to drag before the bell rang. Rebecca stopped by her locker to finally put her backpack and coat away. Because of the shock from the news of Adam's death she completely forgot to stop at her locker earlier. She didn't bother stopping after first period and now she was getting tired of carrying her coat and backpack around all day. She was hot and her backpack was heavy. She didn't know how other students managed. She took her math book and notebook with her before closing her locker. She stood there, staring past it. The tardy bell rang, which partially caught her attention. She walked to class, oblivious to her surroundings. She was still having trouble accepting the news. If she was this upset, how was Nicole handling it? Rebecca passed by Adam's locker on her way to class. The lock was already gone. It was probably already empty. She opened the locker door. Inside was the red-headed girl nonchalantly popping candy pieces into her mouth. "You're late sugar drop," she said. The girl looked at her. "You're not ready. You need to mourn." Rebecca closed the door and shook her head. Tears welled up in her eyes and she couldn't hold it anymore. Her books fell to the ground and she buried her face in her hands and cried.

Rebecca cried for several minutes. She fell to her knees and continued to cry. Hands gripped her shoulders and tried to pull her up. "Not here," Melissa said. "Come on! Come on! Not here! Follow me!" Rebecca followed Melissa into the girl's bathroom. Melissa held Rebecca as she cried. She patted the blonde girl on the back of the head as she said, "I know. I know. Let it out. Let it all out." Rebecca cried for a few minutes before Melissa's teacher came in with Rebecca's dropped books. She was a younger teacher, barely older than her own students. She tried hard to look professional in her skirted beige suit. Her brown hair was braided and twirled into a bun.

"Is everything all right?" the woman asked.

"Yeah," Melissa answered as she motioned to put Rebecca's books on the sink. "We knew Adam. She just needs a good cry."

"Do you need to see a social worker?"

"No," Rebecca replied as she wiped her tears away. "I'm fine. I just needed to cry."

"Are you sure?"

"Yeah," Rebecca reassured her as she pulled some tissue paper and blew her nose. "I'm alright. I'll be okay now. I've just been holding it in all day."

"Are you sure? If you need to speak with someone—"

"Yeah, I'm sure. Thank you."

"Okay. Melissa, you two can take a few more minutes, and then please get back to class."

"We will Mrs. Wilton," Melissa answered.

Rebecca cleaned her face in the mirror. The reflection she saw wasn't her own. It was the red-headed girl. "Did you have a good cry sweetness?" she asked. The girl mimicked every motion Rebecca made. "I hope so. You really needed it. You have to be ready you know."

Rebecca didn't want to go see a social worker and this red-headed girl had been haunting her all day. She wanted to call Melissa to the mirror and ask her if she saw the girl, but she didn't. Rebecca collected her books and turned to her friend. "Thank you, Melissa. I guess I held it in too long."

"Yeah," Melissa answered as she wiped her own tears away. "I had my cry before first period, after we saw Nicole off."

"She didn't stay?"

"No. Peter took her home. He said he'd stay with her for awhile. She said her parents won't be back until this weekend, I think."

"So she has no one right now?"

Melissa shook her head. "Not when Peter leaves. He can't stay with her forever. Come on, we should get to class."

When Rebecca finally made it to class she found that several of its students were missing. "Rebecca, are you okay?" Spencer asked as she took her seat. "Yes," Rebecca answered and didn't utter a word more. Her teacher didn't press. Rebecca looked to her left. Nicole's seat was empty. Rebecca had doubted that she would have stayed, and everyone had said she had gone home. Not seeing her in class just seemed to make it real. Rebecca turned and looked towards Adam's desk. Even if someone took it, it would forever be Adam's desk. It would forever be empty. *One year today,* Rebecca thought. *It would have been their one year anniversary today.* She wiped away her newly forming tears.

Rebecca felt alone in class and barely paid attention to anything Spencer had to say. He didn't call on her when he couldn't get the answers he wanted from class either. Rebecca was relieved for that. She really didn't want to deal with anyone. She thought maybe she should have gone home too, but now the day was almost over. She may as well just stick it out.

Rebecca found herself staring out the window wondering how Nicole was doing. Peter was with her, so she must be okay. It wasn't that he liked her in that way or anything. Peter had known Nicole as long as he had known Rebecca. Though the three didn't meet for years, Peter had grown up alongside both of them. Peter didn't look at either her or Nicole as potential girlfriends. He never had, even when he was asked about why he always hung out with them. He would always answer, "I always wanted a sister. Now I got two." They all knew where they stood. At least Nicole was in good hands if nothing else.

Rebecca could hear faint humming. She recognized the voice of the humming. It was the red-head again. She wasn't close this time, but she was there. Rebecca didn't want to look for her, so just stared out the window. Through the reflection of the glass the red-head skipped along the window panes like she was playing hop-scotch. "One, two, three, four. He only needs one more," she sang. Rebecca looked behind her to see if the girl was in the room. She wasn't. Of course she wasn't. She would have to be skipping over all the desks. "Five, six, seven, eight," the girl continued, drawing Rebecca's attention back to the window. "It's time to accept your fate." Rebecca closed her eyes trying to ignore her.

"One, two, three, four," the girl continued. "He only needs one more. Five, six, seven, eight. He's going to tear down Heaven's Gate. One, two, three, four. He only needs one more."

Rebecca covered her ears. "Please stop," she whispered.

The girl kept skipping across the windows. "You don't like my song? He's choosing now, you know."

"Who?"

"The avatar."

"Avatar?" Rebecca looked to the window for the girl, but she was not there to answer.

"Rebecca?" Spencer asked. "Are you okay?"

"Yeah, I think so. I'm just…I'm fine."

Spencer said something else, but Rebecca didn't catch it. She didn't even notice the release bell ring. It was the leaving students that caught her attention. She gathered her books and headed to her locker before going to lunch. She was not in a rush, even though Adam and Nicole would not be there to let her cut in line. Adam would never be there to let her do that again. When she got to the cafeteria the line was already long. She got in the back and waited. The line moved at a steady pace. When it was her turn she didn't even think. She just pointed to food items and mumbled that or this. Tray of food in hand, Rebecca began to walk towards her usual seat. She was flustered to see that it was already taken. Peter wasn't there to save their spots.

Rebecca took a moment to find a place to sit. One of the small square tables on the side of the cafeteria was free. She sat with her back to the wall and stared down at the food she had bought; a cheeseburger, fries and a can of Coke. She had forgotten the side of ketchup and cookie. Rebecca sighed. Without her friends, she was lonely. Staring at her bland tray of food, she ate her fries, slowly one at a time. "Hey candy cane!" that familiar voice said again, though her accent was gone. The red-headed girl came to Rebecca's table, but this time she was wearing the school's uniform. She plopped down in the seat across from Rebecca. She reached over the table and grabbed a handful of Rebecca's fries and shoved them into her mouth. "So good!" she gleamed.

"Who are you?" Rebecca asked.

The girl swallowed the mouthful of cut up potatoes. "A name? I suppose you do need a name. You humans are so silly that way. Let's see, we're given lots of names. How about Úna? Yeah, Úna; I've always liked that name."

"Úna? What do you want from me? Why are you haunting me?"

"I'm here to prepare you." Úna grabbed another handful of fries and stuffed them un-elegantly into her mouth. "Things are going to get rough for you candy."

"My name is Rebecca."

"We know your name. We know everything. We are everywhere but we are neither here nor there."

"We? We who?"

"You'll see. We're all rooting for you sweetness." She grabbed the last handful of Rebecca's fries and stuffed them two or three at a time into her mouth. "Yesterday was just the beginning," she said around mouthfuls. "The avatar is just starting to taste the power."

"What are you talking about? What's an avatar? Are you talking about Adam?"

"Ah, the little apple. The poor boy had his neck slit, you know? The avatar was fast. He never had a chance."

Rebecca's anger was rising as new tears began to form.

"He ended up flopping around like a dead fish. It was really quite pathetic."

As her tears ran down her face, Rebecca reached over the table and grabbed Úna by the scruff of her shirt and yelled, "Stop it! Whatever you are, just stop it!"

Úna smiled back. "People can see me now sugar plum."

Rebecca looked around her to see her fellow classmates staring back at her and whispering. She could hear some of the closer whispers, about how she was picking on a freshman just because she was upset. She realized it certainly looked that way. She let Úna go and found her demeanor again. She wiped her tears away, trying not to cry.

"Just go away," she pleaded. "Why are you doing this to me?"

"I have to," Úna answered. "You have to be ready." She took Rebecca's cheeseburger and took a big bite. "Apple was only the first."

"Please stop calling him that."

"Sorry," Úna said as she took another big bite. "I have a one track mind."

Rebecca reached for what remained of her sandwich. "Stop eating my food."

Úna held it away. "Why? You're not hungry." She stood up. "There will be another today. The avatar is choosing now. You know who he is. You see him every day." Finishing the rest of the cheeseburger, Úna left the cafeteria.

Rebecca looked at what remained of her lunch. She barely had any at all, but Úna was right. She was no longer hungry. She pushed her tray away and sat with her head resting between her hands. She stared at the table and tried not to think.

"This is a nightmare," she whispered to herself. "It has to be. None of this is happening. It's all a dream."

"Nope!" Úna said, almost gleefully into her ear.

Rebecca looked around, but Úna was nowhere in sight. She groaned. "I just want this day to end."

When the release bell rang, Rebecca was not quick to leave the cafeteria. She dragged her feet. She couldn't help but think about what Úna said. Someone else was going to die. That's what Úna was hinting at. This avatar person was going to kill someone else. What was an avatar? Why did Úna insist that she knew who it was? Who was Úna anyway?

"Rebecca!" Michael called. It brought Rebecca's attention to the here and now. She looked up to find him waving to her by her locker. She whispered his name as a smile crossed her face. She couldn't help but run into his arms. "Rough day, huh?" Michael stated.

"You have no idea," Rebecca replied. "This whole day feels like one big nightmare."

"I know. You look beat. Are you planning on finishing out the day?"

"I've come this far. Why turn back now?"

Michael smiled at her, which brought a stronger smile out of Rebecca. "Always so strong. That's why I love you."

"I love you too."

Rebecca kissed his lips and hugged him. Over his shoulder, she could see Sarah watching them, anger etched into her face. Rebecca held him tighter. Sarah turned hard and walked into her class. *When will she give it up?* Rebecca thought. *No, not today. I won't think about her today.*

"Come on Becca. If you're staying, let's get to class before we're late."

"Right. Let me get my books."

They walked to class holding hands. Rebecca didn't let Michael hold her books because she didn't want to clutch onto his arm like she was glued to it. She didn't like showing too much affection towards him in school. She felt it kept rumors down to a minimum, considering his last girlfriend was Sarah. Today she knew she wouldn't be able to help herself and used her books to keep her arms busy and not need to grab him. Michael didn't much care for that, but could understand her viewpoint. Today of all days, he would not argue with her. She was upset enough. In truth, he wished she would decide to skip their last class and go home. Either his or hers, it didn't matter. He just thought school seemed to be too much for her today. It certainly was for Nicole. She didn't stay.

As they walked into their last class they saw that Santano was still swamped in paperwork. It looked like he hadn't made a dent in the piles of paper on his desk. He had written something on the board in large letters.

NO CLASS TODAY

XTRA CREDIT AVAILABLE

SMALL GROUPS ALLOWED

"Has he been doing this all day?" Michael asked.

"I guess," Rebecca answered as she wiped some remaining tears away. She saw Santano sitting at his desk going over papers. "That's nice of him."

"Come on, Heather and Monica are waiting for us. They already moved our desks."

Rebecca laughed and let Michael lead the way. As they passed by Santano, a chill ran down Rebecca's spine and made her shiver. It caught Santano's attention.

"Is something wrong?" he asked.

"No," she answered as she faced him for a moment, pulling Michael to a stop. "I just got…cold." His eyes were darker and glowing. Rebecca rubbed her eyes and they appeared normal again.

"Are you sure?"

"Yeah. I've just had a bad day, since I heard Adam died."

"Yes, tragic news."

Santano went back to grading his papers without saying another word. Rebecca didn't think much of it, but he didn't sound upset, like the other teachers did. He didn't seem too concerned. Rebecca noticed a pile of packets on his desk. It must have been the extra credit. She took one for herself and Michael. She looked to him and he nodded back. She followed him to their friends.

"How are you doing?" Monica asked Rebecca as she sat down.

"I could be better," Rebecca answered. "I can't even imagine how Nicole is feeling."

"Has anyone even called her yet?" Michael asked.

"I did," Heather answered. "She's doing a little better. She stopped crying at least. Peter stayed with her."

"I know," Rebecca said. "I keep hearing that her parents are gone too."

"Yeah. Her dad's company sent him to New York to take care of some deal. She said her mom went with him."

"Bad timing," Michael said.

"I think her dad's in line for some big promotion, so he's trying to look good to get it."

"What's he do?"

"I have no idea. I never asked."

While her friends spoke, Rebecca caught herself staring at Santano. Something was different about him today. She wanted to talk to her friends about Úna too, but wasn't sure if that would be a good idea. She wasn't even sure if all of that actually happened.

Michael nudged Rebecca's arm. "Hey, you okay?"

"Yeah," she replied. "As good as I can, I guess."

"Sorry, it's just…you were staring at Santano."

"I was?"

"Yeah. Are you sure you're okay? I don't think he'll care too much if we ask to leave early."

"It's okay. I just—Does he look different to you?"

"Different?" He looked at Santano sitting at his desk behind his piles of papers. "Different how?"

Santano wasn't so much grading the papers in front of him as he was going through their names. He thought about each student that he came across; who they were, how they acted and whether or not he even liked them. *Sarah O'Conner,* Santano thought as he looked over one of her assignments. *Flirtatious, slutty bitch. She's always been a problem in class.* He pulled out a list of names that he had hidden under the piles of paper and added her name to the list. Hyphenated next to it he wrote "Cheerleader Bitch". *She went on and on when Michael dumped her.* For an instant he felt Sarah's jealously towards Rebecca. Santano smiled. *I wonder how she would react if he was next?* He wrote down Michael's name next. Hyphenated next to it he wrote "For Sarah". *That could be fun to watch.* Looking at his extensive list of names he rubbed his neck and sighed. *I didn't think picking which punk kid to sacrifice next would be so overwhelming. I would like to just send them all off.* He leafed through a few more and then his brow rose. The name caught his attention and for a moment nervous fear griped him. He stared at the name at the top of the page. Melissa Stouthart. *She has to go next,* he thought. *I probably should have killed her first. With her mob connections she could find out about me before the cops do.* Santano sat nearly dumbfounded. *Wait a minute, how do I know that her uncle is a Capo? Why the hell do I even suddenly know what that is?* He realized it was the knowledge that Satan had spoke of. He accessed it again. It seemed to come and go randomly, but in this instance when he needed it.

Santano couldn't control it and wondered if he ever would. He opened his desk drawer and pulled out a bulky laptop, which he had bought yesterday as a reward to himself for his first sacrifice, and logged onto the school's network.

"How about like that," Rebecca said. "When did Santano get a laptop?"

"I have no idea." Michael answered. "I always thought of him as kind of low tech."

"He chose," Úna sang into Rebecca's ear. Rebecca turned, but Úna was nowhere in sight. Her stomached dropped. That feeling had come back. That sickening dread from yesterday. Something bad was going to happen. She knew it.

"Are you sure you're alright?" Heather asked. "You seem really freaked out."

"I—I don't know," Rebecca answered. "I just have a lot going on right now; and now this whole thing with Adam—I think it's just getting to me."

Michael looked at the clock. "The day's almost over," he said. "Just hang in there."

Santano wrote down Melissa's address on his list and circled it. She would be his next sacrifice. He decided that if he needed to, he would kill everyone in the house. He only needed to buy himself a little time. Once he was Death itself, what could even the Mob do to him? Melissa was as good as dead.

***

In an abandoned warehouse a few miles away, the young man, Angel, sat with legs crossed in silent meditation. The room was filled with a dim light that hung around him, glinting off his silver cross. However, the light radiated from that spot, not a fixture. It seemed to just hang in that sole room, in that particular area. Angel was so deep in mediation that he seemed to be barely breathing at all. Beads of sweat poured down his brow. A white aura began to appear around him, dancing about the outline of his form only slightly. It barely came off his body at all. It simply made the outline of his form seem to glow. Angel began to concentrate harder, trying to make the glowing aura grow. The aura began to fade. "No," he whispered. "I am far from done." He took a breath to clear his thoughts.

"O Lord, give me the desire to pray, and teach me to pray as Thou wouldst have my needs. Sustain me, that I may overcome my weaknesses and strengthen me, that I may have Thine approval. May I be reverent and unselfish as I come to Thee in prayer. Amen." The aura grew slightly and brightened, but not much. Angel's muscles were held taunt and sweat dripped off his nose. Exhausted, Angel breathed and let his body relax. The aura faded. "My power is waning faster than before." He looked at the sheathed sword and dagger resting at his side. "I'm running out of time. What do I do?" Angel lay down and stared skywards. He looked past the light, into the darkness behind it. He touched the silver cross about his neck as he stared into the darkness. His mind was playing tricks on him again. Ruby eyes and a red smile stared back at him. He could hear the sick and decrepit laughter of that diseased creature. "After all this time," he said, "it still hurts."

The sword resting beside him began to hum. It pulled Angel to a sitting position as he gripped it and the dagger. He rose to his feet as he attached the dagger to his side. He pushed his thumb against the sword guard and exposed the rusted metal of the blade. "Show me," Angel said. His mind's eye opened, casting vision over his vision. It was transparent and misty over the vision of the physical world around him. In that second sight he saw Melissa Stouthart. She was in a class room talking to someone. That didn't matter to Angel. "Where will he strike?" The blade hummed and Angel was filled with the knowledge he needed. "Her home. I have time, but not much." He strapped the scabbard to his back. The weapon began to shimmer, but Angel closed his eyes in concentration to stop it. "No," Angel said. "The cloaking will take too much power. I may need to use Quickstep to make it in time, so I'll need all the power I can conserve. I hope I have gathered enough." Angel left the room running. Without him the mysterious light faded, leaving the room in darkness.

***

The final bell rang, telling all the school day was over. Rebecca couldn't be happier. Perhaps now she could escape from the whispers of Úna. Rebecca's stomach stayed tight the rest of class. It was still tight, even as she and her friends boarded the bus. She silently cursed Úna. Why did she have to say that? How was she even managing to talk to her when she was nowhere in sight? Rebecca leaned against Michael. Úna had to be a figment of her imagination. She couldn't be real, could she?

"Do you want to come over for dinner tonight?" Rebecca asked suddenly.

"Tonight?" Michael asked. "Sure, but I thought Heather and Monica were staying late with you tonight."

"They are, but I'm sure Dad can make an extra plate for you."

"Sure thing." He kissed the top of her head before laying his head against hers.

"Did anyone else notice how fast Santano got out of class today?" Monica asked. "Looks like he has some place to be today."

"I noticed that too. He usually stays late. At least, he does during football season. I always saw him leave either during practice or afterwards."

"Maybe he's got a date tonight," Heather joked.

"Is he even married?" Monica asked.

"I have no idea. He's my teacher, why would I care about his romantic life?"

Rebecca had her eyes closed as she listened. She enjoyed the noise. It was something different and uplifting. "One, two, three, four," Úna sang. "You're all going to cry some more." Rebecca eyes shot open and went straight to the window. Úna danced like a gleeful child in the window's reflection. "Five, six, seven, eight. He's going to seal another's fate." Úna laughed as Rebecca shut her eyes tightly and held onto Michael's arm.

"What's wrong?" Michael asked.

"Nothing," Rebecca answered. "I just don't feel right, that's all."

"I know. It's been hard on everyone today."

I want you to stay tonight, Rebecca thought. *I want you to stay with me and not go home. I'm afraid to go to sleep alone tonight.*

Rebecca was expecting Úna to say something in response to her thoughts, but the young girl stayed quiet for once. Rebecca looked at the window. Úna was gone. *I wish my parents would let you stay*, Rebecca thought as she looked at Michael. He smiled back at her and touched his forehead to hers.

"What are you thinking?" he asked.

"Nothing much," she smiled back. "Dinner is at six."

"Isn't it always?"

"Get a room!" Monica called.

All four laughed. Rebecca loved her friends dearly. She would be lost without them.

***

Angel raced down the street as fast as he could. People stopped and stared in awe as he ran with the speed of an Olympic runner, but his stamina was reaching its limit and his speed was declining. Angel could hear the murmurs of conversations as he ran by. Chicago was a major city. With his speed and unhidden weapons, people thought someone was shooting a movie. He had always wondered what a movie was. He had never seen one. Always being on the move, he never had the time to catch even a matinee. He knew he did not have much time and tried to dig into his reserves. Above all else, he wanted to conserve his Celestial Energy. He would need it against the avatar.

The leather clad Amazonian woman ran up next to Angel and kept pace with him, barely breaking a sweat.

"You again," Angel said.

"You will not make it in time," the woman said. "You will fail."

"Why do you haunt me so?"

She looked at him. "You let him steal me."

Angel reached for the blade strapped to his back. "Be gone aberration." He slashed the sword through her. Her form disoriented and she disappeared, but her laughter lingered. "Blasted specter. She has dogged me every day since then. Yet, she always speaks the truth. I cannot afford to be too late." Angel gripped the dagger at his side. "Quickstep!" His form blurred and he leaped great bounds forward, closing the distance he had before him quickly. He hoped it would be quickly enough. He hoped he would have enough power left to fight.

***

Santano pulled into the alley behind Melissa's house. He took a quick look around before opening his glove box and fetching his ski mask and the Blood Dagger. It didn't have a sheath, so he wrapped it in cloth. He pulled the mask over his head before exiting his car. Blood Dagger in hand, Santano advanced to the back door. The back hadn't been shoveled and the snow crunched beneath his feet. He peered through a partially curtained window into the kitchen. Inside he found a woman about a decade his junior milling about. Her hair was cut short and had tints of gray in it. She had far less wrinkles on her face than Santano had. Melissa's mother, he mused. She was carrying a steaming pot of water from the stove to the sink. It seemed she was preparing dinner for the night. Santano decided that it would be the last thing she ever did. She was in his way.

Santano moved to the back door and knocked. Melissa's mother looked towards the door and wondered, "Who could that be? Melissa?" She looked at the clock on the wall. It was around the time her daughter normally came home, but she could not fathom why she would come in through the back door. The woman finished pouring the steaming water into a strainer in the sink, the limp noodles within tumbling into the strainer. She put the pan down on the counter alongside the potholders. She wiped the sweat from her hands on her white apron and went to the door. Without parting the curtains and peering through, she opened the door ready to greet her daughter. Santano burst in and wrapped his hand around her neck as he pushed his way into the house. His heart was racing again, as it had done with Adam. The woman instinctively grasped the hand at her neck as Santano thrust with the Blood Dagger. The opals of the dagger began to glow and the dragons began to growl as the sharp blade pierced through the woman's stomach. Santano stabbed her quickly again and again. Her eyes were wide in shock and pain. The dragons pulled away from the dagger and ripped into their victim with each thrust. Each thrust pulled free chunks of flesh and bone. Blood poured out of the woman's mouth as her stomach was pierced again and again. The dragons roared as the blade found itself in her septum. They drove deep into her body and pierced her lungs and heart.

Melissa's mother stared with empty eyes at Santano. Her grip weakened and fell from Santano's hand and her arms dangled at her sides. Impaled by the dagger, she hung lifelessly in Santano's grasp. He released his grip and she slumped to the floor in a bloody heap. Santano's hand was coated with blood and dripped onto the floor. He looked at the Blood Dagger and watched as the blood dripped off the blade. Satan's words returned to him. "You must have your chosen victim etched in your mind. This blade will only accept the souls of your students, no one else." Santano's eye twitched. It didn't matter. The woman was in his way. It was Melissa he was after. Hers was the soul he wanted.

"Mom, I'm home!" Melissa called out from the other side of the house. "I'll help you with dinner in a minute. I want to put my stuff away first. I need to talk to you anyway." Her voice carried away as she spoke. Wherever it was that she was going, it was further away from the kitchen. Santano smiled. This was going to be easier than he thought; perhaps just as easy as Adam had been.

Angel arrived at the corner of Melissa's block exhausted. Sweat beat down his face and he was breathing his second wind. The sword strapped to his back was humming fiercely. "He's near her," Angel said. "He's within striking distance. So close." Angel could see the house, which only sat about fifty yards away. He took a deep breath and took off as fast as he could towards the house, trying to make every second count. Snow kicked up with every step. As fatigued as he was, Angel hoped to God that he wouldn't have to have a drawn out fight.

Angel saw a shadow of a person through a second floor window. He knew that was where he had to be, regardless of whether it was the avatar or the victim. He had to be there to protect her. Angel ran to the side of Melissa's house and began kicking up between her wall and her neighbor's with hurried persistence. Hand on the dull wooden handle of his sword, Angel focused his sights on the window above and readied to draw his weapon as soon as he found his feet.

Santano climbed the stairs at a steady pace. He was ready to rush up them and strike should Melissa come back down them. The Blood Dagger was pulsing in his hand, but not like before. It was different this time. It wasn't just pulsing; the entire weapon was vibrating in his grip. There was a hum in his ear. Santano did not know what it meant except that it wanted another soul. He did not want to disappoint it. Bloodlust took over and Santano rushed up the remainder of the stairs and through Melissa's unlocked bedroom door. It smashed against the wall as it swung open. Melissa turned around in a start holding some papers she pulled out of her backpack. Santano lashed out with the Blood Dagger. Melissa screamed as she threw herself back and held up the papers as a flimsy shield.

"Mom!" Melissa cried. The Blood Dagger ripped through her feeble attempt at defense. The pages ignited as the blade ripped through them. "Mom, help!" Santano was silent as he reached out for her. His fingers grazed her throat, but she managed to pull back and away from his grip. As she fell out of reach Santano caught hold of the loose blouse of her uniform. He pulled her close and raised the Blood Dagger. He brought it down on her. She screamed as she caught his hand and held the dagger inches from her with all her might. She heard shattering glass as the dagger came down. Following the crash, a large rusted blade appeared beside her head. All was still. Melissa followed the blade's length to the flared tip, held just inches from her attacker's wide eyed face. Her heart was racing. Her breaths were almost to the point of hyperventilation. Two blades were poised by her head. Then she heard the demand of the man behind her. "Let her go Samuel Santano!"

Melissa couldn't believe it. Was this man before her, with the dagger over her head, really her teacher? She stared at the masked man with wide eyes. She was quivering.

Santano gritted his teeth. The pulsing of the dagger had been getting stronger, more urgent. Now it was silent. It was not hungering for a soul. It was trying to warn him. "Who the hell are you?" Santano finally demanded.

Melissa's breathing nearly stopped as he stared at her attacker. She knew that voice. "Mr. Santano?" she asked. "Is that you?"

Santano didn't answer her. He just stared at the man that held a sword to his face.

The young man's face held only seriousness as he eyed Santano down. "Didn't Satan tell you?" he asked. "I'm the one going to stop you. I'm Angel, the demon hunter."

Again, Melissa's face filled with shocked surprise. She turned her head and saw Angel's face. It was the man from the pictures she had gotten for Rebecca. Staring at him she could not help but wonder, *Rebecca, what did you get me into?*

Santano twisted the fabric in his hand, drawing Melissa's attention back to him. She braced herself. "Sorry," he said. "I must have missed that part."

Melissa stared at him. "My God," she realized. "It is you. Santano, let me go!"

Santano took a step back, pulling Melissa forward, but Angel was fast on his feet and came forward as well, his blade even closer to Santano's face.

"Mom!" Melissa cried. "Mom, help!"

"Let her go, Samuel," Angel said. "There is no need for another loss. I can strike you down before you can make another move. If you let me, I can sever your contract."

"How generous of you, but I like my current deal."

"Mom!" Melissa cried again.

"Don't be foolish," Angel said. "I can cleanse you, but it has to be now. If you insist on pursuing his promises, only my blade awaits you."

A vision whisked through Santano's head. The Blood Dagger pulsed and Angel was away. A phrase rang lightly in his ears. Santano did not readily know what it meant, but knew it should be repeated and with purpose. "Pulse." The dagger pulsed strongly in his hand. Just once. A force pushed from the dagger and staggered Angel's stance and buckled Melissa's body, almost breaking her grip on his hand. Santano used that instance to attempt to gain the upper hand. He pulled back quickly, pulling Melissa with him. With her body shaken by the pulse, she offered no resistance. He turned Melissa around and pressed her back to him, turning her into a human shield between himself and Angel. Santano pressed his red blade against her exposed neck. So sharp was the edge that it was already hungrily drawing blood.

Angel pressed forward quickly with a thrust, but pulled back when Melissa was brought between him and Santano. Melissa, finding herself with a dagger at her throat, panicked. "Mom!" she cried out at the top of her lungs.

"About that," Santano said. "Mommy's dead."

Melissa's body went limp. Tears swelled up in her eyes and began to pour. "No, she can't," she said. "You didn't…"

"Angel, was it?" Santano asked. He grinned. "What was it you were saying again?"

Angel glared at Santano as Melissa sobbed and cried for her mother. She couldn't believe that her mother was dead. Angel looked briefly at the blade of his scimitar. He could feel its powers draining quickly now that it was removed from its protective sheath. All the energy he had reserved was now being wasted in this stalemate. This avatar was cocky and very sure of his abilities it seemed. He had already learned one of the Blood Dagger's abilities. Angel was not expecting that. He needed to find some way to lower Santano's guard if he was to rescue Melissa. Angel hoped at this point that that was still a possibility. It was a long shot, but perhaps he could call Santano's bluff. Angel just needed a faltering moment to strike this mortal servant of Hell down. He sheathed his blade, but didn't release the handle. He needed to buy some time and allow his powers to recharge. If he could use Quickstep…

"It seems I underestimated you," Angel answered. "You're a little stronger than I thought, but it will still end the same."

"You're pretty sure of that, aren't you?"

"I've been doing this for a very long time. It always ends the same. If you persist, only Hell awaits you and its lord does not take kindly to failure."

"Then I guess I shouldn't fail."

"I have lost count of how many avatars I have sent. So many corrupt souls, but they can still be saved. I do have the ability to sever your contract and cleanse you of your dealings. Even if you lived a bad life, you can begin again. You will have a clean slate." He needed just a little longer. He had no doubt Santano would deny his help, but he just needed enough power to attack quickly.

"I have led a good life!" Santano screamed. "I devoted my life to children! I took care of them as if they were my own! And what do I get for it? Nothing! No wife! No gratitude! No children of my own! I'll be dead within a year if I don't do this!"

"Understand this avatar," Angel said; his glare cold and icy. "My duty is not to save your victims; it is to stop your ascension. Saving her life is of little consequence in the grand scheme."

"So it doesn't matter if you save her?"

Angel shook his head. His grip on his sword tightened. There was almost enough power stored. Just enough. He had to find a moment of weakness in Santano.

Melissa was suddenly brought back to her situation. She was being held captive by her teacher and he had a very sharp dagger pressed against her neck. Worst of all, Angel had admitted that saving her was not important. "No, please!" she cried; her face red with tears. "Don't do this! I'm sorry I—" Santano silenced her by covering her mouth with his hand. Her hands pried at his, but refused to budge. She stared at Angel with pleading eyes. Angel stared back emotionless, but he was dying inside.

"I didn't realize she was so talkative," Santano said. "If we're done, do you mind if I finish this?"

"If you insist on this course of action," Angel began, "I withdraw my offer. It doesn't matter how many innocents you have sacrificed. Upon your defeat their souls will be released to be allowed judgment. Having sold your soul, yours will already have been determined. If you spare her, I will sever your contract with Satan and allow you to live."

Melissa was desperate. Blood trickled down her neck where the dagger's point had been cutting into her. It hurt. She slammed her heel down on Santano's foot, eliciting a cry from him as he buckled. That was the moment Angel needed! "Quickstep!" he cried. His form blurred across the room. Santano brought the Blood Dagger up and caught Angel's sword as he came back into focus. Surprised fear flooded Santano's face. "Damn!" Angel cried.

"Pulse!" Santano shouted in panic. The Blood Dagger pulsated again and filled the room with an invisible force. It pushed Angel and his sword away. Melissa's knees buckled under its power. Angel pulled his balance back quickly and rushed forward again. Santano panicked and pulled the blade across Melissa's trembling throat as he pushed her forward into Angel. Blood sprayed out from her neck as she stumbled forward. Her hands instantly went to her throat as she gurgled blood from her mouth. "No!" Angel shouted as he caught her. Her blood coated his body. Santano didn't know what to do. He trained the Blood Dagger at Angel and shouted, "Pulse!" It was all he knew to do. The dagger pulsed for a third time, the invisible force thrusting from it stronger this time. Angel braced himself with Melissa still in his arms. He forced his sword's blade forward and cut into the invisible force. His coat flayed about as the force was cut and flew around him.

Pained by the turn of events, Angel threw Melissa away from him as Santano rushed forward. If he was fast enough there may still be a chance to save her. If he could defeat Santano quickly, perhaps he would be granted a miracle and save her life. The Blood Dagger had to be destroyed before her life faded. It was the only way. Santano slashed angrily and desperately with the crimson dagger as he shouted its power again. Angel caught the dagger's blow with his sword and the pulse pushed him back against the window, but he stood his ground. Santano continued forward. Again, Santano used the same motions. Angel, knowing Santano would use the only attack he knew again, readied for it. He cut into Santano's side as he took hold of Santano's hand. The pulse radiated out and shattered the wall. Santano's momentum and the power from the pulse pushed Angel back and with nothing to hold him he tumbled towards the ground and pulled Santano with him.

Angel slammed into the ground first with Santano on top of him. The sword pushed through Santano's side and out of Angel's hands. Dazed, Santano rolled off of Angel. He was wobbly on his feet and tried to stumble away as he held his bleeding side. Angel groaned as he rose to his feet. With his sword gone, Angel drew the dagger at his side. The dagger's blade was thin and flared, like the Blood Dagger's, but it was rusted and dull. The handle was made of dull steel with the wear of age. The hilt was made of a curved hand guard. Angel was in pain and tried to catch his breath, but he was not dazed. He quickly locked onto Santano and rushed forward, his cross swinging freely and glinting off of the bright snow.

"I gave you a chance!" Angel shouted as he cut across Santano's back. Santano screamed as his back arched from the stinging pain. He spun around in a panic and raised his own dagger in a hasty defense, narrowly blocking Angel's blow. With their daggers locked together, Angel took hold of Santano and pulled him close. He spied the spots on Santano's dagger. There were only eight. It had already consumed its second soul. Melissa's life was no more. Angel had failed her mortal existence, but he vowed not to fail her eternal one. Wind began to whip around the two as Angel's rusted dagger began to hum.

"Now I will save their souls," Angel said as energy was gathered into his blade.

"What are you doing?" Santano demanded as he tried in vain to pull away, but Angel held him fast.

Angel's dagger was glowing with the power it had gathered. Strong winds emanated from the dagger and whipped their clothes and hair around.

"Stop it!" Santano shouted. "You can't do this!"

"Dagger of Power!" Angel shouted. "Cosmic Crush!"

Santano's eyes locked on Angel's dagger as its white glow grew out, enveloping the Blood Dagger. He was panicking. He didn't know what was going on. The light pushed against Santano as it grew, then he felt a pull as the light began to recede, pulling the area around itself inward. Santano could feel his arm being pulled into the collapsing light and felt his hand falling under pressure. He tried to pull away but couldn't. His hand was being crushed, his arm pulled away. He screamed.

The light had become a pinpoint atop Angel's rusted dagger, everything that was within the light compressed with it, the area around it, pulled inside. Half of Santano's forearm was gone, destroyed by the implosion, along with the Blood Dagger. He stumbled back. Angel pulled his dagger away and instantly the light threw out. There was an audible but empty boom as everything within the light was destroyed. Angel stood his ground and pulled his dagger away from the pinpoint of light. There was an audible but empty boom as everything within the light was destroyed and threw back out in a violent collapse. Angel shielded himself with one arm as the light threw out everything within it as little more than dust particles. Angel breathed heavily. It had taken a lot out of him. He locked eyes on Santano's screaming form and said through his exhaustion, "Now to deal with you."

Screaming and blinded in pain, Santano rushed forward. He landed a wild punch as Angel thrust with his dagger, hitting his mark. The new pain was nothing compared to what Santano was already feeling and he continued to attack. Angel was struck several times before he was able to counter Santano's blows. Angel grabbed Santano's fist and threw the avatar over his shoulder. *That attack depleted all my powers*, Angel thought. He spied his scimitar in the grass. It would certainly end the battle quicker, but his dagger would have to be enough.

Angel rushed Santano again, determined to deliver the fatal blow. He sliced across Santano's chest. The cut was deep and drew blood, but it did not slow Santano down. He was blinded with pain and rage and struck out at Angel. An adrenaline filled backhand forced Angel to stumble. His dagger stumbled from his hand and a second punch pushed Angel away and nearly to the ground. Blood cascaded down his face. Santano reached for Angel's dagger as he charged. He struck with a wide arch that Angel evaded, but left him off balance. Santano swung again, forcing Angel into an unsteady crouch. Santano thrust with the dagger and Angel caught his arm with both hands; falling the rest of the way to the ground. Angel pressed his feet into Santano's stomach and kicked the avatar over him and onto his back. Both rose to their feet as quickly as they could. The snow covered ground was tossed and askew with blood.

Santano rushed forward as he rose, slamming his head into Angel's chin. Blood escaped as Angel bit his tongue and stumbled back. Santano thrust forward, his eyes wide with pain and panic. Angel spouted blood as his dagger struck high on his stomach. Santano withdrew and struck again as they both tumbled down. The snow crushed beneath them as Santano tried to pull to thrust again, but Angel held his hand still, keeping his dagger buried inside him. If only he had the power for another attack, Angel would use it. He would survive. His weapons wouldn't kill him, but they could certainly hurt him.

Angel looked into Santano's panicked eyes. They were the eyes of insanity. Angel had to get him off. His face close, Angel slammed his head forward, breaking Santano's nose. The battered avatar was driven away. Angel pulled his dagger from his stomach and struggled to his feet. Angel stumbled forward into a puddle. He looked down to see the red of the melted colored snow. *So soon?* Angel thought. Santano screamed forward at Angel's hesitation. Angel swung an upward arc, aiming for a vital vein in Santano's throat as his exit point. Santano struck with a strong punch as the dagger bit into his body. It bit at the wrong angle and missed its intended mark. Santano struck twice and then slammed his bloodied masked head forward. He hit Angel in the mouth, drawing fresh blood. The dagger landed with a sluggish splash in the red watered grass.

Santano's adrenaline was fading. His vision was coming in and out of focus because of his blood loss. He could hear the sirens approaching in the distance. He looked around panicked. He could see the eyes that watched from the safety of their windows. Curtains were hastily pulled shut as his head turned frantically. The whole thing had been witnessed. What was he to do now? "Leave," a voice echoed.

Santano dashed around the house and into the alley, where his car waited in idle. He had to escape. His car was the fastest way. It's all he could think to do. He climbed in as fast as he could, threw it into gear, and tore off. He was not sure if he was noticed. He was not sure if he was being followed. He was in pain and he was frightened. What was he to do now?

Ultimately Angel was able to push through his pain and slowly rise. He had heard Santano flee. Blood dripped from his stomach and face onto the ground beneath him. He heard the sloshing of steps in the melted snow. Painfully, Angel raised his head to be greeted by several policemen. They had their hands on their holsters while two approached. Angel coughed and blood spilled. He could hear them cry out for paramedics as his jacket was torn from him. He let them handle him. He was in no condition to resist.

Angel caught a glimpse of several uniformed men rushing into Melissa's house. They would find her body there. Angel let his body relax as the paramedics rushed to his side. He would survive, but he hated to be in the hands of authority. He could never explain. They would never believe. Angel's gaze went to the street. He watched the bright lights flash as he saw a gurney being rushed to him. Santano would bleed to death before he got back to his Circle. Angel was certain of it. The souls were safe and he would have to contend with Santano one last time.

CHAPTER IV

Monica, Heather, and Rebecca got off at the first stop. Michael waved good-bye to them as the bus drove away. Rebecca stared after the bus as it pulled away. Her attention was not drawn back until Heather touched her shoulder.

"Hey," Heather asked. "Are you okay?"

"Yeah," Rebecca answered. "I'm just looking forward to him coming over tonight."

"Yeah, I bet," Monica said sarcastically. "You can do oh so much with your parents home."

"Like we do anything when they're not!"

"I don't know. That kiss this morning said otherwise."

Rebecca scoffed at the remark. "I was having a bad morning!"

"Aw, quit teasing her Monica," Heather said. "Remember, she's the sweat innocent girl."

"That's what makes it so much fun."

"Keep it up," Rebecca said. "I'll have my dad add extra spice to your plate."

"Okay, okay, I'll stop. I'm not calling your bluff this time. My tongue was on fire."

Laughing, they began their walk to Rebecca's home. As they passed by car windows Rebecca noticed a fourth person in the reflections. She turned to see if someone was following them, but no one was there. Rebecca tried to take a better look without her friends noticing. In the reflection, dressed in the school uniform with a backpack slung over her shoulder, Úna walked with them. *Not her again*, Rebecca thought. She wondered if she took a swing if her reflection would hit the intrusive red head. Rebecca ignored the reflections, all the while expecting Úna to say something, but the young girl never did. She stayed pleasantly quiet.

Rebecca opened her front door and called out to her father, "Dad, I'm home!"

"I'll be right there!" he returned. After a moment he rolled into the living room with a mournful look on his face. "I heard about your friend."

The little joy the girls were enjoying was dashed. "Yeah," Rebecca said. "We found out today in class. Jason told us."

"I'm so sorry."

"We are too." There was an awkward silence. "Hey Dad, can you make an extra plate for dinner? I invited Michael over. I hope you don't mind."

"No, I don't. I thought you would today. I already asked your mom to pick up some extra things from the store on her way home."

"Is Mom coming home early today?"

"Yes. I called her and let her know what happened. They let her go home a couple hours early today."

"That's good. We'll be in my room doing some homework. Let me know if you need anything."

Eric nodded as they walked away. "Rebecca," he said. "Can you come here for a second?"

"Yeah." Rebecca turned to her friends. "I'll meet you guys in a minute." Her friends nodded and went to her room. "What is it Dad?"

"Why didn't you call?"

"About Adam?" Rebecca looked away sheepishly. "I just didn't think about it. My head was all messed up today."

"I bet. This can't be an easy thing for you. Are you going to be up for going to school tomorrow?"

"Yeah. Why wouldn't I be?"

"I'm just saying. I won't make you go if you feel you need to stay."

"Thanks Dad, but I'll be okay."

"Are you sure?"

"Promise!" Rebecca placed her right hand over her heart and held her left hand up, palm open.

Eric laughed. "Okay little trooper. Go be with your friends."

"Thanks Dad." She kissed his cheek. "I love you."

"I love you too honey."

Rebecca ran to meet up with Heather and Monica, who already had their books out and strewn across Rebecca's bed and desk.

"Is everything okay?" Heather asked.

"Yeah," Rebecca responded. "My dad was just worried about me; that's all. Everything's fine."

They tried to focus on their work, but after nearly an hour still had difficulty. They had finally found a light mood, but Eric inadvertently dashed it. Rebecca found herself constantly staring at her phone. Her own line was one of the few privileges her parents allowed her on their dollar, so long as she continued to deserve it. She noticed Heather and Monica eye it periodically as well. She knew they were all thinking the same thing. How was Nicole?

Rebecca sighed. "We should call her," she said, breaking the awkward silence that had developed. "That's what we're all thinking about anyway, isn't it?"

"I know," Monica said as she stretched her neck. "But I don't know what to say to her."

Rebecca shook her head in agreement. "I know, but something is better than nothing, isn't it?"

"Yeah, I guess," Heather said.

"They would have been together for one year today, did you know that?"

"No, I didn't. That's makes it all the worse."

"All the more reason we should call her. Peter can only stay with her for so long."

"Alright," Monica said. "Call her then. We'll talk to her."

Rebecca got up off the floor where she was sitting and reached for her phone. It rang an instant before she picked it up. She jumped a little. She could hear Úna whisper, "Be ready." She and her friends swallowed. Rebecca picked up the receiver, placed it to her ear and answered, "Hello?" Michael was on the other line.

"Rebecca?" he asked. "Where are you?"

"Well, you called my home phone," she replied.

"Home, right. Sorry. You need to turn on your TV."

"The TV?" Her heart sank. She knew what that meant. "Wh—What channel?"

"It doesn't matter. They are all covering it. I'm on my way over now, okay?"

"Okay." Rebecca barely got the word out. She hung up the receiver as she turned to Monica and said, "Turn the TV on."

"What's wrong?" Monica asked.

"Michael said turn it on."

Monica reached behind her for the television. She crawled a bit on the floor before she could reach the power button. The screen brightened into a news broadcast, which was being recorded in front of Melissa's house. There was yellow crime scene tape already surrounding the house and investigators could still be seen moving in the background. Rebecca and her friends gasped when they saw it. The reporter stood listening to someone in her earpiece before speaking.

"The second of two grisly murders has just been discovered," the reporter began. "Less than an hour ago the bodies of Lisa Stouthart and her daughter Melissa were found in their home." Rebecca and her friends stopped breathing as the pure shock of another murder had taken place washed over them; again someone they knew. Tears welled up in Monica's eyes as one of her oldest and closest friends became the evening news. The reporter continued, "It is unknown whether these murders are connected with yesterday's murder of Adam Segulis, who was found dead in his home late last night. On the scene the police discovered a young man bloody and beaten. He was taken to the hospital to be treated for stab wounds. The police are not releasing if he is a suspect or his identity. Currently—"

Monica turned the television off. "I can't," she cried. "I can't watch anymore. How could this be happening?" Heather and Rebecca moved to Monica as tears filled their own eyes. "She was my friend. She was my best friend! Now she's gone!" Heather and Rebecca embraced their friend as she sat on the floor crying. Heather soon joined in the tears. Rebecca tried to hold hers back. She didn't want to cry again, not so soon. First it was Adam, and now Melissa and her mother. Rebecca let out a few sobs as she tried to comfort her friend. She fought hard not to let the sorrow consume her. Then she saw Úna. She was standing by the door, still in the school's uniform, with a mournful look on her face. "Cry now candy," she said. "You won't be able to later." Rebecca wanted to scream at her, to demand why she was following her. Why was she in her room? Instead, Rebecca did what Úna said. She cried. They cried until they had no strength left to cry.

***

A brown station wagon pulled into the driveway. The door opened and Santano fell from the inside of the still running vehicle. He was covered in his own blood and struggled to stand. Stumbling, he approached his front door and fumbled for the keys. The blood from his ski mask was running into his eyes. Santano pulled it off and wiped his face with it, smearing blood all over it before tossing it to the ground. He did not notice the blood sizzle as it touched the ground. He did not notice the blood trail he left behind him bubble and evaporate. He was in too much pain. He was in shock. Blood still dripped from his severed arm. He was matted in fresh snow from the fall from his car.

Santano finally opened the front door and he ambled inside. He leaned against the door to close it. He was beside himself with anger and fear. Knowing that Angel would implicate him in the murders Santano was expecting the police to come knocking on his door soon. With a freshly missing arm and a pavement full of blood, he didn't have much of an alibi to work with. Perhaps he would simply bleed to death before they arrived. Wouldn't that be better than spending the rest of his life in jail? He started to laugh. Jail? What was so important about that? He had failed Satan and lost his gift, the Blood Dagger. Angel had destroyed it. He screamed.

Santano knew he would have to face Satan's wrath sooner or later. He didn't have much of a choice. He had made a deal. Santano would meet with what he was sure would be a very disappointed and angry demon now. There was no escape from that wrath. He had already forfeited his soul. Santano hoped he would still have a chance to get out of the mess he had found himself in. He hoped he could make another deal.

With a blood smeared hand, Santano made his way to his basement stairs. The bloody hand prints he left behind smoked as they evaporated. He was able to take only a few steps before he lost his footing and tumbled down the hard wooden steps. Santano groaned as he looked up. Through blurry vision he saw the flames and the eyes within. Santano tried to pull himself to his feet, but couldn't find the strength. With one hand, he pulled himself towards the burning fire.

"Help me," Santano muttered.

The eyes seemed to smile.

"Some one—" Santano's sentence was caught off by a violent cough.

"His name is Angel," Satan said.

"Who—?"

"He is the last of the demon hunters. He is a mortal servant of Heaven, a sort of avatar, if you will. Like you."

"He—dagger…broken."

"Yes, he destroyed the Blood Dagger. He broke you, leaving you with mortal wounds. You should be dead."

"No…I can't…die yet."

"And that pleases me. Your will is strong. Your faith, stronger." The blood pouring from Santano's arm began to drift and pool, taking on the unrefined form of an arm. "Angel will be expecting to encounter your demonic side, but he will be in for quite the surprise."

"I don't…understand." Santano moved his blood arm, unaware that it was even there until he used it to push himself up. He stared at it through blurred vision. His head was spinning and he was getting cold. "My arm—blood?" He flexed his red liquid arm as if it was flesh and bone.

From the demonic flames lesser streams of fire wafted away, gently caressing Santano's forming blood arm. Slowly it consumed the arm made of blood and worked its way towards Santano's flesh. "Samuel Santano, it is time to fulfill the second half of our bargain." The flames reached for Santano's severed arm and seared it. He winced as the pain grew, his senses coming back enough to feel the pain. "With this the pact will be sealed. I will mend your wounds and unleash your power. I give unto you the second of the Blood Weapons." The fires climbed up Santano's arm as fires surrounded his body and lifted him from the ground. He began to scream. "Prepare for your first steps into Gehenna and for a true taste of power my avatar."

The flames consumed Santano's body limb by limb. His screams echoed throughout his house as the fires consumed every last bit of flesh. The consuming fires grew until Santano's form was lost to their all consuming hunger. A large red blade cut through the flames and dispersed them. The scimitar's blade was a crimson red with eight white spots running along both sides. The handle was etched as flames and the hilt was forged of dragon heads with emerald eyes. In the center of the hilt was a large opal. The flaming handle pulsed with life in Santano's reforged hand. His face was different. Tentatively he touched the muscle and sinew that composed his face. His flesh was completely gone. The meat squished and sloshed under his touch. His hair looked odd and out of place atop his head. The muscles that would have formed and controlled his lips contoured into a smile.

***

Angel sat in the interrogation room. Several hours had passed. He was bandaged and his handcuffed hands rested on the table. With his shirt torn and bloody, he bared only bandages crisscrossing his body. His trench coat was slung over the back of his chair. His weapons were gone and Angel was visibly agitated. Upon admitting that they were his, he was promptly placed in police custody. He stared at his reflection in the two-way mirror. Jason looked at him from the other side of the two-way glass. He was trying to stay impartial, but found that to be very difficult. They wanted to charge this man with the murder of his friends, or at least his best friend's friends. Two other officers sat in the room with Jason, staring at Angel through the glass. The door to the room opened and drew their attention. Another man walked in. He was not dressed as the other officers, but in street clothes. In his hands was a folder containing the incident report. His face was lightly coated with blonde facial hair; a five o'clock shadow. His eyes were dark and his hair loose and slightly long, but not long enough to tie. He needed to cut it.

"Detective," one of the officers said.

The man looked up from the report to address the officer and saw Jason. "Jason, are you okay," he asked.

"Yeah Dad," Jason answered as he turned back to Angel.

Jason's father, Jeff, put the report back in the folder. "You really shouldn't be here son."

Jason shrugged. "Never stopped me before. Besides," he said, nodding to one of the officers in the room. "Davis asked me over. Wanted to know if I knew this guy."

Jeff shot an angry look towards the officer, Davis. "He knows better." The officer became visibly uncomfortable as he broke eye contact with Jeff. "Well, do you know him?"

"Not a clue. Never seen him before in my life." He watched Angel through the glass. His eyes were closed and his lips had been moving. "God, this is harder than I thought."

"You've never been faced with this situation before. This could be the man that killed your friends."

"Technically, they weren't my friends. They were Michael's. I knew them a little through him." He turned towards his father. "I've heard the cliff notes. Do you think he did it?"

Jeff stood beside his son and looked into the interrogation room. "You know I can't make that assumption. Especially since my being on the case is a little touchy. You did know them, even if only through Michael."

Jason looked back to Angel. "Yeah, I guess."

"Has he been doing this the entire time?"

"Yeah. I think he's reciting prayers."

"Kind of what I was afraid of. You should really probably go."

"I want to watch. He's adamant he didn't kill them, but he won't talk to anyone."

"Hopefully he'll talk to me. We have enough to hold him for awhile. If he didn't kill them let's see if he knows who did."

Jeff entered the interrogation room. Angel looked up but said nothing.

"Hello Angel," Jeff said. "I'm Detective Jeffery Cragoff. If you like, you can call me Jeff."

Angel eyed the man before him. He let out a sigh and touched his cross. His eyes closed for a moment, his lips going into motion but no sound escaping them. He opened his eyes and slightly smiled. "I will talk to you," Angel said. "You are not as the others. You are a good person."

"Thank you for saying that," Jeff said as he sat. "But are you implying that the other officers that interviewed you are not?"

"You would not understand."

"Try me."

Angel was silent for a moment. "Very well. I am able to see beyond what the human eye can see."

"What does that mean?"

"You genuinely want to help people. To you, this is a calling, not a job or a position of empowerment. Your reasoning to wear that badge is just, as is your son's."

Jeff was taken aback. "What do you mean? How do you even know if I have a son?"

Angel pointed to the two-way mirror. "He called you father; you, his son. You and he are much alike, and I understand his position. Jason, you said his name was?"

Jeff looked towards the two-way mirror. "Yeah." He looked back to Angel for a moment. "Hold on a second." He left the interrogation room. Jason looked at his father with worry as he checked to make sure the speaker was off. Jeff looked towards the other officers in the room.

"Make sure this stays off, got it?"

"It was never on," one of them said.

"Well he heard every word we said. How else would he know my son was here, or his name? Keep it off and keep quiet. Don't say anything."

Jason and the two other officers in the room nodded. Jeff went back to speak with Angel. "Okay, let's get back to business, shall we Angel? You have no ID. Can you tell me what your full name is? Where are you from?"

Angel looked away almost ashamed. "My place of birth and surname are of no consequence," he said.

"Come on, you can tell me. I told you mine."

"I have no family."

"You don't talk to them anymore, huh? Falling out?"

"They are dead."

"I'm sorry to hear that. What happened to them?"

Angel's hands tightened into fists as he stared at the table. "It was my fault."

"Did you do something? Was it an accident?"

Angel did not speak right away. He could hear the screech of Pestilence in the back of his mind. After so many years, and all he has seen, it was still terrifying. "It was a mistake." His voice broke once. "I tried to save them."

"Sometimes things happen that you can't control."

"I should have. I should have been able to protect my kin."

"Angel, we found you at someone's home. Did you know them?"

"No."

"Then why were you there?"

"I was sent."

"Who sent you?"

"I was too late."

"Angel, did you kill the two women inside?"

Angel's eyes shot up. "Two?"

"Yes. There were two bodies in the house. You didn't know?"

"I didn't know about the other woman. He was only after Melissa."

"You knew her?"

"No. I was sent to try and save her."

"From who?"

"The avatar."

"Avatar?"

"You would best describe him as a Satanist. But he's more than that."

"So, are you telling me he killed Melissa and her mother?"

"Adam as well."

Jeff's brow arched in surprise. The two cases are related and Angel knows how. "So we're dealing with ritualistic sacrifices then?"

"In the most basic sense. He will kill again tomorrow."

"Who will he kill?"

"I don't know. He hasn't chosen yet."

"Why tomorrow? Why not today?"

"It is unsafe for him to take more than one soul a day."

"He took two today."

"No. He ended two lives, but took only one soul."

"Who is he? Do you know? Maybe we can help you. Make sure he doesn't take another."

"You cannot help me. You would only be throwing away your lives."

Jeff reached out and put his hand on Angel's. "My job is to protect people. That's what I do. Please, a name."

Angel looked into Jeff's eyes and sighed. "His name is Samuel Santano."

Shit! Jeff cursed in thought as he pulled his hand away. *That's one of my son's teachers.* He placed his hand to his chin in thought, trying to hide his apprehension. "Samuel Santano." Jeff repeated. "How do you know him?"

"Because of what he is. You can't hurt him."

Jeff looked towards the two-way mirror for a moment. *Jason is hearing this whole thing. I have to wrap this up.* "Angel, can you tell me about Santano? If we go to him, what should we look for?"

"Burns; red puddles. There is snow on the ground. Where his blood falls it will boil."

"His blood will boil?"

"I know how it sounds. I have been saying it long enough to know how it sounds on the outside, but it is what it is."

Jeff sighed. "Angel, let us help you. Give me something I can use."

"You cannot help me. They are safe now, but come the morning they will be in danger again."

"So you know how he targets people? How? We can use that."

"The reasoning is as different as the people that make the contract."

"Angel, how does he pick?"

"I don't know how he picks; just that his victims have some tie to him. They always do. How are Adam Segulis and Melissa Stouthart tied to Samuel? The others will be tied in the same fashion. Those are his targets. Tell me. That would help me."

"This is all new to me. I don't know how they are tied."

Angel cocked his head. "Your breath faltered. You do know, at least you think you do. You don't want to say."

Jeff knew Angel was right. They were Santano's students. As far as he knew, that was the only connection to Santano the two of them had. "You're right, I do have an idea and I won't say. Not yet."

"I understand. Listen to me Jeff. You can't stop him and you won't help me."

"Why won't I help you Angel?"

"Because you can't."

Jeff sighed and rubbed his brow. "Okay, listen. It's late and you're probably in a lot of pain. Honestly I'm surprised you were released to us so quickly. Why don't you get some rest and we'll try this again later? I really do want to help you, Angel. I want to catch the bad guy too."

Angel said nothing as Jeff rose from his seat and left the interrogation room with folder in hand.

Jason looked at his father and scoffed. "My teacher? Seriously? I know he's weird, but a killer? Come on!"

"That's enough Jason. Go home. Don't tell anyone about anything Angel said in there. It could compromise the investigation."

"Yeah, I know." Jason started to leave and hesitated. "He's crazy, you know that?"

"Home, Jason. Now."

Jason went into motion and disappeared through the door.

Jeff looked at the officers in the room. "Get Angel into lock up and get him a mental evaluation. I don't think everything is quite right in his head."

"Don't take a shrink to tell you that," one of the officers laughed.

"No, but it takes a shrink to tell us how much. He knows more than he's telling. I need to know how much more."

"You don't think except for this Santano guy almost everything?" the other officer asked.

"No. There were bloody puddles where we found him and heading behind the house. Get a team out there to sample the puddles behind the house before they're gone. I'm going to report to the chief."

Jeff walked away as the other officers went in to put Angel into lock up. *Samuel Santano?* Jeff thought. *Damn it! I should have made Jason leave before I started. I know he's going to tell at least Michael, who will then probably tell Rebecca.*

Who knows who she'll tell? We have to have a talk. Maybe I should have made him wait for me instead. If Angel is telling the truth, we have a big problem. As Jeff walked into the chief's office the potbellied man stood up to greet him. He was in full uniform with a clean shaven face and a full head of hair, still its natural medium brown color, despite him being almost a decade older than Jeff.

"Did you get anything out of him?" the chief asked.

"Yes, but I think he's holding back."

"Tell me."

"Angel is scared of something, but I'm not sure what. I think he may be working with someone else, who may be giving him information on what to do. His family died and he blames himself."

"What does that have to do with this? Him and the Stoutharts related?"

"No, I don't think so. He said he was there to protect Melissa. She was the target, not her mother."

"Slitting someone's throat is his idea of protection? Make sure I don't ask him to watch my dog."

"He said he was sent to stop the killer. That's why I think he's working with someone."

"We'll know when someone pays his bail. If he's not the whack job that killed them, who did?"

"The same guy that killed Adam Segulis."

"Connected. You're going to make me happy now, right?"

"Angel said the killer's name is Samuel Santano."

"Ring any bells."

"He teaches at my son's high school."

"Are you fucking serious? A teacher? Great, I can see the headlines now. Local teacher makes demonic sacrifices." The older man sighed. "Can this be trusted?"

"I think. Maybe. He called Santano an avatar, or a Satanist. That when his blood touches the ground it boils. There were red puddles leading all the way to the alley and tire tracks."

"Anything lifted?"

"No. I asked for another crew to be sent back to sample the red puddles leading behind the house."

"So Angel roughed this guy up? Good. It'll be easy to get a match that way. What else?"

"According to Angel, Santano is targeting people connected to him in some way. Adam and Melissa were both his students. Angel expects him to kill again tomorrow. One a day for I don't know how long."

"Then why two today?"

"He was after Melissa. Her mother was in the way."

"I hate dealing with the occult."

"Right now we're just waiting for results to come back on the contents of the jars we found in Angel's coat."

"Jars? What jars? Nobody told me about any jars."

"It's mentioned in the report."

The chief gestured to the piles of paper on his desk. "Does it look like I have the time to read every single report that finds its way to my desk?"

Jeff stifled a grin. "Angel had on his person jars with contents of various colors, as well as vials of water and crosses. He thinks he's fighting servants of the devil. I guess it makes sense."

"Makes sense, huh? Then tell me what a priest is doing carrying around a sword."

Jeff shrugged. "Hard to say. If Santano's hurt, he may show up at a hospital. Maybe we should go poking around, have a little chat with him."

"Damn right we are!" the chief shouted as he slammed his hand on his desk. "Figure out where this guy lives too. I want someone there in case we miss him or he skipped the hospital."

"I'll get on that."

"Get a search warrant too. I want in his house. If he's a Satanist we should be able to find something."

"It'll be hard with only Angel's word to go on."

"It'll be easier if another one of his students dies. Find out what else Adam and Melissa had in common besides they had him as a teacher. Let's hope he's not just randomly targeting his students."

"Do you want me to ask Jason?"

The chief shot Jeff a glance. "Jason. He wasn't there when you interrogated Angel, was he? Please tell me he wasn't, just once?"

"I'm sorry. Davis asked him over to ID Angel."

"He did what? I'm going to wring that rookie's neck! Get him in here!"

"He's escorting Angel to a cell."

"Not Davis! Your kid!"

"I already sent him home."

"He can't say anything. We have to go."

"I already told him to keep quiet."

"My kid is twenty-three and doesn't listen to me. Yours is seventeen. You're my best. I want you on this case. If he yaps, I have to yank you. I want you on this as long as I can keep you."

"I was worried you would pull me when you found out."

"Up to Jason," the chief said as he grabbed his jacket from the hanger. "Get your coat."

Angel was escorted from the interrogation room by two officers. His hands were still cuffed in front of him and each officer held an arm. One had Angel's trench coat slung over his shoulder. Angel looked around, searching for a way to escape and retrieve his weapons. He needed to get back on the hunt and finish off Santano before it was too late. Angel caught a glimpse of one officer having trouble with the arrest she made. With one hand clutching a large box she found she was having trouble maintaining control of her charge. The tall red-head threw the box onto a desk and turned to her charge. "You are more trouble than you're worth!" She grabbed him with both hands and walked him out. The box had fallen to its side and was knocked open. Inside were Angel's sheathed weapons, vials, and jars of colored salves. Even his small pocket books were there. His eyes locked on them. "How fortuitous," he whispered.

Angel tested his bonds. The cuffs were sturdy and would not easily break. He needed them removed and removed quickly. He did not have the time to force them off with his limited strength. He whispered a prayer,

"My Father, if my work seems hard today, may I not cease working if I grow weary." His escorts noticed his mumblings. "But may my strength be renewed to continue my work."

"What did you say?" the taller of the two officers asked with a jerk. "What are you talking about?"

"May the aim of my work be to please Thee, and to help in the progress of humanity. Amen."

"Speak up," the shorter escort, Davis, demanded as he gave Angel a hard jerk.

Angel took a deep breath as strength filled his limbs. He tightened his fists and stood his ground. "Let's go!" the taller officer demanded.

"No," Angel answered. He pulled his arms apart, breaking the links in his cuffs and threw his escorts off him in one motion. His jacket went flying and Angel plucked it out of the air.

"Hey!" they shouted as Angel broke away from them and headed for the unguarded box. Papers flew everywhere as Angel leaped over the desks in his way. The surrounding policemen rushed forward to subdue him, but Angel was easily able to knock them down with only a blow or two. Each one that went down was unable to get up immediately. Angel had knocked them senseless. When he reached his weapons the officers pulled away and drew their pistols. They were trained on Angel only for an instant. He muttered something beneath the roar of the room and his form blurred and vanished, along with the box in his hands. He appeared in another part of the room, crouching on a desk with his trench coat donned and his sword almost strapped to his back. Astonished murmurs slowed the room's reactions as Angel filled his pockets with his belongings. When the room had regrouped and trained their guns on Angel again, he blurred and was gone. Again he reappeared elsewhere, this time on the ground behind a desk and not readily in view. Angel finished filling his pockets and was ready to make an escape.

"Over here!" a voice shouted. Angel looked up to see a gun trained on him. He blurred and vanished as the trigger was pulled.

"The hell's going on?" the chief shouted as he burst from his office with Jeff.

"He got away from us!" someone shouted.

The chief and Jeff watched astonished as Angel's blurred form darted around the room, disorientating the officers trying to keep up with him. The chief's eyes tried to keep up with Angel as he yelled, "Someone grab him!" He seemed to pay no attention to the fact that Angel was basically disappearing and reappearing. Jeff rubbed his eyes, wondering if he was really seeing what he was seeing. It should have been impossible, yet he was seeing it. In all his years on the force, he had never seen anything like it before.

With the room of officers confused, Angel appeared before a wall and drew his sword. The rusted blade ignited in flames as Angel shouted, "Meteor Punch!" The flames culminated at the sword's tip and spit forth a fireball with a rock core. Struck at pointblank, the fireball bashed through the wall and to the outside. Angel's coat fluttered from the explosion. Flames burned on the edge of the newly formed hole in the wall. Jaws dropped as Angel burst into a run. A few rounds fired. "What are you louts waiting for?!" the chief shouted as he pushed forward. "Get after him!"

Officer's made their way through the breached wall and opened fire on Angel. He turned sharply as he continued to run backwards. He drew his rusted dagger as he swung his sword in quick motions. Each swing deflected the series of bullets away from his body. One or two managed to graze his arm and he winced. Angel ducked behind a car to shield himself from the increasing barrage of gunfire. Holding his ancient dagger tight, Angel called out, "Dagger of Power! Psionic Camouflage!" A green mist began to waif from the dagger's hilt, surrounding and consuming him.

Officers raced to where Angel had hidden, but he was gone. No one had seen him run and they searched the vicinity for him. Murmurs of shock and disbelief echoed throughout the station. The chief broke through the crowd in anger and looked through the newly formed hole in his wall. "Put out an APB! I want him back! Now!" The chief stormed back towards Jeff. "Get this wall fixed on the double!" Jeff stood dumbfounded. He watched Angel dart around the room in a blur and then throw a fireball from his sword. The evidence for that was the hole in the station's wall. The chief blazing past him drew back Jeff's senses and he shook his head. They still had to talk to his son. This mystery would have to wait.

***

Monica had left Rebecca's house just after Michael arrived and long before Jeanine came home. Jeanine was unaware of Melissa's death and was surprised to learn that Monica had left. Michael had helped Rebecca and her father tell her mother that another friend, and her mother, had been murdered. Dinner that night was quiet. Michael looked around the table as everyone ate in awkward silence. Both Eric and Jeanine sat opposite heads of the table. Heather and Rebecca sat across from each other and Michael sat beside Rebecca. Staring down at his plate, Michael thought he would never see the day where he would not enjoy Jeanine's scalloped potatoes, no matter what she served them with. He found he liked it even better than his own mother's rice. Sided with skirt steak, it should be a meal enjoyed, but like everyone else he had trouble enjoying it. Another friend was gone. He wondered if Jason had already called him with news on what the guy they found had to say. He was sure if it was important, he would have called Rebecca's house to relay the news. Without hearing from his friend, Michael figured either they had found out nothing, or Jason was not allowed to say, which meant what he knew was important. Two days back at school after Christmas Break and all Hell was breaking loose.

After dinner Michael helped Jeanine clear the table.

"Thanks for dinner Jeanine," Heather said. "I guess I should get going. My parents may know I'm here, but I'm sure they're worried. I want to call my brother too."

"Haden?" Rebecca asked. "He went back to his dorm already?"

"Yeah, he left the day before we went back to school."

"What does he say college is like?" Michael asked as he grabbed his jacket. "Does he like it?"

"He loves it. He said he couldn't wait to get back. He kept going on and on about how hot California girls are. I was happy not to have to hear about that anymore."

"We'll see you later Rebecca." Michael kissed her cheek.

"Is your car fixed yet Michael?" Jeanine asked.

"It won't be ready until Monday."

"Then I'll take you both home. It's too dangerous to walk around at night right now, especially with a murderer running around."

"Thank you," Heather said. "I didn't really think about that."

"Mom," Rebecca said. "Before you take them, um…"

"What is it sweetie?" Jeanine grabbed her jacket and keys.

"Well, can Michael…stay tonight?"

Heather leaned into Michael and whispered, "Have you ever stayed here before?"

"She's never even offered," Michael whispered back.

"Then she must be really scared."

Michael nodded in agreement.

Jeanine smiled at her daughter and shook her head. "I understand that you're scared right now, but no. You're safe enough in your room."

"That's not why," Rebecca mumbled.

"Speak up. You know I don't like it when you mumble."

"I just want—"

"The answer is no. You may both be eighteen, but this is still my house. My rules. I don't want one thing leading to another and that's how it starts."

"But Mom—"

Eric touched Rebecca's arm to silence her. "I understand," he said. "Your mother is right, though. I don't have an issue with Michael staying over once in a while, but now I think is a bad time. Okay?"

Rebecca sighed. "Alright."

"We'll talk about this later Rebecca," Jeanine said.

"Alright Mom."

As Jeanine ushered Heather and Michael out the door Michael opened his mouth to talk, but Jeanine interrupted him, "Don't say anything Michael. We can all talk about it later, but tonight you go home."

"Yes, ma'am," Michael answered. He looked to Rebecca and mouthed, "Sorry".

Heather tried to hide her laughter. She wanted to say something, but decided against it lest she be reprimanded as well.

***

Far away from the police station, a green mist began to waft into existence in a dark snow dusted alley. Within the mist a form began to appear. It was Angel. The mist was absorbed back into the dagger as Angel leaned against a garage, exhausted. He slid to the ground as he sighed in fatigue, his breath vaporizing in the cold air. "What am I going to do?" he said. "I can't keep going on like this, but there's no one to replace me.

Using Cosmic Crush has never dazed me so much before." Angel forced himself to stand. "At least it should be easier to defeat Samuel now. He may have the Blood Sword, but his powers will have stagnated as an inner demon." Wearily, Angel walked away. "I need to rest before he chooses his next victim. He will have to start over now."

Angel heard the tapping of heels on the cold ground. He turned to see a tall, curvaceous woman with the build of an Amazon. She was slightly taller than him, wearing all black leather; her halter top connected to the choker around her neck. Her long dark hair whipped around freely in the cold wind. She wore no jacket but seemed unaffected by the cold.

"You," was all Angel said when he saw her.

The Amazonian woman smiled at him. "Poor, poor Traitor. You've met your match with this one."

"I've defeated him once. The second time is always easier."

She crossed her arms and rested one against her face in thought. "This is true, but have you really defeated him? You may be in for an unwelcome surprise Traitor."

"I will win. I must win."

"Yes, you must. Your blood depends on it, but you will not. You will die."

"Another day, but not today."

"Yes, another day. Four days, perhaps." She smiled wickedly at him. "Will you seek Redemption, or will you simply pass?"

Angel looked away. "Redemption…" he whispered. He looked back to her. "You know what that would do."

She nodded. "What will you do, Traitor?"

"Be gone, aberration."

The woman smiled and was gone. Angel looked toward the sky. "Lord, my work is not yet done. I gave my word. Eternity has not yet passed."

CHAPTER V

Rebecca lay in her bed that night, eyes open. She didn't want to go to sleep. She would give anything to be able to hold onto Michael, but her mother was stern in her decision. Rebecca wanted to bring it up during dinner, but she didn't. She thought she would have a better chance after dinner, but Jeanine didn't even give her a chance to say anything. Rebecca looked at her clock. It was just after midnight. She turned away from it and huffed. "This is ridiculous," she said to herself. "I'm afraid to go to sleep because of a dream. It's just a dream." She looked around her room, expecting Úna to chime in. "Stupid bitch. She has me expecting to find her in my room. She's probably not even real. She's probably just some figment of my imagination that took off when I found out Adam died." She sighed as she closed her eyes. "We never got to call Nicole either. I'll have to call her in the morning."

Rebecca tossed and turned all night. She witnessed legions of angels battling against one another in what used to be a lush and green world. The golden streets were tarnished, the trees set ablaze, and the buildings, more beautiful than any she had ever seen, lay in waste. The ground shook and split as fire erupted from the crevices. A slew of angels were knocked back, some of which fell into the fires. A heavily armored angel walked forward from the devastation. He wore armor of shining gold, from his thick and sturdy boots of forward facing roaring lion heads to the gold mane like neck guard. A blue jewel glowed and from it lines of blue power coursed through the armor, filling the runes in the arm and leg pieces. In his right hand he held a massive broadsword that Rebecca thought at first was surrounded by flames, but she realized the blade itself was a flame. In his left was a massive polished mirrored shield that reflected the carnage it saw against its surface. His angelic wings draped around his shoulders like a majestic emerald cape. He tore the pure white lion headed helmet from his head to better view the battlefield. His medium long dark brown hair with golden tones drifted in the battle born wind. His brown eyes filled with anger as he saw the devastation that was around him in this once beautiful kingdom. "Samael," he whispered in disgust. He donned his helmet before unfurling his mighty wings. He took to the skies with such power that the ground buckled beneath the flap of his emerald wings. He held his blazing sword aloft and shouted, "Push them back! Push them to the Gates! Push them into Eden!"

The angels under his command charged forward, chanting the angel's name, pushing their former comrades back as much as they could. Rebecca could hear the chant, feeling it reverberate through her body like a war drum. Michael. Michael. Michael. Rebecca stood frozen as she watched the war unfold. "It could have gone many ways," Úna said, her Irish accent back. Rebecca found the red-headed freckled face girl standing beside her with a concerned look on her face as she watched the devastation.

"What is this?" Rebecca asked.

"You don't know?" Úna asked. "Look around you and see how beautiful this place used to be, before The Fall."

Rebecca looked around. Wherever she looked, for an instant, she could see the world as it once was. Beautiful buildings of brilliant hues of blues, browns, and greens rose high into the sky. The trees were tall and their canopies full; their colors brighter than any Rebecca had seen. Their leaves were not always green, but mixes of greens, reds and browns, as if the leaves were in a constant autumn state. The streets were paved in gold and everyone walked them with smiles on their faces. There was no pain, no anguish. Rebecca could think of but one thing. "Is this Heaven?"

Úna nodded. "This is where the war erupted. It was here that the first blow was struck."

"What happened?"

"The accuser passed his own judgment. He found your kind unworthy of praise. He refused to bow and instead raised up arms."

"Are you talking about…?" Rebecca found she couldn't finish the sentence.

Úna nodded her head. "You call him the devil. He now goes by Satan, but his true name, his Angelic name, is Samael. He was one of the most powerful of angels, perhaps the most powerful. He refused the rank of archangel and his place as one of the twelve rulers of Heaven. He took to his task as the tempter of Man. He did his job well, perhaps too well. He saw humans as fickle beings that were easily swayed. Their faith in their Creator was tentative at best. Lest, that is what he had decided."

"I don't understand."

"Then come. I will show you."

Úna touched Rebecca's arm and the scene of war was replaced with fire and brimstone. Carved caverns with jagged walls and sharp ceilings stretched all around. Deep chasms that belched white hot fires dotted the landscape. In Rebecca's gaze was a burning lake whose flames burned bright and hot; the Lake of Fire. She knew this place at once. Everyone would. It was the place all humans fear the most. "Hell?!" Rebecca exclaimed, her body tensed as she wanted to run and was too terrified to move. Her heart raced and her stomach tightened into knots as her eyes darted around the landscape.

"The Underworld," Úna said. "This is where the traitors were banished, but Samael was not content to his new home of torments. This was a critical turning point in the war. It changed everything." Úna pointed to the Lake of Fire. "Look at the battle raging before you. Even an Olympian found it impossible to control Samael's rage."

Rebecca stared at a war ravaged angel. She could tell, even from the distance that they stood, that he was once very beautiful. His once fair flesh was carved in battle wounds and scars. His long light brown hair was a tangle and matted in blood. His white robe torn and tattered, revealing a slender but strong body beneath. His wings of pure white were stained red. Even with all his hurt, the angel's beauty was great. The being he wrestled with was nearly twice his height and imposing. His body was massive in muscles, even beneath his armor of black and gold. His face was hidden behind long dark hair and a great beard. His armor had small spikes running along its back, knees, elbows, and shoulders. His boots were tipped with spikes, as were the soles. His gauntlets were locked with golden chains and along his fingers and down the gauntlets length were lined sharp spikes. Somehow, Rebecca knew him immediately.

"Hades…"

Úna stared at the battle. "Yes, the god of the Underworld; the Olympian god of death and betrayer of Samael. He offered up his realm to house Samael and his legion in exchange for the souls of Earth. It was agreed upon, but only for the wicked. Righteous souls would not suffer in this place."

"Wait, you mean there wasn't always a Hell?"

"No. Earth had no such place, not naturally. The Eldest could not stand to see his creations in torment. Instead, many humans were doomed to live life over and over again until they were deemed worthy to enter Heaven's Gates. It was not an easy task, so angels were constantly on Earth guiding wayward mortals to their paradise."

Hades knocked Samael to the ground and delivered several powerful blows to his head. Each strike was so strong that Rebecca could feel the vibrations of the strikes and hear each blow as if she were standing next to them. The bone crunching sound made her flinch. She could see the blood of the angel splatter on the god's dark armor and hair.

"Come!" Úna said. "This is important!"

Úna again touched Rebecca and the young blonde girl suddenly found herself standing beside the pair and staring up at the terrifying visage that was Hades. Samael lay on the ground bloody and beaten, but still tried to stand. Hades pressed his foot violently against the fallen angel's back. The spikes of his boots drew fresh blood. His heavily gauntleted hands reached for Samael's blood stained wings and tore them from his back. Samael screamed.

"I will destroy you for this Hades," Samael promised.

"You are but a lowly angel Samael," Hades said. His voice was deep and hallow. "There is nothing you can do against a god. You were foolish to challenge the Eldest and I was a fool to believe that you even stood a chance." Hades lifted Samael overhead. "Since you will not lie in peace I will cast you into the Lake. It is reserved for only the most atrocious of souls, but I believe that it will shatter what is left of your will."

"I will rip your still beating heart from your chest and roast it over these flames god of death."

"None cast into the Lake ever return, Samael. You will not be the first. Farewell Samael."

Hades hurled the fallen angel into the fires below. The roaring crackle of the burning flames was not loud enough to muffle the angel's screams of agony. Hades stood over the Lake for a moment before walking away.

"What happened?" Rebecca asked.

Úna raised her hand and time seemed to speed up. "It took a millennium, but he climbed out."

A burned hand burst from the fires, starling Rebecca. The burned husk of Samael screamed out the ancient god's name as he pulled himself up. His skin was burned red and scarred. His pure white wings, torn from his back a millennium ago, were replaced with seared black and charred flesh that dangled from his back. His legs were mangled and barely moved. His bloody eyes seethed with anger. The Olympian god approached the burned angel bewildered. "This is impossible," he said. "None but the strongest of gods can escape my torturous fires." Samael screamed as blood caked bat-like wings tore from his back. He unfurled them and took to the air. Hades looked up at Samael as he attempted to gather the strength to battle his godly opponent. Dark malignant energy swirled around him in a darkening cocoon.

"Our time runs short," Úna said as she snapped her fingers. "See the strength of the enemy of Man."

Time shifted instantly and a newly formed Samael stood atop the mangled and defeated body of Hades. The armor of the ancient god of death lay shattered, his body battered and broken. His empty eyes stared skyward from a mangled face. Samael's lower limbs had taken the form of a goat with burned red fur and dark hooves. Massive twisted horns grew from his head and curved around his cranium. His dark red body was covered in cuts, blood, and guts. His dark leathery bat wings dripped with blood and gore. In his right hand he held a rapier of silver with a half guard etched as an angel's wing. In his left hand he held a still beating heart.

"Samael is no more," the fallen angel said. "From this day forward I will be known as the Lord of Gehenna. I am Satan."

The alarm sounded and jarred Rebecca from her restless slumber. Hell. She was sure that she was just shown Hell. To witness such a beautiful creature become so evil and vile was disheartening at the very least. Rebecca knew what she had witnessed, but she had trouble believing that she truly saw what she saw; the legendary fall of legions of angels and the seizing of Hell itself. The fiery and bloody birth of the greatest evil the world has ever known, the once proud angel called the devil and Satan. Rebecca had never known that he once had another name.

Rebecca looked at her clock and turned off the alarm. It was six in the morning. Her mind couldn't help but wonder what was happening. Was she seeing events of days gone by? Was she being warned of some great catastrophe that was about to rock the world? Of all people that could be given the warning, "Why me?" Rebecca cried. "What can I do?"

"You will do what you have to do," Úna said. "Just as he has done; just as your blood has always done."

Rebecca looked at Úna standing in the threshold of her door with one foot on the other side. "What?"

"You'll see. Time for school." She closed the door. Rebecca climbed from her bed and threw her door open, but Úna was nowhere in sight. All Rebecca could think to do now was what she had to do. She had to go to school.

Rebecca stood under the pouring water in the shower as she tried to push her troubling thoughts away. She tried to convince herself that she was having these dreams because of the murders. It would be enough to give anyone nightmares. She wondered if maybe she should talk to the school's social worker. Maybe that would help her deal with her dreams. If nothing else, it was someone that she could talk to besides Michael. She didn't want Michael to know about these dreams. They were making her feel like she was going crazy and that's the last thing she wanted anyone to think. At the very least the social worker could suggest something that would help.

Nirvana echoed in Rebecca's ears as she waited for the bus. She decided to bring her headphones this time. If she couldn't be distracted by the outside, maybe she could avoid Úna and any other hallucinations. She nearly jumped out of her skin when a hand lay upon her shoulder. It was Michael. She pulled the coat's hood from her head and the headphones off her ears and let the strap rest against her neck.

"So that's why you couldn't hear me," Michael said. Rebecca thought he looked upset.

"Michael, what's wrong?" Rebecca asked. "What are you doing here?"

"You didn't see the news this morning before you left, did you?"

"I never watch it."

"We're walking today. We need to talk. If Monica saw it this morning, she's probably going to be mad at you."

"Why? What does the news have to do with me?"

"Come on. I'll explain on the way." Michael took her by the hand and led her in the direction of the high school.

"What's going on? You're scaring me."

"Remember how the cops found someone yesterday when Melissa and her mom was murdered?"

"Yes."

"I caught it on the news this morning. He broke out of jail and the police have a warrant for his arrest. They think he did it. It's the guy you had Melissa looking for, Angel."

Rebecca stopped dead in her tracks. Shock washed over her face and dread that she may have gotten her friend killed filled her being. She felt sick to her stomach.

"Yeah," Michael said. "That's what I did. That guy is loose out here right now. I don't want to stay out but I also didn't want you and Monica to get into it on the bus either. We're going to talk to Jason first."

Rebecca stuttered her agreement and picked up her pace with Michael. If what he was saying was true, did that mean Angel would target her next? Was she going to be the next to die? Somehow, that just didn't seem right. Angel wouldn't do that. How she knew that was true, she didn't know. She just felt that it was true. She tightened her grip on Michael's hand. Michael would protect her, wouldn't he? She knew he would try.

The trek to school was uneventful. The sidewalks were clear but the sun's light was cold. Walking with heightened speed and raised blood kept them warm in that cold. They looked for Jason in the weight room first and found him on one of the chest press machines. He had already worked up a good sheen of sweat.

"What are you two doing here?" Jason asked as he continued his routine.

"We came to talk to you about the murders," Michael said.

"I'm sorry. This time I can't. My dad will be taken off the case if I do, suspended too."

Michael held the machine in the up position. "You don't have a choice. We may have a motive for you."

"What are you talking about? Put my weights down."

Michael let the weights fall and Jason stopped his workout. He left his machine and wiped the sweat from his face with his towel. "Now, what are you talking about?" Jason asked.

Jason looked to Rebecca, but she looked away and remained silent. She didn't want to say it. In a way, she thought that if it wasn't said then it wasn't true.

"Rebecca saw Angel on Monday."

"Alright. So what?"

"She asked Melissa to look him up and now she's dead."

Jason's face filled with shock. "Oh shit. What did Melissa say about this guy?"

"Um…" Rebecca said.

"Becca, I need to know. My dad needs to know."

"She said to not ask about him. That he was trouble. She said it was like he didn't exist."

"So she went looking for a guy that didn't want to be found. Definitely shows a motive. What else do you know? Did she give you anything?"

"She gave me some photos of him from—I guess it was a hunting store."

"Do you still have them?"

"They're in my bag."

"Alright, hold on to them. My dad will probably want to look at them. He may be able to find out what store they're from and look further into it. In the meantime, just go about your day. Don't mention this to anyone. I'm going to call my dad before class starts up. At least I'm going to try. I may not be able to get a hold of him this early. Just go about your day normally until me or him tell you otherwise, okay?"

"Yeah."

Jason threw his towel on the machine to mark that he hadn't wiped it down and left the weight room.

"Does…anyone else know?" Rebecca asked.

"I don't know," Michael answered. "Who watches the news, right?"

Rebecca didn't respond, but she heard Úna say, "It's not as it seems." Rebecca looked around the room briefly, but didn't see Úna.

"Hey, Becca. You know the Principal is probably going to tell everyone about this guy, right?"

"You—You think so?"

"They think he killed two students."

"What about Melissa's mom?"

"Jason did tell me something about that yesterday, I guess before he was told to seal his lips, but he told me it was confidential and not to repeat it. She wasn't killed like Adam and Melissa. She was in the way."

"What do you mean?"

"Melissa's mom was stabbed to death. What no one else knows is that Adam and Melissa had their throats slit."

Rebecca gasped and covered her mouth. Úna had told her that Adam had his throat slit yesterday. She knew before anyone else.

"I know you're really against ditching, but I think you should consider skipping biology today. Melissa was Monica's best friend."

"Yeah but—"

"I'll talk to her first, but if I say we should skip class—Please; just this once."

"I'll need to talk to her anyway."

"Yeah, but the middle of class isn't the place. She was as close to Melissa as you are to me or Peter."

"I see what you're saying. Okay, if you think we should leave, I'll skip just this once. But stay with me when I have to explain to my parents why."

"I will." He moved in to kiss Rebecca and she lifted her head to let him give her a quick kiss on the lips. There was no one around to see. There was no one to potentially offend. Lately, she had found she was not caring about that anymore.

Rebecca didn't realize that Michael had left. She heard him tell her to get to class before she was late, but she hadn't realized he had left. The bell rang. Cutting class was looking good to her now. She didn't want to deal with everyone today. She would wait for Michael. If she was going to leave, it wouldn't be without him.

Úna sat with her legs crossed on one of the machines. She was wearing the school's uniform. She smiled as she watched Rebecca leave, who was completely obvious to Úna's presence.

"What do you think?" Úna asked the empty room. "Does she have what it takes?"

"If she doesn't, she will when I'm through with her," a voice answered her back. It came from nowhere and everywhere, all at the same time.

"Are you going to take her now?"

"Absolutely not," a second, older voice said. "That is simply out of the question. As a mere mortal, she would not last more than two minutes with you. You have to wait. She will let you know when she is ready."

"So," Úna said, "when are you two going to make your presence known? Or are you just going to let me deal with the little cookie?"

"Must you refer to everything as food?" the first voice chastised.

"Well, if it bothers you so much, I guess I'll do it more, you sour grape."

"Rusted blade."

"Spoiled milk."

"Enough!" the second voice boomed. The room darkened with the anger in his voice.

"Yes sir," Úna and the first voice replied in unison.

"Are you going to show yourselves to her or not?" Úna asked again.

"In due time," the second voice said. "I see the strands of a short lived future. I can feel the pain and anguish of that loss. One more must fall. Then we will appear to her."

"Poor thing."

"Until then, leave her in peace. You can do no more but torment the girl."

"Fine. Fine." Úna jumped from the machine. "I'll leave her be, but I'm sticking around. The grotesque abomination is nowhere in this region. My underlings will answer to me. They will keep me updated."

"Very well. Do as you please. We will prepare for our arrival. We must decide on names."

"Understood," the first voice said.

"How about Mr. Cranky and Old Guy?" Úna asked as she left.

"Can I hit her? Just once?"

"Now is not the time to fight amongst ourselves. Keep your temper in check. We have much to do and little time to do it in."

Rebecca walked slowly to her history class. The loud speaker kicked on and the Principal's voice filled the hall. "Good morning students. I wish I had more joyous news to relate, but alas, I do not. As many of you may know Lisa Stouthart and her daughter Melissa Stouthart were murdered yesterday afternoon. The police have a suspect, but he has eluded custody. I am to inform you that this man, who has been identified as Angel, should be considered armed and extremely dangerous. He has been described as a Caucasian with short brown hair and brown eyes. He has a muscular build with no apparent scars. He often wears a trench coat and carries a sword with him. If you see someone of this description, please do not approach him and contact the local authorities immediately."

The loud speaker gave an audible click as it was turned off. Rebecca could hear someone running behind her. She turned to see Úna running down the hall carrying a set of books in her arms. "I missed it," Úna said, absent of her accent. "What was he talking about?" She looked at the clock jutting from the wall. "We're so late! Come on!" She ran past Rebecca and headed into her history class. Rebecca questioned what she was doing. She picked up speed and followed the red head in.

"Sorry I'm late!" Úna said. "I completely missed the bus!"

"That's okay Úna," Ms. Dale said. "You and Rebecca please take your seats."

"Wait a second!" Rebecca exclaimed. "Who is she?"

"Úna Devor, your classmate." It was spoken more as a question than a statement.

"Since when?"

"All year. Rebecca, are you sure you're okay?"

Glenda didn't give Rebecca a chance to answer. She rose from her seat to go to her friend. "I think she's just a little overwhelmed, Señora Dale. Úna usually just keeps to herself, sí?" She took Rebecca by her hand and led her to her seat. "Vamos."

Rebecca broke her hand free. "No, I'm okay. You're right, I'm just overwhelmed. I'll be fine. Thank you Glenda."

Rebecca took her seat. She was relieved to learn that Úna was not a member of her group. That at least hadn't changed. Rebecca tried to concentrate on the group project, but found herself distracted by Úna. She was munching away on M&M's one piece at a time, savoring each piece. She seemed involved with her group, more so than Rebecca could say for herself. Austin had even brought a koban to show everyone, but Rebecca couldn't find any interest in it. She had hardly done any research on her end of the project. Austin was researching both military and economy in her stead. Rebecca felt bad, but she couldn't focus.

"Rebecca, are you sure you're okay?" Brian asked.

It took Rebecca a moment to acknowledge him. "I'll be alright. I'm just…distracted."

"I'll say," Glenda said. "You've been staring Úna down like she's some kind of alien or something."

"I have?"

"Did she do something to you o què?"

"I'm…not sure."

"What do you mean you're not sure?" Austin asked.

"It's hard to explain."

"It's because of Adam and Melissa, isn't it?" Brian asked. "The guy that escaped?"

"Something like that."

"I wouldn't worry too much. I'm sure the police will catch him soon."

But will someone die first? Rebecca thought to herself. *What does he want? And he does have a sword. Why could no one see it in the picture?*

Rebecca forced more attentiveness to avoid further questions from her friends. She knew they only wanted to help, but they were only making things worse for her. Rebecca was relieved when the bell rang. She was happy to get out of that class. She stopped at her locker to lighten her bag, since she hadn't had a chance beforehand. She noticed Úna humming away happily and obliviously as she wondered down the hall. Úna had her nose buried in a book while she hummed her tune. Rebecca wasn't sure what the tune was; she had never heard it before. Úna weaved around the passing students with little difficulty, even though she paid no attention to her surroundings. Rebecca saw that she was reading Othello. *Don't tell me she's in my English class too,* Rebecca thought. She gathered what she needed from her locker and then proceeded to English. Sure enough, Úna had already found her seat. It also looked like Nicholas was trying to hit on her, but Úna was paying him no attention. Rebecca really didn't want to deal with all this and thought about finding Michael and leaving. Instead, she took her seat.

The bell rang and everyone took their seats, but Leonato waited the few minutes he had always offered. Rebecca wanted to turn around and see what Úna was doing, but thought that would draw attention to her. She didn't want to do that. She wondered why everyone knew who Úna was but her. Why was she the only one out of the loop? How long was Úna supposed to be in school with them?

"Hey Rebecca," Nicholas said as he tapped her shoulder.

For once, Rebecca was happy to be bothered by him. She turned around to feign a look at Nicholas, but instead fixed her gaze upon Úna. "What is it, Nicholas?" Rebecca asked.

"Are you doing okay?"

"Two of my friends just died. What do you think?" Úna was sitting quietly at her desk reading <u>Othello</u> and munching away on Skittles. She seemed oblivious to what was around her.

"Yeah, I know. I'm really sorry about them."

Úna spied Rebecca staring at her. In response she raised her head, smiled widely, and waved her fingers in a playful greeting.

Realizing that Úna knew, Rebecca quickly fixed her gaze on Nicholas. "Thanks for that, but are you going somewhere with this?"

"Well, kind of. About the tutoring I was asking you to do—"

"Nicholas, stop. I'm really not in the mood for this." Rebecca turned around in her seat.

"No, it's not what you think."

"Please, just leave me alone. I'm dealing with a lot right now."

"Right," Nicholas groaned. "Sorry."

Class began and Leonato began his lecture on Shakespeare and <u>Othello</u>. Much to Rebecca's surprise, Úna answered all Leonato's questions with such knowledge and authority that one would think she was not only an expert on Shakespeare, but that she actually knew the man. More than that, Rebecca thought. She seemed generally proud of him. The bell rang and the class spilled out into the hall. Rebecca walked down the hall to her next class. She was not looking forward to it. Nicole hadn't returned to school yet and seeing the empty seat was hard to bear. Rebecca thought Nicole would transfer out of that class entirely. She would probably transfer out of all the classes she could that she shared with Adam. Looking towards his desk just to find an empty seat would just be too much. It would be harder if someone decided to take that seat. Rebecca knew she wouldn't be able to handle it if she lost Michael like that.

When Rebecca entered class, she found yet again that Úna had found a seat in it. It looked like she was almost done with <u>Othello</u>. *Ignore her,* Rebecca thought to herself. *Just ignore her. Take your seat and pretend like she's not even there.* Rebecca sat in her seat and focused on the lecture. She was astonished to learn that Úna's understanding of mathematics rivaled her own. Rebecca was happy to not be called upon so often to answer questions, but was also annoyed that Úna was stealing her spotlight.

Rebecca found herself doing something she often didn't do, volunteer to solve problems and explain the formulas. She wasn't going to let this stranger outdo her. Years without a decent rival, Rebecca was just learning about her competitive spirit. She was good at math. She didn't want to be second rate to someone else. When Úna noticed Rebecca challenging her, a sly smile crossed her lips.

The lunch bell rang and Úna was one of the first students out of class. Rebecca stopped by her locker to put her books away and found Michael waiting for her.

"Are you ready to go?" he asked.

"Just like that?" Rebecca asked. "You already talked to Monica?"

"I talked to Heather. She said don't come to class until they can talk. Monica did see the news today and she's mad. Heather's been doing her best to keep her calm."

Rebecca bit her lip. She didn't know what to say.

Michael lifted her chin. "I know what it looks like, but that doesn't mean it's your fault."

"But I had Melissa look for him, and now she's dead."

"I know, but how would he know she was looking for him?"

"But you already said—"

"I want to be cautious, that's all. So let's go. We can talk more on the way back to your house."

Rebecca hesitated. "Wouldn't it be better if I talked to her instead of running away from her?"

"It will be better to talk to her when she is willing to listen. Give Jason a chance to get a hold of his dad too."

"Alright." Rebecca conceded and prepared to brave the outside cold.

***

Santano had trained all night and day in the confines of his basement. The demonic flames that housed Satan's essence watched Santano's endless training and corrected his form when it faltered. Santano's face had its flesh returned to it and he appeared as a normal man wielding a blood red scimitar.

"I can't believe how strong and alive I feel," Santano said in mid slash. "I haven't slept in over twenty-four hours and don't feel the least bit tired."

"That is a benefit of my gift," Satan said. "With your powers unleashed and now allowed to grow, you will find that you need less and less rest. We rarely sleep. There is no need except to recover from injury."

"This knowledge…is it a part of that gift as well?"

"Yes. Currently that knowledge is limited to your profession, but as you grow in power you will obtain more. Use this knowledge to help you in your quest. That is why it is there. You have access to everything you could need to know about your potential victims in order to choose your sacrifices more readily."

"There is a lot of strife and misery accompanying the death of Adam and Melissa. Three it seems are being hit especially hard." Santano laughed. "Rebecca seems to blame herself for some reason. Monica seems to agree and is pissed at her. Nicole though…" Santano stopped in thought as he accessed the knowledge. "She is asking for Angel's head on a platter. She is in so much strife and anger. It's rather delicious. Perhaps I should send her to her beloved? Wouldn't it be poetic to learn that it was I that did away with Adam and in turn was doing her the favor of allowing her to see him again?"

"Yes, in a delightfully perverted way."

"Then she is next."

***

Angel lay sleeping on the floor in the warehouse that he made his temporary home. His weapons rested on the ground within arm's reach. The scimitar that Angel called the Sword of Might began to hum in warning and roused him from his slumber quickly. He gripped his weapons as he rose to his feet. He pushed the hilt of the sword away from the base of the sheath, freeing a portion of the rusted and dull blade. "Show me," Angel said. As before, Angel's mind's eye revealed Santano's intended target, the mournful Nicole Amnesty. He could see the anger and sadness dwelling within her. She was walking down the street in her winter coat, but her hood was down. The wind would pick up every now and then and whip her hair around. "Where will he strike?" Angel asked the blade. The blade hummed and his mind's eye vision moved past Nicole and towards her destination, a corner convenience store. It was there that Santano would strike. Angel knew where he needed to be.

Angel strapped his weapons to his being as he began to head out of the warehouse. The Amazonian woman stood in his path. "Why do you try so hard?" she asked. "You can't stop him." Angel ignored her and moved through her. The woman's form faltered as Angel passed. "Do you truly think you can save her Traitor? You can't."

"I will try," Angel answered as he continued on his way out. The woman followed.

"Try as you might, you will not succeed. You have struggled long, Traitor. You have given the Dark One much grief, but your struggle is coming to an end. This avatar will be your undoing. This will be your last hunt."

"Enough!" Angel shouted as he turned with a swing of his blade. He cut through the woman in one motion, the blade passing through as if she were air. Her body distorted and she smiled at him as she disappeared. "It doesn't matter what happens to me," Angel said. "If I am to die, so be it. I will continue to fight. Death will not stop me."

"I never said it would," her voice echoed. "But a dead man has no strength to struggle. Remember that."

Angel stared down at his rusted sword. He was worried. Santano was still trying to accumulate his sacrifices, as expected. His aberration insisted that he would finally die. What was of real concern to him, however, was that the blade never warned him of the arrival of an inner demon. Did Santano in fact actually survive their last encounter? If so, what exactly will he face? It had been so long, he could not readily remember.

***

Nicole walked down the cold snow covered street. She walked with her head down, hands in her pockets and hair blowing in the wind. Where people had yet to shovel their walkway, Nicole kicked the snow with her feet until she was through it. Her face was red with recently shed tears. It made her face cold. She had seen the news that morning. She knew about Angel and that he was not only being charged with Melissa and her mother's death, but also with Adam's. Needless to say, she didn't care much if Angel was caught or simply shot to death on sight.

The door chimed as Nicole entered the small corner shop. She stomped the snow from her boots on the floor mat.

"Hello Nicole," the clerk greeted.

Nicole looked at the young man. He was tall and thin with short jet black hair. His eyes were a soft brown and were heavy with concern. He didn't look as cheerful as he normally did, but then again neither did Nicole. "Hi Burt," she answered.

"How are you feeling? Are you doing alright?"

Nicole gave him an almost insulted glance as she crossed the floor to the bread rack. "When they kill Angel, I'll be much better." Her tone was angry and insulted and she realized this as she grabbed a couple loafs from the shelf. "I'm sorry Burt. It's just really hard for me right now, you know? My boyfriend was murdered, my parents are away. I just feel so alone right now." She rubbed away freshly falling tears. "I'm sorry."

"You know, Nicole, if you need someone to talk to…you can always talk to me."

Nicole offered a weak smile as she laid the bread on the counter. "Thanks Burt, I appreciate that. It's been awhile since we've done much of anything together. But right now, I think I really do just need to be alone."

"Well, you have my number if you need anything."

"Yeah, I still have it, somewhere." She laughed weakly. "I could always come and visit if I can't find it."

Burt offered a small smile. "I'm renting now, but I still live in the area."

"I didn't know you moved."

"I did graduate almost two years ago, you know. Can't stay at home forever."

"Yeah, I suppose not."

Burt looked at the loaves of bread laid on the counter. "You can just take them. On the house this time."

"Are you sure?"

"What's the old man going to do, fire me? That may actually help me."

Nicole laughed a healthier laugh.

"That's more like it."

"Thanks Burt, I needed that."

Burt bagged the bread and handed it to Nicole. "I know you did."

Nicole took the bag and headed for the door. Before opening it she looked back at Burt. "You know, we used to be pretty close friends. When did we grow apart?"

Burt shrugged. "I don't know; my graduation maybe?"

Nicole contemplated his response for a moment. She wiped away a left over tear. "We'll have to take some time to catch up later."

Burt agreed.

Nicole exited the store and bumped into someone that was rushing by. "Hey!" she said. "Watch where—!" Nicole found herself staring into the exhausted face of the man she hated so much, Angel. Her eyes widened in fear and anger as she realized who she was standing in front of. Her heart began to race as her adrenaline began to rise with her anger and fear for her own life.

"Nicole?" Angel panted. "I need to—"

"Get away from me!" Nicole screamed as she slammed her bag of bread across Angel's face.

Angel's face jerked to the side and spittle flew from his mouth. Taken by surprise he was knocked off balance which helped Nicole push past him. Angel quickly found his footing and grabbed Nicole by the arm.

"Hold on!" Angel exclaimed.

"Let me go!" Nicole screamed as she let the ruined bread fall to the ground. She clawed at Angel's hand and kicked him in the shin.

Angel groaned in pain and grabbed her other hand. He wrestled with her while she kicked him in the legs anywhere her booted foot could reach. "Wait! Let me ex—!"

Angel was interrupted when a metal bat slammed into his back, sending him to the ground and forcing him to release his grip on Nicole. "Run!" Burt shouted at Nicole as he swung the bat and hit Angel in the stomach. Nicole took off down the street as Angel rolled away to avoid the next blow. "You won't take her!" Burt yelled at Angel.

"Stop!" Angel called after Nicole. "Samuel Santano—!" Angel was silenced when the bat struck across his face. His blood coated the frost covered ground as it trickled down his face.

Nicole ran down the street. As she reached the alley that was only a couple houses away from the store, a figure quickly emerged from it. A black shirt and jeans hugged his large, muscular body. His face was horrific to look upon; all its flesh stripped away, his pale brown eyes forever locked in a wide stare, his graying brown hair looking odd atop his head. In his left hand he held a blood red scimitar with eight white spots along either side of the blade. His frightening visage halted Nicole in her tracks, but she had no time to let out a scream. He was fast and held Nicole as his sword passed through her body. All she felt was a sharp pain and her clothes become wet with blood. The man whispered into her ear, "Say hello to Adam and Melissa for me."

Nicole took a few struggled breaths as blood trickled out of her mouth. She knew that voice. The realization of who her killer was hit her hard. Tears welled up in her eyes and all she managed to do was whisper his name, "Santano?"

Santano pulled the Blood Scimitar out of Nicole's body and pushed her away, letting her fall to the ground. Burt saw Santano appear seemingly out of nowhere, he had moved so fast, and pierced Nicole in what seemed like an instant. He called out to her as she fell. She hit the ground and stared up at the sky, coughing up blood once as she struggled to breathe. Santano held up the Blood Sword and watched as Nicole's blood swirled around the blade, filling the third white spot. Burt gritted his teeth and gripped his bat tightly. "You monster!" he cried as tears began to flow. Angel rose quickly before Burt could throw his life away. Angel drew the Sword of Might and cried out, "Keen Edge!" The blade shined briefly and sliced through the metal bat, effectively disarming Burt.

Angel rushed forward into battle with the Sword of Might drawn back and ready to strike. Santano stared at his adversary and a fleshless grin crossed his lipless mouth. Burt watched the first collision of blades and felt the shockwave emitted by them. It wasn't strong enough to physically move him, but it was strong enough for him to feel. Realizing there was nothing he could do except call for the police and an ambulance, Burt ran back into the store to dial nine-one-one.

Angel and Santano traded powerful blows, but no matter how quickly Angel struck, Santano was faster in his block. Angel was gripping his sword with both hands and swinging with all his might, but Santano was able to defend against every strike with a single hand on his weapon. He barely moved from his ground. That face; Angel knew that face. Between blows Santano reached out and took hold of Angel's neck. Santano's grip was tight and Angel was lifted off the ground. Angel was jarred and pried at Santano's choke hold with one hand while he held his sword tightly in the other. He found he had trouble finding the strength to lift his sword arm as he struggled to breath in that instant. In one quick motion Santano slid the Blood Scimitar into Angel's side. Angel grunted and dropped the Sword of Might. His hand gripped the red blade and tried to pull it out, but he had no leverage to challenge Santano's newfound strength. "You're out of your league now, Angel," Santano said. "Give it up." With a quick thrust of his hand, Santano threw Angel off of his sword and across the frost covered ground. Angel's blood dotted the frosty pavement. Landing near the store entrance Angel could hear Burt on the phone with the police as he tried to get help. Angel rose to his feet as quickly as he could. Dazed and staggering, he rushed forward again. He drew the Dagger of Power and held it ready to strike as Santano raised his blade horizontal to his body and placed his hand at the base of the blade. As Angel neared, Santano pulled his hand across the blade, leaving behind a trail of flames and said, "Vanish." Angel struck as he called out, "Impact!" The Dagger of Power passed through the smoke that Santano left behind as he disappeared.

Angel winced as a sharp pain shot from his wound. Bewildered, he stared at the dissipating smoke that Santano had left behind. Santano was not an inner demon. Angel knew that face. Death's Visage. It had been so long since an avatar survived their initial encounter. Santano survived and now had his powers unlocked, as well as wielding the Blood Sword. How did he survive those injuries? Angel moved to retrieve his sword and as he did he heard Nicole struggle to stir. His eyes widened in shocked amazement. Somehow, Nicole was still alive. Angel could barely believe that was possible. She was fighting. He kneeled down next to her and took her into his arms. He wanted to help her. He was unsure if any of his prayers would help her and his healing powers left him many years ago. At this point he didn't know what to do. He had never encountered this before.

Angel looked down at Nicole and her lips trembled as she struggled to find the strength to speak. "I'm sorry," she said. "I was…so angry at you, but…it was Santano…all along." She coughed up blood.

Angel looked at her, unsure of what to do. "I'll help you." He said finally, thinking of nothing else to say.

Tears filled Nicole's eyes as she smiled weakly. "The angel says you can't. She looks so sad."

"Angel?" Angel looked behind him and tried to use his diminished Divine Sight to locate the angel Nicole spoke of, but he could not. He focused his powers briefly, trying for just a glimmer, but nothing.

"She's so beautiful…" Nicole breathed one last time and slowly her eyes closed.

Angel sighed in disappointment. "I am sorry," he said. He laid Nicole gently back onto the ground. He could hardly believe that she was so strong willed that she was able to prolong her death to say those simple words. "Don't worry," Angel said as he rose back to his feet, sword in hand. "I will free you, I swear it."

Angel sheathed his sword and turned his attention to the storefront. Burt had come back out and stared at Angel with hurtful and teary eyes. Angel looked away, placed his hand on his dagger and whispered, "Quickstep." His form blurred for a moment and he was gone. Burt ran to Nicole, picked her up into his arms, and after a moment of trying to rouse her, cried.

CHAPTER VI

Rebecca was quiet on the cold walk back to her house. She clung onto Michael's arm and watched her breath turn to vapor as she breathed. It kept her calm. Michael didn't press her to talk. Leaving school early and seemingly hiding from and abandoning her friends was hard enough. He hoped her parents wouldn't be too angry with her. He wasn't worried about himself; it wasn't the first time he had cut class, but it had been awhile since the last time he played hooky. Since he met Rebecca, he had little reason to leave school early. Unlike Sarah, Rebecca never skipped class. This was her first time, as far as Michael knew. In his mind she had good reason. He hoped her parents would understand.

Rebecca undid the lock to her front door. Her mother would still be at work, but her father was always home. In a wheelchair, where could he go; especially in the middle of winter? The ground is either covered in snow or slick. Not the best conditions for a wheelchair to try and operate on. Rebecca was glad that her mother was at work. That gave her time to talk to her dad alone about what she had done. Eric always seemed more understanding of her plights than Jeanine.

"Who's come home so early?" Eric called into the living room from the kitchen.

"Uh, me Dad," Rebecca called back.

"Rebecca?" She could hear him put something down on the table and roll himself towards the living room. "Is everything okay?"

"I'm…not sure."

When Eric entered the living room threshold, he was surprised to see Michael with his daughter. "Michael? You're here too?" He crossed his arms and furrowed his brow in concerned anger. "Please tell me there is a good reason for you to be here instead of class."

"Well—"

"There is," Michael interrupted.

"I would much rather hear it out of my daughter's mouth," Eric said.

"I understand, but it was my idea. Please give me the chance to explain sir."

Eric sighed. "Alright. Rebecca, since you are home, I need some things from the corner store. Go pick them up for me. That'll give me and Michael a chance to talk."

"Yes Dad," Rebecca answered

"I need some green peppers, a leaf of garlic, and some tomato paste. Wait a second and I'll get you some money."

Eric wheeled around and left towards his bedroom. Michael leaned towards Rebecca and whispered, "I'm sorry about getting you in trouble. I'll try to smooth things over."

"I know. It'll probably be easier to talk to my dad instead of my mom anyway."

Once her father returned with some money, Rebecca left to purchase the ingredients that she was asked for. By what he wanted, she figured that he was making spaghetti. As she neared the corner store she could see the flashing lights of police cars. As she drew ever closer she could make out an ambulance and yellow crime scene tape surrounding the area. Fearing that yet another murder had taken place, Rebecca ran over. When she reached the line she was forcibly stopped by an officer before she could cross. Rebecca saw a draped body being hoisted into an ambulance. "What happened?" Rebecca asked as she tried to see around the officer holding her back. "Who is that?"

"It's Nicole," Burt said. Rebecca stopped her struggle and broke away from the officer. She turned towards Burt, who was sitting sorrowfully atop the hood of one of the police cars. He had a blanket wrapped around him. Rebecca could see the blood on his hands.

"What did you say?" she asked him as she closed the distance.

"That's Nicole's body," Burt repeated. Not able to bring himself to look at Rebecca, he stared at the ground instead.

Tears were quickly welling up in Rebecca's eyes. Bloody hand prints marked the blanket where Burt had pulled on it. "What happened?"

Burt hesitated, not sure of how to start, but ultimately said, "Angel…"

"Angel killed—?"

"No!" Burt interrupted, connecting with Rebecca's teary gaze with his own. "Angel didn't do it. He…I think he came here to help her. I think he was trying to warn her."

Rebecca was trying to refrain from crying, almost as much as Burt was. "Burt, please tell me what happened. Why are you covered in blood?"

Unable to continue looking Rebecca in the face, Burt glanced away before telling the story. "She came to buy some bread. She was pretty distraught over Adam's death. We talked a little before she left. When she did, Angel met her at the door and tried to stop her. I think, now, that he was trying to warn her, but she wouldn't listen. Why would she? He's wanted for three murders. While they struggled I grabbed the bat the old man keeps behind the counter and attacked him. Now I wish I didn't."

Already knowing the next part of the story, Rebecca covered her mouth as tears began to flow down her face. "What happened?"

"Someone jumped out of the alley. It was almost like he appeared out of nowhere. He had a big red sword and just slid it into her. She didn't have a chance."

Rebecca gasped. She no longer tried to hold back her tears or sobs. With Rebecca sobbing freely, Burt began to sob anew, but still continued. "Angel attacked him and I called the police. When I came back out, the murderer was gone. I held Nicole until the police came and pulled me away." He sighed and wiped his tears away with the back of his hand. "I don't think Angel killed Melissa and her mother, or Adam. I think it was the other guy, but when Angel ran he got the blame. They're completely ignoring the other guy." He slammed his fist on the hood of the car. "I hate the media!"

Rebecca turned towards the ambulance as it pulled away. As she watched it disappear into the distance, sirens blaring, she sobbed, "Not Nicole too. Why is this happening? Please, tell me why."

"Excuse me," one of the officers said. Rebecca turned to face him as she tried to quell her tears. "You were her friend? I would like to ask you a few questions."

"Yeah, okay." Rebecca answered as she wiped her tears away.

"When was the last time you saw Nicole?"

"Yesterday, when we found out Adam died."

"Adam Segulis? You haven't seen her between then and now?"

"No. He was her boyfriend. When she found out he was dead, she hadn't come back to school."

"Have you called her since?"

"I haven't, but my friends have."

"Was there a relationship between either Adam or Nicole and Melissa you're aware of?"

"Yes. We were all friends. I had known Melissa since about third grade."

"What about Adam and Nicole? How long had you all known each other?"

"They had been dating for about a year. I met them when I was a sophomore. That was about two, three years ago."

"Do you know if they had anyone that they didn't get along with? Anyone at all?"

"No. Melissa kept mostly with her circle of friends, and Adam and Nicole were pretty likable. No one really had issues with them."

"So they didn't draw anyone's attention? No one at all?"

Rebecca hesitated. Melissa had found Angel, who was then charged for her murder. "No," she lied. She decided to wait for Jeff's father to say anything about that.

"Okay. What did you say your name was?"

"Rebecca."

"Rebecca…?"

"Um…Virtue."

"Thank you Ms. Virtue." The officer gave her a card. "If you think of anything else that may be helpful, please call us."

"Okay," Rebecca answered as she took the card.

Burt watched the officer walk away before calling Rebecca over. "There's something else I want to tell you, something they ignored and something I didn't tell them."

"What is it?"

"His face. I told them he wore some kind of horror mask, but I don't think it was a mask. It looked like his face had been skinned. He had no skin at all, just muscle tissue and veins. It didn't look fake to me."

"That's disgusting. You think he skinned his face?"

"I don't know. What bothers me is what Angel called him."

"He knew his name? What was it?"

"He called him Samuel Santano."

Rebecca's eyes widened in shocked surprise and her heart dropped. Úna's words came back to her, "You know who he is. You see him every day."

"No," Rebecca said. "It can't be. Mr. Santano? Our teacher?"

"I don't know if it's the same Santano, but that's the name he said," Burt responded. "He's the only Samuel Santano I know. When I told the cop, he didn't seem to care very much. He scribbled something, but I don't think it was a name."

Rebecca's mind reeled. It couldn't have been the same Santano. He was in school teaching class. He had to have been. How could she know for sure though? She skipped that class. "I…I have to go!" she cried as she ran back towards her house. She needed to get home. That's all she could think. It wasn't for the fact that the murder had just happened and Nicole's killer was still on the loose and probably close by. She needed to know about Santano. She hoped and prayed that Santano was still in school, that the man Angel called was a different Santano. It couldn't be her biology teacher. She couldn't believe it, but if it was, it started to put the things Úna had been saying into perspective. Yesterday, when Santano took out his laptop for the first time in front of class, Úna sang, "He chose." That afternoon Melissa was killed. Úna knew how Adam was murdered, information the police had not leaked. Then last night Úna showed her the taking of Hell and the rise of the devil himself. Just what was Úna? Why was she giving Rebecca these warnings? What fate did she have to accept? What did she have to get ready for? What was she expected to do?

Rebecca burst through the front door crying. She ran right into Michael's arms as Eric wheeled around. Both asked what was wrong over each other.

"Nicole!" Rebecca cried. "She's dead! He killed her!"

"Hold on a second," Michael said. "Who killed her? How do you know?"

"Burt told me. It just happened! The police were there and an ambulance was taking her away!"

"Rebecca, please calm down," Eric said, frustrated that he could do little to help confined to his wheelchair. Michael rocked Rebecca in his arms as he whispered soothingly into her ear. Eventually, Rebecca did calm down and stopped crying.

"When I got to the store," Rebecca said, "the entire area was roped off. The police were removing a body. Burt told me it was Nicole. She came to buy something and when she left, she ran into Angel. Burt tried to help her, but when she did get away from him, someone else jumped out of the alley and killed her. Burt thinks Angel was trying to warn her about him."

Before Michael or Eric could say anything in response the door bell rang.

"Oh for the love of—" Eric grumbled as he rolled over to the door. "Who could that be?"

"Please don't let it be Monica," Rebecca whispered to herself over and over again.

When Eric opened the door, Jeff stood on the other side in full uniform. "Good afternoon, Mr. Virtue."

"You're Jason's father, right?" Eric asked.

"Yes. My name is Detective Jeff Cragoff. I wish we could have met under better circumstances."

"Yes, so do I. I suppose you came to talk to my daughter?"

"Yes. I was told she might have information prudent to this case."

"Come in then. The sooner you catch this guy the sooner my little girl can stop crying."

"Thank you. We are certainly trying our best."

Rebecca was relieved when Jeff came through the threshold. "Um…Dad? Is it okay if me and Michael talk to him alone?"

Eric sighed. "Yes, if that will make it easier for you. I need to make some phone calls anyway."

The trio waited until Eric was out of the room before Jeff said, "If what Jason has already told me is true, I can understand why you don't want your father to hear it."

Rebecca rubbed her arm nervously instead of giving a verbal response.

"So, what exactly is it that happened?"

"Pretty much what we told Jason," Rebecca answered.

"That's fine, but I need to hear it from you, not a second source. Remember, my son is not a cop yet. He can't take statements. He's not on this case either, so please refer information directly to me."

"Well…Alright. I saw Angel on Monday. Something about him bothered me and I mentioned it to my friends. Melissa was brought up and we asked if she would be able to find out who he is. She said yes."

Jeff had taken out a pocket book and was jotting down Rebecca's story. When she had spoken to the officer at the store earlier, he didn't do that. "Okay," he answered. "Go on. What happened next? Did she find him?"

"Yes. Hold on." Rebecca picked up her backpack from where she had tossed it when she first arrived home and dug through it. She retrieved the folder that Melissa had given her earlier. "She gave me these pictures of him. She said his name was Angel." Jeff took the folder and browsed through the pictures. "She told me something was off about him, that it was like he didn't exist or something. She was killed that afternoon."

"I see. Do you mind if I keep these? They may be helpful."

"Not at all. I'm kind of glad to be rid of them."

"Do you have any other information?"

"Well…I know about Nicole. Burt said there was another killer. Angel called him Samuel Santano."

Michael's attention perked.

Great, his name is spreading, Jeff thought while retaining a neutral posture. "Did you hear Angel say this?"

"No, that's what Burt said. I showed up after it all happened. My dad sent me to the store after I got home."

"Yeah, when I didn't find you at school, I decided to come here. Figured you may have left. Can't say I blame you for that. Why did you ask Melissa to find this man? I mean, what made you think she could actually do it?"

Rebecca shrugged. "I guess because she's just kind of nosey. She always knew the latest gossip and rumors, like she was the first to know. I'm not really sure how she does it."

"Alright." Jeff reached into his vest pocket for a card. "While I don't think you are in any immediate danger, stay on your guard. Please call me directly if you notice or remember anything else. I'm going to relay this information to my chief and see what he wants to do."

"Okay. Thank you. Um…"

"Is there something else?"

"They said he carries a sword. Is it true?"

Jeff didn't answer right away, but found himself looking at the pictures of Angel. "Yes, we did confiscate a sword from him."

"In the pictures, does he have it on him in any of them?"

Jeff looked through the pictures. He saw no sword readily. "Which picture do you think you saw a sword?"

"You don't see one?"

"Not readily. It would cause a stir and he probably didn't take it with him." He handed Rebecca a random picture and she looked at him. "What do you see?"

Rebecca looked at the picture. The sword strapped to Angel's back was as clear as day to her, but no one else could see it. She showed it to Michael. He shook his head. He couldn't see it. Rebecca handed the photo back and answered, "Just a man."

Jeff nodded. "Be safe." Jeff let himself out. *That was strange,* he thought as he walked back to his car. He found himself really looking at the pictures. For an instant, in one of them, he thought he could see a sword, but there wasn't one. *Nothing. Just some security photos. I think I know this place. I'll have to pay them a visit.* He put the pictures away and got into his car. *Nicole was just murdered? I should be getting notification of that any minute. Angel didn't kill her, huh? I definitely want to read that report. If Angel was trying to warn her, then it coincides with his alibi. He isn't the killer; he's a vigilante that knows what's going on. It looks like it is the occult.*

Michael put his arm around Rebecca once she was done telling Jeff the story and fidgeting around. He looked at her and asked, "Santano? Are you sure?"

"That's what Burt said," Rebecca answered. "It's all I have to go on."

"What do you think?"

"I don't know. How could Santano kill his own students?"

That's a good question. "I don't know, assuming that it's the same Santano. And why did you go back to the sword thing anyway?"

A knock from the kitchen threshold turned the couple around. "Is it safe to come back in yet?" Eric asked.

"Yes Dad," Rebecca replied, thankful for the interruption to Michael's question. "Thanks for giving me a few minutes."

"I couldn't help but overhear. The Santano that you're talking about, it's not one of your teachers, is it?"

"I don't know."

An awkward silence filled the room. "Well," Eric broke through, "I do have some good news. You're mother is bringing home takeout. Not quite sure what exactly, but she's bringing home something."

"No spaghetti tonight, huh?" Rebecca asked, trying to smile.

"Naw. Changed my mind. I suggested pizza, but Jeanine said absolutely not. Friday's only."

Rebecca and Michael laughed, though Rebecca's laughter was short.

"Rebecca, when you get a chance could you dig out the air mattress."

"The air mattress? Why?"

"I thought maybe you were going to ask if Michael could stay tonight again. You're mother said you'd have to sleep in the living room. Just be aware that Jeanine will probably check in on you."

A huge smile etched itself on Rebecca's face. She wouldn't be afraid to go to sleep tonight. "Thank you, Dad!" Rebecca exclaimed as she threw her arms around Eric. She caught herself quickly and turned to Michael. "You do want to stay, right?"

Michael smiled a lovable smile and answered, "Of course I would. How could I say no?"

The phone began to ring, drawing their attention to it. "How busy we are today," Eric said as he began to turn towards the kitchen.

"Don't trouble yourself sir," Michael said. "I'll get it."

"You can call me Eric you know!" Eric called after Michael as he disappeared through the threshold. Eric smiled to himself. "That boy…"

Michael answered the phone on the third ring. "Virtue residence."

"So you did skip with her?" Monica's angry voice said from the other end.

"I thought you would call. Calm down—"

"I will not calm down! Do you know who killed Melissa? Of course you do! That's why you're at her house instead of class!" Michael could hear someone struggling with Monica over the phone she was using. He guessed it was one of the school's payphones. "I want to talk to Rebecca right now!" Monica shouted.

Michael contorted his face in thought. "Alright," he finally answered.

Monica went silent for a moment. "That fast? You're going to put her on the line just like that? Aren't you avoiding me?"

"Answer me a question first. Is Santano there?"

"What does that have to do with anything? Put her—Heather back off! Put Becca on!"

Michael could hear the two arguing over the phone. When the struggle was over, it was Heather on the other end. "Sorry," she said. "I can't get her calm. Luckily Jason walked by."

"Santano," Michael repeated. "Is he there?"

Rebecca walked into the kitchen. "Who is it?" she asked.

Michael raised his hand in a wait motion. "Is Santano there? It's important."

"No," Heather answered. "I don't think he's been in school all day."

"Put Monica back on. I have something to tell her."

"Okay…"

A moment later Monica's voice came back, "Rebecca?"

"No."

"Put her on! I have something I want to tell her!"

"We just talked to Jason's dad. You know, the detective working the case? It doesn't look like Angel did it."

"What are you talking about?"

Michael hesitated. "Nicole…is dead."

"What?"

"We think Santano did it."

There was silence for a moment. "No way…" The anger in Monica's voice was suddenly gone.

Michael could hear muffled speech for a moment.

"What's happening?" Rebecca asked.

"I'm not sure," Michael replied. "They're talking."

"Hello?" Jason's voice said through the receiver.

"Jason?"

"Who told you about Santano?"

Michael's brow furrowed in anger. *He knew and didn't tell me*, he thought. "It's what Burt said," Michael answered. "Talk to him."

"Did my dad find you yet?"

"Yes, we spoke." He was silent for a moment. "Why didn't you tell me?"

"I told you I couldn't. My dad would have been pulled and suspended."

"Care to fill me in?"

Jason hesitated. "Might as well. Don't think it can do any harm, now that you know. Angel implicated Santano the day he was brought in. He said he was trying to stop Santano. We didn't believe him at first, he sounded kind of crazy, but right now no one can find Santano."

"Why didn't you tell me?"

"I couldn't. The chief pressed me. What could I do?"

Michael sighed. He didn't want to have an argument over police protocol over the phone, especially since Jason wasn't even a cop. "Is Monica okay?"

"Yeah. She's sitting down and crying. What did you tell her?"

"Yeah, you wouldn't know yet. Nicole was murdered not too long ago."

Jason was speechless. "What did my dad say?"

"That Rebecca wasn't in any immediate danger, but I'm not sure I believe him."

"He would have told you if you were." Jason's voice was breaking. "Class is gonna be out soon. I'm going to see if my dad can just come pick us up and take us home."

"Alright. Probably a good idea."

"Hold on, Monica wants the phone back."

After a moment Monica came on the line. Her voice was a little hoarse from crying. "Can you tell Rebecca I'm sorry?"

"Yeah, I can."

"Thank you...for leaving." She and Michael laughed lightly at the remark.

"Yeah, no problem. Be safe guys." Michael hung up the phone and turned to face Rebecca and Eric. "Monica said she was sorry."

"Is...she okay?" Rebecca answered.

"I think she'll be fine. Jason's going to try and call his dad to come get them. I don't think he feels too safe right about now."

"I'm not too sure what's going on, but it has to do with what you told Detective Cragoff, doesn't it?" Eric asked.

"Yeah, it does," Rebecca answered. "I'd like to not talk about it right now."

Eric sighed in defeated frustration. "If that's what you want honey."

Rebecca smiled weakly. "Thanks." She looked towards the phone and then towards Michael. She wondered if she should ask him about Úna, but the last time she sought out a dream figure, people started dying.

"What's wrong?" Michael asked.

"Nothing," Rebecca decided. "I was just thinking." *I won't ask about Úna. Not right now. Maybe she'll even be gone tomorrow.*

***

In the local hospital two officers were standing inside the morgue. The medical examiner was drawing up papers for the officers' reports on the deceased. One of the officer's had Nicole's morgue sheet pulled down and was looking at her body. Her clothes were drenched in dried blood and she didn't look peaceful at all.

"Don't you cut off their clothes or something?" the officer asked.

The medical examiner didn't look up at him but answered, "It depends on the situation. This isn't one of them."

"So she's just going to lay here in bloody clothes?"

"Officer, she just arrived here. We're not going to strip her in front of you."

The other officer laughed.

"Like she'd care," the first grumbled. "She's dead."

"But the family would," the examiner responded as he handed the officers their paperwork. "This is the fourth murder in three days. Very sad."

"Yeah," the second officer said. "They're so young. They hadn't even had a chance to taste life yet."

"Is there anything else you need gentlemen?"

"No, that should do it. Thank you for your time."

The two officers left talking amongst themselves about how good Nicole looked for a dead girl. The examiner closed the door. He shook his head mournfully and said, "No respect at all." He walked over to Nicole and pulled the sheet back over her head. "They had no respect for you at all." He sighed. "I'll be back shortly to start cleaning you up. It's a shame that your parents won't be here to give a positive ID for a couple of days. At least the autopsy will be done by then and you'll look presentable."

The medical examiner left the cold confines of the hospital morgue to prepare his supplies for Nicole's cleaning. A few moments later a green mist slowly appeared in a corner of the room. Within the mist Angel appeared. Once he was fully materialized the mist was absorbed back into the dagger at his side. "Disrespectful indeed," Angel added.

Angel went about examining the name tags on the bodies, bypassing Adam's when he crossed over it. Adam was not the victim he needed to see. It took only a moment to find Melissa's body. Angel pulled the metal sheet she laid upon out of the steel rack confines that housed her. He pulled the sheet covering her head down. The slash in her neck had been cleaned, but not yet closed. It seemed that her clothes had not been replaced yet either, as her shoulders were bare. Her skin already had a tint of blue and was ice cold to the touch, but that fact didn't bother Angel in the least. It was not the first time he had had to do this.

Angel carefully pulled her eye lids apart and peered into her empty green eyes. All he saw within them was pain. Angel shook his head in sorrowful regret. "He survived? How did he survive? He was mortally wounded. This isn't right. She should be free. Santano should have had to start all over again." Angel placed a hand on her eyes and closed his. He breathed in deeply and exhaled slowly. When he opened his eyes a moment later they were brightly glowing white. Angel was seeing the last moments of her time between realms, the moment of what should have been her Judgment. Angel did not like what he saw.

Melissa floated aimlessly in an off white space. She was barely conscious of her surrounding as her blood flowed slowly from the gash in her neck. "What's…happening…?" she whispered. Angel knew this place. It was the realm between that of the physical and spirit world where souls received their chance to go to Judgment. Normally, souls were free of pain and led towards their final resting place, usually by someone close to them that had already passed. Melissa's soul, however, was in torment and strife. It still suffered from the harm caused to her in life. Angel's battle with Santano held her soul captive in that place, unable to transcend to either realm. Heaven, however, did not abandon her. Knowing that she was a satanic sacrifice for Santano, the Archangel Saint Michael was dispatched to try and redeem her. However, he would not go unopposed. Michael was greeted by three fallen angels; Alastor, Azazel, and Nagel. Angel could not help but cringe. He had once fought Nagel himself and barely escaped with his life.

Alastor was a small lithe woman, smaller than her comrades, but not bone thin. Her fair skin was blotched and dark lines fell from her eyes, as if she had been crying and ruined her mascara. Her long dark hair was a tangled mess and damaged. It was not all the same length. Wings of bones stretched from her back with dark flesh filling the gaps. A dark robe with blood splotches barely clung to her body, covering more of her lower body than her top. One strap had broken and exposed one breast and the side of the robe was torn, exposing a shapely leg.

Azazel was taller and fuller than Alastor, but shorter and leaner than Nagel. Azazel's wings were black as night, darker than his long dark hair. His hair fell to nearly his waist and his bangs partially covered his face, falling to his chest. His body was otherwise bare of hair. He was adorned with jewels of gold, silver, and diamonds; bracelets, necklaces and rings adorned him. Strands of his long hair were braided with laces of gold and beautiful ornaments. A black vest hung open, exposing a marred chest, cut and scarred. Tribal tattoos covered his body in an attempt to hide his battle scars. His legs were entwined with a fabric that made for breeches of garnet. His face was adorned with piercings as were the two long gnarled goat horns that grew from his head.

Nagel was as tall and large as Michael, but their similarities ended there. Nagel's skin was a tone of dark with burn scars covering his body. His head was bare and his eyes as dark and deep as opals. Nagel's wings were black and broken; their original color lost forever, as well as their original length. They were tarnished and brittle. Each flap of his wings lost several feathers and stronger flaps lost more, yet Nagel seemed never to run out of feathers. His lips were dry and broken and his eyes burned with hatred. Like Michael, he wore a robe, but it was dark, like his skin, and dirty. Tears dotted it and the edges were tattered. Of the three demons, Nagel was the only one wearing armor. A thin cuirass protected his chest and back, leaving his shoulders completely exposed. The chain shirt he wore under it were exposed beneath the silver metal. The breastplate of the cuirass was dented and had a large crack marring the center. The sleeves of his chain shirt were torn at the elbows and used to partially mend the crack in his breastplate, the melted metal visible when the light hit it a certain way. His backplate was as dented as the breastplate, but wasn't cracked. The guard of vambrace once had effigies carved into the silver metal, but have since worn away. The surface was no longer smooth but dented with the blows of heavy blades and hammers. The cowter that protected his elbows were attached to the guard of vambrace and made the two pieces look like one, protecting the length of his forearm to his elbow. The greaves that protected Nagel's lower legs flowed seamlessly into the poleyn protecting his knees. The greaves had the same damage as the vambrace. The edges of his armors were brittle and the silver color dull. Once it may have been another color, but it had long since faded. Nagel walked on bare feet.

Michael's armor fared far better. The cuirass was composed of both a breast- and backplate, which were lined with slight cracks from its damage in the early days of the War in Heaven. A lion's head and mane flowed from the center of the breastplate and towards the back piece. The vambrace was adorned with fire effigies, as were the greaves that protected his lower legs. The poleyns were clear of adornments and his elbows lay unprotected. A partial gauntlet with an open palm connected to the vambrace. A fauld of four lames connected to his cuirass which protected his hips and waist. The armor itself was colored with gold accents. Michael's feet were not protected by armored boots, but instead were covered by golden sandals. Michael knew a battle was imminent and unavoidable, and though he came prepared he was not expecting such heavy resistance. "If I had known it was going to be like this," Michael said, his voice kind but firm, "I would and brought Gabriel with me." He grasped the air and light began to shine in his grip. "Perhaps if I had opted to bring Unbridled Fury instead." The shining light in his hand expanded the length of a blade and became a solid weapon. The hilt was golden wings but cracked and the blade was as bright and sharp as a diamond, but its edges were chipped and a hairline fracture snaked its way up the blade. It was damaged. As powerful as he was, Michael was uncertain if he could wretch the soul from the devils hands, but he had to try.

Angel was unsure about demon hair, but an angel's hair continued to grow, just like a human's hair. Michael's gold streaked dark brown hair was longer than the last time Angel saw it, about shoulder length. It was tied back with a golden band that left the tail of the hair lose. Michael's emerald wings were partially spread when he arrived, but upon creating his sword, he spread them. They were large and majestic, easily striking fear into nonbelievers and sinners alike. To believers, they inspired awe. Even after seeing Michael's wings completely unfurled twice before, Angel still found himself at once terrified and awed. Michael raised his sword before him and said to it, "Heaven's Flame. Purge." Sparks of flames began to burn from the cracks, seemingly having trouble igniting. Suddenly the blade was consumed by fire, the diamond like blade being completely replaced by divine flame. Michael drew his sword back and prepared for battle.

The three fallen angels chuckled and grinned at the lone angel before them. Melissa rested helplessly between the two groups, barely aware of their presence. The blood that poured from her wound slowly began to stir with life. This tore Michael's attentive gaze from his enemies as he worried about the soul before him. Nagel used that momentary drop in guard to launch his attack.

Nagel spread his dark tattered wings and darted forward at full speed. He gripped the air and cold filled his hand, turning into an ice crystal. He closed the distance quickly, drawing the ice crystal back to strike as it shattered into a sword similar to what Michael's had been. The blade was of silver steel and frost vapors wafted from it. The hilt were as drops of dew and a white blue in color. Melissa could feel Nagel's dark presence pass over her and she quivered. "Freeze!" Nagel shouted in a harsh voice. "Hoarfrost!" The sound of freezing water echoed in the space as the silver steel of the blade was overtaken in a thick layer of frosty dew, becoming hard like ice. The white blue of the hilt became like an ice crystal and drops of dew fell from it. Michael was quick to defend and locked his flaming blade against Nagel's frosted shard. Their height and form were eerily similar and they looked like opposite versions of one another, a true visage of good and evil.

"How long must we contend as such brother?" Michael asked.

"Until one no longer stands," was Nagel's answer. His voice was slow and pained, but eerily reminiscent of Michael's.

Nagel launched a relentless barrage of blows, but Michael was able to match him blow for blow. Dark ragged feathers filled the surrounding area as they fell from Nagel's wings. Each clash of their swords released a violent clash of energy with hallow "thoom"'s as fire and ice clashed. Ice chips cascaded from Nagel's sword as smoke wafted from Michael's. They traded several powerful blows, but neither one gave nor gained ground as their swords met again and again with violent force. Michael pulled away, letting Nagel's blow strike empty space. Michael spread his emerald wings wide as he grew the distance between them. Nagel caught himself quickly and flew forward, feathers molting from his wings like falling rain. A bright blinding light radiated from Michael's spread wings. Nagel was caught in the flash as he tried to close the distance and forced to stop in his tracks with a cry. Michael rushed forward and delivered a powerful punch to his once ally. Nagel was knocked from his aloft position and fell into the seemingly endless space, but hit ground quickly. He tried to stand and focus his sight, but his eyes still burned with Michael's blinding flash. "Damn you, Michael!" he cried. "I'll get you for that!"

Michael rushed towards Melissa's soul, which was enshrouded by her blood. Alastor and Azazel had gripped the enveloping shroud and carried her away from the advancing angel. "You will not take her!" Michael cried as he raised his sword. With a mighty battle cry he swung his fiery blade and released two streams of flames that struck true. The devils were knocked away from Melissa and crashed onto the invisible ground below. Michael reached for Melissa's soul, but the shroud surrounding her lashed out violently at him. It burned and pierced his hand savagely as he fought to reach through it, but was ultimately forced to withdraw. His hand was red with burns and coated in deep gashes. "More powerful than I thought," he said. "The avatar isn't dead yet." Melissa trembled within the shroud, oblivious to the battle that was going on for her soul. "Scared…" she cried. Michael raised flaming sword and shouted, "Finish it, Angel!" He shouted as he brought the burning blade down onto the shroud, but it fought back. It refused to burn and actively fought to hold back Michael's blade. Ultimately the shroud won over and pushed the archangel back. Michael could see the other two devils recovering from his strike. They concentrated and glowing light covered their bodies and filled their hands. They were preparing for battle. Michael was not at full strength in this place and his enemies were further strengthened there because of the avatar. Michael did not like to admit when he found himself outmatched. He readied to attack the shroud again but found the frosted blade of Nagel pressed through his body, slipping in an opening in the backplate and bursting through the lion's face. Nagel put an arm around Michael as he pressed his cold blade further into Michael's body. "You dropped your guard," Nagel said. "Now freeze."

Frost began to cover the surrounding area of the blade, coating Michael's armor in a cold embrace. From the inside, Michael was freezing as his protective armor was coating with a thin sheet of frost. "Blast," Michael grunted. He had allowed Nagel an opening and was wounded. Michael stared at Melissa and hoarsely cursed, "Angel…" Michael closed his eyes and his body turned to light. As light he was able to flee back to Heaven. He had to abandon Melissa.

Nagel flew to Melissa and took a strong grip of the shroud. "The avatar lives," he said. "The soul is ours."

Angel closed his eyes and shook the vision from his sight. When he opened them again they had returned to normal, the white glow gone. He closed Melissa's eyes and pulled the covering back over her head. He pushed the metal sheet back into its confines in the cold room. "Samuel is strong," Angel said. "The Blood Dagger allowed the devils to appear, but I couldn't break his will. He was stronger than I thought. He didn't die. He's an ascended avatar now. His power is escalating and now he has the Blood Sword." Angel reached behind him and gripped the Sword of Might. He pulled it partially from the sheath, freeing only a portion of the blade. "Sword of Might, show me his next target." The sword began to glow, but showed Angel no soul. He returned the blade. Angel's eyes narrowed. "He has the foresight not to choose his victims in advance. This will make it harder, but will give me some time to plan. It's been a long time since I've faced an ascended avatar. I won't be able to defeat him in a head on fight; he's become too strong for that. I have to find another way." Angel gripped the handle of his dagger. "Dagger of Power. Psionic Camouflage." From the dagger's hilt the green mist seeped and covered Angel's body. As it faded away, so too did Angel.

***

Later that night Rebecca made room in the living room and, after finding the spare batteries, filled the air mattress. Michael's parents brought a change of clothes for him and a pair of pajama bottoms. Rebecca had a couple sets of pajamas to choose from, some more revealing than others, but chose one of the more conservative ones. A pink flowered two-piece. It's what she normally wore when she had company over anyway and all she and Michael would be doing was sleeping. She wondered if Michael would try to make any advances while in bed, but with Jeanine checking in on them periodically, she doubted it. As annoying and untrusting as that was to Rebecca, her mother's reasoning was that it wasn't them she didn't trust, it was the situation and hormones. Rebecca still thought it was Michael. After all, it wouldn't be his first time, just Rebecca's. Still, Rebecca's main reasoning for wanting Michael to stay was just something strong to hold onto while she slept in fear of impending nightmares. For the past three days she has had them. Why would tonight be different? Michael was there.

Jeanine didn't like the fact that Michael had no top to wear and tried to get Eric to lend one of his, but he refused. As he pointed out, they were adults and to have a little trust in them. It's not like their bedroom wasn't very far away. If so much as the television was turned on, they would hear it. Jeanine's reaction embarrassed Rebecca red, but Michael took the whole thing with a grain of salt and laughed it off.

After what seemed like an eternity to Rebecca, her parents left them alone and shut off the lights. Michael laid with one arm around Rebecca while she clung lovingly and fearfully to him. He couldn't help but notice her periodic trembles.

"Hey, what are you so worried about?" he whispered.

"Why do you think I'm worried?" she whispered back.

"Your body keeps shaking. I know your boundaries. I'm not going to press."

Rebecca smiled to herself. "Because you don't want to, or because of my mom?"

"It's true your mom would wring my neck, but I don't want to make you do something that you aren't ready to do. The last thing I want to do is push you away like that. Besides, I think we would need more than five minutes."

Rebecca tried not to laugh too loudly. She looked up at Michael. "What was it like; your first time? Was it with Sarah?"

"Why would you ask that?"

"Because I want to know. Was she the only one?"

Michael became uncomfortable. Rebecca could hear it in his breathing and in the way he moved. "She was my first time."

"Was she the only one?"

Michael looked back at Rebecca. "Do you really want to know?"

"Yes."

"You promise you won't look at me differently?"

"I've heard a lot of things Michael. I just want to hear what really happened. You trust me enough to tell me, don't you?"

Michael sighed and looked away from her. "Sarah wasn't the only one."

"How many?"

"Only a couple; two or three."

"When did you first do it? Did you like it?"

Rebecca was rubbing her barefoot against his. Michael caressed her arm as he held her in return. "I'm not...sure if I liked it. We were just out of seventh grade. We were too young."

"But you did it again?"

"After awhile. We talked a lot. Neither one of us knew what we were doing and didn't want to ask our parents. We had no idea about protection. She freaked out the first time she missed her period, but I had no idea what that meant."

Rebecca couldn't help but giggle. "You had a scare then?"

"Yeah, more than one. I started using condoms."

"Who were the other girls?"

Michael hesitated. "Her friends."

"You slept with her friends?"

"Yeah. The first one was because I was mad at her. She cheated on me. I beat him up, but she didn't seem to care. I decided to sleep with one of her friends to show her how it felt. I knew one of her friends had a thing for me and, well, we did it."

"Was it just that one time?"

"That's all that I meant, but when Sarah decided that it didn't bother her, we did it a few more times, until she moved away. I guess really, I was just still mad and she didn't seem to care."

"You said there were two or three."

"Yeah," Michael said as he rubbed the back of his head nervously. "The second one was a little weird. She was another of Sarah's friends."

Rebecca flexed her nails on his chest. "You liked sleeping around with her friends, didn't you?"

"Ow, that hurts. And no, the second one was Sarah's idea."

"What?"

"She thought a threesome would be fun."

"Was it?"

"At the time, I guess."

"Did you do it a lot?"

"Only a couple of times."

"Would you ever do that again?"

"I don't think so. Her friend did become pregnant and I was scared to death that it was mine. It wasn't."

"I had heard things, but I didn't know you were so…experienced."

"I guess if you can call it that."

"You sound like you regret it."

"Doesn't it make you mad? I just told you about all the girls I had sex with. Doesn't that bother you just a little?"

"Why does it bother you?"

Michael chuckled. "Because, I did it all because I thought I was supposed to. Everything I did, I did because I thought that's what was expected of me. I thought that's what a guy like me was supposed to do."

Rebecca pulled herself up and laid her body over his. She rested her chin on her crossed hands over his chest and looked at him with a smiling face. She still rubbed one foot against his while Michael looked back at her dumbfounded. "What kind of guy are you, Michael?"

Michael stared back at her for a moment as his eyes became misty. He laid his head down against the pillow and whispered, "Basura."

He's getting upset, Rebecca thought. *He's starting to talk Spanish.* She reached a hand around his head and pulled it up to make him look at her. "You are not garbage. Even with your flaws and mistakes, you are better than that. I don't care that you've had sex with Sarah and God knows who else. It turned me off at first, but you made me look past that. Someone told me once that I saved you. I didn't understand. I still don't. But you are better than you think you are. I don't know where you came from or how you were before, but you changed. You changed drastically and you did it for me. How can 'basura' do that?"

Michael smiled back as tears flowed down his face. He wrapped his arms around her and said, "Thank you. Somehow, you always know just what to say."

"Isn't that what girlfriends are for?"

Michael looked at her for a moment. "Can I tell you a secret? One I've never told anyone, ever?"

Rebecca's face contorted in confusion. "Of course."

"I've never seen my parents."

"What do you mean? Your father was just here."

Michael shook his head. "That wasn't my dad. That was my tio. I'm an American citizen, but I'm not even sure if I was born in this country. I'm not even sure where my parents are from to be honest. I just know they couldn't afford to keep me, so they sent me away. The two people that raised me are my tios. My dad's sister and her husband. They treat me well, like a son I guess, but I always felt out of place and abandoned."

Rebecca pulled her body over Michael's until she was face-to-face with him. "You weren't abandoned. You're aunt and uncle raised you like their own. They gave you everything you could have ever wanted. Your parents did the best they could for you at the time. They gave you to someone that could protect you. They led you to me."

Michael smiled up at her. "Yeah, that certainly is one way to look at it."

"That's how I look at it." Rebecca kissed him.

Michael looked into her eyes for a long moment. "That's how I'll look at it too. You're right. They made the best choice they could for me. I love you, Rebecca."

"I love you too."

They kissed in each other's embrace, lost to where they were until Rebecca heard the floor creak. "My mom!" she shouted in a whisper as she jumped off of Michael, kneeing him slightly as she did. He cringed, but tried to hide it.

"How's everything going in here?" Jeanine asked as she walked in.

Rebecca stood up. "Fine. Just going to the bathroom."

"That's good. Just checking in."

"I know." Rebecca disappeared towards the bathroom to save face.

Jeanine sat on the arm of the couch and looked down at Michael. "I heard you guys talking about something for a while, then nothing."

Michael carefully sat up, trying to hide the pain that still remained in his lap. "Can't blame you."

"So what were you doing? She got up in quite a hurry."

"We were just talking."

"Really?"

Michael sighed. "I know Sarah has probably told you every nasty little thing she could about me, that's why you don't like me too much. Most of what she said is probably true if not all of it."

"Pray tell."

"I can't change my past, and even if I could, I'm not sure Rebecca would want me to."

"Why do you say that?"

"I do love your daughter very much, Jeanine. She makes me feel like I never felt before. I would die for her." He looked at her, Jeanine's face coated in suppressed shock. "Rebecca is right, you know. She did save me, even if she doesn't understand how or from what."

Almost nervously Jeanine asked, "What did she save you from?"

"Myself. She makes me feel like I'm worth something. I would never do anything to hurt her."

Jeanine looked at him for a moment and then away. When she heard the toilet flush she said, "Be good to my girl, Michael."

"You don't have to worry about that."

"Yeah, I'm starting to feel that."

Jeanine was already gone when Rebecca came back into the room. She climbed back into bed next to Michael without comment about her mother's intrusion, which was partly welcomed. "I guess we should go to sleep now, huh?" Rebecca asked.

Michael laughed softly. "That might be a good idea."

CHAPTER VII

"Sit down," the chief told the young officer in his office. The officer, Davis, sat down uncomfortably in the chair. Jeff was offset to the chief's desk reading the report Davis had wrote.

"Is something wrong, sir?" Davis asked.

"According to my detective here, there is. It seems there is something missing from your report; an important something."

"I put everything that happened in the report, sir."

The chief started to speak but was interrupted.

"Don't give me that crap!" Jeff shouted as he threw the report on the desk in front of Davis. "Your report only mentions Burt's statements and makes no mention that you interviewed someone else."

"Well, I—" Davis stuttered.

"On top of that there is no mention of a second killer or Santano!"

"Now hold on a second!"

"I reinterviewed them both!"

"Why?!"

"Shut up!" the chief shouted over Jeff as he started to speak. "Shouting at my officers is my job Jeff! Let me do it!" Jeff huffed and remained quiet. "He interviewed them both because the girl you talked to and didn't mention has been waiting to talk to him all damn day! It just happens that they talked after the murder!"

"But why would he go and interview the store clerk again?"

"Because she told him the clerk told you about another guy and Santano, as well as a few other things, and none of them were in your report!"

"I didn't think he was telling the whole truth. He was in shock—!"

The chief slammed his hands on his desk as he rose to his feet. He stuck a finger sharply in the young officer's face. "That's not your decision to make Davis! You take statements as given and don't decide what should or shouldn't go in! You falsified your report!"

The officer remained quiet. After a moment he said, "I'm sorry. I'll rewrite it."

"Don't bother," Jeff said. "I already did."

"First you called Jason in, which was asking for trouble," the chief said. "Then you let Angel get away from you. Now you do this? I should have your badge, but I'll settle for this." He took a pile of papers and showed it to the officer sitting sheepishly before him. "This is your report. Make another mistake like that and this is also your career." He pushed the sheets through a shredder and wiped his hands as if cleaning them of dust. "You're suspended for two weeks. When you return, I expect you to know proper protocol. Is that understood?"

"Yes sir," Davis said.

"Good. Now get the Hell out of my office."

The officer rose from his seat and left with his head down. The chief and Jeff remained quiet for a long moment.

"Santano, huh?" the chief asked finally.

"That's what he said," Jeff answered. "Burt said that's what Angel called Nicole's killer. I think Angel was right."

"Great. A higher than thou loony. His face was skinned too? That'll definitely push the warrants."

"I want to interview the clerk at the gun shop. Maybe we can get some leads."

"Angel knows who this guy's targets are. I want to know how."

"You don't think Angel helped in the killings? This could be just a ruse you know?"

"Only Angel's prints and blood was at the double homicide scene. Melissa had hand mark on her face and neck, but there's no prints. Santano was wearing gloves. From the get-go there has been two suspects, be we can only find Angel. Now we have something more definite. Santano was a no call no show."

"Definitely looks like he has something to hide."

"We're not releasing this information. Not until we know for sure." The chief tapped his chin in thought. "See if you can get Angel to trust us. He likes you."

"I don't think it's going to be that simple. Angel believes he's battling the devil."

"Today, so are we. We got to bring Santano down. He's targeting his students, just like Angel said. I would keep Jason home if I were you."

Jeff said nothing, but mentally agreed.

***

The great oaken doors opened into the main hall and processional music began to play. Jeanine and Eric stood from their seats, followed by the guests seated in the pews. Jason stood next to Michael, both in tuxedos. Michael grinned nervously. First Nicole and Adam appeared from the door and made their way to the altar. Once there they parted, Adam standing beside Michael and Jason and Nicole standing across from them. Monica and Peter made their way down the aisle next. Once at the altar, they too parted as Nicole and Adam did. Alone, Heather walked down the aisle next and stood beside her friends. Following her was her brother, Haden. In his hands was a small pillow and resting on them were two golden bands. The processional music rose in volume and tempo. Angel escorted Rebecca down the aisle in a beautiful white bridal gown. She locked eyes with Michael and couldn't keep from smiling.

"Today is a big day," Angel said.

"Yes, it is," Rebecca replied as they made their slow procession. "I couldn't be happier today."

"You move ever forward. Today a new chapter of your life begins."

"Yes. I look forward to the future."

"You continue in the footsteps on your forefathers. Soon you will take up the mantle."

The brightness of the church darkened and it seemed as if with each step they took the altar moved further away. The priest ready to perform the wedding looked up. The flesh of his face was gone. With each step the pulsing muscle was stripped away, leaving ever growing sinew and bone. Rebecca looked around her and the guests had become dark shadows.

Heavy footsteps clanked on the floor as the frightening metallic body of War approached. "The end approaches," his voice boomed. The ground began to shake and Rebecca watched as the bloated and enormous form of Famine approached from the other side of the church. "I will feast on all that you hold dear," he said as he licked his toothy maw. "Nothing will escape my hunger." A dark shadow passed beneath Rebecca and Angel and blocked the way they came. The unstable form of Pestilence rose. "No one will escape. All will fall by my blight." Angel and Rebecca stopped, locked between the three frightful beings. Panicked, Rebecca looked towards Angel who had already drawn his weapons. She looked back towards the altar. Her friends and future lay at the priest's boney feet. He scraped his scythe against the floor. "All will fall to my death and decay," he said. His voice was slow and hallow. "You cannot stop us. The end will come."

"Your time is coming," Angel said as he handed Rebecca his sword. "You must take up the mantle. The end cannot happen. They must be stopped."

"Wait!" Rebecca cried as she took hold of Angel's sword. "I don't understand!"

"Fight!" Úna's Irish voice cried out. Rebecca sought her out and found her standing beside Famine. "It's your destiny! Fight! Defeat them! Do it!"

Rebecca woke up to her mother's footsteps in the early morning. Her heart was beating fast, but aside from gripping Michael's sleeping form tighter, she didn't stir. She remained motionless in a mock sleep for a few moments after the front door was closed. A cold wind snuck in during that brief moment and made Rebecca shiver from beneath the covers. The light of the sun hadn't even broken the horizon yet. She looked at Michael sleeping so peacefully. She remembered seeing him at Death's feet. She remembered him specifically as the monster's enormous scythe scrapped near his body. Rebecca moved to kiss Michael on the cheek and whispered, "Please don't leave me." She stayed awake holding him until they were awoken by Eric a couple hours later.

Rebecca let Michael have the shower first. She knew how long she would take and Michael was a guest in her house. That was the polite thing to do. Besides, she had to put away the air mattress if nothing else. As she used the small machine to deflate the mattress her mind whirled around her dream. It wasn't the first time she had dreamed something similar, but the Horsemen and Úna's presence was new. It bothered her. She could almost feel the hardships the day would bring, almost as if the dream was a forewarning of it. Watching the bed deflate all she could think about was how she wished she and Michael could just lay in it all day. Just to lay safe in his arms. She didn't want to face the new day.

Her angst did not go unnoticed by Eric. He wheeled into the living room and handed Rebecca the box for the mattress and its inflator. "Honey," he started. "Are you alright?"

"Yeah Dad," Rebecca answered as she took the box. "I'm okay."

"Are you sure? You look…distraught."

"Yeah, I'm fine." Rebecca folded the bed into a square small enough to fit into the air mattress box. "There's just a lot going on I guess."

"I understand. You know, I can't speak for Michael, but if you don't feel up to going to school for awhile, you can stay home."

Rebecca thought about that for a moment, but what would she do all day at home besides let her mind wander and terrorize her more? She got up off the floor and hugged her father. "Thanks Dad, but I'm alright. Thank you for letting Michael stay last night."

Eric returned her hug and said, "You're welcome. I thought you needed that. I know Michael is not a bad person, and I think he proved that to Jeanine last night."

"I hope so."

Michael came out of the bathroom fully dressed with wet, but combed, hair. He smiled at Rebecca and said, "I guess it's your turn."

Again the two walked to school hand in hand. Rebecca had trouble shaking the dream from her mind. She kept stealing glimpses of Michael as they walked. She kept seeing him at Death's feet and tried to hide her apprehension from him. The dreams had always haunted her, but never like this. The murders were bad enough, but Santano possibly being the murderer made it that much worse. Just what was he after? Was he just killing randomly or was there a pattern that no one has been able to see? Rebecca wondered how many more were going to die before he would be stopped. Who would he choose next? Heather? Monica? Michael? Herself? She shuddered at the thought and pulled Michael's attention.

"Are you alright?" he asked.

"Yeah," she lied. "Just cold."

"We'll be at school soon. You'll be nice and toasty in no time."

"Yeah," she said as she gripped his arm tighter. "I guess so. It has heat."

Michael laughed. "I'm glad you're feeling better."

"Yeah…" Rebecca knew she wasn't feeling better. If she hadn't had that dream, then maybe…

***

Several squad cars were parked in front of Santano's home. The engines were running, but the lights and sirens were off. One of the officers banged on Santano's door and called out, "Police!" He waited a moment before banging on the door again announcing, "Samuel Santano, this is the police! Open the door! We have a search warrant!" He turned to the pair of officers holding a battering ram. He motioned towards the door and in two short hits broke the door open. The team moved in quickly and scoured the house. With the curtains drawn preventing the morning sun from entering the windows, the house was dark. The team broke into several smaller teams and scattered around the house. Three proceeded to the basement. They tore through the dark basement looking for anything that may be useful in their investigation, but found none. They seemed oblivious to the large fire consumed pentagram on the ground with Satan's eyes watching their every move. A chill ran down their spines and finally one radioed, "The basement's clear. There's nothing down here."

After a moment of static the radio blared and another voice responded, "Negative here too. It looks like he hasn't been back in a few days. All his clothes are here and his bed hasn't been slept in."

"So he skipped town?" another voice crackled. "He definitely has something to hide. Do a thorough search of the house and then get out of there. I'll radio that Santano is gone."

"Ten-four."

The leader of the trio in the basement looked at his partners and said, "This place is giving me the creeps. Let's get out of here."

"We're supposed to do a thorough search," one of his partners said.

The first member looked around and said, "Not much to search. Mostly just junk."

"But everything's been pushed to one side," the third member said. "Doesn't that strike you as strange?"

"It does, but that doesn't change the fact that there's nothing here. There's no reason for all this space, so there's nothing to report back about. Let's get out of here."

The trio left. As each team finished their search of the house they too withdrew. An hour passed before the force was completely withdrawn and heading back to the station. Santano stepped from the basement's shadows with a sinister grin on his face.

"Looks like I just got fired," Santano chuckled. "Just as well, I suppose. I was resigning soon anyway."

"You are adapting well to your new powers," Satan said. "I am pleased."

Santano chortled and flexed his fist.

"Something troubles you my avatar. Surely it is not the humans that were just here."

"It's Angel. When I first met him, I didn't know what to think. He knew who I was and acted like he knew what I was doing. Then he was there when I sacrificed Nicole. I can't help but wonder if he was there when I sacrificed Adam too. I think he's the only one that knows, but why? How can he possibly know what I'm doing or where I'm going?"

"He knows because it is his business to know. He is the last of the demon hunters."

"A demon hunter? But I'm not a demon. Why is he hunting me?"

Satan let out an amused chuckle. "How little you still know, my avatar. It is true that you are not a demon, but that matters not. After all, I am not a demon either."

"You're not? But I thought—"

"I am a fallen angel, a devil if you will. I am the highest of the hierarchy. We fallen angels stand outside others of our kind. We were the only ones that were once blessed by the divine light, before we were cast out. Following us are devils, equivalents to Heaven's archangels. Beyond them are demons, inner demons, avatars; as yourself, and mortal servants. That is a rough breakdown. The term 'demon hunter' is merely a title that in truth has nothing to do with hunting demons. Once they may have had the strength to challenge a devil, but those days have long since passed. Their job is to kill avatars, to keep them from ascending and bringing our war to the breaking point."

"You mean the War in Heaven? It's still going on?"

"That war is over, but a new one has begun here on Earth. Everyone here will fight, whether they want to or not. I am just trying to help it along. My best warriors are failed avatars and the vilest humans the world has ever seen. An example of which would be Attila the Hun."

"Attila the Hun? I didn't even know he was Christian."

"There is but one Gehenna, the place you call Hell. We do not care what your faith is. Why should we when we are at war with our own Creator? Attila was a power hungry mortal. Alas, before I could bargain with him he was struck down by the era's demon hunter."

"So how long has Angel been doing this? He doesn't look that old."

"Angel is centuries old, but his struggle is coming to an end."

"Centuries? Is he immortal or something?"

"His vow prolonged his life, but he is running out of time. He became more than human, but less than a demigod. He is ever quicker becoming mortal. His power is waning. Very soon Angel will be nothing more than a mere mortal man again. When that happens, the power of the demon hunters will forever be lost. Nothing will be able to stand in my way."

"I don't understand. If he's so weak, why haven't you killed him yet? Let's get him out of the way!"

"Though the concept of killing Angel is a simple one, the act of killing him has proved rather difficult. Time and again he has slipped through the hands of death. However, I know of one being that perhaps has the ability to defeat him. Perhaps we will be able to start the collection as well."

"The Collection? What's that?"

"It is nothing you need concern yourself with just yet my avatar. This entity, however, has proved problematic over the years. Stand back, Santano. I must summon this lesser demon from within the abyss. Keep a safe distance. He may lash out and you do not have the strength to defend yourself. This particular demonic is rather powerful for its kind. Angel was mine once."

"Angel was yours?"

Satan did not answer. The uppermost point of the pentagram began to glow as demonic symbols began to encircle it. Santano took a few steps back as the massive flame began to flicker. "I will invoke the power of this Circle to enlist the aid we desire," Satan said as streams of fire began to slither off the flame. "From the bowels of the Underworld, from the depths of the Abyss, I summon thee." The streams encircled the symbols around the glowing point. A man's scream of pain echoed from within the growing flames as a skeleton began to form within the flaming circle. "Come forth! I command you to return from the Abyss!" The flames grew higher as organs, muscles, and flesh began to form on the moving skeleton. "Return to serve your master!" The flames licked the man's naked body and turned to clothes. The flames on his legs became dark jeans. The flames that licked against his torso left behind a black muscle shirt. As the flames continued to caress his form, they consumed the air around him and coated him in a black leather trench coat. "Return to serve me!" The man bent over in pain and groaned. Then with a scream he threw his body out, as if throwing off a great weight. The flames surrounding him burst away and died. The man threw his form forward against an invisible barrier. "Release me!" the man shouted in Angel's voice. The man's hair was ghostly white and his skin gray. His beige eyes were full of rage. Much to Santano's surprise, the man before him was Angel's physical double, allowing the avatar only to gawk. Angel's double pounded on the invisible wall and shouted, "I said release me!"

"What in the world?" Santano finally said.

"This is the demon Demonic Angel," Satan said.

"Demonic Angel?"

"Every demon hunter has a demonic counterpart. A demon hunter cannot hold sin, but because of their...shall we say, special nature...their sins cannot be simply forgiven. Instead they are carried by these demonic counterparts. The longer a demon hunter fights, the more chances he has to sin. Those sins make their demonic half more powerful."

Demonic Angel drew forth a curved sword of dark metal and struck the field. As Demonic Angel drew the curved blade, the red clothed tail wrapped itself around his forearm, anchoring it to his hand. The tip of the curved blade was wild like fire and the hilt curved around his hand in the shape of a protective claw. "Let me go!" he shouted.

"Some time ago, this demonic became troublesome; likely due to his power."

The demon finally stopped his barrage and placed a hand on the field between him and Santano. "You have no idea. I exist, so I know Angel still lives."

"This is true. I have summoned you for a task. I can presume you understand the task?"

He turned to Satan's Presence. "It is the only task I have. Destroy Angel. Once I do that, I will be a full demon, not this lesser creature, tied forever to that semi-mortal."

Santano looked at Demonic Angel for a long moment. "Can he beat Angel?"

Demonic Angel grinned as he lowered his ember glowing weapon and faced towards Santano. "I have beaten Angel. I would have killed him as well, if not for that—beast—that interfered."

"Now you have another chance to succeed where you have failed," Satan said. "Two hundred years have passed since you last graced the Earth, so I cannot release you just yet. You need time to gather your strength or you will find yourself back in the Abyss. Fail again and you will not be given another chance."

"I won't need another chance. As long as there is no one to interfere this time, Angel will be no more." Demonic Angel chuckled. "And the hope of the world dies with him." He faced the flame. "I can sense something else. You would mean to ask something further of me?"

"I do. I can see the strands of fate woven in time. A pure innocent that will fit nicely into the Collection will approach Angel later this afternoon. Angel is not your main task. Bring back the girl you will find with him. She is your priority. Once she is within our grasp, you may do as you please with Angel."

"Tsk. Whatever. You'll get your sacrifice once I am through with Angel."

"Do not think you can order me demon."

Demonic Angel screamed as his body was wracked with pain.

"I have brought you back again and again. It is I that chooses if you ever walk this Earth again, not you."

"A—As you command—my Lord!" The pain stopped and Demonic Angel slumped to the ground.

"Very good."

"What do I do in the meantime?" Santano asked. "With Angel distracted, it would be easy to make the remaining sacrifices." Santano thought for a moment. "Though, with the police looking for me, maybe I don't want to roam around too much."

"That is a wise decision. Even if you had a desire to continue at the moment, the rules of this game are clear. The demon hunter can face but one threat a day. We have released his sins, so you must wait a day."

"Rules? No one said anything about any rules. Why do we have to follow rules?"

"The simple answer is it gives us an advantage. I would never agree to anything that put me at the disadvantage. As long as we play by the rules, you need concern yourself only with Angel. So relax. Let Demonic Angel gather his strength and then do what he was created to do."

***

The wind howled and whipped snow into the cold air. Rebecca stared at the school's front doors as she and Michael approached it. Rebecca knew that more hardships lay beyond it. She was starting to wish she had taken her father's offer and stayed home. As they passed through the doors Rebecca spied a glimpse of Úna walking through the hall. It looked like she was almost done with <u>Othello</u>.

"Michael?" Rebecca asked.

"Yeah?" he answered.

"Do you know Úna?"

"You mean personally? No. We talked a couple of times, but that's it. I don't really know her."

"Do you know who she hangs out with?"

Michael shook his head. "Not really."

"Looking to make some new friends?" Sarah asked as she approached the couple.

Oh God, Rebecca thought. *Not this girl. Not now.*

"Already looking to fill the holes in your circle?"

Rebecca glared angrily at Sarah as her eyes became misty.

Michael put himself between them. "That was uncalled for."

Sarah pointed around Michael at Rebecca. "Rumor is it's her fault that Melissa is dead."

Rebecca gasped. She wondered if Monica had gone on a rant before Michael had spoken to her.

"Where did you hear that bull?" Michael demanded, but like Rebecca, was worried that Monica had inadvertently started a rumor with an angry rant.

"I heard some people saying that you had pictures of the killer and that you had Melissa get them for you."

"Who did you hear?"

"Does it matter?" Sarah turned from Michael to speak to Rebecca. "Never thought you were the kind of person to put a hit on someone. What did they do to you?"

"That's not what happened!" Rebecca cried.

Sarah tried to take Michael's hand. "Michael, I'm worried about you."

Michael broke his hand away. "Don't be. I can take care of myself. And you're wrong about what happened."

Sarah scoffed. "Do you think people are going to care?"

Michael leaned into her and shouted, "I'll make them care! We're done talking!"

Michael led Rebecca, who was on the verge of crying, away by the hand. Sarah stared after them in shock. Michael had never screamed at her like that before. She bit her lip and fought to hold back her tears. "I hope you're next bitch," Sarah whispered. "And I'll make sure everyone thinks this is your fault."

Michael pulled Rebecca along ranting in Spanish. He was speaking so fast that Rebecca was barely able to pick up the words and had no idea what he was saying. His grip was becoming painfully tight. Rebecca jerked back on his arm and forced him to a stop.

"Michael, wait," she said. "You're hurting me."

Michael let go and said, "I'm sorry. She just—that was totally out of place. I'm sorry I lost my temper."

"I know," Rebecca said as she rubbed her hand. "It's okay."

"Who does she think she is anyway? How does she even know about the pictures?"

"Glenda saw them."

"Glenda? Why would she tell Sarah anything?"

"It doesn't take much to start a rumor, Michael. You know that."

"I'll fix this."

Rebecca caressed his face. "Just be there for me. That's all you need to do."

Michael took her hand and kissed it. He sighed. "Alright, if that's all you want. But if you change your mind, just say the word."

She smiled at him. "That's all I need, Michael. I'll talk to Glenda. You don't worry about anything."

"I'll check on you between classes, okay?"

She smiled warmly at him. "Don't worry about me. I can take care of myself. I'm a big girl you know."

"Yeah, I know." He kissed her hand once more before parting ways.

Rebecca made her way to her locker wary of the hardships that lie ahead. Things just seemed to be going from bad to worse. She knew that when the Principal came on with the morning announcements he would talk about Nicole. She didn't want to hear it, but what could she do? She supposed she could just wait outside and go late to class. The dreams weighed heavily on her mind. She needed to talk to someone. It was hard for her to accept, but she needed to talk to the school social worker. If nothing else, she could get at least the dreams off her mind. She wondered if she should report to Jeff about her dreams too and what Sarah had said. Rebecca opened her locker and started preparing for class. She decided to ask for Jeff to be there when she talked to the social worker, just in case anything she said would be helpful.

"Hey Rebecca," Nicholas said. Rebecca peeked from around her locker door to see that Nicholas had snuck up on her. He was definitely not someone she wanted to deal with right now.

"Not now Nicholas," she pleaded. "Please? I'm really not in the mood."

"Look, I know you're going through some stuff right now," Nicholas said. He sounded genuinely concerned, but Rebecca wasn't sure if he was being sincere or just happened to be a really good actor. At the moment, she didn't really care. She just wanted him gone. "I wanted to talk to you about the tutoring I asked—"

Rebecca slammed her locker door in frustration. "Alright!" she shouted. "Is that what you've been trying to talk to me about all week? Is it that important?"

"Hey, calm down. All I was going to say—"

"If you leave me alone for the rest of the week, don't say a word to me, then I'll agree to help you. Okay? Just leave me alone!"

"Okay! Okay!" Nicholas said as he took a step back."

Rebecca took a deep breath. "I've been going through a lot right now, alright. I'm just…I'll tutor you on Saturday, okay? Just leave me alone until then, alright?"

"Yeah, sure. Damn, sorry I said anything."

Nicholas rummaged through his backpack for a sheet of paper and wrote something on it. He handed Rebecca the paper and said, "This is my address. I'll see you around six or seven, I guess?"

"Yeah, that's fine." Rebecca took it already having second thoughts about agreeing to meet him. She wondered why he hadn't already had his address ready for her, like he did with his phone number, but with all the things that were already on her mind, that concern was pushed to the back of the list. She just didn't want to deal with Nicholas anymore. That was at least one concern she had some control over, even if she wasn't sure that was the best way to handle it.

Nicholas picked up his backpack and walked away. He mumbled something under his breath, but Rebecca couldn't make it out. She looked at the paper he had given her. He didn't live terribly far away, but further away than she would have liked. It was probably a fifteen or twenty minute walk from school, but that would make it almost thirty minutes from her house. Michael's car wouldn't be ready until Monday, and Jeanine wouldn't dare leave her at someone's house that she didn't know. "What am I doing?" Rebecca wondered to herself. "What am I getting myself into here?" She folded the paper and put it into her backpack before heading off to the main office. As she walked towards the office she spied the time. Classes were going to start in only a few minutes. The Principal would probably notify the school about Nicole's death, like he did with Adam's and Melissa's. Rebecca didn't want to hear about Nicole's death again. She didn't want to hear about any more deaths at all. She headed to the nearest exit to wait out the announcements outside.

Rebecca waited in the cold for the announcements to end. She caught herself checking her wrist to read the time, but realized she hadn't worn a watch in about a year. It seemed to fly by faster if she tracked it and didn't want time to race by. She sighed. She only wanted to wait about fifteen minutes. She thought that would be enough time, but now she would have to guess. The wind wasn't blowing and she could tell that the temperature had risen a little since she and Michael arrived. She was thankful for that little spike in heat since she hadn't the foresight to bring her jacket. The sky was overcast and threatened snow. They had gotten a snow flurry already, but were still expecting a heavy snowfall. Rebecca was cold and hugged her body, trying to keep warm. She saw a police car pull up a few minutes before she was ready to go back inside. A young officer got out and approached the school. He carried himself strongly and his body looked strong and powerful, especially under his police uniform. He was clean cut with short dark hair. His face had a chiseled look, almost as if it was made from stone. As he approached the school entrance he locked eyes with Rebecca. She swallowed deeply. His eyes were deep and fierce.

"What are you doing out here young lady?" he asked. Though his question was not in anger, his voice was strong and firm and commanded authority.

"I—I didn't want to hear the announcements," Rebecca answered.

"Bad news today?"

"Yes. What are you doing here? Is something wrong?"

The officer gave what Rebecca thought was a forced smile. "Nothing is wrong at the moment, but I was one of the officers asked to patrol the school in light of the homicides. My name is Officer Guerra, under direct orders from Detective Cragoff."

"Jason's dad? He's in charge of the investigation?"

"Yes. I was handpicked by him. Talking to me will be as good as talking to him."

Rebecca looked at him for a moment.

"Is something wrong? You look concerned."

"I am, a little. I wanted to talk to Jason's dad."

"Well, you can talk to me. I'll tell him anything you want him to know."

"I'm not sure how important any of it is. I wanted to talk to the social worker about it first."

"I see. How about this then, I go with you if you like? I'll take your statements while you talk to the social worker. Just tell me what you want to pass on. Does that sound acceptable?"

"Yeah, I guess it does."

"Alright. Let's go then. I'm sure the announcements are over with by now and you seem terribly cold."

Rebecca smiled. "Yeah, I am." She followed Guerra to the main office.

"Good morning," Guerra said. "I'm Officer Guerra, checking in for the day. Have the other officers checked in yet?"

"Oh," the secretary said. "I wasn't aware that you were even coming. No one tells me anything." She rifled through some paper work for something that Rebecca didn't think she even knew if it existed. "Well, I don't think anyone else has checked in yet. So it's just you right now."

"That's fine. This young lady would like to make a request." Guerra motioned towards Rebecca as he spoke.

Rebecca stepped forward. "I was hoping I could talk to one of the social workers," she said.

"Of course. We currently have one available so you don't have to wait. You can go right into room four."

"Thank you."

Guerra followed Rebecca into the room. Sitting behind a desk was an elderly man with long thin gray hair that rested about his shoulders. He had long side burns and his face was lined with wrinkles. His body was small and frail. His dark eyes were sunken into his head. Gray stubble lined his face. He looked at Rebecca and Guerra, smiled and said, "Good morning." His voice was soft and slow and painfully old. "Welcome to my office. I am Dr. Grave."

Wow, Rebecca thought. *Bad name today.* "Good morning," Rebecca said.

"Please, have a seat."

Rebecca sat in one of the chairs at the front of Grave's desk. She was definitely not comfortable.

"Please Guerra, will you close the door?"

"Of course," Guerra answered before turning to close the door.

Rebecca tried to hide her concerned look. Guerra never introduced himself, so how did Grave know his name? Guerra stood on the side of the desk and took out a notepad and pen, ready to write anything Rebecca said.

"Well young lady," Grave said, "what is your name and how may I help you this morning?"

"My name is Rebecca. I wanted to talk about the murders…and some dreams I've had."

"Go on. I will do what I can to help."

Rebecca looked at the pair. Grave didn't seem to care at all that Guerra was in the room ready to start writing down everything she said, even though she had asked him to come. She tried to push it from her mind. Maybe she wasn't the only one that had a cop in the room with her. Maybe Grave realized that she had asked Guerra to stay. "I'm not sure where to start," Rebecca said.

"What is bothering you the most?" Grave asked. "Let's begin with that."

Rebecca tried to laugh. "So many things have first place on that list."

Grave rubbed his stubbly chin. "I see. Then, let us start with the reality. People in this school are turning up dead. That has given you angst, correct?"

"Yeah. They were all my close friends."

"That must be very hard for you. To lose so many friends in as many days is no easy event to deal with."

"No, it's not, and my boyfriend's ex is making it worse."

"Who is she and how is she making it worse?"

"Sarah O'Conner. My boyfriend dumped her for me. She's never let it go and has tried to steal him back from me ever since."

"How long did they date?"

"About five years." Rebecca sighed. "I never really thought about it before. That's a long time."

"And the two of you? How long have you two been dating?"

"Two years in May."

"Your boyfriend, is that the extent of your relationship with Miss O'Conner?"

"Pretty much. She's a stuck up cheerleader. She thinks she's one of the prettiest girls in school. I guess she's pretty popular, but I never really paid any attention to her."

"It's quite common for the rejected from a long relationship to feel hostile towards their ex's new object of affection. This is doubly true if that new object of affection was the cause of their relationship ending, as seems to be your case. As time goes by, Miss O'Conner will move on. Now, how exactly is she making these events worse for you?"

"She's spreading a rumor about me. I'm not sure if she started it, but I'm worried she'll run with it."

"Rumors are rumors and ultimately are only lies."

"This one isn't so much." Rebecca looked down at the desk. "It's about Angel."

"The suspected murderer? What does he have to do with this apparent rumor?"

Rebecca was hesitant to answer. Both Guerra and Grave remained quiet. Every time she spoke, Guerra penned something on his notepad, but the page was never flipped. "I asked Melissa to find him. Then she died."

"Really?" Grave asked. "When did you ask her to do this?"

"Monday, before Adam died. She brought me back pictures of Angel the next day."

"Have you already reported this to the authorities?"

"Yes. I told Jason's dad about it; Detective Cragoff. Officer Guerra said he was leading the investigation."

"When you asked your friend to seek this individual out, no one had died yet, correct?"

"That's right. Adam was found dead that night. But he was in school that day."

"Why would you ask your friend to seek out a man you had never met?"

"That's just it. I knew him, but I've never met him, not in person. I never knew his name."

"What do you mean?"

Rebecca spied Guerra as he took his notes. He had been writing the whole time and if he had flipped through his pad's pages, she missed it. Rebecca swallowed hesitatingly before answering, "I dream about him. I have for as long as I can remember. I've never told anyone."

"This is why you sought him out? You personally witnessed the physical representation of someone from your dreams?"

"Yeah. He even carried the sword I dreamt he always carried. It's even in the pictures Melissa gave me, but no one can see it." Rebecca realized what she had just said. "I sound crazy."

"There are many things in this world that are beyond the understanding of a normal person. Simply because it cannot be seen does not mean that it is not there. Tell me, what sort of dreams did you have about Angel? Were they romantic in nature? Were they nightmares?"

"We were never romantic in the dreams. He acted more like a second father or close uncle. He was always teaching me something, or telling me stories."

Guerra and Grave looked at each other out of the corner of their eyes. Guerra had the splinter of a smile, more genuine than he had outside. "What was he teaching you?" Grave asked. "What kind of stories was he telling you?"

"He would teach me all kinds of things. Sometimes he would teach me the piano, or read me poetry. He would teach me to dance and show me magic tricks." Rebecca laughed nostalgically as she recalled their activities, but then she frowned. "He also taught me to fight. It's the one thing I never wanted to learn, but it's what he said was the most important."

"When he taught you to fight, what did he teach you exactly?"

"He tried to teach me so much. Self defense, hand-to-hand, armed. But none of it was modern. He didn't teach me to use fire arms or anything like that."

"Did he ever tell you the reason for teaching you these things?"

"Yes. To stop the Fourth. But I never knew what that meant. What was the Fourth? All he ever said when it was brought up was I had to stop it. He couldn't do it himself or come with me. He always said one day I would have to take up the mantle, but I have no idea what that is."

Guerra and Grave purposefully looked at each other for a moment. Guerra looked at his notes and nodded. Grave looked back to Rebecca. "The Fourth you say?" he asked.

"That's what Angel talked about. It was coming and we had to stop it. We couldn't let it come. Then, recently, I started dreaming something else. There is a girl in school, Úna. I first saw her in a dream, but everyone acts like she has always been here. It feels like a cruel practical joke. When I dreamed about her, the Four Horsemen were chasing me. Every night I've been dreaming about them. They keep saying Death is coming." Rebecca seemed to have an epiphany. "Wait, is Death the Fourth that Angel kept talking about?"

Grave hummed in thought, tapping his chin. "Perhaps. Have you ever heard of the True Forms?"

"No. What are they?"

"I like to think I am an expert on the True Forms. They are lore of some of the most ancient civilizations in the world, but information on them is scarce in each individual society, so knowledge of them is hard to come by."

"Can you tell me?"

"The True Forms signal a change in the world, for better or worse. For these societies, it has always been for worse. The True Forms are better known as the Four Horsemen."

Shock flooded Rebecca's face.

"They appear one by one. When the Fourth rises, society is forever changed. At least, that is how the legends go." Grave raised a boney finger. "There is more. Warnings that each member is coming and a defender of Mankind to hold their destructive forces back. However, this defender can only hold these forces back for so long; then entire bloodlines die. When these defenders fail in their task, blood will wash over the land and the destructive side of the True Forms will rise one by one. War. Famine. Pestilence. And finally, Death. The Four Horsemen." Grave laughed apologetically. "I apologize. Please forgive an old man's rambling. It is a subject I am highly interested in and have a hard time holding myself back when I start talking about it."

"It's okay," Rebecca said.

"This girl, Úna you said? It is very likely that this is a girl you have often seen but never seen. She has always existed, but because she kept to herself, you just never noticed her. Your mind, needing to make sense of the slayings and requiring a messenger, used the person you barely knew, which in turn made this girl stand out to you."

"Yeah. That makes a lot of sense."

"As for Angel, you saw someone that resembled the person in your dreams. When a dreamer bears witness to a physical representation of their dreams they often over react."

Rebecca chewed on the inside of her lip, feeling like a fool.

"The only other conclusion would be, for most people, an impossibility. He is real."

Rebecca shot a surprised look to Grave.

"As for Miss O'Conner, I would not worry too much about her."

"I agree," Guerra added. "We know about the photographs you handed over to Detective Cragoff. I will personally inform her that spreading of that information will be regarded as obstruction of justice. I doubt she wants that charge."

"I don't think she would," Rebecca laughed. She looked at the clock. First period was almost over and she wanted to talk to Glenda. She felt a little better, but she had more questions than she came in with now. Úna. Rebecca felt like it was Úna that had the answers she really wanted, but she wasn't even sure of what the questions she needed answered were. "Thank you Officer Guerra, Dr. Grave. It was…insightful, but I think I need to get back to class. Officer Guerra, you will let Jason's dad know about what we talked about? I don't know if it'll help, but—"

"I will be sure he gets the notes," Guerra said with a nod. "Be on to class."

Rebecca nodded and made her way out. Guerra followed behind her to the door and closed it. He turned back to Grave and drew his gun. He pulled the clip out as he walked back across the room, tossing it onto Grave's desk. He pressed the barrel against the palm of his hand and pulled the trigger. His hand muffled the gunshot and smoke drifted from his hand. He tossed the discharged bullet onto Grave's desk as well, flattened against his palm. "I never liked these new automatic weapons," Guerra said. His voice was different now; deep and booming. "Cheap and random, but I have to admire their destructive power."

"You really do not like having that bullet in the chamber, do you?" Grave asked, his voice also different. It was no longer so slow and pained, but still echoed of ancient age.

"Not at all. These weapons defeat the whole purpose of weaponry. There is no honor or skill. No strength is necessary or good aim required. Just point and pull the trigger." He mimicked his directions, making the gun give off an empty clicking sound. "There is something wrong when a baby can kill a man."

"Humans have improved the tools of war—"

"These are not tools of war." Guerra threw the gun onto the desk. "These are tools to kill and maim. They are your tools, not mine. They cannot protect or defend. They cannot teach or subdue. They can only destroy. The death of a man is the often unwanted side effect of war, not the mandated, desired outcome. Humans should not want to simply destroy one another, only to protect what they have, or take what they want. It is not necessary to destroy your opponent as an only choice by default. This is why I dislike modern weaponry."

Grave grinned as he picked up the notepad that Guerra had discarded on the desk as he followed Rebecca to the door. "It is easier to kill your enemy to take his land than subdue him and force him to work it for you."

"Yes, it is. However, what good is it to kill for the land you desire if you destroy the land in that pursuit? In their arms race, humans have forgotten the whole point of the race." Guerra looked towards the door. "At least they have filtered the modern idea of warfare from her."

Grave looked at the sketch Guerra was making on his pad; a massive beast on four legs with a fearsome head. "So you approve of their handling of the little prodigy?"

"I do. I believe I can perfect and hone what they have started. She will be the greatest warrior the world has ever seen, should she survive her tribulation."

"We will have to leave that up to little Úna, as she has chosen to call herself. She has but one more part to play before the last piece of the puzzle falls into place."

"Let us hope she does not mess it up. It is almost pathetic to have the three of us dealing with this girl, while the Third trails Angel."

"That is her choice. Leave her be to it. She and his watcher have done much to push him through the ages. They know what they are doing, even as much as they begrudge each other."

"The angels do not trust us."

"Only as much as we trust them." Grave smiled. "I trust them completely. You should have more faith. The girl's guardian is already with her."

"I know. I could feel his presence in the room. A little soon, isn't it?"

"He has been watching over her for some time now, though I think he is only now beginning to understand the reasoning for it."

"I suppose that is a good thing. Do you think she's figured it out?"

"I was rather blunt about it. So were you."

"I did not say a word, as you instructed."

Grave chuckled. "Guerra is not blunt?"

"We do want her to figure it out, don't we?" Guerra smiled. "She has Spanish friends. Someone will tell her and help her put the pieces together. Then, hopefully, she'll confront the little bottomless pit."

Úna's voice echoed throughout the room, "Hey! I heard that!"

Guerra's voice boomed in laughter.

Looking at the time, Rebecca decided that there was little point in actually going to class. All she really wanted to do was talk to Glenda about the pictures of Angel she saw and she couldn't do that until the end of class anyway. Rebecca waited outside the room leaning against the lockers. She stared at the floor as she thought and waited for the bell to ring. She found herself thinking about what Grave had said. *The True Forms are the Four Horsemen*, Rebecca thought. *So there are only four of them. And someone is supposed to fight to hold them back? So can we change the path we are on? Like I could do anything. How could I stop something so powerful that they can completely destroy entire societies?* The bell rang and shortly thereafter the numerous doors opened and hundreds of students filtered into the hall. Rebecca waited for Glenda to walk out of the room. Glenda spied Rebecca first and broke from the flow of students.

"Rebecca!" Glenda called before Rebecca could say anything.

"I was worried about you!"

Glenda hugged Rebecca and she returned the embrace half-heartedly. "You were worried?" Rebecca asked. "Why were you worried?"

"Vamos. Too many ears."

Glenda led Rebecca to the girl's restroom where they could talk more privately. Glenda sighed before beginning. "Estoy preocupado—I mean, I was worried because of Angel. You had pictures of him."

"Thanks for worrying, but that's what I want to talk to you about."

"Oh? What about those pictures?"

"Did you tell anyone about them?"

"Like who?"

"Sarah?"

"¿Por qué tendría que tell her anything? She's done nothing but tease me since grade school."

"She knows about the pictures."

Glenda bit her lip and rubbed her arm nervously.

"Who did you tell?"

"I didn't mean to tell anyone." Glenda took a little time answering, making sure she stayed speaking English so Rebecca would understand what she said. "It slipped. When I found out Angel was the killer, I kind of freaked out because you had pictures of him. I thought you might be getting into trouble. I mentioned pictures you had, but caught myself before I said anything else. Sarah might have overheard." She sighed. "Lo siento."

"So you were talking about them?"

"Yo no dije que ellos—I mean I didn't say they were of Angel or where you got them. Like I said, I caught myself. Sarah must have just run with it since I freaked out. How…right is she?"

"She's not right! She's completely wrong! I didn't…I didn't…"

Rebecca broke into tears as Glenda unwittingly insinuated that Rebecca caused Melissa's death. Glenda held onto Rebecca and said, "Hey now! Hey now! No llores! No llores! I'm sorry! However that came out, I'm sorry! I don't even know what she said."

"What's going on in here?" Úna said as she came into the restroom. "Are you fighting?"

"No," Glenda answered. "We were just talking."

"It looks like you're making Rebecca cry."

"It's not how it looks."

Úna, Rebecca thought as she wiped her tears away and looked at the strange red-head. *Where did you come from? You couldn't have been here all this time. I would have noticed you.*

"You want to hear something funny?" Úna smiled devilishly.

"What?" Rebecca asked.

"Sarah just got chewed out by a cop. Something about obstructing justice? She turned as red as a cherry." Úna burst out into laughter.

"Obstructing justice?" Glenda asked. "For what? Oh, no importa! That is too funny!"

Glenda and Úna laughed for a moment before Úna spoke up, "Do you mind if I pee? I really gotta go!"

"Oh! Sorry." Glenda looked at Rebecca. "Are we done? We okay now?"

Rebecca nodded and followed Glenda out. Rebecca looked back towards the restroom and thought about what Grave said. Before they parted, Rebecca stopped Glenda.

"Do you know Úna?" Rebecca asked.

"What do you mean? Like, are we friends?"

"Do you know her at all? When did you meet?"

Glenda shrugged. "Not sure. She's been around as long as I can remember."

"But you never hung out with her or anything?"

"No. She always kept to herself."

Dr. Grave said Úna was always around, just in the back of my mind. Officer Guerra already told Sarah to back off. Guerra. "Glenda? Is guerra a word?"

"Guerra? Yeah. It means war in Spanish."

The chain leaden metallic body of War flashed before Rebecca's eyes and his booming roar echoed in her ears. "War?" Rebecca repeated. "Thanks."

"Uh, sure?" Glenda responded.

Rebecca left Glenda standing bewildered by her question as she headed to English class. *Guerra is war. Officer War. War; the first of four. Grave, the place where the dead lay. Death? War and Death? Rebecca shook her head. What am I thinking? Do I really think I was talking to the Horsemen of War and Death? They look nothing like the monsters in my dreams. You're thinking too much. The True Forms are just legends that some old man told you.* Rebecca found herself standing in front of the class room door. She stood there for a moment before Úna pushed past her. Úna turned and said, "If you are that out of it, you should go home or something. Go somewhere to get your thoughts straight."

Rebecca watched Úna walk to her desk and take a seat. "Go and think," Rebecca said. "That may do me good." She turned to walk away, looking back only briefly towards class. The bell rang and she walked away. She stopped by Michael's locker and used the spare key Michael had given her to open it. She put her books inside and wrote Michael a note,

Michael,
I had to leave today. Don't be mad that I didn't ask you to come with me. I need to be alone right now to think. Please bring my books home after school.
Love Always,
Rebecca ♥♥♥

Rebecca folded the note and placed it where Michael was sure to see it. She closed his locker and retrieved her jacket from her own. She knew that if her parents knew she had cut out again, and so early, they would be furious. At least she was sure her mother would be. Her father would be more forgiving of that fact. It was the fact that it wasn't home that she intended to go to that would really raise their ire.

***

The door opened and a chime sounded. Jeff entered the gun shop and was greeted by the clerk. Jeff showed the clerk his badge. "Detective Jeffery Cragoff of the Chicago Police," he said.

"What can I do for you officer?" the clerk asked.

Jeff pulled one of the photos of Angel from his pocket. It was folded twice. "Do you remember seeing this man, perhaps a week or two ago?"

The clerk stared at the photo. "He does look familiar." He thought for a moment. "Yes, I do remember him. You're the second person that's come in here looking for him."

"Really? Who was the first?"

"I don't know. He talked to the shop owner and they pulled some security video. I thought he was a cop."

"Neighborhood watch maybe."

"Well, that's a picture from our security camera, so I guess you should know."

"Right. This guy," Jeff tapped the photo. "Did you catch his name?"

"I thought he said his name was Angel."

"What did he come here to buy? Guns? Ammo?"

"Knives."

"Knives?"

"We don't just sell guns here officer. We have some nice hunting knives, among other types. All legal to own, of course."

"Of course. Can I see his purchases?"

"Sorry, there weren't any."

"He was just browsing, huh?"

"I wouldn't sell. He wouldn't produce any ID."

"Did he say why?"

"That he didn't have any. He tried to barter with me, but I wouldn't do it."

Jeff nodded as he folded and pocketed the photo. "Did he act suspicious in any way?"

"Besides the bartering over ID thing? Not really."

"Did he threaten you in any way?"

"No. That's the guy I heard about on the radio, isn't it? The one wanted for three homicides?"

"Yes. You said someone else came asking about him?"

"Yes, but he talked to the store owner."

"Is the owner around?"

"No, sorry. He's going to be gone all weekend I think. He'll be back on Monday though."

"Long time to wait." Jeff produced a card from his jacket pocket. "Give him my card. Tell him to give me a call."

The clerk took the card with a smile. "Sure thing. I'll let him know when I see him. I'll see if I can't dig up his number and give him a call."

"I would appreciate that. Thank you. Have a good day."

"You too."

***

Demonic Angel sat in his fiery prison with eyes closed in silent meditation. Satan's Presence had left and Santano was content to stare at the demon for the better half of an hour. His resemblance to Angel truly was uncanny, even with the explanation Santano was given. Santano crouched on the ground to get a better look at Demonic Angel's face.

"Will you stop staring at me," Demonic Angel demanded.

"How would you know that?" Santano asked.

"I can feel your eyes on me. It's disgusting. Stop it."

"How long have you been around; or Angel for that matter?"

"What does it matter to you, mortal?"

"I'm an avatar."

"You're still mortal." Demonic Angel smiled and opened his eyes. "Though your soul is no longer your own."

"Is that supposed to scare me?"

"I don't really care what it does. I was born immediately after Angel ascended, about nine hundred years ago."

"Nine hundred years? How can Angel not be immortal?"

"It would certainly seem that he is. He's the first demon hunter to be so. Perhaps it's part of his bargain with God; who knows? I certainly don't care. I'm going to kill him."

"If you've been fighting him for nine hundred years what makes you think you can kill him if you haven't already?"

"You're a fool. Demon hunters, though mortal, are divine by nature. You can't just kill them. That's too easy. You have to crush their hope. Angel's has proven difficult to destroy, but I came close."

"What held you back? Couldn't you bring yourself to do it?"

"I was interrupted."

"Interrupted? What do you mean?"

"I had Angel defeated; his hope crushed. I was about to deliver my coup de grace when someone intervened. He protected Angel and proceeded to steal my relic. Apparently, it belonged to him and he was hell-bent on retrieving it from me. Can't say I blame him. It gave me control over space time. It made it impossible for Angel to ever defeat me. I couldn't be exorcized."

"Is that how you kill a demon?"

Demonic Angel stood up. "You'll find out." He looked towards the outside. "There you are. Looks like our little innocent is on the move." Demonic Angel flexed his fist. "And just in time, too. My strength has returned." He drew his dark metal blade and with a single stroke shattered his prison. "Finally. I can finish what I started two hundred years ago. Though, I suppose I should abduct this innocent first." He chuckled. "I guess we'll see." Demonic Angel swung his sword around wildly, his hand slipping from the handle to hold the tail. Spinning, the entirety of the sword was consumed in flame. He pulled the tail down, slamming the flaming weapon into the ground. The flames burst around the demon and consumed him. Santano jumped back and shielded himself. As quickly as the flames were born they were gone and along with them Demonic Angel.

***

Rebecca got off the public bus a few miles from her house. She walked a few blocks from there to her secret place. She liked to visit this place when she needed time to be alone with her thoughts. It was this place where she had made some of her life's most important decisions, such as dating Michael. Rebecca stood before the old warehouse. It looked in worse condition than it actually was and was never condemned by the city. In reality, it was just abandoned and a little work would get it back to working order. A summer was all she thought it would really take for someone to renovate it, but for the last several years it had remained dormant and alone. For the most part, it was safe. Within the entrance Rebecca sought out her hidden flashlight. She had always promised herself that when it was discovered she would never come back. She thought at that point other people had decided to move in and it would no longer be safe for her to venture to. It had remained exactly where she had left it, untouched. She turned it on and ventured within. She noticed immediately, it was unusually warm.

Angel's coat lay on the floor with the sheathed Dagger of Power resting within it. The Sword of Might cut through the air and sweat dripped from his brow. He was hard at training within the abandoned building, but he was worried. Santano was the strongest avatar he had ever faced before and he was having doubts he could win. It had been a long time since Angel had not defeated an avatar in their initial encounter. Following that initial defeat they would return wielding the Blood Sword, just as Santano had done, but with their inner demon released. Sometimes Angel was able to exorcize the demon and other times he couldn't, but that wasn't important. Simply banishing the demon back to Hell was enough to save the souls it had collected. Santano never had his demon released, which meant the souls he was collecting were adding to his hellish powers. He was getting stronger. Already Angel worried that Santano was stronger than he. If that was true, what chance would he have? As Santano grew stronger with each collected soul, Angel grew weaker with each passing moment. How much longer could he hope to hold out?

Angel knew that if he could not hold his ground, that if he failed, Satan would win; he would have his final Horseman and launch his attack on Heaven. The world would be lost. Angel would have to fight with more than he ever had before; perhaps with more than he did have. His powers were rapidly weakening. Soon, perhaps within the next couple of weeks, his luck would run out. He would lose all his powers and the demon hunter would be gone forever. Without a demon hunter there would be nothing that could stop Satan. Heaven would be lost. Before that, he would have to make one last ditch effort against Hell. No matter what happened, Angel knew the aberration was right. His death was quickly approaching.

Even as Angel's powers drained, including his enhanced senses, his hearing seemed to be the last to wither. In the vast silence of loneliness, it was still superhuman. Rooms away he could hear the creaking of the main door opening. The sound halted his training in mid slash. Angel gripped his sword tight. He had company. He focused his senses and could make out the faint sound of footsteps heading his way. He tried to reach out to it, to discover just who was intruding upon him, but he could divine nothing. He just knew that it was time to fight and in his weakened condition he would have to get the drop on whomever his challenger was. He hoped Santano would be foolish enough to seek him out. It may be the only chance Angel had to defeat him.

Angel sheathed his sword in the scabbard strapped to his back as he scanned the large storeroom. On one side he spied stacks of shipping crates. They climbed high into the air and above them he could make out exposed rafters beyond the divine light he had blessed the room with. He dashed towards the crates and leaped up their stair like face towards the top, almost forty feet high. From there Angel focused the strength in his legs and jumped nearly thirty feet towards the exposed rafters. His leap fell short and he grasped the rafter with his hands. "Blast," he cursed as he pulled himself up. He crouched on the beam and reached for the handles of his sword and dagger, only to discover that his dagger was not at his side. He gasped as his eyes locked onto his jacket which nestled his dagger. He had forgotten that he had removed it.

Angel looked towards the door as the footsteps came to echo just outside of it. He had no time to retrieve the dagger before the owner of the footsteps entered the room. He crouched low and gripped the handle of his sword tightly. Angel sighed a breath of relief when Rebecca crossed the threshold. It was not Santano. That final battle was postponed a bit longer. Angel released his grip on his sword as he calmed, but his tension quickly rose when Rebecca noticed the unnatural light in the center of the room. She turned off her flashlight as she approached it. When she noticed Angel's jacket lying on the floor she looked around in confusion as fear started to build inside of her. She looked around for an explanation for the lighting, but the few fixtures that she knew did work remained off. There was no lantern or other external light source to explain the seven foot radius of lit area she found herself in. The light that came in through the high windows had always done little to light the room, and with the light Rebecca found herself in, she could barely see those windows, it was so bright.

Angel crouched low to hide from Rebecca's view. She scanned the room and called out, "Hello? Is—Is anybody there?"

"Go away," Angel whispered. "You don't need to be here. Just listen to your instincts and leave."

"Hello?" Rebecca called again.

Rebecca glanced down at Angel's jacket as he ran across the rafter quickly but silently. He positioned himself over her and crouched low again. "I guess they left," Rebecca concluded. She picked up the jacket and

Angel's dagger fell from its confines. The sound of it hitting against the floor startled her, but she relaxed when she saw the sheathed weapon at her feet. Rebecca put the jacket down and picked up the dagger. "No," Angel whispered. "Leave it alone." Rebecca unsheathed the rusted blade and looked at it in surprise. "Where did this come from?" she wondered aloud. "It's so rusted." Angel's tension was rising again as Rebecca looked over his weapon, draining it of its powers as she kept it from its sheath.

"I wonder how old it is." Rebecca asked herself.

Angel could stay silent no longer. "Put it back!" he shouted

Rebecca glanced upwards as she took a fearful step back. Angel dropped from the rafter and tumbled the near seventy feet back to the ground. Rebecca stepped further back as he came down and watched in awe as he was pressed to one knee following the motion of his decent. Angel seemed unharmed, but his hands and feet ached from the force of the landing. He did not wait long to regain his composure and rise, barely letting the pain in his hands and feet subside. His head spun and his body ached. He looked at Rebecca as non-menacingly as he could and repeated, "Put it back, please."

Rebecca stared at Angel in awe. She could not believe the height from which he had fallen and seemed totally unharmed. He had landed on his feet. It was impossible. Finally able to see him face-to-face sent a cold chill down her spine. It really was the same Angel from her dreams. This was the man she had dreamt about all her life.

"You—You're Angel," Rebecca stuttered. "Bu—But how did you—I mean—What are you?"

"Put the dagger back," Angel said. "Please. I won't ask you again."

Rebecca realized that the dagger belonged to him. It was rusted now, but it was the same dagger he always carried in her dreams. Her grip tightened on it. "No way!" she shouted as she held the dagger threateningly. "Tell me what's going on! Who are you? Why have you been haunting me?"

"Haunting you?" Angel mumbled. He dismissed it and let out a sigh. "What's going on? I've been asked that before, once or twice here and there. I could tell you, but I doubt you're ready to hear the truth. No one is ever ready for it."

"My friends are dead! They started dying right after you showed up! You know why, I know you do! Tell me!"

Angel looked at her with a frown. "They are your friends? Yes, I'm afraid I do know why they are dying. I'm trying to save them, but it's difficult. He's stronger than the others were."

"What others? Who are you talking about?"

"He's an avatar. His name is Samuel Santano."

Fear ran through Rebecca. Fear that everything she has already figured out will be supported by Angel. "Santano? You mean my teacher?"

"I'm afraid so. I knew his name and where he would be. I've come to stop him."

"Why would he kill my friends? It doesn't make any sense!"

"Samuel made a deal with Satan. In return for power, he must offer up ten human sacrifices. He's already made three. I wasn't able to stop him."

"This is ridiculous!" Rebecca shouted. She was getting scared. Not because Angel was standing before her, but because she believed him and sorely did not want to. "You're telling me that my teacher made a deal with the devil and is killing off my friends? It can't be true! It just can't!"

"Why can't it be?"

Angel's sudden remark took Rebecca aback and she stuttered. Finally, through breaking tears she whispered, "Because I don't want it to be."

"I'm sorry, but it is."

Rebecca's tears ran down her face. "But then…that means…" She tried to hold back her sobs. "Why my friends? Why choose my friends?"

"I'm afraid that is just bad luck. His victims are tied to him in some way, and for at least a little while longer, will be chosen at random. I'm running out of time."

"What does that mean?"

As Angel opened his mouth to speak, his laughter filled the room. "Guess who's back!" his voice echoed. Rebecca stared at Angel in confusion as the voice spoke. Angel's lips never moved. His face filled with shocked dread. "It can't be," he said.

The ceiling tore open, flooding the room in light as the grey skinned white haired Demonic Angel plummeted to the ground. He landed with a loud thud on his feet and quickly stood erect. Angel turned in a start as Rebecca took a few steps backwards. Demonic Angel grinned and said, "Did you miss me?"

Angel immediately drew his sword and shouted, "This isn't possible! You were exorcized!"

"You'll never be rid of me," Demonic Angel grinned. He reached back for the handle of his sword. The red cloth tail came alive as he drew it and wrapped around his forearm. As he drew his sword, he also reached with his other hand for the silver handle at his side. He pulled free a thick blade, a mix between a large dagger and small sword. It had no hand guard and was the same dark metal as the sword in his right hand. Demonic Angel let the sword slip through his fingers and began to twirl it by the cloth tail. "It's been a long time, Angel," the demon said. "Do you remember these?"

Angel gripped his sword tighter. "Yes, I remember them." Angel thought. *Without the Dagger of Power I'm at a disadvantage against the Hellish Weapons. This girl still has the Dagger of Power and by now it's been drained!*

Demonic Angel chuckled softly as the blade of his sword began to glow red hot. Sparks flew from it as it spun around, making a red hot blur. "You're dead this time Angel." He let the tail go and the handle fell into his hand. "Magma Punch!" He slashed horizontally with his demonic sword and it spit forth from the blade a ball of molten magma.

Angel quickly retaliated. He held the Sword of Might horizontally and shouted, "Meteor Punch!"

A rock core fireball shot out of the fire consumed blade and raced towards Demonic Angel's attack. The two balls of molten rock and fire met and detonated in a violent explosion, creating a cloud of thick black smoke. The two warriors dashed into the smoke to meet with a violent clash that erupted energy that scattered the smoke from them. They traded blows quickly, great sparks flying as they did so. Demonic Angel's sparks of power were far larger and Angel was having difficulty keeping up with his speed. Demonic Angel fought with both blades and made it difficult for Angel to defend Cloth and blood flew from Angel's body as he was repeatedly cut by the Hellish Weapons.

Rebecca stared on in amazed fear as her nightmares were becoming real right before her eyes. She couldn't believe what she was seeing. They were moving faster than she thought a normal human could move. Even with Angel being cut repeatedly by the seax in his left hand—she knew that's what it was—he was still in relatively one piece. Anyone else would have been cut to ribbons. Their erupting energy flustered her blonde locks. Their weapons were not normal. Nothing could erupt with sparks of power like that. She contemplated the notion that they were magical. Would that be possible? Her eyes glanced down at the dagger in her hand. Angel was protective of it. Did it have the same kind of power? She could have sworn for a moment she saw the pure steel shine from beneath the rust.

Angel released his dual grip on his sword and caught Demonic Angel's dagger hand before he could land a good thrust. Using his sword, Angel locked Demonic Angel's flamed tipped dao sword to the ground. Before they had a chance to struggle between each other, Angel reared his head back and slammed his forehead into his demonic double's face. Pure black blood squirted from his nostril's as Demonic Angel grunted and took a step back. With a twist of his waist, Angel drew his fist back and delivered a powerful backhand to Demonic Angel. The demon was knocked off balance and fumbled backwards. Angel leaped several feet back as he shouted, "Sword of Might!" He raised his sword aloft. "Eternal Fire!" A puff of fire spewed forth from the blade and died as soon as it hit the air. "No!" Angel shouted. "Not now!" Demonic Angel grinned. "Out of gas already?" he taunted. He let his sword slip from his hand again and twirled it by the cloth tail. It creating a spinning motion of fire. "You do it like this," he grinned. "Hell Fire!"

With a flick of his wrist Demonic Angel sent the spinning sword slamming into the ground. It bounced off the floor as the fire roared up and forward with an almost living hunger. Angel fell back while quickly gripping his cross. "Halo!" Angel shouted. A white light surrounded him and protected him from the demonic flames as the force knocked him to the ground. The heat of the fires broke sweat from his brow.

With an evil chuckle Demonic Angel leaped high into the air, his sword pulling up with him to find his hand. He trained his seax upon Angel.

"Demonic Sting!" he shouted. A hail of thorns shot from the thick pointed blade in a cone formation. Angel found the strength to roll to safety just inches away from the thorns as they trailed after him. Demonic Angel landed amidst the thorns with a grin. Both weapons were trained on Angel's weakly rising body, but something else caught his attention. "What's this?" the demon asked. "I sense something…divine." He looked towards a shocked Rebecca, still standing with dagger in hand. "Ah yes, the 'priority' task. I see, so you're important to Heaven. I guess I should focus on you after all." Demonic Angel rushed Rebecca at top speed. "Poison Sting!" Rebecca screamed in panic as Demonic Angel struck. Her instincts instantly took over, but they did not make her run, as she would have thought. No, she had been taught better. Angel had taught her better.

Rebecca stood her ground, twirling the dagger in her hand to catch the opposing blade and steadying the block with her free hand. He was strong; Rebecca could feel it in their lock. He was strong enough to push her back, but something was holding her in place, unmoving. She could feel something—a presence—to help steady her, adding strength and stability to her stance.

"Feisty," Demonic Angel said. "I like that." He tried to press forward, but found he met unnatural resistance as Rebecca only took one step back. "Your little angel can only do so much to protect you." Demonic Angel reached back with his sword and caught Angel's sword in mid strike. Demonic Angel looked towards Angel with a grin on his face. He was at a disadvantage locked between two opponents, but Demonic Angel knew his light counterpart would not risk hurting Rebecca with an assault barrage. The flame tipped sword began to vibrate with power. The blade began to glow as dark clouds appeared and spun around it. Demonic Angel chuckled and said in nearly a whisper, "Cataclysm." The power his sword gathered was released in an explosive force that threw Angel across the room. Now free of its lock, the demonic sword continued to the ground and released a second wave of energy that raced after Angel.

Rebecca's heart was racing. She had no explanation for what she was witnessing. All she wanted to do was get away, to get to safety. Whatever was helping Rebecca stand her ground had released its hold. She was free to move and wasted no time letting her common sense take over and made a run for the door. She didn't want to fight. Why did she even think she could? She didn't like the answer. Because she knew she could.

Demonic Angel returned his attention to Rebecca and chased after her. Using his demonic speed and strength he closed the distance quickly and leaped over her and cut off her escape. Rebecca came to an abrupt stop as Demonic Angel lashed out at her again, this time attacking her with his sword. She threw herself to one side to avoid the attack, but with her balance already challenged from her sudden stop, she found herself on the ground and vulnerable to her attacker. Demonic Angel thrust the seax forward and called out, "Vine Snare!" From the base of the blade vibrant green vines erupted and began to ensnare around Rebecca. She tried to crawl away from them as they quickly ensnared her body.

Angel's sword raced through the vines and cut them with one stroke. The vines withered and died with their roots severed. Angel's sword flew past them and skidded across the ground. Demonic Angel frowned as he looked towards Angel. Rebecca backed as far away from Demonic Angel as she could, afraid that he would attack her again, but she couldn't manage to find her feet.

"Leave her alone!" Angel shouted from across the room. "Your fight is with me!"

Demonic Angel smiled. "You are my primary objective, but unfortunately I have orders. However…" Demonic Angel relaxed his stance and faced Angel, tapping the tip of his seax against his chin. "If you insist on interfering, then I guess I have no choice but to deal with you first. What to do, what to do?"

He's too confident. Angel thought. *What does he want with this girl? Santano has only made three sacrifices. Are they starting the Collection so soon? Can they do that?*

Demonic Angel let his sword loose again, slowly beginning its spin. He took a few steps forward, slowly. His grin was evil. Angel advanced in kind, unarmed. Demonic Angel burst into a charge. Angel did the same. The demon flicked his wrist with a swing of his arm, releasing his grip on the swords tail to sending it darting across the space between them. Angel shifted his weight to let the blade fly past him and took hold of the tail. He jerked the sword back around and into his hand as they closed the distance between them. Demonic Angel shifted his weight to avoid a blow that never came. Angel thrust the sword into the ground as he darted past his doppelganger and jerked the tail towards him, pulling the demon off his feet. Angel pivoted with an elbow blow as Demonic Angel was pulled into it, but the demon caught the attack with his sword arm, his hand tangled in the red tail of his sword.

Rebecca returned to her feet and found herself staring at the rusted sword in front of her only a few yards away. The urge to take it was powerful, almost as if it were beckoning to her. Her eyes went to the door and she took a few quick steps to it before stopping and returning her gaze to the sword. She could almost feel the sword begging for her. She could almost feel the pull of the dagger in her hand towards that sword. She took a few slow steps towards it. Rebecca found herself struggling against two very powerful urges, one she didn't understand. It was more than wanting that sword or needing that sword. It was hers.

Demonic Angel noticed Rebecca's struggle. *What is she doing?* he thought. *Is she actually thinking about fighting me?* He grinned. *Well, I shouldn't disappoint her.* Demonic Angel shouted, creating a violent sonic burst that knocked Angel off balance. A powerful kick to Angel's stomach pushed him across the floor as he tried to brace himself and stay on his feet. With a quick flick of his arm, Demonic Angel let the sword from his grip and across the space between them. Angel was too off balance to avoid it and found his stomach pierced. He fell to his knees. "Poison Sting!" Demonic Angel called out as he twisted at the waist and threw the seax at Rebecca. She was only a few paces from Angel's sword when the thick blade that was almost too big to be a dagger, but almost too small to be a sword, struck her shoulder. Rebecca spun once as she fell to the ground with a scream. Her grip around Angel's dagger was tight as she tried to keep herself up right. "Are you still holding that dagger?" Demonic Angel laughed. "You're persistent, I'll give you that, but you're not going anywhere now." He turned to Angel, who was trying to pull the sword from his stomach. "Now I get to finish what I started. You lose, again." Demonic Angel approached

Angel triumphantly as he jerked back on the tail, pulling the sword from Angel's stomach. "Not surprising though. You're weak!" He kicked Angel across the chin and knocked him onto his back. "You were always weak." Demonic Angel kneeled down and drove his sword into Angel again. With a devilish grin, he slowly pushed the blade deeper into Angel, gleefully watching the demon hunter writhe in agony. He savored every moment of Angel's pain.

Rebecca looked at the blade buried in her shoulder. She wasn't sure how far it had penetrated, but a good portion of the blade was still exposed. The pain went straight through, but she wasn't sure if the blade did. It burned and the burning was slowly growing out from her shoulder and into her arm. "Pull it out," Rebecca heard a voice whisper. It was soothing and masculine. It wasn't Úna. Rebecca gripped the demonic blade's handle and grimaced as the burning intensified. She steeled herself, breathing fast before holding it and pulled the blade free. The flaming pain progressing through her body was making it numb. Her shoulder tingled as her nerves went to sleep or died. She wasn't sure which.

Rebecca let the demon blade slip from her fingers and clang on the floor. She rose to her feet and took the last few steps towards Angel's sword. She looked towards the two men fighting before reaching down to grip the rusted sword. For an instant, Rebecca thought she saw metal beneath shine through the rust. It felt surprisingly good in her hand and as weak as she felt with the burning numbness that was filling her body, it was light. She turned back towards the two warriors and watched as Demonic Angel wrapped his hands around Angel's neck and began to strangle him.

"There's no one here to save you this time Angel," Demonic Angel taunted as Angel struggled against him.

"Don't forget about me," Rebecca rasped defiantly as she took a few slow steps towards them.

Demonic Angel loosened his grip on Angel and turned his amused attention to Rebecca. He watched for a moment as Rebecca painfully advanced with sword and dagger in hand. The right shoulder of her coat was red with blood. "Are you serious?" Demonic Angel laughed. "Honestly, I'm surprised you're still standing at all."

"Run," Angel gargled.

Demonic Angel gripped his sword and pulled it from Angel's bloodied middle. "So you want to fight me, is that it?" The demon approached Rebecca until he was only a few yards away. He chuckled. "Take your best shot. You may be human, so you can hold those, but only the blood of a demon hunter can harness their powers, and the Virtues have long since been dead."

"Really? Is that a fact? Then you should know my name." She raised the rusted sword horizontally before her. Hers. This was her sword. This was her fight.

"Hm?"

"It's Rebecca Virtue."

Demonic Angel's cocky face turned to one of shock instantly.

Rebecca didn't think. She followed her instincts. "Eternal Fire!" Flames erupted from the blade. Demonic Angel raised his sword in a panicked defense. The flames broke through his hastily raised shield and burned his flesh. "Impossible!" he shouted as he tried to defend against the flames. Angel's struggle to stand was halted as he stared in shocked disbelief. Demonic Angel broke through the flames and struck at Rebecca. She braced herself and caught his sword with the sword in her hand. Her heart was racing as she stared into the crazed eyes of her enemy. "You can't be!" Demonic Angel shouted. Flames danced across his form and slowly consumed him. He struck again as Rebecca took a step back, but again Rebecca caught his strike. "The Virtues are dead!" he exclaimed. "All dead!" Rebecca gritted her teeth and lashed out with the dagger in her opposite hand. It cut into Demonic Angel's flesh like fire and forced him to back away. He held his burning wound as black blood covered his hand. He growled and attacked again. Rebecca braced her sword with her arm and stopped Demonic Angel's attack with the sword's flat. He pushed his sight past the physical and was shocked at what he found. "An archangel?!" Rebecca pushed back and cut him with her sword.

Angel tried to push his sight forward, but could barely make out the aura of the divine around Rebecca. "She can't be," Angel thought aloud. "How is she doing this? No guardian angel has this kind of power."

Rebecca held her ground against Demonic Angel's relentless assault. *He's so strong!* Rebecca thought. *I can barely feel my body, it's so numb.* Rebecca pushed him back and swung the sword. "Meteor Punch!" A fiery rock core rocketed from the blade and pushed Demonic Angel back. His body was beginning to crack and light escape. *How in the world am I doing this? Am I going crazy?*

Angel closed his eyes and lightly touched them with his fingertips. "Help my eyes to see," he whispered, "all the good Thou sendest me." He opened them again and the divine light around Rebecca began to slowly take shape. Angel recognized the form. "Raphael?"

"You bitch!" Demonic Angel screamed as he raised his ignited sword high. "Pestilence killed all of you!" He brought the sword down and washed a wave of flames over Rebecca. She screamed and tried to brace herself against the demonic flames. Angel saw Raphael's wings wrap around Rebecca and the angel protect her in an embrace against the flames. They never touched her. Demonic Angel rushed forward and thrust his blade by Rebecca's head. Angel saw Raphael wince as he was stabbed, as well as Demonic Angel. Rebecca had thrust with her own blade and ran the demon through. "No," Demonic Angel whispered as he dropped his sword. His hands went to Rebecca's neck in a weak hold. "Baraqyal."

"Ho—Holy Strike…" Rebecca stammered the words in her head. The rusted sword began to glow white.

Demonic Angel's face was flooded with pain. "Damn…Pestilence…"

Angel saw lightning rocket from the ground and bathe the area in fire. From the lightning burst flew what at first looked like an angel, but Angel knew otherwise. She was Baraqyal, one of the Executives and fallen chief angels of Heaven. Her hair was long and the color of tarnished silver. It covered half her face and from behind the silvery covering, lightning danced from her right eye. Her skin was fair and lovely and wings of silver moved on her back, whisking her quickly across the storehouse floor. In each hand was a massive hammer with a lightning bolt handle and sparks of electricity crackling on the silver white heads. She wore pants of silver silk with a slit on the outside of her legs from her ankles to her knees. Her silver vest covered a shirt of dark blue hues. The shirt had long sleeves with long slits on her arms, staying connected at the wrist. Her eyes locked with the angel beside Rebecca and her body started to spout lightning bolts. She was donning her devilish armor.

On the astral plane, Rebecca could not see the devil that appeared or the angel beside her, only the breaking body of Demonic Angel before her. He was on the physical plane with her. Demonic Angel scream as the sword in Rebecca's hand released its energy and vaporized him. Nothing remained as holy energy erupted from within him. His weapons drifted away into dust. Baraqyal stopped dead in her tracks and stared down Raphael. The archangel returned the stare for a long moment, trying to read Baraqyal's thoughts. Rebecca stood quivering. She stared at the smoke that wafted around the rusted blade. Demonic Angel was gone, like he had never been there in the first place. She could no longer feel her body and her weapons had grown heavy. She let them fall. Her legs could no longer support her weight and she slipped to her knees. She didn't fall. Someone had helped her down. She couldn't see Raphael holding her, but she could feel his embrace. She felt safe in it. She could rest. She closed her eyes and let the poison running through her finish its work. She wouldn't have to fight anymore. Raphael gently laid Rebecca on the ground, keeping his eyes on Baraqyal as he made sure Rebecca lay in a comfortable position. He then took his green stained wing and wrung a green liquid from it. The liquid steamed as soon as it hit the ground. Angel knew then that Raphael had protected Rebecca and absorbed much of the poison, which is how she must have had so much strength to fight. Raphael's gold plated sword materialized in his right hand, and still kneeling on the ground beside the worn out Rebecca, stared at Baraqyal. The fallen angel returned the stare for a long moment. Lightning danced around her and with a central strike and flash, she was gone. The threat was gone. Raphael looked towards Angel, then to Rebecca. The two were equally concerned. Raphael opened his mouth to speak, but didn't. His eyes narrowed disdainfully on Angel and slowly vanished from Angel's sight.

Finally finding the strength to stand, Angel rose to his feet and approached the sleeping girl. His eyes were misty. He stared at the girl on the ground, sleeping almost peacefully. Blood from her shoulder was soaking her jacket and beginning to make a small pool around her. A voice long since past filled the back of Angel's mind. "Angel, my darling…" it giggled. Tears began to pour from Angel's eyes. "Amanda…" he choked. "Is it true?" He wiped his tears. "I remember…I am…a Virtue. My love, did you truly live?" Angel slumped to the ground and smiled through his sobs.

Angel could feel a tentative touch. "Do you remember?" a soft voice whispered. "On that day nine hundred years ago."

"On that day," Angel said as his eyes swelled with tears. "Pestilence rose; all my family slain." Angel's tears slid down his face from the painful memory. Echoes of the past invaded his mind, images and voices long since forgotten.

"You will follow me, won't you?" Amanda had asked him. Angel sobbed at his broken promise to come for her.

"That man…is a man no longer," Angel's father had warned. "I love you my dearest son. My boy…" Angel cried for his father, the final words he spoke with his last breath.

"You are the last," Pestilence's sickly voice said. His visage was clear in Angel's mind. Two long, powerful arms supported a small, thin frame, two small legs giving it an almost ape-like posture. It's entire being like darkness itself. Angel could see its crimson eyes and smile the clearest. "No Virtue blood has escaped me."

"My blood," Angel whispered. He looked at Rebecca. "Uri. My promise."

"Death shall not rise," the soft voice whispered. "Your blood depends on it."

Angel caressed Rebecca's face. "She is of my blood? I was not the last?"

Angel took in Rebecca's sleeping face. As peaceful as she lay sleeping, the look of exhaustion was evident. About her neck Angel noticed the cross nine centuries ago. "As long as you carry this my love will always protect you," Angel recited. "I will always be with you." A solemn smile found its way to Angel's lips. "It is true, isn't it? She lived. My love hid you, protected you and our son."

Angel laid the cross back against Rebecca's body with trembling hands. "Her cross, the Heavenly Weapons, Raphael," Angel rambled. "You really are a Virtue. I wasn't the last. You are the next in line. You are the next to rise."

CHAPTER VIII

Deep within the bowels of the Underworld, in the shattered remains of Hades' fortress, rested a massive throne of bones. The bones cried out and from the various eye sockets, blood tears poured. Seated atop that grotesque thrown was Satan himself. One hand, clenched in a fist, propped his head up. The other drummed atop the skull arm rest. Screams of agony and begs for mercy echoed throughout the shattered halls. Hanging upon the walls were torn tapestries depicting the forgotten age of the Olympians. Shattered and broken statues of Hades and his servitors lined the various halls, though some were so badly damaged that it was unsure what they were previously. Tormented souls hung like portraits along the walls of these halls and from the ceiling souls hung as living chandeliers. Satan sat silently on his throne. Except for his drumming fingers, he was unmoving as he read through and visualized the endless battle plans held like files in his mind; plans that after millennia of manipulation would soon see fruition.

From time to time Satan's eyes would wander and he would find himself watching one of the many torments around him. People's worst fears and pains were enacted upon them, as well as being subjected to their tormentors' perversity, almost in show like fashion.

An athletic man in a shimmering black robe walked through the tormenting shows. His black feather wings were folded against his back. Even at five foot eight, he seemed small beside some of the tormentors. His hair was short and dark. His brown eyes looked only at Satan, even when the tormented souls managed to tear at his robe. He was handsome, far too handsome for what he was; Lucifer, the fallen light bearer. Satan stared blindly past Lucifer as he approached.

Lucifer climbed the mound of bones and leaned in close to Satan. Into his ear Lucifer whispered, "Baraqyal was called. She came to report the defeat of Demonic Angel by a blonde young girl." Satan's nostril's flared.

"She stated that Raphael was there as well, protecting this girl; the same girl you sent Demonic Angel after. She used the powers of the Heavenly Weapons."

Satan sat quietly, motionless and, except for his flaring nostrils, devoid of emotion. This was very unexpected news. It meant but one thing; Pestilence failed. Satan leaned forward on his throne and rubbed his chin in thought. How did an entire bloodline slink past them through the ages? How is it they were able to hide? How is it that this girl's linage had managed to slip past him completely when he handpicked her for the Collection? This changed his plans dramatically.

"Where is Pestilence?" Satan finally asked.

Lucifer placed his hands together. When he pulled them apart speckled light the size of a scroll appeared between them. This speckled light turned into a scroll. Lucifer opened the seal and unfurled it. He glanced at the angelic letters and symbols. "It seems Pestilence is keeping himself busy in the Middle Eastern regions," Lucifer said.

"Summon him."

Lucifer re-rolled the scroll. "With all due respect my Lord—"

"Do it. We need to have a discussion."

"If it is your desire my Lord, I will do what I can."

"Santano's victims have been the girl's friends thus far?"

With a flick of his wrist, a parchment blazed into existence in Lucifer's left hand. Again he glanced at the angelic letters and symbols. "Yes, they have been."

"Summon Inquisitor as well. Tell him to prepare for an inquisition. Bring her friends to me."

The parchment burned away as quickly as it came into being. "As you command, my Lord."

Lucifer gripped the air and touched his fists together. As he pulled them apart, a beam of light expanded between and beyond them, becoming a long staff. Atop the staff sat an orb of clear crystal. The crystal orb began to glow brightly, enshrouding Lucifer in a bright light. In a flash, Lucifer was gone. Satan stood with crossed arms. His mind raced as it searched for answers to his questions. There must be a reason they were hidden all these years, he knew there had to be. Humans cannot simply slip from divine sight.

At the base of the bone mound, a bright light filled the area. The light was pulled back into Lucifer's crystal orb. With him were three animal-like demons, each carrying impassionedly one of Santano's victims, nude and barely conscious. Their bodies were marred and bruised but possessed no open wounds or blood, but were covered in a sheen of sweat. Even those marks were quickly healing. Each of the demons was large and muscular with all their chiseled and hard limbs to bear without shame. Three distinct animals stood. The first demon had Adam slung over his shoulder. Its head was of a fierce lion with a red mane that tapered into its chest. Its body was the color of red clay. In place of hands and feet it had the paws of a lion, each toe sporting a deadly sharp claw. The bear headed demon squatted over Melissa with its massive bear claw pressed on her back. Its flesh was as dark as its fur. Its claws flexed on Melissa's flesh impatiently. Its other paw scratched its side. Nicole sat, with the help of the serpent headed demon, in front of it. Her head lolled slightly as she tried to focus. The serpent demon had, for the most part, human hands and feet. Its hands, however, were equipped with long sharp nails and its long emerald tail partially encircled the two. The tail's tip caressed Nicole's leg. The serpent's head had a pair of almost saber-like fangs. It was the only demon with a tail.

"I have brought the bestials 'caring' for them my Lord," Lucifer said. "Is there anything else you would like of me?"

"Yes," Satan said as he settled back into his throne. "Bring me the Chalice of All Souls Blood."

Lucifer bowed and again his crystal orb glowed. In that flash of light he was gone.

Satan relaxed into his throne and said, "Wake them."

The man-bear tossed Adam onto the ground with a loud thud. He roared as he raised his massive claw and drove it through Adam's body. Adam awoke in a gargled cry. The man-bear lifted Adam off the ground and faced him towards Satan, adjusting his head with the other paw. No blood. No guts. Only pain. Adam's hands clutched weakly at the protruding paw. Tears ran down his face and he sobbed.

The lion-man took his paw off Melissa's back and leaned towards her. He sank his sharp teeth painfully deep into her neck and shoulder. A barely audible scream escaped her as she awoke. The lion-man pulled her to her feet. As weakly as Adam, she clutched at the demon's snout, trying to find the strength to pry his maw open. No blood ran down her body, only tears.

The serpent-man hissed as his tail lifted and entwined around Nicole's neck. Her hands clutched at the tail as it tightly entwined about her throat. She tried to dig her nails into his tail, but in an instant found herself flung into the air and slammed face first into the ground. The serpent-man grabbed her wrists and pulled her arms abruptly back and forced her to her knees. There he held her, pulling her arms back with his powerful hands and pushing her forward and strangling her with his tail. The end of the tail wrapped around her hair and pulled her head back to stare up at Satan. Pained tears filled her eyes, but she did not cry.

Satan's eyes trailed over the anguished bodies before him. "Inquisitor is on his way," Satan said. "As the Tormentor of Hell, he can pry any knowledge from your unwilling lips. But I am not at all unreasonable." Satan grinned. "I offer you a chance to avoid his torments, which will be far greater than anything you have yet to experience. Just tell me about your friend, Rebecca. Who is she; her background; her wants and needs? Tell me everything."

"Fuck you," Nicole croaked. "We won't tell you anything."

All eyes turned to Nicole in stunned amazement. Fear found itself on the serpent-man's face. Satan smiled. "My Master—" the serpent-man began in a hissing voice. Satan raised his hand and the bestial silenced himself. Flicking his tongue into the air, he tried to taste what his Master was thinking.

"I see," Satan said. "I think I understand why you were able to prolong your death." Nicole glared at him without fear, feeling pain only from her torments. "You have a very strong will. You're not afraid of me."

Satan motioned for Nicole's release. Without hesitation the serpent-man released Nicole's wrists and unwound his tail from her neck. Nicole supported herself with one hand on the hot ground and one hand went to her throat. She coughed. She glared up angrily at Satan. He smiled and said,

"I will fix that. I will break your will and teach you true fear." Nicole struggled to stand, her body weak and exhausted. A bright light filled her vision and she was blinded. The light faded quickly and her eyes began to adjust, but almost instantly she found a powerful hand at her throat. Satan had closed the distance in that time and, wings partially spread, gripped her by the throat and slowly lifted her off the ground. Her hands tried to pry his off. Her feet dangled as she tried to find footing. Lucifer looked quizzically at the display holding a large golden, emerald laden chalice filled with a deep red liquid. "What did I miss?" he mumbled. Nicole stared at Satan defiantly, taking in deep pained breaths. Satan stared into her eyes, reading them, but spoke to Lucifer. "Gather our forces Lucifer. Pestilence's mistake may be costly." Then he smiled. "Today has been very stressful and full of unwelcome surprises, don't you think? It has been a very long time since I have partaken in these 'festivities'. I think some stress relief is in order." He brought Nicole close to him. She stared back with angry, defiant eyes. "You will learn to fear me." Satan tightened his grip, forcing a hoarse yelp from Nicole. "Make no mistake about that. What your bestial has done, and what Inquisitor will do to your friends, is nothing compared to what I will do to you." Nicole stared at him, gathering her strength. She spat in his face. Satan did not flinch or wipe the spittle away. He just grinned at her.

***

When Rebecca awoke her body ached and she was chilly. Her shoulders and back were cold. The stab wound in her shoulder throbbed, but it was more uncomfortable than painful. She had trouble opening her eyes from her deep sleep and they had to take a moment to adjust. The floor was uncomfortably cold against her bare back. She realized she was topless but for something draped over her. She thought she felt her bra, but wasn't sure. Finally her eyes adjusted to the light filled room. She was still in the warehouse. An old leather trench coat covered her. She tried to move and found that her muscles, especially in her arms, were sore. She held the coat in place and sat up. She found her shirt and jacket were within reach, but they were bloody. Off the ground her bare back was colder. She slipped the jacket on to keep warm. She was relieved to find that her bra was in fact still on. Her shoulder was also bandaged. Stains of red dotted it. She looked around and found Angel a few yards away. He had his back to her and was putting back on a blood stained and torn shirt. Almost his entire body was bandaged.

Rebecca hesitated at first. "What happened?"

Angel flinched as he put an arm through his shirt. "The poison finally wore off," he answered.

"Poison?"

"It's not a fatal poison. It's a neurotoxin that knocks out all motor functions. In short, it paralyzes you."

"What about you?" Rebecca asked as she got to her feet. "Are you okay? Who was that guy; your brother? He looked just like you."

"I've seen better days," Angel answered as he began to strap his dagger to his side. "I'll live though. What you saw was my demonic double."

"Demonic? You mean he was a demon?"

"Sort of. I guess yes would be a simpler answer."

"You're saying—"

"That he was a demon? Yes. You asked me for the truth and I can tell you the truth, but will you accept it?"

Rebecca hesitated as Angel reached down for the sheathed sword at his feet. "Tell me what's going on," she said. "Why is this happening?"

Angel nodded as he began to strap his sword to his back. He hadn't turned to face her and he moved so solemnly. "Can I ask you a question first? Your necklace; where did you get it?"

Rebecca touched the cross hanging about her neck. "This? My father gave it to me when I was little. It's an heirloom that's been handed down for generations."

"It looks to be eleventh century."

"It is. How did you know that?"

Angel didn't answer. He was thinking about how to handle this new information. For so long he had thought he was the last.

"It's said whoever wears this cross is protected by an angel's love."

Angel perked at the saying. It had changed a little, but that's what he had told Amanda when he gave it to her over nine hundred years ago. Angel turned around and looked at Rebecca for a long moment. His heart was pounding in his chest and his throat was sore from the tears he had wept. How much should he tell her? Is he even right? He saw her use the powers of the Sword of Might. He saw her use them to slay Demonic Angel. He saw Raphael protecting her, like a guardian would. Like Uriel had protected him on that day. "Rebecca Virtue?" Angel asked. "That is what you said your name was?"

"Yes," Rebecca nodded.

Angel opened his mouth to recite his name, but chose against it. Perhaps it was too soon. His guardian was not there to guide him. Even the aberration that haunted him would have given welcome insight. No. He mustn't tell her too much too soon. The truth coupled with her lineage may be too much for her to handle right now.

"Heaven and Hell," Angel finally began, "are very real places. And they are at war with each other."

Rebecca swallowed. Hard.

"What you saw and managed to kill was not a true demon, but the physical manifestation of my sins."

Rebecca's eyes widened in astonishment; almost in disbelief. "He was—your sins?"

Angel nodded. "I am a demon hunter; the last of my kind. My family was murdered a very long time ago. That left me the sole heir to a legacy that spanned generations. I am God's only mortal soldier. My task is to keep the Fourth from rising."

Shock flooded Rebecca's face. Even in real life, away from her dreams, Angel insisted on stopping the Fourth from rising.

"I'm afraid that is why your friends are dying. Samuel Santano is sacrificing them to become that trump card; that final piece of the puzzle that would give Satan the advantage. He needs to make seven more sacrifices, ten in all, to complete his ascension. He'll become stronger with each sacrifice he makes."

Tears were running down Rebecca's face. It was all so surreal and so hard to believe. She wiped her tears away. "But why my friends?" she asked. "What is so special about all of my friends?"

"They are all innocent souls, for the most part. The fact that they are your friends is just bad luck. I'm sorry." He looked at her bloodied clothes on the ground. As he turned to walk away he said, "You can keep my jacket."

"Wait!" Rebecca called. "What's going to happen to my friends?"

Angel hesitated. With a half-turned head he said, "I'm sorry. There is no easy way to say this. Until I defeat Samuel, the souls of your friends will remain in Hell."

"What?" Rebecca gasped.

Angel placed his hand on his dagger as he began to walk away, towards the border of the illumination and the entryway.

"Wait!" Rebecca called as she reached out for him. Angel's form blurred and he disappeared into the darkness. Rebecca fell to her knees and began to cry. Slowly the light faded from the room, leaving Rebecca alone with her tears in the darkness but for the rays of sunlight that peeked in through the battered ceiling. All around her, Rebecca's world was falling apart. She wasn't sure how to even attempt to pick up the pieces.

***

Angel's form was a blur as he raced across the building rooftops, three, four, even five stories high above the street. The sun was still held high in the sky, but it had already begun its decent into night. Angel, unsure of exactly where he was going, finally stopped. He was breathing heavy and out of breath. His breath turned into vapor with each exhale into the cold air. The cold wind bit into his flesh. He looked back from whence he came. He had traveled farther than he intended. Farther than he thought he could with Quickstep. He looked back and saw the raven haired woman sitting on the building's edge. Her hands rested on the edge of the building and her shoulders were cocked to one side. The wind whipped her hair about. She didn't seem cold at all. The cold hadn't caught up to Angel yet. The woman, Angel's aberration, looked at him over her shoulder with a sly smile.

"Another Virtue," she said teasingly. "Whatever shall you do?"

Angel stared at her, but did not answer.

The woman grinned, showing her teeth. She looked back over the city. "Do you believe her?"

Angel pondered for a moment.

"Well?"

"I'm not sure."

"Such a dilemma Traitor," the woman said as, very graciously and without fear of falling, she stood. "Has your bloodline really flourished?" She turned and walked towards Angel. No mists escaped her lips. "Were all of your hardships really unnecessary?" She stopped and stared into Angel's eyes, a snide smile on her face. "Do you believe this girl?"

Staring into this woman's eyes, Angel found it hard to lie to himself. Still, he tried. "Pestilence killed them all."

The woman laughed. "The abomination could only kill who he could find and he found every named Virtue in the world."

Tears were running down Angel's face. "She wasn't a Virtue," he croaked.

"No, she wasn't."

"He was unnamed."

"Yes, he was."

Angel's face was marred with pain, guilt, and sorrow. He sobbed deep sobs that shook his body. "I never got to see my son."

"No, you didn't." The woman let Angel cry for a long moment. She laid her hand on his shoulder. "You needed that, didn't you?"

Angel forced himself to stop. His eyes were red with tears.

"What are you going to do now, last of the demon hunters?"

"She must be trained. They'll come after her. She must be protected."

The woman nodded. "Good." With an effortless shove, she pushed Angel onto his back. Before Angel could rise, her foot was pressed to his chest. "Do you know who I am Traitor?"

Angel stared up at her and shook his head.

"You let me fall and I have never forgiven you for it. Half of what I am now runs unchecked. With my remaining half, I had gifted you health. I take it away today. Another will need it. Today we strip all our gifts from you. Today, you become mortal."

Angel's eyes widened in realization. "You're...Pestilence."

"Close. I am the Third."

Angel blinked and the woman was gone. On the howling wind he heard her voice. "We leave you now, Angel Virtue. Your time is done."

Angel closed his eyes. His body was warm, even against the cold wind. The aches in his body were subsiding. Faintly, on the roaring winter wind, Angel could hear the hum of a familiar and ancient melody. Its origin was on the tip of his tongue, but escaped him. Just before he caught it, the cold blasted his body and he lost it. A scratching feeling began to form in the back of his throat. He looked at his clothes. They were still torn, but the blood was gone. The wind battered Angel's body and made his bones ache. He needed something to keep warm.

***

Nicole screamed long and never ran out of breath. She felt the scream lasted an hour. Each felt longer than the last. Her third rib clattered into the bowl before her. A bone stand held the bowl at her waist level. Panting and with tears running down her face, she looked down. Her body had no marks, but three of her ribs lay in the bowl between her and Satan. Her tongue was pinched painfully between his fingers and pulled farther out of her mouth than she thought possible. She thought he was going to pull it out completely, but he hadn't. He just kept it pulled taunt, like the bone spikes piercing through her hands and feet kept her body spread eagle against two boney pillars. Twice the pillars had moved and twice the nails had moved, pulling at the joints along her arms and legs. Satan twirled his sharp bone tool between his fingers as he stared into Nicole's pained but angry eyes. "You're a very stubborn girl," Satan said with a grin. "This is much worse than what the Bestial had done to you, isn't it?" Nicole didn't attempt to respond. "I wonder if your friends are as strong as you. They are going through this very same torment as well, but probably with much more narrative."

"I 'on't 'ite' i 'ongue," she said defiantly around her stretched tongue.

Satan smiled. "Not so soon I hope. Though, time is ticking." Satan placed the tip of the bone tool between her heaving breasts and pierced her as easily as piercing a pin cushion. Again, Nicole screamed an endless breath scream. When she stopped, Satan continued. "Let me show you something that even Inquisitor doesn't know." He took up one of her plucked ribs from the bowel and raised it to eye level. He placed his thumb against the tip and snapped it. Nicole screamed in intense pain. "These spiritual bones are still very much connected to your body." Fresh tears ran down Nicole's face and she sobbed slightly as Satan repositioned the rib to snap another small piece off.

Suddenly, barbed chains whipped around and entangled him. It forced Satan's hand to tug on Nicole's tongue and drop her rib back into the bowl. "How dare you?!" a voice boomed. Unable to see past Satan, Nicole stared in painful fear at his smug face. What in Hell would have the audacity to attack Satan himself?

Satan flexed his wings and broke the chains. "War," he said before releasing Nicole's tongue, as if answering her unspoken question. Her head bobbed as her tongue became comfortable in her mouth again. Her head was much heavier than she thought it should be. Satan turned and folded his leathery wings. Nicole lifted her head and saw what had attacked Satan. Its chains were still whipping about its body. It stood bigger than Satan in every way, but was also the smallest of the three. It was a man; at least she thought it was a man, wearing heavy armor of slick black. Not a piece of his flesh was exposed. He looked more like a living suit of armor than a man. He stood at least a foot over Satan and his torso armor was jagged and vicious looking. The paldrons on his shoulders curved into sharp spikes and the length of his vambrace was almost bladelike. The gauntlet had a sharp spike over each joint on his fingers and the tips of his hands were like sharp claws. The bands of the gauntlet looked more like three sharp waves. Even the cowter had two saber like spikes, as did the poleyn that connected the greave with cuisse, making the illusion that his leg armor was one piece, not three. Staring at the savagery that matched the vambrace, perhaps it was one piece. Nicole saw no way to remove any of the pieces since they all seemed to lock together. The poleyn looked almost like a saber-toothed skull with the two divots resembling eye sockets. The sabaton were brutally spiked all around. The helmet was the most terrifying of the suit, even as the entire thing seemed to breathe. It looked bigger than was necessary for a man, even one big enough to wear that suit of armor. Three sharp points curved off the top of his head. The metal tail that came off the back of the helmet was like rows of spiked hair, unmoving. The top of the helmet looked at once separate from the gorget and at once part of it, the two interlocking like a jaw with large dreadful teeth. It was what attacked Satan. That was War.

Staggered behind War were two other creatures. To its left was a creature slightly larger than him and composed of shifting black energy. Long arms supported its body. Its crimson eyes squinted with its gapping crimson maw. To War's right was the third creature was much larger, and much rounder, than the other two. A pair of upward tusks stuck out of its massive maw. Pointed ears framed its head; one of the ears had been torn, as if a bite had been taken out of it. A knotted braid sat atop its pierced head. Staring at these things, Nicole could not help but feel fear.

"I only summoned Pestilence," Satan said.

The biggest one pointed a sausage finger at Satan and spoke in a slurping, engorged voice, "You have no right to summon any of us! Be glad we came at all!" He spoke almost as if he had a mouth full of food. Spittle rained from his maw as he spoke.

"I am well aware of the agreement, but I thought Pestilence may want to know."

War's chains shot at Satan and stopped short, the beaked heads snapping at Satan's unflinching face. "Know what?" War bellowed. The deep eyes of his helmet were naturally red and glowed as he spoke, the mouth of the helmet never moving. "Make it quick Dark Angel!"

"The Virtues yet live."

"They are dead save one!" Pestilence shouted in annoyance. "He is of no concern to us."

Satan stepped aside and motioned to Nicole. "This girl says you are wrong."

Panicked, Nicole looked at Satan and yelped, "What?"

War stomped up the mound, bones cracking and crunching beneath his heavy boots. He bent down and held his face frighteningly close to Nicole. She could see the whole of his helmet was one piece, not several put together. His eyes were not eyes or jewels, but hate and anger. "What do you know?"

"I don't know anything!"

War peered into her eyes. "Liar. You know a name." A pair of beaked chains rose to either side of Nicole's head and opened four ways. "Tell me this name." Nicole grimaced as the open beaks locked onto the sides of her head.

"I won't!" she shouted.

"I am not a patient being," War said as Nicole felt something poke against the sides of her head. "You will tell me now."

Nicole could feel something sharp pushing into her head, digging into her brain. Visions, words, phrases and names flashed in her mind. She shut her eyes tightly, trying to push the mental invader out. Trying to protect the secret they wanted to know. "Tell me," War growled. Opened beaks assaulted her body, clamping down on her legs, arms, and body. The hooks dug painfully into her flesh. Her eyes shot open in pain. Fresh tears rolled down her face as the face of her friend filled her mind.

"The name," War said.

"Rebecca—Virtue," Nicole said against her will.

The painful chains withdrew. Nicole's body lost its will to fight and she whimpered. War turned and walked back towards his allies. The dark form, Pestilence, slammed his hands into the ground. The force of his slam split the ground and erupted magma and fire from below, shooting it up into the air around him. "She lies!" he bellowed. "I killed them all! My plague hounds hunted them all down! I hunted the blood! Not the name, the blood!"

"Obviously," Satan began, "one or two slipped by you."

"No!" Pestilence shrieked. "I created the Black Plague that day! My hounds infected them with condensed strands! They were dead within minutes!"

The large one, Famine, scratched his massive belly in amusement. "Guess you can't hold your boast anymore, huh?" he chuckled.

Pestilence rose up to Famine's eye level. "Shut up!"

Barbed chains ripped between them. "Enough." War rumbled. He turned back to Satan. "This girl has the name of the demon hunters, yes, but how can you be sure she is of the blood?"

"That is simple," Satan said.

Nicole was pouting, but watched the progression before her with interest; especially when Satan motioned back to her.

"I am certain this girl has more vital information I will retrieve. As for proving Rebecca's lineage..." he showed the three Horsemen the golden, emerald jeweled chalice Lucifer had brought. "This is the Chalice of All Souls Blood." Satan dipped a finger into the bloody liquid to the first joint. "It possesses a drop of blood from every human that is alive and has ever lived, even for a moment." Satan pulled out his blood coated finger. He put it to his lips and sucked the blood clean. He pondered for a moment. "Angel had a child. A son."

Pestilence shook with fury. "Give me that!" He reached out his arms the long distance and stole the chalice from Satan's grasp. He then emptied the contents of the chalice into his maw. After a half-moment Pestilence gripped his head and reeled over in pain.

"Only a few drops can be drunk at a time," Satan said as he motioned the chalice to return to him. A black energy ring appeared around it and returned it to him. "You are overwhelmed by the lives otherwise." He shook his head. "It will take a year and a day to refill now."

"That wench!" Pestilence bellowed. "It was her! The babe in her belly; Angel hid it from me! How did he hide it?!" Pestilence struck the ground again. Flames and magma erupted around him. "I won't be made the fool of! I won't! I'll kill them! All of them! Again!" A smile crossed his crimson lips and he chuckled. "Oh yes, such a marvelous disease. Attuned specifically to their DNA. Waterborne. Airborne. Sexually transmitted. Highly contagious." He chuckled evilly. "I won't make the same mistake." He looked at his brethren. "Would you like the stragglers?"

Famine clawed at his belly and hummed in thought. "What say you War?"

War turned his gaze to Satan. "Clever, Dark Angel. You got your desire without issuing a command. Famine and Pestilence will do what they may. I will follow along with great interest." He turned to Famine and Pestilence. "Whatever it is you do, do not interfere with the Collection. Leave the immediate blood for last, after the Collection has started. Death is long overdue." War began to walk away. "I will pick off those that remain." His chains ripped from his body and sliced into the surrounding tormenters and tormented. "It is so easy to die a violent death."

Pestilence looked back to Satan. "This disease will take some time. As War said, I will leave the avatar's region alone—for now. Within forty-eight hours no one that has even touched a Virtue will live. Another babe will not slip by me."

Pestilence and Famine then took their leave. Satan returned his attention to Nicole. She gasped when he picked up one of her ribs. "Where were we?" Satan asked with an evil grin. He pressed his thumb and broke off another small fragment.

***

Rebecca left her bloody shirt and jacket behind. It would be hard enough to explain the trench coat she was now wearing. She wasn't sure what time it was, but the sun was still up. She thought it would be for a few hours more. She might be able to beat Michael to her house. She hoped she could slip in unnoticed through the back door. She didn't want anyone to see her like this. Her shoulder still throbbed with a dull pain, but it wasn't too bad. She thought it would be worse. The blade was big. Touching it made it hurt more. She wanted to look at it. She was worried it would need stitches. How would she explain this?

Rebecca got off the bus and walked the few blocks back to her house. She turned into the alley and made her way to her back gate. She tried to open it only to find it locked. She looked down at the pad lock. *Shoot,* she thought. *I forgot Dad locked it for the winter.* Wincing from the pain in her shoulder, Rebecca climbed the fence. Hidden beneath the light layer of snow, the frozen grass crunched beneath her boots. At the back door she tried to peer into the window, but she couldn't see past the icy glass. It was hard enough to peer into the window in the door considering her height, but she could do it, barely.

Rebecca didn't bother scraping away the ice. It would be too much trouble for too little reward. She just had to hope no one was in the kitchen. She took her key and undid the lock. Slowly, she cracked the door ajar. She peeked inside. No one was around. The clock on the stove said it was just after two. Jeanine wasn't home yet. She wasn't sure where Eric might be. School hadn't gotten out yet, so Michael, hopefully, hadn't been by.

Silently and quickly, Rebecca made her way upstairs to her bedroom. She locked the door behind her. Finally in the safe confines of her room she sighed in relief as she rested her weight against the door. She hadn't been caught. Her lips trembled and she slid to the floor. She tried to control her sobs so Eric wouldn't hear her. Did this nightmare know no end? Demonic Angel. A demon? It was simply beyond human comprehension. Everyone knew about demons, but there was no proof anything like them existed. They stayed safely in the confines of books and movies. At least they did. Rebecca apparently not only saw one, she fought and killed one. That notion alone was almost more than she could handle.

Rebecca sat on the floor with her head against the door for some time, just letting it all sink in. Seven more. Angel said Santano would kill seven more. She shook her head. She couldn't think about it, not yet at least. When Rebecca finally regained her nerves she rose to her feet. Angel's trench coat was heavy on her and applied unwanted pressure to the stab wound, keeping it at a constant throb. She undid the jacket and slipped it off her shoulders, remembering how naked she was underneath it. The red dots on the bandages had gotten a little bigger, a little redder. This was the first time Rebecca had actually looked at the bandages. They were done very well and a sweet scent wafted off them. She tested the motion of her arm. She had full function and motion of it, but the more extreme motions sent her jolts of pain. She needed to see the damage.

Rebecca rummaged through her dresser for new clothes. She was down one shirt and her only coat. Her bra had blood stains on it, so it was ruined. She had to get rid of it. Rebecca found a new bra and settled on a long sleeved shirt. She hoped she wouldn't have to go to the hospital, but deep down she knew she was kidding herself. She was stabbed. She knew she would need stitches.

Clothes in hand, Rebecca peeked around her door and crept to the bathroom in only bandages and a bra. She locked the door behind her and took a moment to dig out the first aid kit. She ran warm water in the sink and wet a washcloth in it. She looked at herself in the mirror. A long, hard look. She was visibly shaken. She noticed her hands were shaking. Was she shaking on the bus? She took a deep breath to calm her nerves. "The worst is over," she said to herself. "This is just clean up." She opened the first aid kit and picked up the scissors. She cut the fabric of the bra and pulled it off. She then cut off the bandages. She dumped both in the trash can. Dry blood masked the stab wound, but it was nowhere near as bad as Rebecca thought it would be. Angel did a very good job of cleaning her up. She used the cloth to wipe the blood away. She was careful not to aggravate the wound too much. She didn't want to experience more pain than she had to.

With the blood gone, Rebecca was finally able to take a look at the stab. She was surprised to see that it wasn't bad at all. It wasn't a deep and nasty cut, or a gash. She was sure that the dagger pierced her deeper than that, but it wasn't deep at all. She trailed her fingers over it, feeling the bumps and split flesh. No, it was bad, but it was healing. It wasn't bad enough to need stitches, but her fingers trailed over the forming scar. It was going to be long and very visible. The ends looked old and healed, while towards the center it looked newer and still bleed. She certainly wasn't going to the hospital now, how would she explain this? Rebecca's self examination had caused the wound to start bleeding fresh from the center and send a jolt of pain through her. Rebecca continued to the wound and noticed a faint sweet smell waif from it. She rubbed her bloody fingers together and realized there was something else, something thick. She sniffed her fingers. The smell was on them too, mixed with the blood. It must have been coming from a salve Angel had used on her. It was in the wound. Maybe, she thought, to fight infection. Or neutralize the poison he was talking about. Rebecca shivered at the thought and pushed it away. She didn't want to know about it. There was too much to explain.

Rebecca leaned over the sink and poured alcohol over the wound to clean it out. She winced as the liquid burned every bit of the open wound. The outside may be closing, but it still ran deep. She didn't need heavy bandages, like Angel had used, at least, she didn't anymore. It had healed too much. Rebecca took a few gauze pads and taped them over the wound. She breathed and took a step back. She needed to see the back before she put a length of bandage around it. She wasn't sure if the blade and gone completely through. Turning, she looked at her back in the mirror. Nothing. It was clean. Rebecca sighed. There was no scaring of a healing wound. It hadn't gone through at all. She guessed she was lucky that it didn't hit bone. Would she even know if it did?

Rebecca shook the thoughts away and finished her first aid by wrapping the pads in a length of bandage. She gathered the remains of her first aid and threw the odds and ends into the trash. She closed and tied the bag, then replaced it. She would take it out to the trash later. She put the first aid kit away and dressed herself. With her first aid done, Rebecca looked at herself in the mirror. She wasn't shaking anymore, not much, but her face looked tired. She still couldn't believe what happened. She just couldn't get her mind around it. She looked at the sink full of bloody water. The washcloth lay crumbled on the side. Rebecca pressed down on the stopper lever and watched the red water drain. She turned on the faucet and washed her face, trying to wash the memories away. It was no use. She knew it wouldn't help, but she did it anyway. She could still see Demonic Angel's stunned and burned face. "Baraqyal," he had moaned. Rebecca wondered what that meant.

Rebecca took the cloth and threw it in the hamper, beneath a few dirty towels. Maybe nobody would notice it. Maybe she'll do laundry this week. She wished she had used a red one instead of the burgundy in hindsight. She just reached blindly, not thinking. It was too late now. Rebecca grabbed the trash bag and as quietly as she had come, headed back to her room.

Rebecca sat atop her bed cross-legged. She had thrown Angel's jacket on the floor and stared at it in silence. She didn't know what to do. She wanted to turn to someone for guidance and comfort, but who? Who would believe her; especially when she wasn't really sure she believed it herself? Would Michael believe her? Is this something she even wanted to tell him? "No," she whispered to herself. "Don't do that to him. He confided his dark secret to you." She thought silently. She would tell him, she decided, when was she ready.

Rebecca nearly jumped out of her skin when her phone rang. She stared at it, almost worriedly. It was Michael, she was sure of it. Who else would be dialing that number? How many times had he already called? She didn't have an answering machine. Jeanine insisted that the phone was enough. Rebecca had no way to check, unless Michael called the house phone too. Rebecca reached for her phone but hesitated. It stopped ringing. Even if she didn't answer, he would come. That thought made her smile and brought her some peace. Michael would come.

Rebecca watched the time tick by. School let out at three o'clock. A few minutes after her phone rang again. She didn't answer. She would wait for Michael to come instead of talking to him over the phone. Instead, she decided to rummage through her new trench coat. She dug through the many pockets and threw what she found on her bed. Holding it in one hand, Rebecca was reminded of how heavy it was. Her mind cataloged what she pulled out and threw on her bed; a few crosses of various sizes, but none too big, a few vials of what she could only assume was holy water, a small pocket bible that had seen better day and several jars and bags full of colored powders and ointments. One of the small pouches held ash. Pieces of a first aid kit were strewn about the various pockets, rolls of bandages, scissors, and tweezers of varying size; even needle and thread and several lighters. She opened one of the jars of colored ointment, one of the pink ones. A familiar sweet scent wafted from it. It was the ointment Angel had used on her. Looking at Angel's belongings Rebecca knew that, if nothing else, he truly believed he was a demon hunter. The pocket bible was brimming with bookmarks and folded pages. The biggest pocket book Rebecca realized was several tied together. She flipped through the many pages. They were all hand written, each book different from the one before it. The pages were yellow with age and waterlogged. It smelled faintly of mold. Rebecca saw that many of the passages had been written over as the ink faded or washed away. It was Angel's diary. The first entry was dated 'March 1408'.

Rebecca gasped in shock. Was this a joke? 1408? This first hand sewn book was supposed to be over six hundred years old? If it was, then it couldn't belong to Angel. Rebecca sat on her bed and read it while she waited for Michael. She had about half an hour before he would knock on the door.

I have decided to write my most important memories down in, what I am sure will be a futile attempt to remember. How long has it been? Two, three hundred years? I have forgotten so much, but that is probably my punishment. I am but a shadow of myself, after all. Angel. That's all I can remember of my name. If not for the demons constantly calling me that, I would have forgotten that too. Probably. How ironic my name. I am far from an angel. How many lives have ended by my hands? How many lives have my hands fail to save? I truly do not know. I would not trust the name the demons call me, but the aberration calls me the same. Strangely, I trust her, though all she does is torment me. Another punishment, I suppose. Justly deserved as well. Alas, the pain she brings seems to keep me going.

Some days have passed now. I think it is still March. I'm not sure. The ship docked today. This should be India. I don't think the avatar has risen yet. I have to wait until night fall before I can leave the ship. I don't want this to become a daily log, but a journal of my thoughts. I have no mentor to teach me. No guardian to guard me. Everything I know, everything I learn is of my own accord. This is so I don't forget what I learn. This is so I don't forget what is important.

My Quickstep has slowed, but with effort I can still reach top speed. This is the first evidence that my power is deteriorating. I feared this. My power isn't forever. Eventually it will fade away. What am I to do? I can't father, raise, and protect a child while combating Hell. No. That child, and possibly his mother, would be dead before his first year. I will have to think of something. For now, I will rest.

Rebecca swallowed hard. What was this? Was Angel delusional? She flipped through the pages.

October 1426

It is All Hallows Eve. The avatar has been slain, as well as his demonic companions. I wasn't able to exorcise any of them, but he was defeated. I stopped him in the middle of his gathering of the Collection. It was close. Pestilence was unhappy. Again, he tried to get me to drink from his chalice of blood. To forsake all that I am, all that remains. Every day I am reminded of her. Some days I remember her name. Most days I don't. Her face, her smile, her laughter. I wish I could remember. The aberration cautions me never to mention her. To leave the past where it is; the past. Nothing good will ever come of it. But I want to remember her. I want to remember her face. Her smile. Her laugh. Her name. Most of all I want to remember her love. Love. It's been so long since I've felt its warm touch. I fear I've forgotten what it feels like. All I feel now is cold, empty, and alone.

Rebecca closed the book. "He feels abandoned," she whispered. "What happened in his life to make him feel so alone?" The door bell rang. "Michael!" Rebecca threw the bound booklets onto the bed as she leaped from it and bolted down the stairs. She ran to the door and threw it open. Michael stood with Rebecca's backpack slung over his shoulder. "Hey ditcher," he smiled. She smiled back. Seeing him, after all she had gone through, made her want to cry. She threw her arms around him in a hug and let her tears flow, now that he couldn't see. Her embrace threw Michael off balance and he was forced to grip the doorframe to keep from falling.

"Did you miss me that much?" Michael teased as he found his balance. Rebecca didn't answer. She just hugged him tighter. Michael let her bag hit the ground and returned her embrace. He knew something was wrong. "Hey, Becca, did something happen? You're kind of shaking."

"Rebecca?" Eric said as he came down the stair lift. "How long have you been home?"

Rebecca wiped her tears away before turning to face her father. "Um, an hour or two. I left school early. Sorry, I just—"

"How early?" Eric interrupted.

"Um—" Rebecca thought two o'clock. "Lunch?"

Eric's face did not show amusement. "Really? Are you sure?"

"Um, I—"

"Because I got a call around nine this morning that you never showed up at school. All day I checked your room. You were never there."

Rebecca rubbed her arm like a sheepish child. She ignored the throb in her shoulder from hugging Michael.

"Michael," Eric said, "you can come in and warm up. Rebecca, please come into the kitchen."

Neither one said a word; they just did as they were instructed. Michael closed the door behind him as he laid Rebecca's backpack off to the side. He sat on the couch as Rebecca followed her father into the kitchen. He asked her to sit down. She did.

"I thought you were with Michael," Eric said, "but I see that you weren't. Why didn't you come home Rebecca?"

"I just wanted some time to think," Rebecca replied.

"And you couldn't do that here? Where did you go?"

"Where I usually go to think."

"Not this time. I want to know where that place is."

Rebecca didn't answer. No one knew about that place. Her parents would never let her go if they knew.

"Rebecca, there is a murderer out there. You could have been killed."

Rebecca opened her mouth to say something, but stopped herself. She almost was.

Eric waited and sighed. "When did you take up lying to me? Don't I give you enough trust, enough freedom?"

"It's nothing like that, Dad."

"Then what? Rebecca, if something happened to you, it would have been hours before we knew you were in trouble."

"The primary target," Demonic Angel's voice echoed in Rebecca's mind. She flushed. She was in trouble.

"I know you're eighteen and technically an adult," Eric continued, "but you're still my child. And still under my roof."

Rebecca looked at Eric. She wondered if he was going to try and ground her.

"I won't tell your mother about this, but in exchange Michael goes home. I don't want to see him here until next weekend. You go to school and come home. Nothing else. At least while this guy is running around. Is that a deal?"

"Yes," Rebecca replied.

"Good. I'm sorry, but I'm taking the phone out of your room too."

Rebecca said nothing. She just looked at the ground.

Eric sighed. "Are you going to school tomorrow?"

She nodded.

"Are you going to stay?"

She nodded again. She felt like she was five again. Her father hardly ever yelled at her. She was much more likely to bump heads with Jeanine than Eric.

"Alright. Your mother will drop you off tomorrow."

"She's not going to work tomorrow?"

"No, she took the day off. I have to see a specialist tomorrow."

"Is something wrong?"

"My legs have been tingling."

"You're getting feeling back in them?"

"I don't know; maybe. The doctor wants to run some tests." Eric smiled and shrugged. "Who knows, maybe I'll be walking again in a few years."

Rebecca smiled. "That would be nice."

"Wouldn't it? Now, I'm not sure when we'll be back, so I don't want to catch Michael here, got it?"

"Got it."

"No Houdini's either."

Rebecca nodded, but frowned. When would she be able to talk to Michael now?

"Okay," Eric said when Rebecca didn't respond. "I'll send Michael home. Put your phone in my room please."

"I'll tell Michael," Rebecca said.

Eric didn't respond.

"Please?"

He sighed. "Alright. Don't take too long."

"We won't."

They left the kitchen. Michael stood up when they entered the living room. Eric hung back while Rebecca approached Michael. He could tell by the look on her face that things didn't go well with Eric.

"In trouble, huh?" Michael asked softly.

"Yeah," Rebecca answered.

"I guess I have to go?"

She nodded.

"Don't worry. I'll call you when I get home." They walked to the door.

"He's taking my phone for awhile."

"Wow. He must really be pissed. Sorry."

"It's alright. He is. I wanted to talk to you, but—"

"Bus."

Rebecca shook her head. "My mom's driving me tomorrow. I'll see you at school."

"Make it early. I'm cutting out early to get my car. They finished early."

"Before class then. Wait for me?"

"You know it."

Eric cleared his throat.

"I guess I should go," Michael said. "I'll see you tomorrow." He kissed her good-bye. "One more thing, before I go. Jason told me Santano has a warrant for his arrest. Be careful."

Rebecca tried to hide her shock and nodded. Angel was telling the truth. "Bye, Michael. See you tomorrow," Rebecca said as he left through the door. She closed the door and set out to remove her phone.

CHAPTER IX

Rebecca's sleep was dreamless that night. She was glad. No more nightmares. The waking world had become nightmare enough. Rebecca was quiet all morning. It was becoming too much to handle. Santano was a killer and a devil worshipper. Angel was some kind of demon hunter. Magic swords and dangerous demons. Her jacket was gone and Jeanine and Eric questioned where she had gotten the trench coat. Rebecca lied and said she had borrowed it from Peter once. That she had found it in her closet the night before. She had forgotten about it. They seemed satisfied enough with the story.

Rebecca stared out the window of the car at the cold world as it passed by. She was quiet. Very quiet.

"Are you alright hon?" Jeanine asked as she drove.

"Yes," Rebecca answered as she watched Úna dance in the frosted window. "I just have a lot on my mind."

"Well, we won't be home until later on tonight. I'll leave something to eat in the fridge for you."

"Okay. Thank you." Úna was dancing towards her, laughing. Rebecca was able to hear it, like a far away laughter.

"His appointment isn't until three, but it's in Indiana. Are you sure you're okay?"

"Yes. Just tired."

Jeanine said no more. She knew something was wrong, but didn't know what. Úna put her hands on the window and drew her face close. She breathed out, fogging the window. She giggled as she zigzagged her finger through the frost. "Make sure you say your good-byes," Úna said in her Irish accent. "They'll all die soon. Tomorrow. It will all end tomorrow. Are you ready?"

Rebecca took her gloved hand and struck it through the misty frost, making Úna finally go away.

Rebecca said good-bye to Jeanine. Her mind was distracted. Everything that was happening was just too hard to comprehend. She saw Michael waiting for her in the cold at the school's entrance. She smiled. He was leaving early and so were her parents. She didn't want to go to school, but it was the only chance she had to talk to Michael.

"You made it," Michael said as he took Rebecca's gloved hand.

"I said I would," she replied as they entered the building together. She was silent for a moment. "Is it true?" she asked.

"Is what true?"

"About Santano? Do they really think he's the killer?"

"I just know what Jason's told me. So far, no one but us knows Santano even has a warrant for his arrest. I'm not sure if it's made the news yet."

"What about Angel?"

Michael shrugged. "Dunno. Haven't heard anything about him. They probably don't know where he is."

"I—" Rebecca caught herself.

Demonic Angel's voice screamed in her mind. "You Virtues are dead!"

Rebecca shook her head, trying to quiet the demon's wail.

"Hey Becca?" Michael asked. "Are you okay?"

"No," she said flatly.

"You want to talk about it?"

"Yes." She looked up at him. "But not here."

The first bell rang. "Where?" Michael asked.

"Come get me before you leave. I don't want to stay here."

Michael nodded. "Alright, but to where?"

Angel. Rebecca wanted to talk to Angel. She had so many questions to ask him. "Come to my house, after you pick up your car."

"What about your dad? I kinda got thrown out yesterday."

"The house will be empty. He has to see a specialist in Indiana. He'll be gone for awhile."

"Alright. I'll meet you at your locker before third period."

She kissed his lips and parted ways. Michael watched her go and disappear into a class room. He was worried about her. He hoped he could help her with whatever was wrong.

***

Santano sat patiently in his basement. He watched as the upper most candle's flame extinguished. He watched as the candle melted and the wax pooled on the floor. The other four point candles remained lit, as well as the center, but the flames flickered violently. Santano wondered what had happened. He waited for Satan to return and give him leave to continue. "Rules," Santano mumbled. "What rules?" Suddenly, the center of the pentagram was consumed by a ring of flames that grew into a fire plumb. The eyes of the fallen angel opened. Satan's Presence returned and called out,

"Santano!"

Santano rose to his feet and held the Blood Sword at his side. "I'm here," he answered.

"Have you chosen your fourth sacrifice yet?"

"No. You told me to wait. I saw the candle that you used to summon Demonic Angel go out. What happened?"

"Demonic Angel was defeated. That gate was in turn closed."

"I guess he wasn't as tough as he thought."

"It wasn't Angel that defeated him. It was another."

"Another demon hunter? I'm going to have two after me now?"

"No, there can be only one at a time. You will not have two demon hunters to contend with. I am currently assessing the situation, but Angel may have discovered a trump card. We will have more opposition than I originally anticipated."

"Then let me just sacrifice the last seven and be done with it."

"It is not so simple. As I said, there are rules—"

"Screw the rules! Angel can't beat me! Every time he tries he barely gets out with his life! Let him come!"

"With a host of angels to fight alongside him?"

"A host of angels?"

"Angel may be forsaken, but his position is not. We can fudge the rules a little, but we cannot break them. You may kill ten today, or twenty, or thirty. It does not matter. The Blood Weapons will only drink in one soul a day. If it drank more, you would deal with an angel sent from Heaven. That angel would stay; perhaps even help Angel, until you were defeated. You can force your sword to drink more, but don't. Grave penalties will be applied."

Santano kicked the ground. "I wish I knew how this shit worked."

"Just do as you are told and everything will go smoothly. One sacrifice today, then get back here. Something very dire is going to happen soon. You do not want to be caught in the crossfire."

Santano huffed and thought. "What's today? Friday?" He looked at his watch. "About eight, huh? Let me think. Who's at home right now?" Santano thought. Names and faces began to appear in his mind. Potential victims. He was astonished at their vividness, how fast they raced through his mind. He was trying to pick at a few clear names, not a mosaic of people. The images of names raced in his mind, boggled, tangled. It was difficult at first to discern them. The knowledge was becoming easier and easier to come by, but remained difficult to control. He had to concentrate. The names and faces slowed, many removed. Santano started rambling, mumbling. He was listing his particular dislike for each person he saw. "Fat kid. Stupid kid. Slut. Asshole. Kiss ass. Whiner. Makes excuses. A nobody." Then he stopped. A face cleared in his head. "Nice guy. Stayed with Nicole, didn't he?" Santano drew the Blood Sword from its sheath. "Show me Peter Skolic." The blade of the Blood Sword ignited in flames. Santano pointed the blade downward and released the handle. The hilt was in turn consumed by the flame, which then opened into a large ring. The surface within the ring was mirror like and on its surface Santano observed Peter in his home. He was dressed and his hair was wet and combed. He was heading to the kitchen. Santano touched the surface. His eyes rolled back as his lids closed. After a short moment he pulled his hand back and his eyes flung open. "You intend to stay home today?" Santano asked the image. "Good." The flaming mirror closed and Santano took hold of the sword's handle. The flames died from base to tip as soon as Santano touched the sword.

"I guess I should get going before Angel meets me there," Santano said.

"I will occupy Angel for a time, but I cannot guarantee how long," Satan said.

"What about the one threat a day thing?"

"I am not approaching him as a threat. I merely want to talk."

"Alright. You know the rules better than I do. Just keep him off my back if you can."

"Leave under stealth. Your house is being watched."

The large flame died, leaving only the center candle burning. Santano looked at the pentagram for a moment. With a hand on the sword's hilt, a green mist began to waif from the enclosed blade, engulfing Santano into its magic.

***

Angel had returned to the warehouse late that night. Enough time for Rebecca to leave. For the first time in a long time, he had cried himself to sleep. His sleep, however, was restless. He shivered all night from the cold in the room. From time to time he would cough. They weren't deep hacking coughs, but they left a painful scratch in the back of his throat. He stayed in a half waking state. The Sword of Might began to hum in warning, rousing Angel from his fitful slumber in the early morning. He groaned as he picked the sword up and cracked it from its sheath. "Show me," his said.

Angel's mind's eye opened and he saw Peter. He was eating a bowl of cereal and walking out of the kitchen. His location came to Angel's mind and his mind's eye closed. He enclosed the sword back into its sheath and picked up the Dagger of Power. He turned to leave when fire sprang up from the ground in front of him. Angel jumped back and instinctively gripped the handles of the Heavenly Weapons. The fire died, leaving in its place the Lord of Gehenna, Satan himself. Angel gasped and drew his blades.

Satan?! Angel thought in worry. *What is he doing here?*

Satan smiled. "Angel, do you really intend to raise your weapons against me; the greatest of all?"

"Only in your eyes," Angel replied. He was worried, but not visibly shaken. "Having fallen the furthest you are the worst of all."

"If I had a heart, your words would hurt."

"Allow me to cut you open to place one."

Satan bellowed in laughter. "I will do without. Sheath your blades Angel, you only drain them. Besides, I come on peaceful terms. I mean you no harm."

"Why should I trust the Master of Lies?"

"You confuse me with another, but don't all lies come from some truth?"

"Lies are spouted to cover the truth."

"Ah," Satan said with glee. "And there lies the devil in the details. All lies are spoken to cover some truth, so it is the truth that a lie stems from. Come now, Angel. Put your weapons away."

"And give you on open shot? I think not."

"That is rather humorous. Do you think you actually have the power to take me on? Seriously? Angel, your power is almost depleted. You are the last of your kin. A valiant effort you have given, surely, but why continue? This is a lost cause."

"Miracles can happen."

Satan rubbed his chin and nodded in thought. "This is true, but not for you. God only gave you one miracle. One. He gave you the power of the demon hunter, a title you were unworthy to obtain."

"That may be so, but—"

"But what, Angel? Open your eyes boy! God granted you one miracle, but what has He done for you since?"

Angel was silent. In truth, he had nothing to say.

"Was He there when your entire family was slaughtered? A family that had dedicated their entire lives, their entire being, to Him? Was He there for you when Leviathan stranded you in the ocean? Was He there for you during your battles with your sins, Demonic Angel? Hm? What about during all the wars you fought in? What about when Ifreet nearly killed you?

Tell me, Angel, of one instance in which help was there for you. To carry you. Not even your guardian was there to give you a shoulder to lean on."

Slowly, Angel lowered his weapons as Satan spoke. He didn't want to admit it. He wanted to lie to himself, but Satan was speaking the truth.

"Angel, my boy, don't delude yourself. He was never there for you. He left you to your fate." Satan began to walk a calm, nonthreatening circle around Angel. "Now I, on the other hand, have been far kinder to you. I have adhered to the rules strictly, not bending them when I could, or as far as I could. I have called back my forces and even tipped the scales in your favor from time to time. And you, my cleaver little Angel, have always deciphered the cryptic advice and hints I sent your way. I have helped you far more than the so-called all loving God." Satan spat on the ground. "So you worshipped me. So what? Your heart wasn't in it. When you spoke I could barely hear you, even if I strained. You have sacrificed so much to atone for that, and still He turns a blind eye to you."

Each word felt like it cut Angel. Each cut brought to question his role. Did his life even matter in the grand scheme of things?

"Do you know what the truth is, Angel?"

Angel did not respond. He was too busy trying to stand strong against the cutting words. He just watched as Satan circled him.

"The truth is your God no longer cares about what happens to this world. It was His oyster once, yes, but now? It is ugly and filthy and full of rot and decay. It really is an eye sore. So He is drawing His forces back one by one; day by day. And the more He does this, the greater my grip on this decaying mud ball. You are fighting a losing battle Angel." Satan stood still before Angel. "You are fighting on the losing side. As always, I can give you an out." Satan twirled his hand, trailing black smoke behind it that formed into a golden ruby laden chalice.

"The Chalice of the Fallen Ones," Angel said.

"Yes Angel. I know it's been some time since you last saw it, but we can't offer it to you every day."

"Why do you still insist that I drink from it?"

"You'll die if you don't. I am trying to save you." Satan extended the chalice. "Only Hell awaits you my friend. I don't want you to spend eternity in torment. A few drops, remember?"

"I remember," Angel whispered. His sword barely touched the floor. His mind flashed back nearly two hundred years ago. He had just woken up.

"Thought I lost you there," the young man with dark hair said.

"What happened?" Angel had asked.

The young man, in his early twenties maybe, helped Angel to his feet. "I'm surprised that's all Satan sent after us."

Angel saw a gem or stone about his neck. It was glowing a bright white. "What are you talking about?"

"You must have hit your head or something when we jumped out of Hell."

Angel was dumbfounded. "I was...in Hell?"

The man wondered the area, looking for something. "You don't remember? Well, you were pretty beat up. That thing, whatever it was; looked like you—"

"My demonic..."

"Yeah. He was about to drag your ass back when I showed up." He found what he was searching for and picked it up.

"I go...to Hell?"

The man attached the glowing fragment he found to his necklace and frowned. "What century is this?"

"Eighteenth." Angel sighed. "There is no salvation for me, is there?"

"Sorry man, I made a mistake. You're the wrong guy, but I did save you." He walked up to Angel and placed a comforting hand on his shoulder. The glow of his gemmed necklace was gone. It was smooth for the most part, with what looked like pieces missing. "Forget about what I said," the man continued. "I made a mistake. Thought you were someone else. Don't worry, things will work out." He turned and began to walk away.

"When...will I go?" Angel asked.

"Like I said," the man said as he waved Angel off, "you're the wrong guy. Sorry about that. Things will work out. Well, see you around Angel. Stay strong."

Angel was going to call out to him, but the Sword of Might sent him a warning that drew his attention. When he looked back the man was gone.

"Well?" Satan said as he offered the chalice, pulling Angel back to the present. "Do this and you can lead my armies to the one that has forsaken you. Angel, you have been so alone and so lost these past nine centuries, but you no longer have to be. Join me Angel. The power I offer you is greater than that of any demon hunter. You know what I say is true."

"You're right," Angel said in almost a whisper. "It is all true. I have been offered no miracles. I have spent far too much time wandering lost and alone. If not for my first battle being against Pestilence, the angels were not going to come."

"That's right Angel. You gain no boon as a demon hunter. You have fought a brave and valiant battle and I applaud you, but it was a battle you had no hope of winning. You always knew that."

"You're right. I always knew. I was content to fight endlessly for eternity, but I grew so tired."

"Now it can all end." Satan extended the cup. "Drink and you can rest."

Angel stared at the chalice and steeled his nerve. He glared at Satan. "But there is something you have to know too." Angel again raised his sword. "Hope is the last thing to die."

Satan frowned. "And what, exactly, is it that you hope?"

"I can still do right. His angels are not withdrawing. The Four Angels would be the first and they are still here. I have seen them!"

"I am willing to offer you forgiveness Angel, something your God has denied you time and time again. You are a blasphemous traitor Angel, to both of us. Think this over. In the end you will be mine. You belong to me. You will go to Gehenna."

"You are not the first to tell me this, but I still have a chance and you know it! It doesn't matter how forsaken I am. I can still do good in this world. I will not fall for your silver tongue."

Satan grinned. "My Silver Tongue? Funny you should mention it." He looked at the blood filled chalice. "Is this your final decision Angel?"

Angel nodded and gripped his sword tightly.

"I see." Slowly, Satan tipped the chalice over and let the blood spill from it. It poured onto the floor, sizzled, crackled, and popped. "I hold no delusions. This chalice is no longer necessary." He crushed the empty chalice between his hands. It fell to the floor with a loud clang and then proceeded to melt into a golden red swirl of a puddle that bubbled and evaporated. "You know what I never understood about humans, especially recently? Their desire to make my weapon a pitchfork. Not even a trident, a pitchfork, a farmer's tool." Satan chuckled. "Of all the things they could have chosen for me; a whip, a chain, a dagger, anything at all. But a pitchfork?" He sighed, but still he grinned. "So, do you really want to spar with me?"

Angel strengthened his stance.

"I see." Satan rubbed his chin thoughtfully, searching for Santano's whereabouts. He hadn't arrived at Peter's yet. He still needed more time. As long as he didn't use too much power, as long as Angel allowed his time to be wasted, Satan could draw it out. "You know," Satan said, "all angels and devils have a specialized weapon; an embodiment of themselves. Though they may sport different names and designs, many are the same. Flametongue. Sunblade. Flameblade. All the same sword. Mine, however, is rather unique. I do not wield it in its true form often and only one other copy exists. The number of eyes that have lain upon it I can count on one hand." He began to count them off. "God. Michael. Hades. Only these three have seen my true blade. Would you like to be the fourth?"

Angel readied himself. Fear swirled in his stomach. He was unaware that Satan even had a weapon.

Satan opened his mouth and stuck out his tongue. He gripped the red flesh with thumb and forefinger and then he pulled away. A long, thin piece of metal trailed between his fingers and tongue. As his arm came to be nearly fully extended, he flicked his wrist. The metal pulled and snapped from his tongue and molded into a form. A half-hand guard covered Satan's hand; the guard and handle were golden. A white angel's wing stemmed across the unguarded part of his hand. The blade was long, slender, and silver. Satan smiled. "This is the Silver Tongue." Satan took a loose stance and danced the blade around before him in show. "Come. Let us dance."

Angel lunged forward and slashed with the Sword of Might. Satan thrust the Silver Tongue and caught the blade in mid swing, deflecting it. Angel slashed again, bringing the sword down at a different angle. Again, Satan thrust and deflected Angel's blow. No matter the angle or speed of his swings, Angel's blows were always deflected.

"You disappoint me son," Aurick's voice said from Satan's lips. Satan's form shifted into that of Aurick.

"Father—" Angel muttered in surprise.

"Have you forgotten everything I taught you?"

Aurick thrust repeatedly with the Silver Tongue. Angel tried to defend but his defense was all too easy to break. His arm was cut. "A rapier is designed to counter the slash of a heavy weapon," Aurick said. "You never did listen." Aurick thrust again, breaking Angel's defense easily, sliding up the hefty blade of the Sword of Might. Again and again Angel was cut.

Angel backed away. Blood seeped from several cuts on his body. "I may not have been a good son, but I did listen," Angel said under heavy breaths. "Especially when it counted."

"When it counted?" Aurick thrust his sword. Angel deflected with sword and dagger. "If you had listened when it counted, maybe none of us would have died." Try as Angel might to defend against the piercing attacks of the Silver Tongue, it still managed to find openings and slice him. They were not deep but they stung. They stung almost as much as the words, as what his eyes were seeing. "You should have been by my side Angel," Aurick continued. "Maybe we could have defeated John together. We could have stopped him!"

"No!" Angel shouted as he swung with a horizontal blow. Aurick raised the Silver Tongue and let the Sword of Might scrape across it and push him back. "I did the best I could!" Angel cried as he took another swing.

Aurick thrust and deflected. "It wasn't good enough!" Aurick returned. Angel thrust with the Dagger of Power, but Aurick caught his arm by the wrist. A second thrust and Angel's shoulder was pierced. "You're the reason they're all dead."

Tears flowed from Angel's eyes. "I know."

"Why Angel?" Amanda's voice spoke. Angel watched in horror as Aurick's form became that of his lost love. "Why did you leave me?"

"Amanda!" Angel cried as he pulled himself off the silvered blade. He winced in pain as he came off. He was feeling light headed.

"You left me Angel. I thought you loved me."

"I did." Angel wiped his tears. "I still do."

The Silver Tongue was in motion again. Angel backed away as he deflected it, but every few thrusts it scored. "You never came to see me Angel. Not once. You abandoned us Angel."

"I didn't mean to!" Angel shouted. The swords locked and Angel found himself staring into Amanda's emotionless face.

"You never even came to see your son," she said.

"My son. What was…his name?"

Amanda's brow creased. Rebecca's voice said, "You don't deserve to know his name." Amanda's form shifted into Rebecca. She pushed Angel away and continued the barrage of thrusts. "And you have no right to drag me into this!" Rebecca shouted.

"Wait!" Angel shouted. More and more thrusts got through. Small cuts laced his body. Blood stained his clothes.

"What makes you think I even trust you? You tried to kill me!"

"No! That was—my demonic!" The barrage stopped and Angel found he had no strength to stand. He fell to his knees and stared up at Rebecca's friendless face. "You killed him. Remember?"

"What makes you think I even want to be like you? I don't."

Angel's lips quivered. Tears rolled down his face and the Heavenly Weapons clattered on the floor. "Then…it's over," Angel whispered. "There's no hope left." He lowered his head. "There's no reason to go on."

"No, there isn't."

Rebecca thrust the Silver Tongue one last time, aimed at Angel's heart. The blade stopped just short. A massive, gnarled hand held Rebecca's strike. "Enough," a deep voice stated. Smoke grew behind Rebecca and thick black chains came from the smoke and ensnared her. Angel stared on in awe.

"Carried away I see," Rebecca said with a grin. Then her body became that of Satan. "So you came to fetch me?" Satan asked.

The chains tightened around him. "You attacked the demon hunter," the entity within the smoke said. "Should I have waited? Should another angel have come? Michael perhaps?"

"We were just having a friendly sparing match."

A tendril seeped from the smoke and encircled the Silver Tongue. "So, this is your blade's true form. Exquisite. Powerful. You bent the rules very far today."

The smoke began to envelop the fallen angel. With a little struggle, Satan returned the sword to his mouth and stuck out his tongue. He pushed the metal into the flesh, returning it to its hidden sheath. "It seems I must be going Angel. It's a pity you are such a foolish mortal. I will have something special waiting for you when you arrive. Remember Angel, you belong to me."

The shadow and smoke consumed Satan until he was gone. Only the smoke with the dark shadowy figure within remained. Angel looked up at it, his face red with tears.

"Who are you?" Angel asked. "I can't see you."

"None shall see me," the entity said. "I am the Angel of the Abyss, Hell's Gate Keeper; replacement to Uriel, leader of the punishing angels."

Angel struggled to stand. "And what do you call yourself?"

The smoke moved forward. "Abaddon." It stood before Angel. "You are too hurt to fight. Too tired. Too old."

"I will be fine."

Serpentine heads stretched from the smoke. Their flesh was gray, their tongues ruby and thick; their eyes yellow and green. They licked the blood from Angel's body and the open wounds. It burned and Angel winced, but he did not fight.

"What are you doing?" Angel asked.

"Mending you. I have now seen the Silver Tongue's true form, felt its power. It will not slip by again."

"Why are you helping me? I'm a damned man."

"That is the Silver Tongue talking. I will remove its influence as well." The heads bit down. "That sword is very dangerous. It is why only two were ever forged. Only two angels had the strength to make such a weapon."

"I turned my back to God."

"And atoned for nine centuries. I am a neutral angel. I care not for your vices or virtues. I did not fight in the War in Heaven. I watched. The outcome is of no concern to me."

"Then why help?"

"I have no desire to see Samael's victory, but I will not be involved." The heads released Angel and retreated back into the smoke. Angel checked himself. He felt much better, his mind clearer. "Now go, demon hunter. Samael only sought to waste your time." The smoke descended into the cracks in the ground and left the human world.

Angel picked up the Heavenly Weapons and sheathed them. He could not stand around and absorb what had happened. Satan wanted to buy Santano some time and he succeeded. Angel dashed out of the room and out of the building. He had to hurry. There was much distance to cover and little time to cover it in. Even with his strength renewed by Abaddon, Angel was fearful that Satan managed to occupy his time just long enough. He could not allow a fourth sacrifice. He had to save Peter.

***

The snow fell lightly. Santano's breath fogged in the air. His coat hung open and flapped in the wind. It was cold, but not too cold. Just enough to snow. They were still warning blizzard, but it had not come. Santano could barely feel the wind and found himself wondering why he brought his jacket. He was standing in front of Peter's front door. He was able to feel something tugging at him only a moment ago, but it was gone now. Santano was sure something big was happening, but he wasn't sure what. He looked around. No one was on the street. No eyes looked his way. The day had already started. Nobody would find Peter for hours, as long as Angel didn't show up and make a commotion. His face stripped of flesh. Only strands of hair remained on his head and the meat and sinew of his face was becoming dry. Santano's body shimmered as his cloaking ability deactivated. He raised the Blood Sword and with one mighty blow the door was gone.

Standing at the kitchen sink washing the dishes he had used, Peter heard the crash from the living room. With no pets immediately he thought intruder. Peter turned the running water off and took a hand cloth from over the sink to dry his hands. He pulled a knife from the knife block on the counter and cautiously approached the living room. Peter thought of calling out 'Whose there?' but thought better of it. What if this person had a gun? What if there was more than one? Peter was a big guy, but several burglars, probably big guys themselves, could very likely overpower him. He pulled his cell phone from his pocket; a Star Wars-esque black item with a button touch face and yellow screen. The battery was dangerously low, but enough to make a call to the police.

Peter peeked around the threshold into the living room. Standing before the threshold of the front door, facing towards the outside, was the fleshless faced Santano. Peter's stomach dropped in disgust at Santano's face, believing it to be a gaudy mask. Then Santano raised his crimson sword. He hadn't noticed Peter. In one motion he slashed across the doorframe. From the splintered cuts a thick red fluid seeped. It spread across the frame, covering it and creating a fluid mass of redness for a door.

Peter stared in shock and awe. Such a display of unnatural power; he had never seen anything like it. His hands and knees were shaking. He was scared. Who was this? The knife fell from his grip and clanged on the floor. The sound turned Santano's head towards Peter. He stared at the frightened boy. His lip muscles contoured into a grin. He began to move forward, sword fully exposed to Peter's vision. He had nothing to hide. Peter glanced at the knife at his feet and then at the massive blade in Santano's hand. "Shit no," Peter said. He turned and headed for the back door. Santano's form blurred and he vanished. Quickstep. He covered the distance to the back door in a split second. His form blurred into existence between Peter and the door and solidified. He was still learning. It was still an adrenaline rush that he had trouble controlling. He hadn't learned how to turn in mid-use and still faced forward, towards the door and away from Peter. He was closer to the door than he intended.

Santano turned and swung, but Peter was well out of reach. Peter nearly fell as he forced his momentum to a halt. "Holy shit!" he shouted and turned to flee. Santano's head spun. He wasn't used to it yet. Such a quick motion after coming out of it. At least now Peter had no way out.

Peter was unsure of what Santano had done to the front door and didn't want to risk finding out. He ran up the stairs to the second floor. Santano followed behind in a slow walk that became quicker as the room slowed its spinning. He could have closed the distance quickly and run Peter through, but he was confident the fourth sacrifice could not escape him. Peter was only delaying the inevitable.

At the top of the stairs Peter stopped as he passed a decorative shelf full of glass knick-knacks. Eyeing it in his panic he did not see years of collections. He did not see the glass angels his mother and him had picked out over the years. He did not see the plates with his father's favorite personalities adorned on them. He did not see the statues that were gifted to his family. His bronze booties. His first Christmas. His first trophy. He saw none of these. He only saw a heavy and deadly weapon to use against the advancing intruder that was intent on killing him.

Santano began his slow climb as Peter moved behind the shelf and tipped it over. His feet danced as everything inside tumbled to the ground and shattered into thousands of pieces. Santano stopped and looked up the stairs. "What was that?" he mumbled. The shelf appeared inch by inch over the landing. Santano's face flooded with shock. "You've got to be kidding me."

The shelf went over and tumbled down the steps. Santano raised the Blood Sword and thrust as he called out, "Corrosion!" The blade pierced the shelf and offered no resistance to Santano. In that instant it turned to ash and flew harmlessly around him. Peter watched in horror as the meat and bone faced Santano dusted the ash from his body. Peter's senses returned quickly. Whatever was chasing him was not human. Peter ran towards his room before Santano continued his advance. Peter slammed the door behind him. He pulled his heavy dresser in front of the door. His desk he tipped over and braced the door with it as well. He tore the mattress from his bed and flung it over his barricade. He pulled free his box spring and threw it onto the pile as well. A metal bat had lay hidden beneath. Peter took it into his hands and realized he still had his cell phone. "Fuck!" he cursed as he began to dial nine-one-one. "So stupid! I almost deserve to be killed!" He put the phone to his ear and it made half a ring. "What?!" Peter shouted as he peered down at his phone. The battery had died. "Fuck you! I wasn't serious!" The crimson blade pierced through the door and Peter's barricade. Peter threw his phone aside and prepared to defend himself.

Angel could feel Santano closing in for the kill. He gripped the Dagger of Power. It should be charged enough. He didn't want to, but he resorted to using Quickstep. His blurred form darted forward from place to place. The minutes long journey now took only seconds. Angel was breathing heavy by the time he arrived. He had caught his second wind. He was surprised he had only just obtained his second wind, but he didn't have the time to think about it.

Angel could see the red barrier at Peter's door. He coughed as he tried to focus his sight. It was slightly blurred. His keen eyes seemed to be no longer so keen. Angel knew the barrier. It wasn't the first time he encountered it. It would shock any that touched it. Its purpose was not to kill, but to keep whoever was on one side of it on that side. It looked like it confined itself to the front door. It seemed Santano yet had to attain the strength to expand it, or yet to learn that he could. In the past Angel could make short work of it, but with his quickly waning powers, he wasn't sure if he still had the strength to shatter it. He had to find another way inside.

Angel surveyed the house and noted a white fence entwined with dead vines scaling the side of the house, just off side the windows. It would be the quickest way inside. Angel just hoped he wasn't too late.

The crimson blade pierced the barricaded door several times. Peter gripped his bat, ready to swing for a home run. His breathing was frightful and nervous. Sweat was forming on his brow. The blade began to hum and faintly glow. Peter looked about in confusion as a breeze entered the room. He looked to the window. It was closed. He realized it wasn't a breeze. The sword was gathering some kind of energy. Air was pulled towards it in a powerful vortex of force. Peter looked at the window again. He could escape through there, maybe. Bat in hand, he ran to the window and pulled it open. As soon as he did, a hand gripped its side and Angel pulled himself up. Peter backed away and shouted, "Can't just one of you try to kill me?" He swung the bat at Angel's head with all his might. Angel quickly pulled the Dagger of Power from its scabbard and caught the bat. "Wait!" he shouted back. "I'm here to help you."

Peter heard Santano mumble something from the other side of the door, and then everything was blown out. Angel threw Peter onto the floor and shielded him with his own body. Santano came boldly through the threshold. "Angel!" he exclaimed. "I wasn't expecting to see you here."

Peter's eyes flew open. *Wait, I recognize that voice!* Peter thought.

Angel rose to his feet and pulled the Sword of Might from his back. "Whenever you are ready to kill," he said, "expect me to be there to stop you."

Santano's fleshless lips smiled. "Try all you like Angel," Santano said. Peter stared up at him in shock and awe from the ground. "I'm too strong for you now. You have to realize that."

Angel readied his stance and prepared to strike.

"Alright, but before we dance, let me do what I came here to do."

"Santano?" Peter whispered. "No way."

Santano charged and swung a single mighty blow. Angel realized almost too late that it was not a normal blow. He traded a strike with Santano and was pushed back, but he planted his feet firmly on the ground and stopped short of the window. It wasn't as strong as Angel feared, but it was strong enough. Santano swung again and blasted the sword from Angel's hand. The Sword of Might clanked across the floor. Peter had already moved away from the pair, bat still in hand. Angel brought the Dagger of Power forward as Santano pulled back for his next strike and shouted, "Psionic Shield!" From the hilt of the dagger a field of transparent green energy with dark splotches cascading over it grew, creating a large shield with jagged, unruly edges. Santano struck it twice. The shield rippled with each blow, but absorbed most of the shock. Suddenly, Santano realized how to increase his sword's power. He now knew the name of the attack he was using. "Force Shock!" His third blow erupted with a bright flash of energy. Angel's shield shattered, as did the window glass as he flew through it.

With Angel gone, at least for a short moment, there was no one left to protect Peter. Santano turned towards his future sacrifice and was greeted with a steel blow to his face. His head jerked to the side. Blood splattered against the wall and began to sizzle. Peter stared in feared awe as Santano slowly turned his head. The sound of snapping bone could be heard. The tissue in Santano's face was torn. Blood dripped down his chin. His teeth were shattered, broken, and loose. Peter watched in terror as the blood dried, as the tissue mended and the teeth reformed. Santano lolled his head from side to side, snapping his bones audibly back into place. Then he smiled.

Terror gripped Peter. He realized Santano wasn't human. He forced his reserve of courage. He had to survive. He gritted his teeth and swung again. Santano saw it coming this time, before Peter even swung. The blade of the Blood Sword shined and in one motion cut through the metal bat, severing it in two. The business end of the bat went flying in a random direction and made a loud thunk as it hit the wall and then the floor. Peter backed away, astonished that Santano's sword was sharp enough to cleave through steel.

Santano was enjoying the look of fear on Peter's face and his frustration, but he knew he could not drag it out. As much as he may have wanted to, he did not have the time to mentally torment his victim. Angel would be returning very soon, so he knew he had to make quick work of this sacrifice.

Santano raised the Blood Sword in an attempt to end the skirmish in one stroke. He brought the blade down where Peter stood, but much to Santano's frustration, he discovered Peter's nimbleness. Peter evaded Santano's attack with a quick side step and then led in with a hard right hook. Santano's head jerked with the punch's force, but because of his superhuman stamina, he felt only a sting. Santano caught Peter's second punch with his open hand and squeezed. Peter grunted and groaned as his fist was crushed. He was forced to his knees as he tried to pry his hand free. Santano kicked Peter in the chest and sent him sprawling across the room and into the wall behind him. His hand landed on Angel's sword.

Santano raised the Blood Sword as he dashed forward. Peter gripped the Sword of Might, and able to only raise to one knee, blocked Santano's blow with the sword. His hands stung as the sword vibrated in his grip. The Blood Sword bounced back, but Santano was quick. He repositioned the blade and thrust before Peter had time to reposition the sword and defend himself. The crimson blade pierced Peter's chest and exited his back. Shock flooded his face and his grip on the Sword of Might failed. The rusted blade clanked as it hit the ground. Peter's hands went to the blade in his chest. He coughed weak wet coughs. He looked up at his killer. Flesh crawled up his neck and over his face. Hair grew back atop his head. He stared into the face of Santano. Peter could feel the life draining from him. He watched as Santano's sword absorbed his blood into one of its white spots. His body was becoming hot. In the distance he could hear tormented screams. He stared at Santano. He was right; it was Santano's voice he had heard. Santano was the killer. He had been all along.

Peter struggled to his feet, even as the smell of burning embers filled his senses. Unseen hands tugged at his body; tugged at his soul. He reached for Santano, gripping his shirt even as Santano continued to laugh. Peter's sight was becoming blurred. Unearthly sounds filled his ears. He impaled his own body deeper on the sword just to get closer. Blood poured from his mouth. Santano came in and out of focus. Through deep, troubled breaths Peter said, "Rot…in Hell…you…bastard!" Peter exhaled. His eyes closed and his head fell forward. His body went limp; his hands fell to his side. He was gone.

Santano pushed Peter away and off his Sword. It maintained one fewer white spot. Santano placed his hand at the sword's base. "Another time Angel," he said. Santano pulled his hand across the blade, fire trailing behind it. "Vanish." He disappeared, leaving behind only smoke. Angel pulled himself through the window and found his feet quickly. He prepared the Dagger of Power for attack, but lowered his guard when he saw the dissipating smoke. Lying on the ground, Angel saw Peter. The little hope that he held for Peter's survival was dashed. He was too late. Peter lay motionless as his blood pooled around him. The Sword of Might lay next to him. Angel reclaimed his weapon and sheathed both sword and dagger. He kneeled down beside Peter and touched his face, trailing his fingers upon Peter's eyes and closing their lids. "You fought bravely," Angel said. "Don't worry. Just keep fighting. I will save you; all of you. Just have faith." Angel made the sign of the cross and offered a silent prayer.

**

History passed by uneventful. Rebecca remained quiet and didn't participate much in the group discussions. They were almost done with the project. What Úna said kept playing back in her head. "Make sure you say your good-byes. It ends tomorrow." Rebecca was terrified of what tomorrow would bring. She looked at her friends; Glenda, Brian, Austin. Would she see them again? Would they be dead by tomorrow? Would she? They knew she was in agony. It was apparent on each of their faces. They thought they knew the problem, but what could they do about it? The bell rang. The desks were put back into place. Glenda approached Rebecca.

"Hey," she said. "¿Estas bien? You okay?"

Rebecca looked at her. "Yeah, I guess," she answered. "There's just a lot on my mind."

"I'm surprised you've been coming to school."

Rebecca waved good-bye to Brian and Austin as they left. They waved back. "I thought it would be easier instead of staying home."

"How would it be—?"

Rebecca threw her arms around Glenda in a tight embrace. A little stunned, Glenda returned the hug. "Are you sure you're okay?" Glenda asked.

"You've been a good friend to me Glenda," Rebecca said. "You helped me a lot this week. Thank you."

"Uh, si. Of course. What are friends for?"

Rebecca released her embrace and Glenda followed suit. "I just wanted you to know that. Good-bye Glenda." Rebecca nearly broke. It felt like the final good-bye.

"Hey, I'll see you next week."

Rebecca smiled. "Yeah." It felt like a lie.

Rebecca left the class. As she headed towards English class, she passed by Brian. He was fighting with his locker. The lock wouldn't open. She tapped his shoulder.

"Want me to try?" she asked.

"Sure," he answered. "Maybe you'll have better luck. Nine, thirty-five, sixteen."

Rebecca spun the wheel to the right several times, stopping on nine before spinning it once to the left, passed nine to thirty-five. "Don't be so rough with it." She spun it back to the right and stopped on sixteen. She pulled and the lock came open. "You have to be gentle, like with a girl."

Brian laughed. "I'll remember that. Thanks Rebecca."

"Thank you."

"For what?"

"For understanding. For you and Austin always trying to make me laugh. You guys made the class fun. Tell Austin that, when you see him."

"Uh, sure. Is everything alright?"

"I guess. Good-bye Brian."

"Uh, later?" Brian said as Rebecca walked away.

Rebecca sat at her desk and wanted to cry. She felt as if these were her last good-byes. English. She would have to say good-bye to Samantha and Rene too. Why was she so compelled to say good-bye? Was she really seeing her time slipping away? Nicholas came in and didn't say a word. Tomorrow. She had a study date with him tomorrow. No, not a date. Just a tutoring session. She didn't like him. Not one bit, but he had been kind to her all week and all she did was act like a bitch towards him. She didn't apologize though. She kept quiet. Úna came in and took her seat in the back. She was a quiet one, Úna. Rebecca still didn't understand how she had gone unnoticed by her all these years.

The bell rang. They had a test on <u>Othello</u>. Rebecca realized she hadn't even finished reading Scene 1. She hadn't done any homework the whole week. She wrote at the top 'Didn't Read' and didn't even try. What did one 'F' matter if it was all ending? She squeezed her pencil so hard that she snapped it. She let the pieces roll on the desk. It didn't matter. She and Michael were leaving after class. She couldn't wait for class to be done with.

The bell rang. It was over. Nicholas left. He didn't say anything at all during class. He left Rebecca alone. Samantha came up to her.

"Hey," Samantha said. "Are you okay? You seem really distant today."

"I have?" Rebecca asked. "I guess my mind has just been reeling with everything that's been happening."

"I bet. I heard you were going to see Nicholas later."

"He asked for some help in math. I agreed."

"Are you sure that's smart? I mean—the rumors."

"I know, but really, he's been nice to me all week. He hasn't really acted all that much like his usual ass-self. But, I've been kind of a bitch to him."

"You're under a lot of stress. I would be careful though."

Rebecca watched Úna leave and looked for Rene. "I will. Rene left already?"

"Yeah. She has lunch now."

"Okay. Tell her good-bye for me?"

"Uh, sure. You going somewhere?"

"I don't know. Maybe. Good-bye Sam."

"Bye. Enjoy the trip. You need it."

Rebecca tried to smile before she left. It was hard and felt fake. Walking down the hall to meet up with Michael, she realized she needed a few minutes. She stopped in the girl's washroom. She looked at herself in the mirror. Her agony was quite clear on her face. She realized she really was ready to cry. A few tears managed to break free. She wiped them away. Úna stopped behind her reflection in the mirror. She was wearing the school's uniform and carried a backpack. "You been saying your good-byes sugar cube?" Úna asked in her accent. Rebecca nodded absently. "That's good. Now's the time to cry if you're going to."

Rebecca realized the voice wasn't coming from the mirror or her head. It was behind her. She turned around to find Úna standing behind her looking worried.

"Are you okay?" Úna asked, her accent suddenly gone.

"Who are you?" Rebecca asked.

Úna looked at her quizzically. "Úna Devor. We've met."

Rebecca's anger started to rise. She let her bag fall to the ground. "Who are you? Where did you come from?"

"Rebecca, that's not funny. I've always been here. You know me. I know we're not, like, friends or anything but—"

Rebecca stomped her foot. "You know what I mean!" Úna jumped back. "You didn't exist a week ago! Who are you? Why are you following me?"

"I'm not fol—"

"Stop it!" Tears were flowing down Rebecca's face. "My friends started dying and then you showed up! What do you have to do with this?"

"Rebecca, calm down. You're scaring me."

Rebecca crossed the distance between them quickly. She threw Úna against the wall and picked her up by the scruff of her collar. "What do you want with me?"

Úna stared fearfully into Rebecca's eyes. Rebecca's anger did not subside. With what she had seen, she was certain either Úna was not human or she was going crazy. Then Úna smiled.

"Ah, there it is," Úna said in her accent. "Your fire. We've been looking for it."

"Who are you?" Rebecca asked. "What do you want with me?"

"You're almost ready. Not long now."

Rebecca slammed Úna against the wall. "Stop it!"

"Yes, that's good. You'll need that."

"What are you?"

"Do you really want to know? Are you sure?"

"Tell me."

Úna raised her hand. "Then let me show you—" She placed her hand sharply on Rebecca's head. "My fall!"

Rebecca blinked and the world spun. She was falling back. Backwards. Time was unraveling, reversing. Centuries slipped by in an instant. Rebecca was in an amphitheater carved into a mountainside, but then she wasn't. Fear ran through her. It was a strange feeling. The fear. It was a new sensation. She didn't like it. That felt weird to Rebecca. She's been afraid before, but it was like the first time.

A man hung nailed to a cross. He was in agony. His skin was dark, his hair long and knotty. Tribal markings covered his body and strange piercings dotted his face. Another man stood on the ground. His skin was dark too, covered in tattoos. His pierced face was engorged. Sharp, massive teeth grew from his jaws. He carried a strange sword the color of crimson blood. A single white spot was etched on the curved blade. Rebecca had never seen that kind of sword before. The man raised his sword. He spoke in a tribal tongue Rebecca had never heard, but understood.

"I offer this last sacrifice," he said. "This innocent crucified. Open the gate." He pierced the man's side with his sword. The man refused to cry out, even as his blood swirled around the white spot. "Bring onto me the hungry, the starving, the insatiable!"

Rebecca's fear was mounting. "No!" she cried out, but it wasn't her voice.

"Bring onto me the desolate, the thirsty, the desperate!"

"Stop it you fool!" Rebecca recognized the voice she cried out in. It belonged to Úna.

The blood pooled into the white spot, making the entire sword glow crimson. The hanging man's head fell and he breathed no more. The man holding the sword faced the blade downward and released it. The sword hovered in the air and drops of blood fell onto the floor. A pentagram enclosed in a circle, surrounded by strange makings painted itself onto the ground with each drop, ten in all. The sword then dropped, slowly, into the circle and disappeared. Space inside the circle distorted and Rebecca appeared, but it wasn't her. She was Úna. Physically, Úna didn't look different from how Rebecca knew her. Úna was still physically small and thin, her red hair was still wild, but was longer at this time. The main difference was her clothes. It was ancient, made of wool and hide, covering less of her than her contemporary clothes did. Really, Úna wore little more than a skirt. Only a strap covered her small chested top and she was barefoot. Her hair fell below her shoulders. Úna looked frightened. She was terrified. "You can't!" Úna screamed. The space distorted and Rebecca felt pain. She suddenly realized she was seeing things through Úna's eyes. She was Úna. She was in pain. She screamed.

"Give it to me!" the man cried out. "Give me your destruction!"

Úna couldn't move; her body locked in a painful grasp. She was in pain. Rebecca could feel it. "It's...not...yours!" Úna cried. She was fighting. "You can't...have it!"

The man opened his maw wide. "Give me!"

Úna screamed. Dark energy began to emanate from her. The energy wafted away into the maw of the man. "Stop!" Úna cried. "You can't...do this!" The man's form began to bulge. His body was becoming engorged. "You don't know...what you're...doing! Leave me alone!" The man's size grew. Pain. Úna was in so much pain. So much fear. She thought she was dying. She wondered if that's what death felt like. "Somebody help me!" she cried.

A flash of searing light whisked across the amphitheater. It hit the man, but the energy just rocked around him. He didn't budge. Úna looked across the space. A light skinned man stood at the other end. In his hands were a curved dagger and a sword of similar design as the dark skinned man's. Úna cried out to him. "Don't let him...take me! Save me!" She was crying. It was strange, to cry. She was almost ashamed. The First didn't cry. He stood strong. She feared. She felt pathetic. "Please save me!"

The light skinned man touched the pommels of his sword and dagger together. A fine, but sturdy silver chain appeared and linked them together. He took the sword chain and began to twirl his sword overhead. He threw the sword at the dark skinned man and shouted, "Impact!" He spoke Latin. The sword struck and in a blast of energy the light bounced off its target. The last of Úna's energy left her. Weakly, miserably, she fell to the floor. She simply lay there, crying. She couldn't move. She felt ashamed, but she couldn't stop crying. The last of her energy entered the man's toothy maw and his massive jaws slammed shut. Dark energy surrounded him. The light skinned man stared on. "I'm too late," he said.

The dark skinned man's body pulsed. The energy grew thicker, darker. He disappeared into it. The darkness grew and formed. Fat arms moved. Stubby legs turned the bloated mass. The darkness faded. A pale green hue covered the rippling, fatty flesh. A braid of long black, knotty hair whipped about his head. Dirty nails sat atop short, stubby sausage-like fingers. With each step he took with his blubbery legs, the ground shook. Pointed ears framed his large head, half of which comprised of a large toothy maw. Úna tried to stand. "Give...it back," she said weakly. The creature stomped a massive foot onto her back. Her scream was breathless. New pain. She wondered; is this what pain feels like? How does anyone tolerate it? She cried and reached for the light skinned man. "Gerald…help…me. Save…me."

The bloated figure roared and turned to face the light skinned man, Gerald. "Hungry," the creature said, still in its tribal tongue. "Gonna eat you!"

"So, you are Famine," Gerald said as he placed the chain behind him.

"Gonna eat you!" Famine roared, spittle erupting from his mouth, the words coming out as several languages at once. "Then gonna eat your blood!" Rebecca had never heard the languages before, but knew them. Latin. Hebrew. Sumerian.

"Not likely," Gerald first let go of his dagger and spun the chain around his arm before grabbing his dagger again. He then did the same with his sword. "I won't let you stay in this world."

Famine laughed as he slowly approached. The ground shook with each wobbly step. Three, four, five languages at once he spoke. Arabic. Croatian. "First gonna eat you!" English. Pig Latin. "Then gonna eat your wife!" Portuguese. Angelic. "Then gonna eat your sons!" His language changed solely to Latin. "Then gonna eat all the Virtues!"

Gerald raised his sword. "No," he said. Thunder roared. "I think not."

Lightning struck the blade, engulfing it in electrical rage. A single swing erupted a lightning bolt, pure and strong. Famine's body surged in the dancing electrical light. He roared and wobbled back. Gerald swung the Dagger of Power in a wide arc, releasing the handle and letting the chain slide between his fingers. The length of the chain seemed endless as it stretched across the theater. "Shock!" Gerald shouted. A shock rocked Famine's body as the dagger ripped across his protruding gut. Gerald pulled the dagger back as he released his sword. "Thunder!" he shouted. A boom rocked Famine's ears as the sword cut his flesh. He covered his ears and roared. Gerald pulled his arms apart, sending the blades towards Famine. "Tempest!" The blades struck Famine's engorged belly, releasing a bolt of lightning and a crash of thunder. Winds erupted and brought the blades down again. Another lightning bolt. Gerald pulled the blades back and sent them down again. "Cataclysmic Tempest!" The ground rocked as the blades came down. Bolts of lightning flooded the centralized storm as water rained down on Famine. A loud and bright crash boomed as the blades hit. Thunder roared and Famine was hurdled backwards through the stone walls of the theater built into a mountain.

Gerald pulled his weapons back and grabbed their handles. He stood panting, his energy used. Such powerful attacks were tiring. He thought it over. Úna struggled to stand. She was tired and she hurt. She didn't understand. The ground shook and Famine burst from his cave. Gerald stared on in shocked disbelief, Famine's belly had erupted. His innards were hanging out, his intestines dangled at his feet, yet he stood. He stood and roared. "So hungry," he said. "Can't think. Must eat!" He tore a chunk of stone from the mountain wall and shoved it into his mouth. Dirt and dust fell from his maw as he chewed.

Gerald could not believe his eyes. "What manner of creature is this?" he asked. "Does it not know it's hurt?"

Famine uprooted a block of stone and dirt from the ground and began to eat it. To Gerald's horror, he saw that the creature was healing. He gritted his teeth and held his sword to the side. He would not allow it. He gripped the handle tightly and the blade crackled to life. An electrical pulse danced on its surface. He swung the blade and released the handle, the ever lengthening chain kissing his palm and fingers. Famine saw the incoming blade and opened his maw wide. Down his gullet it went and his jaws snapped shut. Gerald couldn't believe it. Famine swallowed the Sword of Might.

Famine seemed in discomfort. Smoke wafted from his mouth. The smell of burning fat began to fill the air. Famine groaned in annoyed discomfort, clutching his almost healed belly. "Burns…" he moaned. "It burns!" His pudgy fingers gripped the chain. Almost instantly his hands began to smoke. He trudged about in agony, pulling at the chain. Gerald tried to stand his ground, but was being pulled with relative ease. He threw the dagger into the ground as an anchor. For a moment, Gerald had his feet and could fight against the pull. Suddenly, Famine wailed. "It burns!" Famine jerked and Gerald found himself stretched between his anchor and Famine. He screamed. He felt as if his arms would sever long before the anchor broke. Famine pulled desperately at the chain with his burning hands. He was gagging, trying to regurgitate the blade.

Úna found her strength slowly returning. Her pain and fear were replaced with anger. Anger towards the monstrosity before her. The abomination that bore one of her names. Unthinking, she leapt onto Famine and sank her teeth into his tender ear. She pulled and yanked, trying to rip it from his head. Famine roared and the sword finally came loose. Suddenly free of tension, Gerald fell to the ground. The Sword of Might flew hazardly, randomly in the air. Famine gripped Úna in his fat fingers and pulled her from his head. Blood spattered from his ear as Úna was torn away. Green flesh dangled from her lips and blood splattered on her jaw. Famine slammed her into the ground. She clenched her teeth and held onto the dangling flesh. She took it into her mouth and began to chew.

Rebecca could taste the fatty tissue. The coppery blood. She could feel as it squished in Úna's mouth; in her mouth. Rebecca wanted to vomit. It was disgusting. Úna swallowed. It was important. Somehow, Rebecca knew eating was important. Not eating in general. Eating the flesh. Úna tried to reach Famine's hand, but only bit air. A roar of thunder drew Famine's attention from her. Again, lightning danced on Gerald's blade. Famine discarded Úna violently to the side. Gerald hurled the lightning drenched blade forward. Famine leaped forward in a large arc. Lightning discharged behind him. Gerald darted to the side with Quickstep as Famine came down. The ground buckled beneath his weight and he released a potent fart as he landed. An opaque brown gas filled the air. It was putrid. Gerald reeled and tried to wave it away as he stumbled out of the gaseous mist. His weapons dragged on the ground. His lungs burned and he coughed. Famine expedited Gerald's retreat with a backhanded swat. Gerald tumbled across the stone stage plateau.

Famine smiled and slowly wobbled forward. "I'm going to eat you, demon hunter."

Úna stood up, battered, but not beaten. Blood dripped from her chin. "Devours!" Úna cried out. "Come to me! Your Mistress needs you!"

Nothing came. Famine came to a standstill and looked towards Úna. Finally, Gerald seemed to notice her. "Run child!" he called out as he began to spin the Sword of Might overhead and the Dagger of Power at his side. "Get away from here! Go!"

Famine grinned. "Hey, that's a good idea."

Úna's heart dropped. It couldn't be. They didn't answer her. That was why the First didn't summon aid, wasn't it? They wouldn't listen to him anymore. "No!" Úna screamed.

"Devours!" Famine exclaimed. "Come and eat!"

Distorted waves of energy spotted the landscape. Small creatures leaped from them, chattering and smiling. Their large mouths were filled with hundred of tiny, sharp teeth. Thin hair tied tightly and knotted in a single braid atop their head. Small boney bodies with dark brown skin stretched tight about their frame. Their eyes were black and empty. Famine pointed his pudgy finger at Gerald. "Eat him."

The small creatures let out a shriek and darted forward. Úna watched in horrified helplessness as they descended upon Gerald in a toothy wave. Lightning roared. The creatures were thrown, charred and burned. The wave did not stop. It kept coming, overwhelming Gerald. Those blasted by lightning were healed, reformed and on their feet again in moments. Úna ran into the wave and pulled at them, commanding them to stop. Tears ran down her face. They would not listen. She watched as Gerald disappeared beneath the wave. Her fault. His death was her fault. Gerald shouted something. His sword raised high over the mob. Lightning struck the steel. Bolts of lightning struck the ground in a dome formation, pushing the wave away. An angel with emerald wings and holding an earth toned mace stood beside Gerald. He wore white, gold accented armor with a lion's head etched on his breastplate. Fire effigies adorned the greaves and lower cannon of vambraces. The devours surrounded them, chattering ceaselessly as they sized up the angel. Gerald struggled to his feet. "Just hold them off for a few minutes Michael," Gerald said between ragged breaths. The archangel stared at Úna and nodded.

Gerald took the Dagger of Power and threw it into the ground, anchoring himself. He gripped the chain tightly. The devours advanced. With a battle cry, Michael slammed his mace into the ground. The stone floor bent and a wave of power erupted, throwing the advancing devours back. Michael gripped his mace with both hands and darted forward. Gerald let the Sword of Might slip from his hand and held the chain. Slowly at first, he began to twirl the blade overhead. As it began to spin in a vortex, Gerald increased the speed. A low rumble of thunder echoed. The sky began to darken. The sword spun faster and faster. Dark clouds filled the sky. Famine watched the sky light up with flashes of light. Thunder could be heard in the distance. Úna watched as Michael kept the devours at bay, even as their advancing numbers grew. His right vambrace began to glow. Gerald shouted, "Divine Storm!" Lightning danced across the sky. Thunder flashed and was earsplitting. Michael's lower cannon vambrace had changed; become more sturdy and the fire effigies being replaced with heavenly runes. The vambrace was now coupled with a rerebrace and connected at the elbow by a spiked cowter. The runes were etched along the gauntlet all the way to the paldron in the form of a lion's claw. Each swing of his mace now seemed to possess more power.

Michael struck upon the descending wave. Úna was unsure if the flash came from Michael or the lightning, but Michael's left arm now matched his right. The ground began to shake. The devours backed away. Michael turned his attention to the approaching mass that was Famine. The Horseman grinned and said, "Angel sounds like a divine dish." Michael dashed forward, flying up to meet Famine. Hard rain began to fall. Lightning flashed. Thunder roared. Michael reared his weapon back as a thick golden cuirass covered his torso. The lion's head was replaced with a blue gem. It glowed and energy surged through the grooves in the armor to light the runes on the paldrons, vambraces and gauntlets.

Michael struck Famine atop his head, sending the titan tumbling to the ground. Michael raised his mace high to strike again. Famine reached out his fist and knocked the archangel back. Famine rose to all fours and threw himself, maw open, at Michael. His mace struck the roof of Famine's mouth while his off-hand gripped the beast's lower jaw. Famine pushed forward, trying to close his mouth upon the archangel. Michael struggled to keep the beast's mouth open. The storm's intensity increased with each passing moment. The amphitheater was flooding. The devours were being washed away. A flash of lightning and Michael's right greave was changed.

A thick golden greave and cuisse was connected by a spiked poleyn, making the piece whole. Holy symbols glowed blue as the energy from the breastplate's gem coursed through the leg armor and into the boot. The top of the armored boot was decorated with a roaring lion's head with a thick flowing mane.

"Gerald!" Michael shouted over the storm.

"Just a little longer!" Gerald shouted back.

Famine's tongue shot out of his mouth and wrapped around Michael's neck, choking him and pulling him forward. Famine moved forward on all fours, pushing the archangel back through the rising water. Michael was tiring. His wings flexed and arched towards Famine. His primary feathers struck Famine's eyes and forced the Horseman to reel back. Michael found his feet and struck at Famine's gut, ripping his entrails out with a single blow. Famine clutched his wound and roared in pain. Michael's full armor was almost donned, his full power almost released. From neck to toe, he shined in glistening gold and pulsating blue energy. "Now Gerald!" he shouted, taking his eyes off Famine for an instant. "Release the storm!" It was all the behemoth needed. Famine reeled forward and tried to bite down on Michael's head. Michael turned and brought his mace up and connected with Famine's chin. His mouth slammed shut and he reeled back. Michael took to the sky and brought his mace down again. Famine reached out with his fatty fingers and caught the mace. A sonic boom echoed. Úna shielded herself from the wave. Famine was getting stronger. They had to end it soon. Then she heard Michael scream. When she looked back, Michael clutched a stump of an arm. Famine munched on flesh and steel as blood rolled down his massive chin. His healing became almost instant after feasting on Michael's flesh.

Úna screamed something into the roar of thunder. She heard Gerald. She and Famine looked at him. He was held to the ground only by the dagger anchor. A tornado swirled around him. Lightning danced around the tornado and stones were whipped into a swirl. Famine began to advance. "Hand of God!" Gerald screamed.

Lighting struck the spinning vortex. The storm was drawn into it. Gerald completely disappeared. Famine watched unimpressed as the raging storm was pulled into the vortex. Michael chuckled. Famine looked at him.

"What's so funny?" the Horseman asked.

"You will now face his full fury," Michael answered.

"You couldn't beat me. What chance does a mortal have?"

"Gerald now wields the entire wrath of Heaven. He has unleashed his miracle. He is now a Force of Nature."

"I am an all powerful Horseman. I will devour that storm." Famine wiped the spittle from his chin.

There was a clash of thunder and the storm vortex took a more humanoid form. The dark storm clouds whirled within the form. Its limbs were composed of stone laced water. Thunder rumbled with its motion and lightning flashed and danced across its swirling body. Famine pointed at it. "Eat it," he said flatly. The devours shrieked and darted forward. The Force of Nature raised a swirling arm of stone and water at them. A cascade of lightning erupted from the blunt, fingerless hand. The ground shattered and burned with each numerous lightning strike. The devours were burned, charred, and thrown into the air. The lightning strikes continued, sending the burned husks flying. Famine gritted his teeth angrily as he watched his devours laid waste to. He roared and moved forward, wobbling at an increased speed, struggling to keep his balance with each step.

The Force of Nature threw its other fingerless limb forward. Lightning raced outward. Famine roared as he came to a complete halt. His body flashed and burned as the lightning struck him. Famine raised a pudgy hand and caught the main bolt. The bolt pushed against his hand, stopping the barrage. The Force of Nature attacked with its other limb. Famine raised his other hand and caught the second bolt as well. Famine advanced. A howl escaped the Force of Nature's featureless head. Powerful winds and rain pelted Famine, whose advance slowed but did not stop.

Famine peered into the storm. Within he could see a small figure. The Force of Nature reacted to its movements in the calm center. A large belch escaped Famine, blowing away the Force of Nature's center, exposing Gerald. "I see you!" Famine shouted as he leaped into the air. The storm closed back around Gerald as he raised his hands, guiding the storm's limbs. Famine flashed and burned as lightning struck, but he landed on the Force of Nature. Their hands locked. "I will eat you!" Famine exclaimed. A limb broke free of Famine's grasp and drove itself into Famine's mouth. Famine inhaled, drawing the storm into him, devouring it.

Gerald stood at the center of a swirling sphere, his Force of Nature almost completely consumed by Famine. Gerald raised his sword and pointed it at Famine. From within the horror, an unimaginable force of lightning struck; an entire storm's furry unleashed in seconds. Famine's thick bones flashed through his flesh. He shook and smoked. The storm passed. Famine stood motionless and charred. Gerald descended back to the ground and the sphere left him. With a pained struggle, Gerald turned his gaze upwards towards Famine. Black smoke billowed from the creature's mouth. He fell back. The ground trembled as his weight fell, the surrounding water casting outwards in a powerful wave meters high. His flesh began to decay and fall to ash. The devours scurried forward, awaiting orders. Michael approached Gerald and Famine spoke. "One for every member of your blood. How many can you save?"

The devours began to chatter.

"Michael," Gerald said as he braced himself for one final fight. "Fetch my son. It is his time now."

"I will not leave you," Michael said as he raised his mace. Blood dripped from his torn and severed arm.

"My time is over. Go, Michael. I will do what I can. I will face my fate alone."

"Devour them all," Famine gargled.

"I will see you on the other side," Michael said as he was enshrouded in light. He was gone.

Gerald twirled his sword overhead. "Not too soon I hope."

Úna watched helplessly as the devours overwhelmed him. She cried out for them to stop. They wouldn't listen. Lightning flashed and flesh burned. Gerald only lasted against the endless wave for a few moments. He sent dozens from this world, but dozens still remained. He screamed and blood coated the ground. Famine was little more than a head. He sneered at Úna. "She took my ear," he said. "Now take her flesh."

The remaining devours, numbering in the dozens, turned towards Úna and surrounded her. Úna could feel their sorrow and regret. She pleaded with them, begged them to desist. Famine uttered his last command before his descent into the Underworld. Úna heard their collective 'sorry'. She screamed and they were upon her, ripping and tearing into her flesh. Pulling her limps from her body. They devoured every inch. Úna's body was gone, yet still she felt. Would the pain ever cease? Would she ever be whole again?

***

Rebecca pulled away and backed into the sink. Her heart was racing, her breathing heavy. Her face was red with tears; her throat was sore. Her body ached.

"Now you see," Úna said. "You see what it is we face. Do not disappoint us, Giver of Life." Úna walked out, leaving her bag behind. "Tomorrow it comes to an end, one way or another. Can you prevent World's End?"

Rebecca watched Úna disappear around the carrousel of wood that created the illusion of a door. She watched Úna's feet simply disappear, as if she had never stood there in the first place. Rebecca stared at Úna's bag. She went to it and sat on her knees. She opened the bag. It was full of books and paper. <u>Othello</u> was gone, but everything else was present. Rebecca looked through the graded papers. They were unnamed. Written comments strangely omitted a name where a name should be. It was just empty space. Room enough for about three letters. It was as if the student Úna Devor no longer existed. Any trace that she had existed at all was now gone.

Rebecca sat alone in the bathroom. She wiped her tears away. What had she seen? What was Úna? Didn't she see Úna die? Wasn't Úna eaten alive? Rebecca shuddered. What were those things? They were very prevalent in her mind, when she was witnessing the event. When she was Úna. Now that she was Rebecca again, all those things eluded her. Just vague, frightful images remained. A storm. She could remember an intense storm. She could remember something very big and gluttonous too. She remembered its visage was frightful, a monster of a creature. She tried to remember it, but only heard a slobbering laughter and large teeth. Someone called out to her. Someone touched her. She turned her head. It was Michael.

"Are you okay?" he asked.

Rebecca smiled at him. "You're in the girl's washroom," she said weakly.

"Hm. So I am." Michael helped Rebecca to her feet. "I waited by your locker, but you never came."

"I was…talking to Úna."

Michael looked at her quizzically. "Who's Úna?"

Rebecca looked at Michael in dumbfounded shock. She looked down at the ownerless backpack. Was she really gone, just like that? "No one," Rebecca answered. "Let's just go. I want to get out of here."

Michael nodded and they left the building.

CHAPTER X

Rebecca saw Michael onto the public bus. She kissed him good-bye and wished him a safe trip. When the bus left, she went to catch her own. She didn't want Michael to know where she was going or why she was going. She was just glad Michael hadn't asked about her new coat.

Rebecca approached her secret place for what she thought would probably be the last time. The week had been bad, but her life took a major trip downhill when she came here yesterday. She found herself wondering if it was such a good idea to come back. Rebecca searched for the flash light. It wasn't there. She remembered leaving with it. When Angel left the room the light had died. She searched the trench coat pockets. She found it on an inside pocket. She must have forgotten to leave it. She flipped the switch and shined the light ahead of her as she entered.

Rebecca approached the threshold of the room where she had last seen Angel. It was colder now. Except for the light of day that peaked in from the hole in the ceiling and high windows, there was only darkness. "Hello?" Rebecca called out as she crossed the threshold. "Angel, are you here?" She received no answer. The light of her flashlight leading the way, she ventured to the point where she first encountered Angel. The light of day that ventured within did little to hide the evidence of a bloody brawl. Angel's blood dotted the floor, as well as some of her own. Rebecca was sure of that. She was stabbed. She touched the wound, remembering the battle. She saw her bloody jacket and uniform top lying on the ground. She was one top short now and the school had only given her three at the beginning of the year. She was going to have to replace that. Rebecca shined her light upwards. She could see nothing upon the rafters. "Angel!" she called out. "I need to talk to you! Answer me!"

Only the echo of her own voice answered her. She began to pace the floor, scanning the room with her flashlight. It seemed as if Angel wasn't there. A scorch mark was burned onto the floor. Rebecca wondered if that was the place where Demonic Angel had died. She swept the light across the room. Several yards away, something glimmered in the light and caught her eye. She approached it. Rebecca thought it was the spot she had battled Demonic Angel. Drops of blood dotted the area. Burn marks graced the ground. She was almost certain. Her light shined down on a feather of pure white. Rebecca picked it up. The feather was ruffled and at least a foot in length, maybe longer. She stared at it in amazement. How did a feather get into the room? There weren't even pigeon nests in that part of the warehouse. Rebecca's heart started to race. It was the wrong question. What on Earth had foot long pure white feathers?

Rebecca swallowed hard and let the feather drop to the floor. She swept the flashlight through the room, calling out to Angel again and suddenly realized the only logical, but improbable answer to her question. She looked back at the feather. Improbable? Unlikely with the things she had seen. She called out to Angel one last time, demanding that he answer her. An answer she did not receive. Rebecca thought that perhaps after Demonic Angel's attack, Angel found a new place to rest to avoid another attack. A chill ran down her spine at the thought of being caught alone with another demon-like opponent. This time she would have no weapons, how would she fight? Rebecca shook her head. Fight? Why would she even consider the notion of fighting anything even resembling a demon?

Rebecca knew she had to leave. If Angel had fled because it was now unsafe, what chance did she really have against anyone or anything that came looking for him? Rebecca swept the light one last time across the room before leaving the warehouse for the final time. No matter what happened tomorrow, whether it was World's End or not, if she managed to survive, she would never return to this place. All she wanted to do was get home before Michael. They had a lot to talk about. Above all, she just wanted to feel safe in his arms, even if just for a little while.

***

Rebecca slid her key into the front door. The car was gone, so Rebecca was sure her parents had already left. She didn't see Michael's car so was fairly certain he hadn't arrived yet. That was good. She wanted to check the answering machine and delete the school's message. She left her bag by the door and hung the trench coat up. She looked at the answering machine resting on the end table by the couch. It flashed one message. Her parents hadn't gotten Caller ID yet, so without that message, there was no way to know if anyone called at all. She pressed play.

Static played at first. "Good afternoon," a voice said. "This is Andy Harold calling from—" Rebecca pressed delete. She knew Andy Harold. He was in charge of attendance in the school. She didn't need to hear the rest of the message, that she had cut class.

Rebecca looked at her uniform and wondered if she had time to change before Michael came. He probably wouldn't stop at home and change first, but there was no reason for Rebecca to keep wearing her uniform. She was done for the week. With luck, she'd get to wear it again on Monday. She had never looked forward to the opportunity to wear her uniform before, but everything lately was pointing to the fact that it may be the last time.

Rebecca climbed the stairs to her room. She was alone in the house and had the blouse unbuttoned and off by the time she entered her room. She threw the blouse on the bed and touched the gauze pad on her shoulder. She had changed it that morning after her shower and applied some of the ointment she had found in Angel's coat. She hoped that was the right thing to do. It had healed further and a dull throb that she didn't always notice was present. It didn't hurt unless she touched it or raised her arm too high. It was healing fast, but was scaring. She opened her drawer and put on a random shirt. She looked at herself in the mirror. A casual weekend shirt, nothing fancy. Rebecca realized that she wanted something fancy, at least fancier. She wanted to look nice for Michael. Did she have time? She went to her closet, where she kept some of her nicer clothes. She looked through the hangers and chose three of her favorite tops. She went to the mirror and held each against her body. The first one was bare shouldered with long satin sleeves. Michael liked that one, but it would leave her bandage bare. She didn't think about it until she looked at it in the mirror. She laid it on her vanity and modeled the second top, blue silk and sleeveless. Just enough fabric to cover the bandage. Jeanine thought the V-neck was cut too deep, but Rebecca didn't think so. Maybe for a fifteen or sixteen year old, but

Rebecca was eighteen. She wasn't sure if Michael had seen her in it yet. She thought her mother disliked it because it accented her cleavage. Most of her tops didn't do that. The third top was a violet button up with short sleeves. It was one of her more conservative tops. Rebecca wanted to look nice, not conservative. She chose the V-neck.

Rebecca put the top on. Now she needed something to go with it. She undid the uniform skirt and let it fall to the floor. She picked up the two tops and took them back to her closet, where she hung them back up and began to search for a pair of bottoms. Maybe a skirt? Rebecca almost felt like she was getting ready to go out dancing or something. How nice she thought it would be just to get away from it all. Away from the killings, the angels, the demons. The door bell rang. "Shoot!" Rebecca whispered harshly. She flipped through her closet quickly and nabbed a slender pair of black pants. Not what she was looking for, but they would do.

Rebecca hobbled out of her room as she put her pants on, stumbling with them as she tried to walk with one leg in. She had them up and was buttoning them as she came down the stairs. "Just a second!" she called out. Rebecca stood before the door and adjusted her quickly thrown together outfit. She opened the door. Michael was waiting on the other side. She smiled at him. "Hey beautiful," Michael smiled back. "Was I supposed to stop and change?"

Rebecca shook her head as she tucked her blonde hair behind her ears. "Come in."

Michael closed the door behind him and hung his jacket up. "You said you wanted to talk," Michael said. "Is everything alright?"

"No, but—Let's talk in my room."

"Your room?" Michael asked in a voice of slight shock. Rebecca nodded and led the way.

Michael swallowed worriedly. His stomach twisted. He had never been on the second floor, where her bedroom was. He was never really left alone with Rebecca at her house for an extended length of time. This past week was the first time he had even stayed the night. Public passionate kisses, asking about people he did not know. Sneaking into her house while her parents were away. Nothing foreign to Michael, but very unlike Rebecca.

He was starting to seriously worry about her. Were the murders really getting to her this much? Did she really blame herself for Melissa's death? Rebecca had been acting strange all week. Maybe now Michael would get some answers.

Rebecca picked up her uniform from the floor and asked Michael to close the door. He obliged. As Rebecca tossed her discarded uniform into her closet, Michael scanned her room for the first time. A twin sized bed rested in the center of the room, its headboard against the wall. A Kurt Cobain poster hung over her bed. A pegasus poster was affixed to Rebecca's closet door. A hand drawn and colored Tinker Bell smiled into the room from the bedroom door. A desk sat at one end of the room. A vanity with perfumes and make-up sat at the other. Most of her bed reflected the mirror. Next to her bed rested a night stand with an alarm clock, an antique lamp, and a picture of them on one of their first dates.

"It's nice in here," Michael said.

"Thank you."

"Did you make this picture?" he asked as he pointed at Tinker Bell.

Rebecca shook her head. "No. Peter gave it to me a few birthdays back."

"It's pretty good. I didn't know he could draw."

"Yeah. He loves it. He always talks about being an independent artist or something. You can sit down." She walked to the window and, wrapping her arms about herself, stared out it. She watched as the naked trees danced in the wind. The ground glistened in snow and frost. The sky was clearing after the light snowfall. The world looked peaceful.

Michael looked about the room. Three choices. Her bed, the desk chair, or the oval vanity cushion seat. Michael opted to stand. "It's alright. Becca, what's wrong? Talk to me, please."

Rebecca stayed silent for a moment staring out at the world, trying to figure out how to say it. She was still hesitant to admit what she had seen, trying to find the courage to believe it herself. Michael waited patiently as Rebecca fretfully altered her weight from foot to foot. Finally, she spoke.

"I'm scared...and confused. I—" Her sentence broke.

"Becca," Michael said as he went to her and wrapped his arms around her waist. "I know you're scared. Heck, I am too. But what is it you're confused about?"

"I'm confused about everything. I'm not sure what to believe...or even what's real."

"I don't understand."

"The murders for one."

"The murders? It's because of Santano, isn't it?"

Rebecca laid back into Michael, allowing herself to feel a little safer in his arms. She lowered her hands to his and rested her head against his shoulder. "Hasn't Santano been acting strange lately? He hasn't been around the last couple of days, and even when he was here, he just ignored us."

"I admit Santano has been acting strange. I mean, I know most won't notice or care, but I noticed. Do you really think he helped kill our friends though?"

"I don't think he helped. I think he may have done it alone."

"Hold on a second, Becca. What about Angel? He was arrested at Melissa's house. He had viable murder weapons. You can't just rule him out."

Rebecca turned in his embrace without breaking it, but put some space between their bodies. "I don't think Angel had any part in killing them."

"It's because of Nicole, isn't it?"

"It's more than that. I...I met him Michael."

"You met him?!" Michael exclaimed. "Geez, that's what's been wrong." He pulled her close in a tight embrace. "My God, are you oaky?"

Pain dug into Rebecca's shoulder. "Ow!" she cried as she pushed away.

"Did I hurt you? I'm sorry."

"No, I—" Rebecca sighed. She gripped the shoulder strap. "Angel didn't do this." She pulled it over her shoulder and exposed the gauze taped to it.

Shock and fear flooded Michael's face. "What happened? Are you okay?"

"I'm okay," she said as she put it back into place. "There was a place I used to go to be alone. I know it was dumb, but it was always empty and nothing had ever happened. Not until yesterday."

Michael raised her chin with a finger. "What happened, Becca? Tell me. It's not like you to keep secrets."

Tears swelled up in Rebecca's eyes. "I'm not sure what happened. It was all so…surreal."

"Just start at the beginning."

Rebecca sighed and wiped her tears away. "This is hard to tell you. It's just hard to say."

"I'm not going to judge you, Becca. Just tell me."

Rebecca looked at Michael's concerned face. "I love you, Michael."

"I love you too."

Rebecca smiled through her sorrow and fear. "Just remember that, okay?"

Michael nodded. "Okay." He was worried. What deep dark secret was she about to tell him?

"I was obsessed with Angel because…I've dreamt about him all my life."

"What?" Michael's hold weakened tremendously and he started to take steps back. Rebecca held him and stopped him.

"Not like that!" she cried. "It was nothing like what we have! He was someone I could trust, someone that helped raise and guide me. He was family!"

Rebecca could see that Michael was emotionally hurt. "He was just family," she continued. "He watched me grow up. He—He helped raise me."

"How can a dream raise you?" Michael asked. His voice was hurt, his eyes moist.

"I don't know, but—I was ten the first time I ever went fishing. My dad took me. He was so surprised when I just picked up the rod, bated it, and cast it like I had been fishing for years. He couldn't understand it. I just shrugged it off. I didn't tell him that when I was six I dreamt I was fishing at a lake with Angel. I have no idea where and back then I didn't know

Angel's name. A few times a month I would dream we were fishing. Angel taught me how to fish. He taught me how to cast, how to bait, how to untangle a line. Everything in my life that I had done for the first time but already knew, Angel taught me."

Michael struggled for the words. "This is hard to take."

"So was being told no one could see the sword on his back."

Michael thought for a moment. "You met him. So what happened?"

"He told me Santano was a Satanist. He said unless he can kill Santano, our friends will be trapped in Hell."

"Do you believe him?"

"A lot of things make it hard not to."

"I don't understand."

"Úna. You really don't know her; short red-head with freckles?"

"No."

"You see why I'm confused? She was here. Just two days ago you said you knew her, now you don't! How do people just disappear like that?!"

"Rebecca, calm down!" Michael said as he pulled her closer. She was on the verge of crying. Michael caressed her cheeks. "Just calm down. Tell me what happened with Angel. How did you get hurt?"

"Someone—or something—attacked us. It said it was a demon. It spit fire! It really spit fire!"

Michael pulled Rebecca into an embrace, being careful not to agitate her wound. "It's okay. It's okay." Rebecca threw her arms around him and buried her face into his shoulder. She was sobbing.

"I don't know what to think!" Rebecca cried. "I don't know what to do! They both dropped from the ceiling. Their weapons spit fireballs! The way they fought; it was inhuman. They were inhuman."

"But they were human," Michael said. "I don't know how—"

"Why Michael?" Rebecca shot back as she raised her head and looked at him. "Why do they have to be human? Because angels and demons don't exist; because there's no such thing as Heaven or Hell?"

"I didn't say that. It's just—What are the chances you would meet an angel or demon?"

"But there's a chance, isn't there? Michael, it came for me."

"How do you know that?"

"Because it said it did."

Michael swallowed hard. He knew Rebecca believed what she was saying and it wasn't like her to make up such a spectacular story. Still, it was hard for him to believe. He was agnostic. Rebecca's story brought to focus everything he even thought he believed. What was it Rebecca had seen?

"I don't know what to think anymore. I don't know what to believe. I had always thought that if I had proof…" She buried her face into his shoulder again and cried. "I found proof Michael. I found proof and it all says that the end is coming. What do I do? I can't stop the end of the world, but Úna said I have to."

Úna. It sounded familiar to Michael. "Don't worry," Michael said as he tried to comfort Rebecca, swaying her back and forth in his embrace. "We'll figure something out."

"You believe me, don't you?" Rebecca asked. "Tell me I'm not crazy."

A voice echoed in Michael's head. "Believe her. Cherish every moment with her." He recognized the voice, only barely.

"Úna," Michael mumbled.

"What?" Rebecca asked as she forced herself to stop crying and look at him.

"I believe you. You're not crazy. I don't know what exactly you saw or what happened, but you saw something. Something extraordinary happened."

"We survived Y2K. The world isn't supposed to end a week later."

"It's not. The world isn't going to end any time soon."

"How do you know?"

"I'll stop it myself if I have to."

A giggle broke through Rebecca's fear and she smiled.

"That's what I want to see."

Michael moved to kiss Rebecca. Their lips met and Rebecca pulled his head towards her for a deep kiss. Her kiss wasn't aggressive, but was long and passionate. Even when it was over, the kiss lingered. Their heads rested against each other.

"Whatever happens," Michael whispered, "I'll be there with you. You won't have to face anything alone."

Rebecca stared into his eyes. Michael saw a desire in them that he had not seem in them before. The desire itself he had seen before, but not in Rebecca and for her it seemed…different.

"I want…to do something," Rebecca said.

"Name it."

Rebecca hesitated. She was nervous, but at the same time excited. "It's sudden, but…make love to me."

Michael's body tingled. It wasn't something new to him, but for the first time since his first time, he was nervous. "Are you sure?"

"Yes." Rebecca said as she kissed his lips again.

"I don't carry protection anymore."

"I don't care. Just love me like you used to love Sarah. Show me what it's like."

Michael stared into Rebecca's eyes. The hunger in them was also in Sarah's. It still was, but for Rebecca it seemed different. Her desire wasn't simple lust. His feelings weren't simple lust. Suddenly, he realized the difference. "No," Michael said. "I can love you better."

Michael kissed Rebecca once more and then, by both hands, gently pulled her across the room. Rebecca let Michael guide her as he laid her atop her bed. Michael supported himself next to her and caressed her cheek, admiring her flushed face and excited breaths. Sarah had never looked so beautiful. There wasn't a comparison between the two, Michael realized. There never was. Sarah could be cute or sexy, but Rebecca was just beautiful.

Michael's face was intimately close and he whispered, "I love you, Rebecca."

Rebecca gazed up into Michael's eyes, one arm around his waist, the other caressing his arm. "And I love you, Michael."

Michael leaned forward and softly kissed Rebecca's lips, slow and sensuous. Simple lip locks, not deep and hungry. It sent charges throughout their bodies. Michael couldn't recall ever feeling that kind of charge. Rebecca's hands gripped and caressed his back, not knowing exactly what to do, wanting to do both at once. She found her hands traversing his back beneath his shirt. Her legs shifted restlessly. Michael rose away and pulled his shirt off over his head. Rebecca admired his body with a new want. Lean and cut; a runner. Not all muscle. Rebecca ran her hands up Michael's torso, feeling the warm hard flesh, every divot and bump. She reached up behind his neck and pulled him back down.

Their kiss was deeper now. One of Rebecca's hands grabbed onto Michael's back. He could feel her nails tentatively claw at him. Her other hand matted through his hair. She was beginning to shift impatiently beneath him. Michael slid his hand down the front of Rebecca's shirt, then up again beneath it. His hand slipped beneath her breasts' cotton guard and cupped it in gentle caresses. Soft moans echoed from the back of Rebecca's throat. She arched her back and began to pull up on her shirt. Michael broke their kiss long enough to slide her shirt up and over her head. He tossed the shirt onto the floor as he leaned back down into a kiss. Rebecca arched her back again as she felt Michael's hand trail behind her. He unlatched her bra strap in only a few motions. He pulled the shoulder straps down one by one, being careful not to aggravate Rebecca's stab wound, before removing it gently and letting it fall to the floor.

Michael's kiss traveled down Rebecca's neck and chest, each kiss slow, loving, and lingering. He kissed and plucked each pink bud softly with his lips before continuing down her stomach. Rebecca struggled to remain still, her breaths deep. Michael blew softly into her belly button, cause Rebecca to elicit a moan and arch her back. He continued down her stomach, kissing the button of her pants and down the zipper before repeating his kissing descent in reverse.

As Michael's lips traveled back up Rebecca's body, his hands traveled up her legs. One stopped at her thigh while the other continued up the side of her body. His hand trailed across the top of her pants and playfully pulled at its button before undoing it. His kisses trailed upon her neck as his fingers pulled the zipper down. Rebecca had her arms wrapped around Michael, pulling his body closer to hers. His hand slipped beneath her clothing and she turned her head from his kiss, enjoying the new feel of his lips everywhere on her body. Her breaths had become deep and heavy. The world beyond the two of them was fast becoming an illusion as his fingers teased the most sensuous parts of her body. Her legs instinctively closed together, wanting and not wanting the sensation all at once. Michael's lips settled on her neck, his hand upon her breast.

Rebecca became increasingly flustered. Her hands clawed down Michael's back, leaving red marks in their wake, before pulling her pants down and kicking them off. Rebecca held Michael tight and entangled her legs with his. Her breaths were deeper and faster. Her moans climbed higher and higher, every muscle in her body spasm. She was on the verge of exploding. She grabbed Michael's hand and pulled it away, letting the cascade of pleasure fade away. They locked eyes and Rebecca smiled up at him, her chest heaving. "You are good," Rebecca mewed. She pulled Michael's smiling face towards her and kissed him.

Rebecca sighed.

"I hope it's everything you've imagined it to be," Michael said.

"It's more," Rebecca replied. "I've never imagined anything like this."

"I've waited for this day a long time. I thought about it a lot. I wanted it to be perfect for you. I wanted to make your fondest memory. I'm so in love with you Rebecca, you have no idea."

"Why do you love me so much?"

"You have no idea how much you glow. You're like a beacon of hope in a world of darkness. From the first time I saw you, it was like you shined a light on my dark world, a light that was always missing. I could never find it. You helped me stumble out of the darkness into a world I had never seen. You stirred something in me that I just didn't understand. From the first time you swatted my hand away, I had wanted you like I had never wanted anyone. I just wanted to be near you. Just being next to you made me happy."

Rebecca looked at Michael with new eyes. Her heart fluttered. "I was your love at first sight, wasn't I?" Rebecca croaked.

"You're more than that. Sarah isn't my first love, Rebecca. You are."

Rebecca smiled up at him, her eyes misty. Rebecca had always had her doubts in the very back of her mind. She was always worried, always thought deep down that one day Michael would break her heart; that one day Sarah would steal him back. Suddenly, all those doubts went away. They vanished without a trace. It was Sarah that was the passing phase, not her. Rebecca knew, beyond the shadow of a doubt, that Michael would never hurt her like that. He would never walk away. Her lips were trembling when she kissed him. "I'm ready," she whispered.

"I'll be gentle," Michael whispered back.

Michael kicked his shoes off before pulling Rebecca's panties down her legs and throwing them onto the floor. He kissed her as he undid the button of his pants and pulled them off. All they had left were their socks.

Rebecca laid back and watched with both fear and excitement. Michael felt her warmth envelope him, hug him tight. Rebecca let out a yelp as she let Michael have her innocence. "Did I hurt you?" Michael asked. Rebecca smiled and shook her head. She wrapped her arms around him and pulled him close into a kiss. She broke the kiss with a gasp as Michael began to move. His thrusts were slow. Rebecca held him with her eyes closed, the world around the two gone. Her soft gasps blew into his ear. "Faster," she whispered. Michael moved faster, his thrusts becoming harder. Rebecca's body shuddered beneath him, her gasps becoming faster. Her hands clung onto his back, her toes curling as the moments went by. She rode the waves of emotion and pleasure as they grew within her. Michael's breathing intensified with Rebecca's. "I have to pull out soon," he said. Rebecca's nails clung to his back and she embraced him tightly against her. She wrapped her legs tightly around his waist. "Don't stop!" she cried out. "Don't you dare stop!" Michael whispered her name. They rode the increasing waves together. Michael winced as Rebecca's teeth tugged at his flesh, but it drove him further. Rebecca's moans were quick and loud, her body quivered. Michael's arms clung tight around her.

They rode the climaxing wave together. Rebecca tore her teeth away as she screamed alongside Michael in ecstasy. Michael's body relaxed atop her, but he did not let his full weight fall. Rebecca kissed across Michael's neck and shoulder, her body still shuddering, her breaths still falling. Michael kissed her lips; slow kisses.

"I love you Rebecca," Michael said.

"I love you too," Rebecca said. "Don't leave me."

"Never. I would die for you."

"Please don't."

They rolled over on the bed, kissing and pulling the covers over them. Their undying passion took them again and again. Each session of love making seemed better than the one before it. Nothing existed beyond them. Time didn't exist. The world and all its worries and troubles didn't exist. All that mattered was their two beating hearts. Their bodies entangled in a passionate kiss beneath the covers. Their heads rested against one another and sleep overcame them.

***

Rebecca and Michael walked through Millennium Park. Spring was well under way. They walked hand-in-hand on that warm spring day. They laughed and joked. The horrors Rebecca had known were gone. The birds sung. They watched the bustle of the city around them, the children running through the park. The park had just opened, missing its new millennium date. Michael stopped in the center of the park. They were talking. He had Rebecca close her eyes. He had a present. She wondered what it could be. It was their anniversary. Rebecca covered her eyes. When she opened them, Michael was down on one knee. In his hand was a box with a ring in it. A small diamond rested on the band.

"Rebecca Virtue," Michael said as shocked tears filled Rebecca's eyes. "You mean the world to me. My love knows no end for you. Would you be my wife? Will you marry me?"

Rebecca smiled as joyful tears ran down her face. It was the happiest moment of her life. The world around her stood still. "Yes, Michael," she answered. "I'll marry you." She reached for the ring, but a hand stopped her. Rebecca stared into Úna's sorrowful face.

"They won't let you have this," she said.

The ground began to rumble and the sky darkened. Spiked chains burst from the ground all around. Michael pulled Rebecca close. Screams filled the air as the chains lashed out, spilling blood and rending flesh. Rebecca's eyes darted panic stricken around the park. War advanced. Police confronted him and opened fire. War continued unharmed. Blades grew from his arms and sundered the officers as he passed. A mother's scream pulled Rebecca's eyes away. Famine had his hands gripped around small squirming forms. Rebecca cried as he stuffed them, crying, into his mouth. Rebecca spied Pestilence's dark visage. The military fired upon him. His form distorted as the bullets struck. A bazooka boom roared and a missile struck his face. His head jerked to the side. He wailed and spat vile green bile that washed over them. The soldiers sweated, hacked up blood and mucus, and turned a sickly green. The shadow of Death grew and enveloped the park.

Rebecca held Michael tight and cried. Chains ripped from War's body and raced forward. Michael pushed her away and became entangled in the sharp chains. Blood trickled down his body. "Michael!" Rebecca cried out. Michael screamed as his body was torn asunder. Rebecca watched as her entire future was torn from her. She fell to the ground and War continued to advance, sharp spikes and blades enveloped his fists and forearms.

"They will steal any hope of a future away from you," Úna said. "They will steal the world's future from it. Will you let them? Will all these deaths be in vain?"

With tear filled eyes, Rebecca watched as War approached. Slowly, she rose to her feet. "They will destroy everything, if you let them." Úna said. "Will you let them? Will you stand by and die?"

Fear filled Rebecca as she stared up at the massive form of War. He pulled his spiked fist back. Rebecca's left hand raised. Her eyes filled with dread. Gone. It was all gone. Her life was at an end. He swung. The erupting force, the released energy washed over Rebecca. Her raised hand had stopped his blow. Her hand was small against his fist. Her face was red with tears. Her eyes, filled with rage, stared up at the behemoth. Her teeth clenched tightly. Her right hand folded into a fist. Her body trembled in anger. Gone. It was all gone. They stole everything she had ever wanted. She wouldn't stand for it! She screamed and let her fist fly.

Rebecca's fist struck War squarely; his body buckled and shattered. The pieces blew away into oblivion. The ground shook and Famine roared. He was charging. Rebecca turned to face him. He leaped into the air. Rebecca threw herself to the side, away from Famine as he came down, buckling the ground beneath him. He turned towards Rebecca and inhaled deeply. Trees and benches uprooted from the force of the vacuum and descended into Famine's bottomless maw. Rebecca dug her fingers into the concrete ground, driving them in as an anchor. She would not budge.

Famine swallowed the refuse and charged. Rebecca stood her ground. The massive being swung its open hand down. Rebecca dashed forward and drove her fist into his gut. Famine reeled and took a few steps back. He swung his massive hands, trying to squash Rebecca between them. She braced herself and caught them. She screamed and delivered a kick that shattered the ground. Famine's form ripped in half and vanished without a trace.

Pestilence wailed as his unstable form raced across the field. His form circled Rebecca for a moment. She readied to fend off this new threat. His form reared up and descended upon her in a wave. She could not push him off and her body was enveloped. Pestilence's form stabilized. His middle began to bulge as a white glow came from within. Rebecca screamed and Pestilence's form was thrown to the four winds. She was glowing now. A gown of white covered her body and pure white wings stretched across her back. She hovered above the ground. Death's form advanced. They stood toe-to-toe. Death's empty eyes stared at Rebecca. She stared back unafraid. Slowly, Death began to open his mouth. A bright light began to glow from within his empty eye sockets and jaw. "No," Rebecca said simply. She raised her hand and placed it on the skull face of Death. Then she closed her fist. Death crumbled into dust.

Rebecca stared at the tattered robes of Death and watched as the wind whisked them away as they turned to ash and smoke. Rebecca looked up and Úna smiled back. "Giver of Life," she said. "I think you're ready."

***

Rebecca awoke in Michael's arms. She hugged him tightly. It was a dream. She had become so tired of dreams. She looked over her shoulder at the clock. It was almost five. Her parents would be home soon. Rebecca thought she would have perhaps another half hour with Michael. She felt strange. She felt ready, though she didn't know for what. Was it the end that she was ready for? She moved beneath the covers and kissed Michael. He stirred, but did not wake. He smiled in his sleep. Rebecca wondered what he was dreaming about. She smiled. She didn't mind that he didn't wake up. All she really wanted to do was hold him. That was enough. All she wanted to do was hold him for as long as she could.

CHAPTER XI

Rebecca let Michael sleep and clung to him for as long as she thought she could get away with. When she thought any longer risked being caught, she reluctantly woke him. Michael slowly stirred and clung to Rebecca.

"Hey beautiful," he smiled.

"Sleep well?" Rebecca smiled back.

"Best I've ever had. How much time do we have?"

Rebecca giggled. "You want to go again?"

"I just wanted to stay like this for awhile, if you can believe that."

Rebecca grinned her 'Tell me the truth' grin.

Michael laughed. "Honest, unless you want to go again."

"Three times is good."

Michael kissed her nose. "Honestly, I thought snuggling would be nice. Never really tried it."

Rebecca hummed satisfaction at his response. "Movie Night doesn't count?"

"Not the same. Your mom was always watching. We've never really been alone like this you know."

Rebecca smiled. "Yeah, I know. I wish we had more time, but my parents could be back any minute."

Michael hummed in thought. "I guess if I had the foresight, I should have parked on a different block. Then I could just sneak out the window."

Rebecca laughed. "Me too. Now come on, before they come home."

They rose and dressed. Rebecca kept eyeing the clock, hoping her parents wouldn't pull up as Michael was leaving. She was cutting it very close. At the last minute, Rebecca chose the original top she wore before choosing the V-neck. They walked hand-in-hand to the door.

"Do you think there's any way I can see you over the weekend?" Michael asked.

"I don't know," Rebecca answered. "I can ask."

"I don't want you to get into any more trouble. If worse comes to worse, I'll see you Monday."

"Yeah…Monday." That didn't sound real to Rebecca. Anything beyond the next day, Saturday, didn't sound real.

Michael stole a kiss, breaking her somberness. "Hey, I'll see you again," he said. "I'm not going anywhere."

Rebecca smiled and nodded. She watched Michael get into his car and drive away. She stood in the doorway long after he was out of sight. The cold wind blew into the house, but she didn't flinch. Goosebumps covered her skin, but she just clenched her fists, almost as if willing herself warm. Her heart was breaking.

"Come back," Rebecca whispered.

"He certainly is a rare fellow," Úna said.

Rebecca did not look for her. "I love him," she answered softly.

"And he you. Truly, his kind of love is rare. You pulled him from a life of sin. I wonder though, can you pull him from the Maw of Hell?"

Rebecca clenched her teeth tight. "I won't let him die."

"I'm sorry pumpkin. That's just not your decision to make."

Tears filled Rebecca's eyes and she closed the door. She didn't want to argue with the specter anymore. Rebecca sat on the couch and stared at the blank television screen. The only light came from the table lamp next to her. On the end table sat the television remote. She picked it up and continued to stare at the television. Waiting. That's all she was doing now. She was waiting for World's End.

Rebecca heard her parents at the front door and turned the television on. She started flipping through the channels, not really wanting to watch anything.

"Rebecca," Jeanine said. "We brought home food."

"Okay," Rebecca replied. She could smell the odor of cheeseburgers and highly salted French fries.

"Have you just been watching TV all day?" Jeanine put her jacket up before taking Eric's.

"I was bored," Rebecca answered as she stood up to take the drinks.

"The weather is so crazy right now," Eric said. "There is so much snow in Indiana."

Rebecca took the tray of drinks. "What did the doctor say?"

"He won't say much yet, not until the results of the MRI come back." He started to cough.

"Are you catching a cold?"

"Nothing I can't handle," Eric smiled as he followed his family into the kitchen. "I'm not going anywhere."

Rebecca smiled as she put the drinks on the table, but it felt forced and her heart sank. She threw her arms around Eric in a tight hug. "I love you Dad," she said.

"I love you too."

Rebecca turned and embraced her mother next. "I love you Mom."

"I love you too Rebecca," Jeanine said. "I know it's scary right now, but don't worry. Everything will turn out alright, you'll see." She started to cough. "I guess we caught something at the doctor's."

Rebecca's stomach tightened as Pestilence's grinning visage permeated into her mind. She felt that the end was coming ever so quickly. She wanted to hold onto as much as she could. As they ate dinner, Rebecca talked and laughed about the past. She talked first about their Christmas' together. She talked about their trips to Europe; to London, Rome, and Paris. She was five or six when they first visited London. She always liked hearing the story of how the giant clock tower, Big Ben, had mesmerized her. Their first night in the city, she fell asleep in the window after staring at the clock tower for hours. She remembered doing the same with the Eiffel Tower in Paris. She could also remember seeing giant winged creatures flying around it, but her parents passed what she saw as birds. They could not see them like she could. Now she wonders if they had seen them at all.

That memory brought out the story of Rebecca's first word. "It's a funny story," Jeanine said. "You had just turned one. It was nice out still so I thought it would be a good idea to take you out for awhile. I'm sure I just needed to get out of the house too." They all laughed. "Anyway, I dressed you up in your coat and all; it was October after all, and put you in your stroller and started to walk. Somewhere along the way we stopped and I sat down. We had been trying to get you to say momma or papa. You started to laugh and reached your tiny hands up into the air, like you were trying to grab something. Then you said your first word."

"Birdie?" Rebecca asked with a laugh.

Jeanine shook her head. "Angel. Your first word was angel."

The color flushed from Rebecca's face. Her first word was angel? Was that what she was reaching for, an angel? The table fell silent. Rebecca finished her drink, the empty slurp of the straw drowning the silence.

"Angel, huh?" Rebecca asked.

"You used to see angels everywhere," Eric said. "You always used to say, 'Can you see the angels, Daddy? Can you see the angels, Mommy?' Must run in the family."

"What do you mean?"

"My parents told me my brother and I used to do it all the time. My grandfather said my dad used to do it."

"I never realized your family was such angel fanatics," Jeanine laughed.

Eric shrugged. "I don't know. Maybe once, back in the day, we were very close with the church. I never really looked into it."

Rebecca touched her cross and remembered Demonic Angel's words, "Only a Virtue can use the powers of the Heavenly Weapons."

"Well, I'm tired," Jeanine said as she stood up and coughed. "I'm going to turn in early."

Rebecca helped her mother clear the table and they walked back into the living room. Rebecca had left the TV on. The seven o'clock news was playing. The title of the report was "Murders Continue". Rebecca came to a sudden halt. It was a picture of Peter that filled the screen. "A fifth body linked to the Angel Killings was discovered earlier this afternoon," the reporter said. "The body of Peter Skolic was found in his room by his parents. There were signs of forced entry and—" Jeanine pushed the power button on the remote, turning the television off. She turned to her daughter, whose eyes had filled with tears.

"Rebecca," she said.

Rebecca shook her head. "No," she whispered. "Not him too." Her hands became fists. "Why are you doing this?"

"Honey—" Eric started, but Rebecca screamed.

"Angel!"

***

Angel awoke with a start. The foyer of the church was chilly, but the heat was on. He stretched into a sitting position on the floor. He looked around. He was alone. He thought he had heard someone call out to him. He sighed. His imagination it seemed. Angel was worried. He had spent the day inside the church praying for strength, but feared his prayers simply fell on deaf ears. He had seen himself in the reflection of the church's windows; gray streaked the sides of his head. His face was beginning to wrinkle. He was aging.

Angel didn't know how much time he had left, but he knew what he had to do. His biggest concern was how to do it. If Rebecca really was of his blood, and all the evidence said that she was, then it was time for her to take over. Angel worried about her though. She had stood against his demonic with aid from an archangel, but would she be able to defeat Santano if he could not? Who would train her? Rebecca would become demon hunter under even worse circumstances than he. At least he had the training. The demon hunter had been dead to his bloodline for nine centuries. She was hope, but a frail hope.

Angel yawned and stretched. There was nothing more he could do so late in the day. He was tired. His vigor was deteriorating. He had to rest. Tomorrow he would return to the warehouse and plan out his next course of action. Tomorrow he would seek out Rebecca and try to convince her to fight. He had to convince her to fight. She was Earth's last hope.

Angel slipped out of the church with the early dawn. He did not want to be seen by the morning clergymen. He would be looked upon as little more than a squatter. He did not want to deal with their desire to help the unfortunate. He did not have the time. As Angel left the building, the harsh winds of Chicago's winter attacked his body. It was a painful reminder of his quickly waning powers. He was cold without his jacket to offer him warmth. He checked a small billfold in his back pocket. It contained a few twenties. It would be enough to buy a jacket or thick sweater. It would be better than nothing. Then he would make his way back to the warehouse.

***

Santano swung the Blood Sword with quick precision. He had been growing ever more proficient with it, training every day. With each sacrifice his skills and powers grew stronger. When donning Death's Visage, his powers jumped even more. He could only imagine his power when it was all done, when he was finally the most powerful and feared Horseman of all; Death. Satan's Presence watched Santano's ever growing training regimen. It had been the night before since Santano last slept, but he showed no signs of fatigue. Instead, he was anxious and Satan could feel it. Santano was at the half way mark. His powers were growing steadily.

After each swing Santano spoke a name, listing his possible victims aloud, "Brenda. Jeremy. Austin. Samantha. Camilla." Each named flashed information into his head. Each student's social ties. Their goals and location. Santano found most to be lackluster. All he cared about was his goal. He wanted his immortality.

"Remember my warning," Satan said. "Pace yourself. Your power will come."

"Can you blame me?" Santano asked. He relaxed his form and faced the flames. "I want to hurry and get this over with before Angel gets lucky."

"Angel's powers are rapidly draining. He stands little chance against you."

"It's a chance I don't want to give him." Santano thought for a moment. "What about that trump card you were talking about? Is that something I have to worry about?"

"At the moment, no. Our goal at current is to begin the Collection. She will be dealt with then."

"You mentioned that when you turned Demonic Angel loose. What is it?"

"The Collection is the gathering of the final sacrifices to begin the ceremony to seal your power."

"I have to take the last five alive?"

"Yes. They will not be of your choice, but of my choosing, pure souls. Souls of innocence, faith, even redemption."

"How do I go about kidnapping five people? What is this ceremony? What's so special about it?"

"Patience, my avatar. You will not undertake this task alone. I will send you reinforcements in the form of the current Horsemen's Underlings. They will help you in this task."

"What about Angel and his trump card?"

"His trump card I will use to my advantage. When she interfered with Angel's battle against his demonic, she opened a loop hole in the rules."

"A loop hole?"

"As I told you, the demon hunter may be faced with only one threat a day. The only aid he can garner is from his angelic guardian, who Angel was abandoned by. As you are aware, if you force the Blood Sword to drink in extra souls, Heaven will release an angel against you. There is a similar clause for the demon hunter. I had chosen Rebecca Virtue as one of my Chosen, and it was she that defeated Demonic Angel. In doing so, she has awarded us an additional threat to face Angel with. I will summon this threat now."

Remembering the power of the first summoning, Santano stepped back. The top left point of the pentagram began to glow as demonic symbols encircled it, just as the top point had done during Demonic Angel's summoning. The massive flame of the Circle flickered violently and the room began to rise in temperature. Santano noted that didn't happen the last time. Streams of fire began to slither off the massive flame and encircle the glowing point, surrounding it in a ring of fire. "Fires of rage, flames of lust," Satan spoke. The circling flames grew. "Embers of insanity, sparks of vengeance." The candle within melted, leaving only the length of the burning wick. "Forsaken inferno and lost light. I call you through the Gates." The flames of the wick grew into a flaming oval. "I activate this second pact and summon forth the flames of arson." A pair of funnels the color of red flames burst from the center and began to pull the oval open. "Your master calls you. Come forth minion of the flame." A small form began to push through the tight opening. "Flamers, send me one of your own! Your Lord commands it!" The red flaming demon within struggled with the burning portal. "Come onto the mortal world! Burn and consume! Flamer, answer my call!"

The demon shouted and tore the flaming portal asunder. Flames scattered about the room and died into cold embers. Santano shielded himself from the flames as the demon came through. He looked the small grinning demon over. It stood with a hunch, but had no physical abnormalities to cause this. Its flesh was the color of red flames and its body masculine in appearance, its body thin with a toned frame. In place of hands it had funnels instead. Flames licked the edges. Its dark eyes held burning flames within. Flames burned atop its head as hair. The demon stretched and shivered.

"Why is the Earth always so cold?" it asked in a male voice that crackled like flames.

"What is that?" Santano asked.

The demon grinned at him. It aimed a funnel-hand at its own body and began to bathe itself in flames. "I am a flamer," it said. "A demon born of sinful flames and careless arson. Flames are my domain." It shrugged. "I'm one of the basic fire demons."

"And you can beat Angel?"

"Probably. He's weak now, even by demon hunter standards. I should be able to hold my own."

"Not as confidant as that Demonic Angel."

"He was very strong. I'm a low level demon, but I have a little surprise for Angel. It's something I can only do on Earth."

"And what would that be?"

The demon smiled. "Well now, that's the surprise, isn't it?" Fire spilled from his funnels and wrapped around his body, enveloping him. Once he was consumed, the flames died and the demon was gone.

Santano crossed his arms and thought. "Rebecca huh?" An image of her flashed in his mind. "Yeah, she's defiantly a good kid. The only trouble she's ever been in is being late for class."

"Yes." Satan said. "The purest soul of the five. It is her sacrifice that will seal your power."

"So after one more sacrifice, we can begin this Collection thing?"

"Yes."

"So I could kidnap her after making this next sacrifice?"

"That is correct."

Santano closed his eyes. "Alright, where are you going to be?"

Santano found it hard to delve into her mind. It was almost as if some force was trying to block him. All he seemed able to glean were fragments of her surface thoughts. Fear. Angel. Confusion. Nicholas. In the flurry of fragmented thoughts that caught Santano's attention. He gleaned something about a meeting. He wondered why Rebecca would meet with someone she never conversed with? It proved too difficult to pull information from her mind. Santano thought perhaps because of her purity. He tried Nicholas instead. Santano found Nicholas' mind much easier to probe. He quickly poked about the youth's mind for his meeting with Rebecca.

Santano opened his eyes. "She's going to tutor him, but he has something else in mind." Santano chuckled. "I guess the rumors are true after all." Santano looked at Satan's Presence and sighed. "He's not really a pure soul though, is he? His sacrifice would mean nothing, wouldn't it?"

"You should probe deeper," Satan said. "Though Nicholas may be a derelict by mortal standards, he is far from a corrupted soul. He is young and driven by hormones. It is this time that a human is most susceptible to sin, Nicholas' being lust. Look again."

Santano closed his eyes and looked back into Nicholas' mind. He focused more, reading more than just surface thoughts. Fear, or perhaps nervousness, filled Nicholas' core. He delved deeper. He saw drinking and flashes of light. He saw Stacy and Marcy, and their flushed faces. He saw one passed out on the floor, he wasn't sure which. Nicholas' body mingled with another. Santano witnessed an argument and threats; then photographs and blackmail.

Santano opened his eyes. "He didn't rape anyone. They got drunk and frisky. Nicholas took pictures of them. Then one found out she may be pregnant and started the rumor to cover her ass." Santano laughed. "Are you kidding?"

"It was unacceptable to her parents," Satan said, "so they decided to blame Nicholas for rape. She claimed she had no choice. Nicholas threatened releasing the pictures online and made her retract her statement."

"Was she pregnant?"

"Does it matter? She tried to destroy his life to keep up her appearance. In return for that attempt, Nicholas has managed to keep them both under his thumb. But he has not pressed his luck, until now."

"So he would count? His soul isn't corrupt?"

"Not enough to make a difference."

"Then I'll defiantly target Nicholas. That way we can get Rebecca for the Collection."

"An excellent strategy."

"What about the other four? How does the ceremony even work? Why can't I just cut them up like the rest?"

"The first five sacrifices set up and empower the five seals that you need to break to receive the True Form's destructive power. The seals are protected by the four natural elements. Only the purest of souls can break the seals. This is why you cannot choose them."

"Alright, but can't you—"

"Not yet. Soon. Today it will be done. We both have much preparation to make, so no more questions. Angel now knows about your intended target, so let us hope the flamer can grant us the time we need."

***

Angel pulled the burgundy sweater over his head in the confines of an alley. The Sword of Might rested against a wall beside the light suede coat he had bought. He pulled the jacket on before strapping the Sword of Might to his back. He gathered up the store bags and threw them into a nearby trashcan. The cold wind raced down the alley. The sweater and jacket shielded him from the worst of it. He raised the jacket's hood and faced his back to the wind. He was broke now, but hopefully it wouldn't matter. This may be his last crusade. In the meantime he had to prepare for his next course of action. He had to prepare for a final confrontation with Santano and convince Rebecca to train under him, at least for a short while.

Angel made his way back to the warehouse with the power of Quickstep. He didn't exert himself too much, keeping the pace to a minimum. He didn't want to drain his power, but he didn't want to waste his time either. Angel arrived at the warehouse in several minutes, a fraction of the time it would have taken him at a mortal pace. He entered the main room. Rays of sunlight peeked into the room from the high windows, but the room was still dark. Angel held his rusted, dull dagger aloft and said, "Dagger of Power. Light." The Dagger of Power's blade began to glow and the light spread to fill a quarter of the room, far from the small space it had illuminated only a few days before.

Angel's jaw dropped. Before Rebecca had held it, it hadn't radiated such light without considerable effort on his part in decades. Angel examined the dagger's blade. The rust had lessened and the lighter parts had chipped away to reveal the pure steel beneath. Angel could hardly believe what he was seeing. Was Rebecca's mere touch enough to repair and strengthen the Heavenly Weapons? Was she that strong? Angel raised the Dagger of Power high overhead. It should not have enough power left between Quickstep and Light. "Dagger of Power!" Angel called out. "Eternal Light!" The dagger's blade glowed brightly and stretched out across the room, drowning every corner in light as bright as day. Angel eyed the room in awe. It still had that much power? How much did it still have?

Angel drew the Sword of Might from its sheath and examined its blade. It had the same kind of repairs as the Dagger of Power. He could barely believe his eyes. Angel brought his weapons close to him. He closed his eyes and let out a long exhale, clearing his mind. As he entered a meditated state, a white aura appeared around his body, clinging to his form and making his outline glow. He concentrated harder. Beads of sweat began to dot his forehead. The glow passed onto the Heavenly Weapons. The aura clung to the edges of the weapons and began to waif off into a mist. As their aura's unified, Angel's aura drew from the Heavenly Weapons, drawing in the mist and making his glow slightly brighter and slightly larger. The difference wasn't much visibly, but Angel could feel it. The weapons, and by extension his own power, was drawing strength from Rebecca. It drew strength from her very blood and faith. Angel could feel his lost powers still closed to him, but the blades powers were not draining as quickly. He wagered that perhaps their powers had actually increased.

Angel breathed, breaking the mediation and with it the white aura. He stared at the Heavenly Weapons before sheathing them, allowing them to replenish their power. Angel looked about the lighted room. Completely lit, he had found that the warehouse was in fact a factory. He was not sure what they built, but machinery rested across the room to his left. Long beltways and crates ran the length of the room. Crates stacked to his right and near them stairs leading up to a set of offices to oversee the work below. The ceiling above was decorated with hanging lights attached to rafters and support beams. All around, targets aplenty. At first, Angel didn't notice the smile that crept across his lips. Though it needed to be done, Angel found himself surprised that he was preparing to do it. He had not done it since the sixteenth century. He had always tried to conserve his powers since then. Angel faced the crates and reached back to grip the handle of the Sword of Might. Yes, it made him feel young again, even with his rapidly graying hair and waning vitality, but it was more than that. It gave him hope that he stood a fighting chance. He was going to see just what he could do.

Angel charged the crates. So excited and full of vigor that he could not help but cry out a battle cry. The Sword of Might was drawn and struck. The crate splintered in half as its top flew off into the air. Angel drew the Dagger of Power and faced it to the crates. Cutting the command phrase, Angel found his muscles flexed as he shouted, "Whirlwind!" He could feel his will force the attack over the edge and unleash the gusting winds. He had not been able to do that in so long. As the powerful hurricane winds whipped the crates into the air, Angel found he liked the long forgotten rush and wanted to do it again. He focused his power and shouted, "Holy Strike!" A white glow appeared on the sword's blade. The glow was bright, making the blade almost appear as if it was made of that glow, save for the rust that peeked through and marred the light.

Angel crouched low, focusing strength in his legs. He leaped into the air, into the swirling crates above him. With one strike to a single target, the glow of the sword unleashed into a chaotic energy, jumping around the various targets in a chain effect, destroying each crate as the divine energy ripped through them. Angel's leap aimed for the beams dozen of feet above. He used the crates as they fell as landings to keep his momentum up. His leaps brought him to an unbalanced landing on the rafter beams.

Angel was amazed that he was actually able to pull that off, even if it did take extra effort. It took only a few seconds for Angel to find his balance on the thin beam. He began to sprint down the narrow planks. In his path were roof supports. Angel held the Heavenly Weapons to his side as balancers and shouted, "Heavenly Weapons! Dual Impact!" The weapons hummed with power. As Angel neared the supports he swung. The beam blew out, leaving an opening for Angel to move through. As he ran down the beams he struck the supports that would not overly damage the integrity of the roof and simply leaped to a nearby beam when he could not strike. Each leap fought his balance but he did not fall.

Angel looked down as he approached the machinery. He leaped towards them and shouted, "Meteor Strike!" He could feel his will force the sword's power. The blade was consumed in flames and with a single swing several flaming rock cores rained down upon the machines. The small meteors smashed the machines effortlessly, igniting flames and smoke. Angel landed in the destruction's midst and unleashed Whirlwind to kill the fires. Smoke fumes rose into the air. Angel looked around exhausted and admired his handiwork. He could not help but smile. Some of his power had in fact returned and the Heavenly Weapons were strengthened. Angel could feel the drain on his body, but for three such powerful consecutive attacks and to still have power left was amazing.

Angel admired his weapons. "That was amazing," he said between breaths. "There is still some power left. Not much, but some. Holy Strike and Meteor Strike alone should have drained their powers for hours. I have no doubt now. She is a Virtue. There is still hope." The Sword of Might began to hum in warning. Angel's smile instantly faded and his face became stern. "Show me," Angel said. In his mind's eye several images began to form. The images were ripped away as a wall of flames sprang up before him. Angel leaped away and sheathed his weapons to replenish their strength. He needed time and distance from the demon that had come to challenge him. Santano had chosen; Angel was sure of it. But why send a demon to occupy his time? If the demon did not come to fight, Angel would simply leave. He would not allow his time to be wasted again.

The demon stood erect as it adjusted its shoulders. Angel could hear its bones pop. He recognized the demon. It was not his first encounter with its kind.

"A flamer," Angel said.

The flamer hunched back over and looked about the room. "Looks like it's true," he said. "She is a Virtue. She powered up those weapons nicely, didn't she? This should be fun."

"I don't have time for you. Be gone demon."

"Too bad. I wanna play."

The flamer lifted his funnels and from them spewed forth cones of flame. Still too close to rely solely on his own agility, Angel used Quickstep to evade the flames and put greater distance between the two.

"You're attacking me?" Angel shouted. "I'm dealing with the avatar! You would risk Heaven's wrath?"

The flamer wagged his funnel-hand as if he were wagging a finger. "What risk? This is legal. Rebecca aided you. Don't you know? Your blood counts as Heavenly help."

Shock washed over Angel's face. Was that true? Help from his kin had never been an option before. Humans had helped him in the past, but never his own kin. He thought them to be dead. "It's true," a soft voice whispered. "Fight." Angel realized that the flamer did not come to attempt to occupy his time, as Satan had done. It came with a purpose. It would not give Angel the choice.

Angel pulled his blades free and darted forward. The flamer raised his funnels in retaliation and spewed flames from his flamethrower-like arms. Angel gathered the strength in his legs and leaped over the fire plumb. The flamer raised a funnel towards Angel and unleashed a new flame torrent. Angel shifted his weight in his descent and barely evaded the flames in a spin. He landed only a few short yards away from the flamer and pivoted the instant his foot touched down and charged. The flamer turned and raised his funnels in defense. The Sword of Might scrapped across the red flesh. The sounds of grinding metal echoed and small sparks flew from the impact zone. Angel continued to press forward as each blow was blocked. Blow after blow bounced off the dense funnel flesh, each blow pushing the grinning demon back. Already dangerously close to his second breath each swing slowed. The flamer evaded Angel's slowest swing and used a funnel to pin the Sword of Might to the ground.

Angel saw the opening and thrust the Dagger of Power. The flamer, taken by surprise, shifted his body and the dagger's blade cut into his face. The demon struck Angel in the stomach with the funnel's side and knocked the air from his lungs, as well as pushing him back. The hit was strong. Angel managed to stay on his feet, but slid across the ground. He used the Sword of Might as an anchor and slowed his motion. The flamer trained his funnels on Angel and fired. Angel brought the dagger forward and shouted, "Psionic Shield!" His will, tiring, forced the ability over. A tarnished translucent green field grew from the dagger's hilt before Angel and blocked the flames. The flamer laughed as Angel used all his strength to keep the shield intact.

The shield soon began to crack under the constant assault. Angel knew it would break at any moment. He was pinned and had little options available to him. His Halo wasn't strong enough to protect him from such a direct assault, even if he had the holy dust needed to strengthen it. Rebecca had all that now. So excited by the prospect that she was his descendent that he didn't think to empty his pockets before leaving his coat behind. Now Angel regretted it. It limited his defensive abilities. Even without them, he had to do something. He did not survive nine centuries and rediscover his bloodline just to be bested by such a lowly demon.

Angel glanced around, looking for something to use to his advantage. The shield was cracking quickly and becoming difficult to maintain. Above, Angel noticed the rafters he had run across. They were splintered and weak. A main support beam held the structure in place. If he destroyed that beam it would cause the roof to collapse, hopefully atop the flamer. If nothing else, it would break the attack. Angel had to act fast. He used much of his weapons power already and hadn't given them ample time to recharge. He could feel their power slipping away. Angel took aim and focused his energy into the sword. It was barely enough. "Sword of Might!" he shouted. "Holy

Strike!" The blade glowed white and Angel hurled it at his target. The flamer's eyes trailed the twirling sword as it flew through the air. It hit the support beam and bright flashes of light blazed around and struck the surrounding structure. The remaining creaked and swayed with their support gone.

The flamer's face flooded with the realization of what Angel's intent was. All at once, the pieces of wood began to fall and then the roof followed suit. The flamer's assault halted and both he and Angel leaped away from the collapsing roof. Angel quickly sheathed his dagger but kept his grip on it. It needed more time to regain its strength, more time than Angel could afford to give. He also needed to retrieve the Sword of Might. The flamer stood erect and popped its back before hunching over again. It looked about the room and then towards Angel across the debris barrier.

"That wouldn't have hurt me, you know," the flamer said. "Not much, anyway."

"I know, but it would have slowed you down," Angel answered.

The demon sighed. "This is boring. I can see without some luck we're going to be at a stalemate." Then he smiled. "Why don't I liven things up? I've been waiting to come back to Earth so I could evolve."

Angel's face filled with concerned shock. He had heard the phrase 'evolve' before. He had known of the phrase even before Charles Darwin had coined it. It was how lesser demons became stronger, turning into more powerful entities. Angel knew a demon could only evolve on Earth, but the process was long and not easy. They had to accumulate enough evil deeds or innocent souls before a demon could evolve. That was the basics, though Angel was sure it was more involved than that. It took at least a century to accomplish that though, so this demon was no amateur. It had experience. Part of Angel was concerned about what kind of power the flamer would gain after it evolved, while another part of him was curious of how a demon went about their evolution. In nine centuries, he had never witnessed it. Either way, Angel was torn. Allow the flamer the time it needed to allow the Dagger of Power a little more time, or attack it outright? In the end, neither was a good alternative.

"Are you ready?" the flamer asked with a grin. He stood erect and pointed his funnels at the ground. The flames licking the funnel's edge turned black. "I call upon the flames of darkness," he said. Plumbs of black fire spewed from the funnels and painted an encircled pentagram on the floor around him. "Look upon me and my deeds. Accept my sins." The flames grew up around the flamer, towering. The towering flames twisted around the demon. "Fires of darkness, give me the power to incinerate!" The towering streams converged into one mass and then compressed against the demon within. Inside the flamer cried out, almost painfully, in an ever deepening tone. The flames absorbed into a large featureless mass. The mass slowly became humanoid, crouched over and in pain. The demon's scream had drowned into a low roar. Suddenly, the form threw its body out, scattering the dark flames across the room and setting the warehouse ablaze. Angel dove behind the fallen debris to shield himself from the unholy flames even as it caught fire. Angel peered over the debris and through the flames.

This demon was larger in all ways than the flamer; taller than Angel, at least six feet. His body was large and toned. His skin was the color of ash and soot and burning flames danced about his massive frame. Powerful hands flexed where funnels once were. His head was bald and free of flames, but his ember eyes had flames dancing within. Angel knew this demon as an incinerator and vastly more powerful than a flamer. The incinerator looked back at Angel with a vindictive grin.

Angel held tight his sheathed dagger and whispered, "Dagger of Power." He leaped to his feet and drew the dagger. "Whirlwind!" With the blade pointed toward the incinerator, hurricane-like winds ripped free. The incinerator stood fast against the winds but gave ground. He tried to advance, taking a few slow steps. Angel concentrated, increasing the ferocity of the winds. The flames on the incinerator's arms intensified as he was pushed further back. He slammed his fist into the ground and a line of fire erupted. Angel leaped back and shouted, "Quickstep!" The fire stream ripped through Angel's image and he appeared several yards away on the demon's flank. The demon pivoted as Angel rushed forward and slammed both blazing fists into the ground. A wave of flames erupted. Angel's form blurred again and he circled the demon once more, appearing behind him and several more yards away. The incinerator slid his hands down his arms, catching the flames on it as he pivoted again and spun the flames into a ball. The flaming sphere quickly grew to the size of a basketball. Cupping a large portion in one hand, the incinerator thrust the larger sphere forward, sending the fireball towards Angel. The fireball passed through Angel's blurred form and exploded when it struck the machine belt. Angel appeared a few yards away from that point and a little closer to the demon. The incinerator quickly spun the fireball large again and, repeating the process, thrust the larger portion forward, leaving a little behind in his other hand. The sphere ripped through Angel's afterimage and stuck the ground. The explosion rocked the fanning flames.

Again and again the incinerator would spin and hurl a fireball as Angel Quickstepped away. Angel spied the Sword of Might amongst the ruble and made his way to it in a few leaps. Moving as he was, he couldn't stand still long enough to call it to him. He gripped the sword and shouted, "Keen Edge!" One swing and the fireball was cut in half, hurdling in two different directions and exploding when they hit the ground. The demon's barrage stopped. Angel was breathing heavily and out of breath. He only had a few more jumps left in him. The flame in the incinerator's hands burned back into his arms. "You're good at evading," the demon said, "but you look tired. If I'm boring you, I'll liven things up." The incinerator kneeled and touched his hand to the ground. "Let's get this party really cookin'."

The flames on the incinerator's body intensified again and burned down his arm. The flames climbed onto his hand and encircled him in a ring of fire. The circle's flames burned high, about a foot or so. "Incinerate," the demon said. The flames suddenly spanned out in an ever growing wave that struck all sides of the room and licked the roof, setting the entire structure ablaze. Angel leaped back as his hand went to his silver cross. He touched it and shouted, "Halo!" With the hasty halo in place, Angel split the wave with Whirlwind. The halo absorbed the flames and heat that caressed his body as it passed.

Smoke quickly filled the room and obscured visibility. Angel used Whirlwind in an attempt to scatter the smoke and kill the fire, but it did little good. Under the veil of smoke the incinerator had gone on the move. The smoke was becoming thick and filled Angel's lungs.

"Where is he?!" Angel demanded between coughs. Weapons at the ready, Angel looked around, trying to find so much as a silhouette.

"I'm right here!" the incinerator shouted as he rammed his shoulder into Angel's back.

Angel felt the sudden explosion of heat on his back as he was sent skidding across the floor. He could only maintain his grip on the Heavenly Weapons during the first few connections with the ground before each went flying in a different direction. Angel had bounced over half the length of the room by the time his momentum came to a stop. His back burning and his body aching, Angel tired to stand. He could hear the incinerator charging as if he were a train. Pain jolted through Angel's face as his head turned sharply from the hot kick. Blood flew from his mouth. Strong, hot hands gripped his back and lifted him off the ground. "Ready to go for a ride?" The incinerator spun Angel around a few times, quickly building speed. The demon's grip was burning and Angel was in a daze. The incinerator threw Angel across the room and through a burning wall.

Smoke and debris filled Angel's lungs. He could hear the incinerator's slow approach. He coughed and struggled to stand. He felt a hand on his back, pushing him back to the ground. It was warm, but not like the incinerator's touch. He felt a presence cover his body as he was pressed down. "I'm going to burn you alive!" the incinerator shouted. Even with the Heavenly Weapons empowered by Rebecca, Angel was still overpowered.

"I must fight," Angel muttered.

A voice softly cooed in his ear. "Rest," it said. Then darkness enshrouded him.

Angel awoke in an unfamiliar bed. He wasn't sure how long he had been unconscious or where he was. He could hear the murmurs of conversations and the tic-tac of key strokes. Monotonous beeps sounded nearby. As Angel's eyes focused in the light, he realized he was in a hospital room. His wounds were bandaged and he was wired to various machines tracking his vitals. One hand was handcuffed to the bed. He was still wearing his jeans and shoes, but his shirt and jacket had been removed. He found them resting inside a clear bag on the floor. Angel looked towards the partially closed door. A red-headed female officer stood guard. She was talking and laughing with someone else that kept coming in and out of view.

Angel's body ached, a constant reminder of his defeat at the hands of the incinerator. He tested the cuff, readying to break it, when he noticed it had some slack around his wrist. With some pain and effort, he slipped the cuff over his hand. The guard was occupied, so Angel would be able to move around unhindered for a short while. He climbed out of bed and turned the machines off before disconnecting the wires. He put his clothes back on, keeping an eye on the guard, praying she wouldn't turn around. His weapons were gone, as Angel had expected, but were they still in the hospital? He looked at the guard again. She was still talking to what appeared to be an intern. Angel took a deep breath, closed his eyes, and focused. He reached out his senses, searching for the radiation that the Heavenly Weapons gave off. Some lingered, but it was weak. They had been taken only recently. Angel would be able to track them easily.

Angel went to the window and looked out it. Four stories up. It was not a jump he wanted to make, but one he feared he would have to. The window was sealed and had to be broken. He looked around the room. Only one chair. The door opened in, so if he was lucky he could block it with the chair. If he was fast enough. He looked back towards the door. The officer and intern were laughing. She seemed confident that Angel was still unconscious and would be for awhile. Angel looked at the clock. It was after seven. The sky was already dark. Hours had passed. He was certain the Collection had already begun. The sacrifices may well be underway. He had to hurry and retrieve the Heavenly Weapons.

Angel took hold of the chair and approached the window. With an overhead swing, the glass shattered. The officer shouted at Angel as she threw the door open. Angel turned and whipped the chair across the room. The officer pulled the door closed as the chair struck. Angel darted across the room and threw this weight into the door as she tried to open it again. Angel could hear her shouting and felt the door shutter as she threw her weight into it. Angel took the chair and propped it under the handle, blocking the door. The door and chair shook with each ram of the officer. It would not hold long. Angel made his way to the shattered window and began to scale down the building, dropping from window to window. Escape was the easy part. He still had to retrieve his weapons and he had a good idea of where to start looking.

Angel pried open a manhole cover and descended beneath the streets. In the sewers he would be unmolested and could lock onto the Heavenly Weapons location. He just hoped he wasn't too late.

Angel raced through the cramped sewer system at full speed. He was grateful for the viaducts and open basins he passed along the way. He felt out the celestial radiation of the Heavenly Weapons as he traversed the underground system. Angel was very much out of breath by the time he reached his destination. He lifted the manhole cover slightly, allowing him to peer and listen for vehicles. He heard only the howl of the wind. Angel slide the heavy cover aside and found he had emerged in an alley behind the police station. The radiation's pull was strongest from inside. The cold air bit at his face and lungs, causing him to cough. Chicago's winter wind raced down the alley's wind tunnel and chilled Angel. He used his sleeve to wipe the run from his nose.

Angel peered through a barred window that looked down into the basement of the station. The halls were deserted. Angel tested the bars. They were sturdy and bolted in place. He tugged them. The bars shook, but Angel could not pull them free. He exhaled, closed his eyes and bowed his head in prayer. "Lord God," Angel whispered, "help me to know my ability, that I may not attempt with weakness that which requires strength to undertake. Amen." Angel could feel his arms fill with strength. He planted his feet firmly and began to pull on the bars. The iron began to bend under the pressure and the bolts broke. The barred shielding broke free in Angel's hands. The momentum forced Angel a few steps back before he put the bars down. He tried the window and found it was unlocked. He slid it open and entered the station.

Angel made the three or four foot drop and slid the window closed. He waved a hand slowly through the air, seeking out the pull and feel of the

Heavenly Weapons. Once he found it, he followed it to a small storage area. The door read "Evidence Room" and was locked with a deadbolt and padlock. Angel's arms still surged with celestial strength, but he could feel it fading. He gripped the padlock and concentrated the remaining strength into his hand. He twisted until the lock broke free in his grip. He let it fall to the ground and rubbed the pain from his fingers and palm. Angel took a step back and delivered a powerful kick, removing his next obstacle. The wood frame splintered as the deadbolt broke free. Leg throbbing, Angel limped inside and felt for his weapons. He found them waiting patiently behind a chain linked fence. The lock was weak and after a moment Angel tore the fence open. He strapped the Dagger of Power to his waist and exposed the Sword of Might's blade. "Show me Santano and his target," he said. Several images entered his mind's eye. He saw Santano slinking into a home. He saw Rebecca and Nicholas. There was something wrong with Rebecca. She was on the ground and Nicholas was standing over her. Three shadows entered his mind and approached slowly. The elements began to wail.

Angel shook his head. The visions vanished. Santano was on the move, Rebecca was in danger, and the Collection was about to begin. Angel knew where he had to be and had little time to waste.

CHAPTER XII

Eric was looking pale that evening. When Rebecca kissed him good-bye, she noticed that his skin was dry. He wasn't looking well, but he assured her that he was fine. He was just coming down with the flu and would make it to bed early. Rebecca was worried. She thought it was more than that. She wanted to cry when she kissed him and told him good-bye.

Jeanine wasn't fairing much better than Eric, though her symptoms were different. Rebecca really noticed on the drive to Nicholas' house. It was cold out and Jeanine had the window cracked open. There were beads of sweat on her forehead and she had not turned on the heater. Rebecca turned it on because she was cold. Jeanine insisted she was just having a hot flash and was fine. Rebecca didn't think that kind of hot flash was normal. She looked to the window, expecting to see Úna come in its reflection. The only reflection she saw as the street lights lit up the window was her own. Úna never came.

Jeanine pulled up to Nicholas' house. Rebecca stared out at it for a moment. It looked normal enough. The lights were on and it looked inviting enough. It really wasn't creepy at all, but that didn't stop Rebecca's stomach from twisting. She really wasn't sure about this, but wasn't entirely sure her apprehension wasn't from something else.

"Just call me when you're done," Jeanine said.

"It shouldn't be more than an hour or two," Rebecca said. "Just come get me around eight."

Jeanine smiled at her daughter. "Alright. I'll be back at eight."

Rebecca moved to give Jeanine a hug and could feel the heat coming off her body. When she kissed Jeanine's cheek, she was very hot. "Be careful Mom," Rebecca said. "You're burning up."

"Don't worry. I'm alright."

Rebecca wanted to protest, but didn't. "Alright. Good-bye Mom."

"Bye sweetie."

Rebecca gathered her belongings; her backpack and thermus of tea, and exited the car. She slowly approached the house, looking back to Jeanine sitting in the car. Rebecca knew she wouldn't leave until she was safely inside. Rebecca rang the door bell and waited. A moment passed. She hadn't heard the bell through the door and wondered if it worked. What luck would it be if it didn't? She motioned to ring it again when the handle jiggled.

Nicholas threw the door open, almost in a panic. "Sorry," he whispered. "My parents are asleep. They weren't feeling well."

"I'm sorry. I don't think mine are either. Maybe we should reschedule?"

"Naw. I'm sure it's nothing. Just some bug going around probably. We just have to be quiet."

"Right," Rebecca said, disappointed.

Nicholas invited Rebecca in and waved to Jeanine. Rebecca turned to wave. The car windows were fogged as the car pulled away. "Good-bye Mom," Rebecca whispered. It felt like her last good-bye.

Santano sat in the dark of his car just down the street and watched the events transpire. The car was off; it had been off for nearly an hour. Vapors escaped Santano's mouth with each breath, but he wasn't cold, not much. He poured more coffee from his thermus into its cap cup. The Blood Sword rested in the passenger seat beside him. Santano smiled. "Looks like the show's about to begin," he mused. "I hope it's entertaining." He looked to the Blood Sword. "I think I'll watch some of it first. Angel is occupied, and even if he does get here in time to interfere, I can beat him."

Nicholas began touring Rebecca through his house, talking in a low tone. First he showed her the coat closet to hang her coat up. He had commented on it, saying the trench coat wasn't her usual affair. Rebecca had answered that she had borrowed it from Peter, keeping to the same story she had told her parents, but now that he was gone she guessed it was hers. There was an awkward silence for a moment before Nicholas offered his condolences.

The front door entered into the living room, so Rebecca was toured there first. There was a tanned couch against one wall facing a large television at the other end of the room. The television sat in a black burnished stand with two tall towers on either side. The towers were made of glass and housed football memorabilia in one and statues and trinkets of tigers and lions in the other. A loveseat sat at an angle towards the television with an end table on either side. In the center of the room was a coffee table. In the corner of the room was a recliner with a reading lamp over it and a bookshelf full of various books against the wall.

"Someone likes to read." Rebecca said.

"My mom," Nicholas said. He pointed across the room towards one of the thresholds. "The kitchen's that way."

Rebecca nodded and started towards it.

"There's not really much to show," Nicholas said. "It's a kitchen. They're all pretty much the same."

"It's a good place to study," Rebecca answered.

"Yeah, I guess, but I thought my study would be better."

Rebecca turned with an almost insulted scoff. "You're bedroom doesn't count as a study."

"My bedroom? Wait—" Nicholas laughed. "You think I'm talking about my bedroom?" He pointed to a closed door. "That's there and a mess. My study is upstairs, by my parents' room and the full bathroom."

Rebecca started to turn red. "Full bath—?"

"Yeah. There's a half-bath on this floor. My study has a large desk, a small fridge, pretty much everything I could need when I'm studying. You thought I wanted to take you to my room?"

Rebecca looked away and bit her lower lip. "Well—I'm sorry."

"Like I said, they were rumors; as in not true." Nicholas began towards the curved staircase. He turned around at the steps and said, "My parents' room and study are on the second floor. Or would you rather be in the kitchen? It's up to you. I just think the study would be more comfortable."

Rebecca felt terrible. Nicholas was trying to be a good host, but all she did was act as if he was acting like a jerk. He must have been used to it since he managed to keep his composure throughout it all. Still, something felt wrong to her, but she wasn't sure if it was Nicholas and the rumors, or just everything that's happened to her this past week. What she had been going through would make anyone jumpy. She tried to push the feelings away, deciding that it was all the murders and dreams making her on edge. Besides, his parents were upstairs. With them that close by, she doubted he would try anything. "No, we can go up," Rebecca said. "I'd like to see your study at least. Having one is kind of cool."

Nicholas smiled a nod and led her up the stairs. He pointed out the bathroom and his parents' room, his voice low to not disturb them. They passed by and continued down the hall. He pointed out what he said was a walk-in closet and opened the door to his study. He flipped a switch in the dark and the room became awash with light. Rebecca walked in and took in the sight. There was a small refrigerator against one wall. On a short table next to it rested a coffee pot, sugar, and tea bags, as well as a can of coffee. In a corner was a computer desk, set up with a computer and printer. Near it, against the wall was a study desk. On a stand of its own was a stereo with two speakers sitting beside it. The desk was certainly big enough for two or three people to sit at. Nicholas had a cushioned seat at the desk and as Rebecca continued to look around the room found two cushioned folding chairs resting against the wall by a bookcase filled with what looked like old text books and paper. Rebecca walked to the window and looked out it. The dark outside yielded only to the street lights, which reflected off a couple inches of snow.

Rebecca turned back to Nicholas. "It's nice," she said. "You and your father share this?"

"No," Nicholas answered. "It's just for me. Everything in here is mine."

"Even the computer? Wow. Lucky."

Nicholas shrugged. "I got a second phone line just for dial-up, so I can get online."

"I don't get the internet at all. I was barely able to make an e-mail address."

They both laughed, though it didn't release any of the tension Rebecca felt. "I'm not too good with it myself," Nicholas continued. "I'm still learning. So you don't mind studying in here?"

Rebecca shook her head. "No, it's fine. But, do you mind if we keep the door open?"

Nicholas looked at the door. It was plainly obvious that Rebecca didn't trust him. He thought about making a comment, but decided against it. Instead he said, "Sure, I guess we'll just keep the radio off."

Santano sat in his car, still drinking his coffee. The Blood Sword had painted the happenings between Rebecca and Nicholas on the car's windshield, making viewing the events seem more like watching a television show. Santano watched the uneventful show with disinterest. Rebecca had moved from discussing how to find the slope of a triangle to helping Nicholas solve for x in various problems. Santano yawned. He looked at his watch. Half past six. He groaned. "You better hurry. You may have all night, but I don't. I'm being nice by letting you have one last run, so do something before I change my mind."

Almost as if on Santano's quo, Nicholas rose from his chair and started for his refrigerator. "I'm thirsty," he said. "What about you? You want anything?"

"No," Rebecca said as she waved her thermus to him. "I brought tea."

"Okay," Nicholas said.

Santano watched Nicholas' face contort with annoyance as he turned and reached for a can of pop. The look left his face when he turned back around and popped the top. He watched as Rebecca poured herself a cup of tea into the thermus' cap and noticed the rising steam. It was still hot. Rebecca blew on it before taking a small sip.

"You want some ice to cool it off?" Nicholas asked.

"Ice?" Rebecca thought. She looked at the steam rising from her cap cup. It was rather hot, and what harm could ice do? "Sure," she said. "That sounds good."

Nicholas nodded with a smile. It turned to a smirk as he faced his back to her again and reached for a tray of ice. He brought her the tray and let her use as much as she wanted. She put one into her cup, which quickly melted. She put several more into the thermus to cool down the entirety of the tea. Santano's curiosity rose. Nicholas' hidden smile at Rebecca's use of ice seemed more like a victory smile. Santano continued to watch with increasing interest. Another twenty minutes passed and Rebecca was already on her second cup, well on her way to a third. The cap was small, after all. It was apparent she had been having trouble focusing for several minutes. Rebecca rubbed her eyes, trying to focus her distorting vision.

"You look tired," Nicholas said nonchalantly. "Maybe you need a quick nap?"

"What?" Rebecca asked. She shook her head. Should she be mad at that remark or thankful? She wasn't sure. What did he say? "I think I need some air." Rebecca rose from her seat and was wobbly on her legs. After a few steps she lost her balance and tumbled to the ground. Or did she trip? She looked up at Nicholas, still sitting in his chair and looking at the worksheet.

"Going to sleep there?" he asked.

Rebecca's vision was going in and out of focus. She was struggling to keep her eyes open. She looked at her thermus. She realized what happened, but had yet to realize what it meant. "You...drugged the ice?" she said in nearly a slur. She rested her head on the ground and her eyes could stay open no longer. Nicolas looked at Rebecca's unconscious form and smiled. Santano could not contain his laughter. He watched as Nicholas took Rebecca into his arms and left the study.

***

The incinerator had returned to Santano's home after his battle with Angel. He had taken the ensuing hours to admire his new form and await a new command. When Satan's Presence roared to life, the incinerator fell to one knee and lowered his head. Satan's eyes opened within the flames and stared down at the demon before him

"Angel is on the move," Satan said. "He has healed faster than I expected."

"I am sorry my liege," the incinerator said. "It seems he was stronger than I gave him credit for."

"It is easy to underestimate him. We are underestimating Rebecca as well. Not only was she able to defeat a demonic, it seems she and Angel they have developed a bond. She is giving him strength."

"Let me face him again. This time I will kill him. It's what I should have done when I first fought him."

"I wanted him to see the end of his power and the end of his struggles. However, with the recent revelations Angel seems to pose a threat, as does Rebecca. They must be dealt with."

"Perhaps it is Rebecca that should be sacrificed in place of Nicholas?"

"I have already made my Chosen. I cannot change it without stripping Santano of all his powers."

"Then let me end Angel's life."

"So you wish the honor of killing a demon hunter?"

"Angel is nothing but a thorn in our sides. I will receive nothing for his removal but the pleasure of assisting the forward motions of our plans."

Satan chuckled. "Santano is bidding his time, unaware that Angel approaches. Very well incinerator. Find Angel and end him."

The incinerator stood and black flames rose from the ground and entwined around his form. "With pleasure, my Lord." The flames consumed him and the fire demon was gone. Satan closed his eyes and the flames of his Presence died.

***

Angel raced through the sewer system to avoid police detection. Small bursts of speed left after images as he blurred and appeared yards ahead. These small burst of Quickstep Angel hoped would help conserve his power. He was traversing one of the larger tunnels. A foul smell wafted from the sewage basin running between the brick lined corridor. After a speed burst an ashen colored hand burst from the ground and gripped Angel's ankle. He fell face first, unable to prevent or cushion his fall. Flames burst from around the hand as the incinerator rose from the ground. With Angel's ankle in hand, the demon slammed him into the nearby wall and with a quick twist threw Angel across the basin into the other wall. His body dented both brick structures. Agonized in pain, Angel spit out blood as he tried to stand. The incinerator circled his hands before him, creating a ball of flames between them as he brought them together. With a thrust of his hands the flame released in a torrent. Angel dove for the ground. The flames licked his back and shattered on the bricks behind him, burning and darkening them. Angel leaped to his feet again, gripping his weapons and ready to draw them in an instant.

"Did you think you could get away from me that easily?" the incinerator asked.

Angel answered only with a glare.

The demon knocked on the brick wall. "We won't be interrupted down here Angel. No sirens will save you this time. You're mine."

Angel let out a calm exhale as a faint field of white energy began to appear around him. "I don't have time for this," he said.

"Then I suggest you make time."

The incinerator leaped over the basin to engage Angel. Angel's eyes narrowed and he prayed it would work. He drew the Sword of Might in a slashing motion, sparks of flame trailing the blade, and struck the ground. Energy surged through the rusted blade as it flew through the air. "Angelic Flames!" Angel shouted as the blade struck. A massive flame erupted from the strike zone and engulfed the very surprised demon. The flames pushed the incinerator back across the basin and slammed him into the wall. The force was so powerful that the demon's body collapsed the wall and he lay in a freshly made cave.

The attack had drained Angel immensely and drained the Sword of Might's power completely. He knew he had little time. With the sword drained of all its power, he lost a large part of his arsenal. Angel leaped across the basin and brought his sword down upon the incinerator. He didn't have time, materials, or the power to exorcize it. He just needed to defeat and banish it back to Hell. The incinerator's hands reached up and caught the blade. The rusted metal cut deep into the demon's ashen flesh and burned. Blood dripped down his arms and smoke rose from his burning hands. The demon lifted a foot and kicked Angel back across the basin with one powerful blow. Angel struck the far wall and found himself on hands and knees.

The incinerator pulled himself free and found his footing quickly. The flames on his body burned strongly. The demon threw his arms out and shouted. The flames on his body fanned out in all directions, searing everything in their wake. Angel touched his cross and hastily raised a Halo as he dove into the filthy water through the intense heat and flames. There, at least for a moment, he would be safe.

The incinerator flexed his wounded and aching hands as he looked at them. Their healing was slow to begin. He walked to the basin and looked into the dirty water. Angel could make out the demon's body through the murky waters. A smile crept onto the incinerator's lips. He kneeled and placed a hand over the water's surface. The flames on his arm came alive and crawled down his arm and spread onto the water. "Boiled alive or burned to a crisp," the incinerator said. "It makes no difference to me. Either way, you're dead."

Angel could feel the temperature of the water rapidly rising. He was short on air and his lungs burned. He needed to surface to breath and vacate the rapidly boiling water. An exhale escaped him as he struggled not to breathe. Angel did not realize he was descending deeper into the basin until his feet touched the bottom. He crouched low and gathered his strength. He was calm and tightened his grip on the Sword of Might. He had but one shot.

Angel pushed off the ground and shot through the water. There was a presence around him. He could barely feel it. Was he subconsciously drawing strength from Rebecca? He burst from the water's surface in a twist, bringing his blade down in an arc. The surprised demon backed away and stared at Angel as he spun in the air, sword drawn. It wasn't Angel that had the demon awestruck. It was something else. "Ur—!" was all the incinerator managed to say before the blade connected with his neck and removed his head. The fires on his body died and his form fell into ash.

Angel landed on the edge of the basin, but his balance was challenged. His arms flailed as he fought to remain on his feet, but he only came closer to falling into the burning filthy water below. As he was about to lose his balance he felt a gentle touch on his back that pushed him forward. He was not allowed to fall. Angel stood dumbfounded as tears began to well up in his eyes. He realized what the demon was trying to say. "Uri?" Angel asked. The warm loving touch on his back also crossed over his shoulder and held him. Then the feeling covered his body as he could feel the angel's embrace.

He could hear Uriel's long lost voice whisper into his ear. "She is in danger."

It was that instant that any doubt of Rebecca's lineage that lingered in Angel's mind was shattered. The girl was truly a Virtue. Heaven's long wait for a real hero to carry on the fight had come to an end. Rebecca would rise as the next demon hunter, but Angel had to survive long enough to help her to that ascension. He had felt Uriel's guiding hand as he fought the incinerator, but had mistaken it for Rebecca's power. The incinerator was the first real demon that Angel had defeated in nearly two centuries. Perhaps it was Uriel that allowed Angel to use such a long dormant power. Was the Light truly shining on him again? In Uriel's embrace, Angel felt no pain or hurt; only comfort and love. Luxuries he thought he would never feel again.

Angel shook his head and wiped his tears away. Rebecca was in danger. He had to hurry! "Quickstep!"

***

Rebecca awoke to a foul smell in her nose. She was lying in a bed, but didn't remember going home. Her arms were resting above her head and when she tried to move them she found that she couldn't. Something held her arms spread over her head. She quickly found that she could not move her legs either, but before she could really take in what was happening she was bombarded with flashes of light. She tried to turn away from the flashes but couldn't. Her arms were pulled overhead towards the bedposts. Her legs were tied together at the ankle and unable to move. She felt bindings around both ankles and at each wrist. She was tied to the bed. "Stop it!" she shouted. "Let me go!"

The flashes stopped and she heard Nicholas emit a short chuckle. Rebecca's eyes were able to adjust to the light in the room. She was no longer in Nicholas' study, but inside a bedroom. The bed she was lying in was a queen at least. A nightstand was at the side of the bed. Resting against the wall was a dresser with a mirror affixed to it. It faced the bed and Rebecca could see the leather straps that bound her. To her brief relief, she was still wearing all her clothes, even her shoes. Nicholas hadn't done anything to her yet. A wardrobe rested alone against the wall.

"Of course," Nicholas said. He was holding an instant camera. On the nightstand were several Polaroid's developing. Nicholas shook the Polaroid of the last shot he took before laying it on the nightstand. "You just looked so pretty sleeping like that. I'm glad you woke up."

"What do you think you're doing?" Rebecca demanded. She pulled in vain at the straps on her arms. "Let me go! Are you crazy?"

"Crazy about you," Nicholas said playfully.

"If I scream, I'll wake up everyone in this house."

"But everyone in the house is already awake."

"They'll still wonder what is making your guest scream."

"Babe, I live alone."

Shocked fear washed over her face. "What do you mean?"

"I live alone. It's just you and me here. Not bad for an inheritance, huh?"

"You can't keep me here forever. My mom is coming back at eight. We'll go to the police!"

Nicholas picked up his camera and snapped another photo. It spit out the white edged grayed out picture. "You could, but Marcy or Stacy will vouch that you're full of it. Two against one. I'll win. Besides, do you really want dirty pictures of yourself on the internet? They're nearly impossible to remove you know."

"You—You're going to blackmail me?"

Nicholas put the camera down and opened the nightstand drawer. He took something out of it. Most was hidden in his hand, but Rebecca could see that it was red and had a strap. Nicholas got on the bed and straddled her. Rebecca's head was whirling. With everything that had been going on, this was just too much. She was angry, but the fear of her helplessness to Nicholas overwhelmed it. Nicholas then showed her the ball gag in his hand. "Thanks for being such a good sport so far," he said, "but I still have neighbors."

Rebecca realized too late that if she made enough noise it may cause his neighbors to call the police. When she opened her mouth to scream, Nicholas pressed the gag between her teeth. Rebecca struggled, trying to push the ball out with her tongue as Nicholas fastened the latch snuggly behind her head. He swayed with the motions of her body, but didn't move beyond that. She stopped when she felt his hands on her arms. He bent closer to her. He tried to show annoyance but his smirk broke through.

"Calm down," Nicholas laughed. "I just want to have a little fun. There's no harm in that, right?"

Nicholas couldn't contain his smile and Rebecca's anger was starting to override her fear. She tried to yell at him, but only muffled sounds came from behind the gag.

"I always thought you were hot," he said as he trailed his fingers down the front of her body. "When you went with the jock I thought, 'Figures'. Wasn't expecting you to steal someone else's boyfriend though."

Rebecca tried to defend herself against the accusation, but again nothing akin to words came out.

Nicholas took his camera and took a shot of Rebecca's half-scared, half-angered face. "So sexy," he laughed. "I guess you're not so innocent. How is it you can keep that good girl rep?" He peeked from behind the camera. "You do want to keep that, don't you?"

Rebecca didn't say anything. Her nostrils flared as she stared at him. Her face was angered, but tears filled her eyes. He would try to destroy her reputation to keep her quiet. She wondered if that's what he threatened Stacy and Marcy with too, to get them to stop the "rumor".

"That's what I thought," Nicholas said. He laid the camera back on the nightstand after taking one more shot. He leaned forward with a smile on his face and began kissing Rebecca's neck. She tightened her fists and stayed still at first, until his hands moved up her body and explored her breasts through her shirt. She began to thrash beneath him, trying to knock him off. Nicholas chuckled in delight but didn't stop. There was no doubt he was enjoying himself. Rebecca began to pull hard at her wrist bonds. She just needed one hand free. That's all she wanted. She could do something with that. Tears began flowing down Rebecca's face as she felt Nicholas' hand travel down her stomach and to her pants. She thrashed harder, not allowing him to slide his hand in too much. Her shoulder was throbbing as she aggravated her healing wound.

Finally Nicholas sat up and smiled down at her. Rebecca's face was wet with tears and her face flooded with panic. "I want to feel you against me," Nicholas said. Rebecca began to scream at Nicholas in panic as he pulled his shirt off over his head. He tossed it on the floor and pulled on Rebecca's shirt. She was screaming frantically at him. She was trying to warn him. They weren't alone in the room.

"Your turn," Nicholas said, but it was too late. As he started to pull up on Rebecca's shirt the crimson blade of the Blood Sword burst through his chest. Blood splattered across Rebecca and she stopped screaming. All her anger went away and was replaced by fear. Nicholas' blood was being pulled into one of the blade's white spots. He stared down at it in disbelief. Rebecca watched as a horrific sight came into view beside Nicholas' head. The man's face was absent all flesh. His hair was gone and the meat and sinew face was dry. Every now and again his veins would pulse as blood was pushed through them. The voice of Santano whispered into Nicholas' ear, "You took too long." Nicholas turned his head to look at the horror next to him. He recognized the voice and stuttered his teacher's name. The muscles on Santano's face contoured into a smile.

Santano sliced into Nicholas and then threw him off of Rebecca and his sword in one motion. Nicholas flew against the wall, blood splattering on it, and lay crumbled on the ground. He gargled and tried to move. Santano bared his sword and he and Rebecca watched as Nicholas' blood swirled into a white spot. When it was filled, Nicholas' motions and gargled sounds ceased. Terrified, Rebecca watched as the veins in Santano's face pulsed quickly and then ceased. She watched as the muscle and sinew began to rot. Santano stared down at her with a smile and said, "Only five left."

It was true. Everything Angel had said was true. There was no escaping that fact now. The man before Rebecca was Samuel Santano, her teacher turned Satanist. It was he that had been killing her friends and now it seemed she was next. Staring into the decrepit face of Santano and seeing the end of her life at hand, Rebecca found herself wishing that Nicholas was still alive. Santano held the Blood Sword over her and said, "Shall we begin?" The crimson blade began to glow. Rebecca's eyes widened in fear and she began to struggle violently. "It'll be over soon." Santano raised the

Blood Sword, ready to strike. He had no desire to kill her, not yet. He needed her alive for the time being, but he needed her free of Nicholas' restraints. A swing of the sword with a field around it would shield her body from harm. It would simply cut her bonds and knock her out. Santano brought the blade down and Rebecca screamed.

Glass shattered into the room. The Blood Sword was caught by the Sword of Might. Angel had arrived. The Dagger of Power was already generating its whirlwind, which caught all the glass as it flew into the room. Angel pushed the crimson blade away and trained his dagger on Santano, releasing the full force of the winds. The wind and glass flew over Rebecca harmlessly and rocked Santano. He shielded his face with his arms as glass shards pierced his body and the powerful winds pushed him back. Only yielding a few steps, Santano stood his ground against the winds. With only a few steps Angel climbed over Rebecca and swung his sword. "Force Shock!" he shouted. Santano defended Angel's attack, but when their blades touched, the Sword of Might released a pushing force that pushed Santano back, his feet dragging on the floor as he tried to hold his position. "Keen Edge!" Angel exclaimed as he sliced through a strap holding Rebecca's arm with the Dagger of Power. With her hand free, Rebecca pulled at the gag, trying to take it out. She quickly realized she needed both hands to undo the strap and went to work releasing her other arm.

Santano and Angel stared at each other in silence. Santano's flayed face showed little emotion, despite the crease in what remained of his brow. The remaining tissue simply wasn't capable of subtle emotion. Angel's face was determined. He knew he was incapable of defeating Santano, but at least he could hold the avatar back.

Santano slashed with the Blood Sword, producing a powerful wind in its wake. Rebecca shielded herself as the winds hit her. Angel held his blade into the wind and shouted, "Disrupt!" The winds blew back and dispersed before they could knock him down. Angel charged across the small space between them. It was a Master Bedroom, so had decent space to fight, but only if they remained in close quarters. Angel attacked with the Sword of Might, but Santano deflected. There was a loud clash and sparks flew from the metal as their blades collided.

Santano went on the offensive and attacked wildly with the Blood Sword. Angel blocked each blow with his sword and struggled to hold his ground against Santano's powerful strikes. Each deflection pushed Angel back. Her arms and mouth free, Rebecca undid her leg bindings as she watched Angel being pushed back towards her. Angel couldn't gauge how close he was and knew he needed to regain the offensive. He added his dagger into the blocks, trying to catch the Blood Sword between the Heavenly Weapons. On a downward blow, Angel caught Santano's blade and pushed it back up. Taking a single step forward, Angel slid the Dagger of Power across the length of the crimson blade and down across Santano. The dagger sliced Santano's shirt, but missed his flesh. Santano moved back to attack with his wind attack again, but Angel moved forward with him and caught the Blood Sword in mid-slash with the Dagger of Power. Angel tilted his sword for an upward strike and shouted, "Flame Strike!" A small flame burned the edges of the Sword of Might as Angel struck, but the flames would not hold. The flames died almost as quickly as they were born. Santano sidestepped as the blade grazed his body, but without the flames he was untouched, leaving barely enough room to avoid Angel's blow in his evasion. Santano instinctively moved back, close to the wall and brandished the Blood Sword defensively. "Damn!" Angel cursed as he sheathed his weapons. The last ounce of their power had been drained on his hasty arrival. Seeing what he had arrived to, he was glad he hurried, but now he was essentially defenseless until the Heavenly Weapons regained their power. A little, that's all he needed.

Rebecca's heart raced as she watched the two superhumans fight from behind the relative safety of the bed. Superhuman. That's the best she could describe them as. The wounds she had witnessed Angel receive in his battle with his sins were gone. She knew that should be impossible, but every cut and gash was gone. He shouldn't even have survived, yet here he stood, defending her. If Angel still had those wounds buried beneath his clothes, he showed no signs. With the exertion he was putting his body through, they should have reopened, but there was no blood anywhere on his being. She realized she was nursing the pain from her shoulder. She wondered if it had started bleeding again. Her wound had healed fast. Did Angel's heal even faster? Her eyes went to Santano. His body looked the same, but his face was missing its skin and hair, like it was expertly removed. He showed no pain from something obviously so painful. He killed Nicholas and she watched as Santano's face lost more of its humanity. Nicholas. Rebecca's eyes found him lying lifeless in a corner. His eyes were open and he looked on with a face of shock and confusion. Nicholas was in Hell now with her friends. Santano had sent him there. Even with what he was going to do to her, Rebecca felt sorry for him. An eternity in Hell is not a punishment she would wish on anyone. She looked at the superhumans before her. It's exactly what they were, more than human. Thinking about what Santano had done, Rebecca's heart broke, but her tears were dry. She gritted her teeth and gripped the bed sheets tightly. "Get him Angel," she whispered.

Santano gripped the Blood Sword in both hands and began to swing wildly. If Angel drew his weapons in defense, they would not charge. Angel knew he had to revert to unarmed combat and hope Santano didn't realize that he was out of power, even if only temporarily. If Santano used his sword's powers, Angel would not be able to defend against it.

Santano's blows were fast but uncoordinated, allowing Angel to evade them without much difficulty, but each evasion pushed him back. He had to protect Rebecca, but he was distracted. Even though the Sword of Might's power had been depleted, it sent constant warnings. Something was happening, but Angel didn't know what nor did he have the time to ponder. Rebecca had called out to him. He was about to fall over the bed.

Angel twisted his body to avoid Santano's powerful blow and lunged forward with an open palm thrust. An empty thud sounded as Angel's thrust struck Santano's sternum, knocking the air out of him. Santano was forced back from the sternum blow. Angel stepped forward again with a closed fist and collided with Santano's sternum again. The Avatar flew back into the wall and held his chest. Santano smiled at Angel and said, "I've felt worse."

Santano gripped his sword with both hands and stepped forward in a thrust. Santano knew he could follow Angel's evasion. His reflexes were fast enough to follow suit to a right or left feint. Angel did something unexpected. He vaulted into the air and landed his hands on the Blood

Sword. Santano was not expecting the extra weight and couldn't compensate with his strength fast enough. His blade headed towards the ground. Angel twisted his hands deftly on the blade, turning in the air and kicking Santano's face with both feet before landing on the floor, Santano's blade piercing the ground.

Santano pulled his sword free only to find Angel's hand pressed against his face. With all his might, Angel threw Santano back against the wall. In one fluid motion, Angel drew the Dagger of Power and hurled it at Santano, crying out, "Impact!" Santano slammed against the wall and rolled, evading the dagger. A small amount of power released, scorching one side of Santano's face and the wall, but doing little else. Angel hoped it would be enough. He turned to Rebecca and shouted, "We have to go!"

"Look out!" Rebecca warned.

Angel turned to see Santano's blurred form dash across the room with the Blood Sword poised in a thrust. Angel didn't have the time to draw his sword in retaliation or effectively evade. Santano was moving much too fast. Angel reached for the crimson sword as it pierced his stomach. He spat blood as the piercing pain rocked his body. "There is nowhere for you to run," Santano said. "You can't beat me Angel. Now die."

Before Santano could deliver the fatal blow, Rebecca threw herself at him and knocked him to the ground. She dug her nails into his flesh and clawed his face. Santano howled in pain and with a powerful kick, threw Rebecca off him and against the bed. She hit the frame with great force, but the clang was muffled. Something had cushioned her fall and she was only dazed. The meaty tissue on Santano's face had torn, but blood no longer filled the veins. "You little bitch!" Santano shouted as he rose to his feet. Santano took a few long strides towards the wardrobe that Nicholas lay beside. He lifted it overhead as if it weighted nothing at all and turned to face Rebecca. She was awestruck by his strength and could think only to raise her arms in defense. Santano motioned to throw but hesitated. He could make out a dim light form around her. He wasn't sure what it was. His eyes locked on Angel. He had removed the Blood Sword with a scream and hurled it at Santano.

Santano repositioned himself to hold the wardrobe with a single hand and caught the Blood Sword. Now supported by only half Santano's strength, the wardrobe suddenly became weighted. Angel dove at Santano before he could get a chance to re-grip the wardrobe. Santano was tackled to the ground and the wardrobe came crashing down with them. Another powerful kick and Angel slammed into the dresser and mirror. Glass shards rained down as the mirror shattered.

Santano moved forward and caught the glint of a weapon drawn. Rebecca had stood, but was unarmed. He turned towards her when Satan spoke into his mind, "That is enough Santano." The Avatar stopped in his tracks. "You are being reckless. If you kill Rebecca now, it will ruin your ascension." Santano took a step away from Rebecca at that. "Leave Angel to his fate and return at once. There is much left to do." Santano looked at Rebecca and Angel for a moment. Angel was hurt, but had his sword drawn. Rebecca was scared, but stood her ground. Both were willing to fight. Santano could hear sirens outside and the slam of car doors. He had not heard the police approach. Perhaps it was time to leave. Santano ran his hand along his sword, igniting it. He then vanished in a veil of smoke.

Angel lowered his sword and stammered, "Rebecca. Take the dagger."

Rebecca's head turned furiously trying to remember where it had landed.

"There," Angel pointed. "Take it. Protect it. It'll protect you."

Rebecca found the dagger and ran to it. As she pulled it free she said, "That was Santano! What happened to him?" She turned to help Angel, but as she did several officers stormed the room. All had their guns trained on Angel and ordered him to stand down. Everything happened so fast, Rebecca didn't have time to react. Angel was surrounded as the police swarmed in. Rebecca was grabbed and pulled back. "Rebecca, stay back!" the officer said. Even looking at the officer that stood to protect her, she didn't immediately realize that it was Jason's father. Rebecca's mind was still reeling from her revelations that she was slow to register the events as they rapidly unfolded.

Jeff spoke into the receiver clipped to his uniform. "Requesting paramedics. Suspect and two victims injured."

Rebecca's mind finally caught up. "N—No!" she shouted. "Angel didn't do this!"

"Drop the sword!" someone shouted.

Blood drowned Angel's clothes. He had trouble focusing, but he kept his eyes on Rebecca.

"He'll come back," Angel said. "He'll come back for you."

"I said drop it!" the officer shouted again as Rebecca called out to them to stop.

"Rebecca, stay back!" Jeff said as he shielded her. He turned to Angel. "Who's coming back for her?"

"Samuel will bring help," Angel continued. "They will be dangerous."

Angel was shouted at again. "Stop talking!" Jeff demanded of the unit. He realized Angel was completely ignoring them and talking to Rebecca. It seemed like he was warning her. "We'll protect Rebecca," he told Angel.

Angel locked eyes with him. He struggled a smile. "You'll try, but you can't." He could no longer hold his sword and it clanged on the ground. The officers fidgeted. "You asked me my name once. Now I remember, after meeting this girl." He looked at Rebecca. "I am Angel Virtue. We are the only ones they fear." Angel's strength left him. He fell to his knees first, then onto his face on the floor. His unconsciousness would only be a brief reprieve.

"Damn, it's straight through," someone shouted. "Get pressure on it!"

"Paramedics E.T.A two minutes," another officer informed Jeff.

"Check that guy in the corner," Jeff ordered.

The officer ran to Nicholas and pressed his fingers to his neck. After a short moment he shook his head and said, "No pulse. He's gone."

"Martin. Randal. Stay with Angel," Jeff ordered. "Everyone else, clear out. Secure the area! Santano was here! Find him!"

Most of the officers rushed out while Martin and Randal pulled the sheets from the bed to try and suppress Angel's bleeding. Finally, Jeff turned his full attention to Rebecca.

"Rebecca, are you okay?" Jeff asked. "Are you hurt?"

"No," Rebecca said frantically. "Angel didn't do this!"

"Calm down. Just tell me what happened."

"Santano killed Nicholas, not Angel!"

"You saw him—?" Jeff caught sight of the dagger in her hand. "Is that Angel's dagger? How did you get it?"

"Angel gave it to me."

Jeff shook his head. "Rebecca, no. It's a murder weapon. It's evidence; we need it."

Rebecca held it protectively against her body. "I can't."

"Cragoff!" One of the two officers called out. "The paramedics are here, but we don't see his dagger."

Jeff turned to answer them, "Yeah I—" He stopped suddenly. A strong force grabbed his arm, but when he looked, his arm was bare. Rebecca hadn't grabbed him, but he could feel the grip tightening. Vaguely, in his ear he heard a voice whisper, "Leave it with her." It was a voice he didn't recognize, but somehow warranted his trust.

"Cragoff!" the officer called back.

Jeff shook his head as the paramedics rifled into the room; two by Angel's side and two towards Nicholas. "Okay, don't worry about it. Get out of their way." The two officers left Angel to the paramedics. Jeff looked back at Rebecca who returned with a pleading face.

The voice echoed again, "Leave it."

"Let's get out of here so you can tell me what happened."

"What about Angel?" Rebecca questioned.

"I'm not sure. Let's just worry about you now." He escorted her out, sheet draped over her shoulders and pulled close to him to help hide the dagger. They sat in his car for a long moment.

"Mr. Cragoff, please," Rebecca pleaded. "You have to let Angel go."

Jeff rubbed the arm the invisible force had grabbed. It had released him with a sense of appeasement. "We'll see."

CHAPTER XIII

Smoke wafted into Santano's basement. Within its obscured mists Santano appeared. The smoke quickly dispersed. The flame of Satan's Presence was already burning and his eyes waited. Santano saw that the second candle's flame had died leaving the naked wick on the pool of cooled wax. The summoned demon had been defeated. This time Santano knew it was Angel because he had been watching Rebecca all day.

"I should have grabbed her," Santano said. "I had the chance."

"It would have been difficult," Satan said. "She was not unguarded. An archangel was by her side."

"Is that what that light around her was?"

"Yes. Her guardian is already protecting her. Baraqyal had informed me that Raphael was at her side when she fought Demonic Angel. Luckily, she cannot summon him and he cannot attack you."

"Well, something was ready to; I thought I saw a weapon drawn, but Rebecca didn't have one."

"Unfortunately, Angel's guardian either never abandoned him, as the rest of Heaven did, or she returned. Knowing Uriel and the circumstances, I doubt she left. You are lucky Angel did not realize she would answer his cry. She can attack you."

"Can I beat her?"

"Doubtful, but you will not continue on alone. The Collection proper can now begin."

"You said Rebecca was the final sacrifice. How am I going to do that if I can't get her?"

"She will come to you; with or without Angel. The Collection is her friends. With the fire of the demon hunter beginning to burn strong in her, I am certain she will come to rescue them. She will be the last to feel this flame."

"If the Virtues are the demon hunters, won't another member of her family take up arms? Her parents? Aunt or uncle? Cousins?"

"Rebecca no longer has a family. Pestilence is making sure of that."

Santano absorbed those words. Pestilence would ensure Rebecca had no family. A single Horseman was wiping out an entire bloodline in only a matter of hours. That was the kind of power he would soon have.

"I'm ready to begin the Collection. What do I have to do?"

"First we will summon your aid. Step back."

Santano stepped back. He was excited. It would be over soon. A week ago he was desperate to cure his heart disease. He quivered in fear as he killed Adam, the first sacrifice. Now, he gazed into the eyes of Hell with a smile. He would not simply overcome his disease; he would overcome the chains of life itself.

"Horsemen of Apocalypse!" Satan bellowed. "I, Samael, exercise our agreement! War! Famine! Pestilence! Send onto me each an underling to give birth to your brother!" The remaining candles plumbed to life, six feet in height in the least, with three distinct roars. "War, send to us a commander of pain and dissolution!"

The voice of War growled, "I will send you aid as agreed. This girl seems strong. I want to see her power. I will send you one that destroys. I will send to you my destruction."

The first flame blew out of existence from within. The candle melted, pooling on the floor and sealing the gate. The creature that was born from the flames was very much human. He stood shorter than Santano by a few inches, but his toned body was naturally larger. With no clothes to cover his body, every crisp muscle was exposed. He stood tall and proud. His dark skin shined like polished steel, as did his long raven hair. The whole of his eyes were a deep crimson with no visible pupils. Though his body was very much male, he was sexless.

Famine slurped his words, "To capture I will send what can be satisfied, if only temporarily. I will give up one of the bottomless pits. I will give to you my hunger."

The second flame flickered and then pulled inward. The being within became clear as it devoured the summoning flame, candle and all. His belch spewed a small flame and he chuckled. As the previous creature, this one appeared male and dressed in old dirty clothes that just covered his body; a tattered shirt and shorts, which may have once been pants. "Spicy," he laughed. His accent was thick and foreign, though Santano didn't know from where. His flesh was black as charcoal, his fingernails short and dirty. His hair was thin and his eyes were glossed with a sickly film. The brown of his iris sat on eyes of pearl white. He was much shorter than the destruction, even shorter than Rebecca; perhaps five foot or five foot one. His body was thin and frail, the bones poking out where the joints met. The hunger looked around the room licking his dry lips.

Pestilence let out a wail. "Disease for my greatest disease! Use his plagues well avatar!"

A loud thud echoed in the room and the flame was snuffed. A staff buried itself into the summoning candle and extinguished the flame. The wax pooled from beneath the butt of the withered staff. Haggard breaths escaped the naked man. His genitals were shriveled and crusted. From the tip of the foreskin leaked a green milky substance. His body was thin, but not like the predecessor creature, and several inches taller as well. Patches of hair were missing, his eyes sickly with mucus. His nose and mouth were crusted and snot ran from his nose. His pale skin was a tint of green and rough with boils and rashes. Open sores covered his body and an unpleasant scent wafted from him.

The hunger waved his hand in front of his nose. "Great, he sent us the stinky one," he said. The pale man eyed the hunger and growled. The destruction slammed his fist into his palm, echoing a boom which his voice matched, "Stop it. We are here to do a job."

The disease turned away while the hunger giggled to itself. Santano looked the trio up and down. "This is the help?" he asked. "I think I'll be better off with just the big guy."

"Do not let hunger and disease's appearance fool you my avatar," Satan said. "They are far stronger than they appear. Now I will reveal my Chosen." Satan's eyes closed and images of his chosen appeared within the large flame as he named them off. "The earth will accept only the strong, stout, and loyal. To the earth we will offer Monica Silvia. The air is felt but unseen and desires one that can see what cannot be seen. It desires what never stops and always seeks answers. To the air we offer Jason Cragoff. Fire is fickle and all consuming. It knows no limits in what it does and will change direction as desired. Nearly no force can stop it. To the unquenchable fire we will offer Michael Riviera. The passive, subtle water accepts only limitless possibilities. It can destroy and create and will accept only one whose qualities match its own. To the water we will offer Heather Lusha. Finally, a sacrifice of purity must be made. Only the pure will bring out the destructive forces of the Fourth. Through the sacrifice of the cross, the innocence of Rebecca Virtue will be offered. The location for the ceremony will be a place intimately familiar to the Avatar. Samuel Santano, take these allies and gather up the Chosen Five and take them to the high school. Only when all five have been gathered may the sacrifices begin. Offer these souls to the four elements and then offer the purest soul to the Fourth."

"My master wants the girl's strength tested," the destruction said. "She currently resides with the air sacrifice. I will fetch them."

"I care not for who I retrieve," the disease said. "However, earth can be stubborn, so I will retrieve her."

"I'm feeling thirsty," the hunger said. "I'll fetch the water girl."

"That leaves Michael," Santano said. "I'll get him and meet you all at the school."

***

Sitting in his living room with Rebecca, Jeff wondered why he didn't take her to the station. If there was a second killer, that's where he should have taken her. She had witnessed a murder. It's where he should have taken her. She was going to be the next victim. It's where he should have taken her. It's where he should have taken her, so why didn't he? Why was he compelled to take her to his house? It was highly unethical. At the very least, he should have taken her home.

Jeff was informed via radio that Angel was rushed to the hospital. If the doctors allowed, which they would be pressed, Angel would then be transferred to a private cell under heavy guard. They didn't want him to sneak away again.

Jeff was dismissive of his son as they came in. He told Jason simply to offer Rebecca something to drink and stay quiet. This was official police business and Jason was not involved. Of course, Jeff knew his son would not listen and didn't bother making him leave when he sat in the living room with them. Jason may go out of sight, but not out of earshot.

Jeff watched Rebecca for a moment while she drank the water Jason had brought. He had brought a wet towel too so Rebecca could wash the blood off herself. She was quiet, obviously upset, but she wasn't shaken in any sense of the word. Jeff could tell she was gathering her thoughts. His police instincts told him she was figuring out her alibi, but she wasn't that kind of person and he always thought he was a good judge of character. Jeff's radio had been keeping him up to date on Angel's condition and the search for Santano. Angel had arrived at the hospital and entered into the emergency room already. The search for Santano was fruitless. He could not be found in the area. His car had never left his house and no one had come or gone since their stakeout began. Rebecca downed the first cup of water Jason had brought her and listened to the radio as she drank through her second cup. By her third the radio notified Jeff that after a surgery and stitches, Angel was deemed in good condition, despite his wounds, and released into police custody. That struck Jeff as strange. How was Angel released so soon? Rebecca looked up at Jeff. She was ready to talk.

Jeff had Jason go to his office and retrieve an audio recorder. He wasn't sure what Rebecca was going to tell him, but he was sure it was something he may not want to report truthfully. This way he could pick and choose what he would report back. Worse case; he had everything on tape. When Jason returned, Jeff set the recorder on the coffee table between them and turned off his radio. He turned the recorder on and took a deep breath.

"Okay, tell me what happened," Jeff said.

"Angel didn't kill Nicholas," Rebecca said. She said it with conviction. "Santano did."

"Nicholas Rannulf?" Jason asked. "He's dead?"

Rebecca nodded her head.

"Oh damn. I never liked the guy—but damn."

"Jason, what did I say?" Jeff asked. "This is official business. Stay quiet. You're not here."

"Right, but damn."

"Rebecca, start from the beginning. Tell me what you were doing there in the first place."

"Nicholas asked me to tutor him earlier in the week, just before the murders started. I didn't give him an answer, but he was insistent on talking to me after that. He was nice about it, he wasn't acting like a jerk, but with the nightmares I was having and the murders, I was frustrated and on edge. I acted like a bitch to him and agreed out of frustration. I felt bad so I didn't back out. That's why I was there."

"You went there to tutor him? How did you two end up in the bedroom?"

Jason bit his lip. The way Jeff phrased it sounded very negative.

"He drugged me," Rebecca answered angrily. "When I woke up, I was tied to the bed."

"How did he drug you?"

"I had brought tea from home because, frankly, I didn't trust him. But I never thought about drugging ice. The tea was hot and melted it fast, then I put more into my thermus to cool it all off."

Jeff turned his radio back on. "Where did this happen?"

"His study."

Jeff clicked the radio on. "Who's still at the crime scene?"

A voice radioed back, "I am."

"Rebecca, where's the study?"

"The second floor," she answered, "near where you found us."

Jeff pressed a button on the radio. "Check the second floor. There is a study. There should be a thermus there. Find it and have its contents tested. The survivor thinks it may have been drugged."

"Ten-four," the voice radioed back.

Jeff returned his attention to Rebecca. "You woke up tied to the bed? Then what happened?"

"Nicholas was going to rape me and try to blackmail me with pictures he was taking. He didn't get far though. Santano had snuck in and killed him."

"You saw his face?"

"He didn't have a face anymore," Rebecca cringed, "but I knew his voice."

"So he was wearing a mask?"

"No, I mean his skin was gone!"

"He skinned his face?" Jason asked in shock, forgetting that he was to remain silent.

Jeff swallowed. Angel had said that the killings were ritualistic. Was the skinning too? "Then what happened?"

"Angel," Rebecca answered. "He came in through the window and pushed Santano back. He cut one of the straps. I did the rest."

"This all happened just before we arrived?"

"Yes."

"Santano might still be in the area. If he skinned his face he'll have to go to a hospital soon."

"Please, Santano isn't human anymore."

"Don't get caught up in their delusions. Santano is crazy and so is Angel."

"You wouldn't say that if you've seen what I've seen."

"What did you see?"

Rebecca swallowed, ready to admit what she had known all along. "Demons."

Before Jeff could say anything in response a loud boom rocked the house. "What was that?" Jason exclaimed as Jeff rose to his feet with his gun drawn.

"It came from the next room," Jeff answered. "Get behind me."

Jason and Rebecca moved behind Jeff as he took a few steps forward. Rebecca held the Dagger of Power close. She felt safer with it. Suddenly the wall between the two rooms blew out and the destruction stood in the newly opened threshold.

"Ah, there you are," he said in a booming voice. "The air and the pure. You were a little more difficult to pinpoint than I thought." He pointed past the trio. "And I see why. No matter, you can't attack me. Even if you did…" He chuckled and began to slowly advance.

Jeff trained his gun on the intruder and shouted, "Stop or I'll shoot!"

"Go ahead human."

Jeff cocked his gun. "I won't warn you again! Stop!"

The destruction chuckled. "Shoot me."

"Fine."

Jeff fired several rapid rounds that struck their target. The being before him jostled slightly from each hit, but each bullet wound and force of impact was felt by Jeff. Bloody wounds opened on his body in the spots the bullets had struck the destruction.

"Dad!" Jason cried as he and Rebecca tried to break Jeff's fall.

Jeff groaned in agony. "I don't understand," he said as he watched destruction's unharmed form advance. "I hit him!"

"Yes, you did," the destruction said. "But I am the embodiment of destruction itself. Any harm done to me is returned to the attacker."

Jeff raised his gun again. "I said stop moving!" He fired two more rounds, but the wounds opened on his own body.

"Mortal weapons may be able to keep most demons at bay, but I am so much more. You cannot harm me." The creature stopped a few feet away. "Air. Innocence. Please do not come peacefully."

Jason's anger rose fast. In a growl he shouted, "I'll show you peaceful!"

The destruction grinned as Jason rushed him. Rebecca called out to him to stop, but she wasn't fast enough to grab him. Jason punched the destruction in the stomach as hard as he could and the air was knocked out of himself. Holding his stomach and trying to catch his breath, Jason took a few tiny staggered steps back.

"Surprised at your own strength?" the destruction gloated. He then delivered his own stomach punch, stronger than Jason's, then a blow to the back of the head, knocking Jason out. With one foot on Jason's back, he motioned to Rebecca. "Your turn, Innocence."

Rebecca gripped the Dagger of Power tightly and stood, standing between Jeff and the destruction.

"Rebecca, don't!" Jeff cried out. He reached for his receiver. "Requesting back up! Abduction in process! Suspect armed! Man down!"

"Get off him," Rebecca demanded. She was tearing.

The destruction raised his hand and silvery steel threads laced his palm. "Make me," he said. The silvery lace shot from the destruction's hand like a bullet and ensnared Rebecca in a steel threaded net. The velocity of the net threw Rebecca across the room and slammed her into the wall. The hanging pictures fell and cracked. A thin line was attached from the net to the destruction's hand and he began to pull Rebecca's struggling form towards him.

Jeff struggled to support himself and aim his gun. "Get off my son!" he shouted "Let her go!"

"Don't shoot!" Rebecca cried. "You'll just get hurt again!"

Jeff's arm shook, unable to pull the trigger but wanting to so badly. He knew she was right.

"Very smart," the destruction said. "Mortal weapons cannot harm me." He reached down for Rebecca but hadn't noticed she was cutting through the net with the Dagger of Power. The blade cut across the destruction's hand and forced him to pull back. Rebecca wasn't hurt and thought only of protecting her friend. She pulled herself out of the remains of the net and thrust the dagger at the destruction. He raised his hand to stop the attack and the blade pierced through. He grunted in pain and Rebecca stared at him in shock. She had stabbed him and she wasn't hurt. The destruction used that moment of hesitation to free his hand and backhanded Rebecca across the room. She hit the floor hard and continued until she hit the wall. The destruction looked at his bleeding hand. "Celestial weapons are another matter," he said. "So the demon hunter did not leave you unarmed. A wise decision, but futile. You will still come to us. If you wish to save your friends you will come to us. The demon hunter will know where to find us. We will be waiting for you."

Red glowing cracks filled the destruction's body until he detonated, leaving behind a scorch mark on the floor. Jason and the destruction were gone.

"Jason!" Jeff screamed. "Bring back my son!"

Rebecca wiped the blood from her lips and ran to Jeff's side. "Mr. Cragoff, please," she begged. "We need Angel. Help me rescue him."

Jeff stared at her for a long minute. He looked at the dagger in her hand, rusted and dull. It had done what his gun could not. He placed his gun down on the ground and reached for his keys. "Do you know where the station is?" he asked.

"Yes," Rebecca answered.

He handed her the keys. "Take the squad car. Turn the sirens on and be careful. Not everyone stops."

"What about you?"

"I'll be fine. Help is coming. Please, save my son. He's all we have."

Rebecca could see the fear in his eyes. "We will."

***

Michael lay on his bed staring up at the ceiling. His mind kept going over and over what Rebecca had said. Angels and demons. The War for Heaven. Was it true? There was a knock on his door.

"Adelante, (Come in.)" Michael said.

An older woman's head with silver stranded hair peeked in. "¿Mijo, estas bien? (Honey, are you okay?)"

"No lo se. (I don't know.)"

¿Que tienes? (What's wrong?)"

"Es deficil. (It's difficult.)"

"Habla conmigo. (Talk to me.)"

Michael sighed and sat up. "¿Por qué crees en Dios? (Why do you believe in God?)"

She came into the room. "¿Por qué crees en el aire? (Why do you believe in the air?)"

Michael laughed softly. "Mamá." He looked at the woman he called mother, his aunt. "Estoy preocupado por Rebecca, (I'm worried about Rebecca.)" he said.

His adoptive mother smiled. "Y que pasa con Rebecca mijo? (And what is wrong with Rebecca hon?)"

"Es difícil de decir Mamá. (It's hard to say Mom.)"

"Mijo, tu me puedes decir. (Hon, you can tell me.)"

Michael sighed and threw his legs over the bed. "Ella tiene miedo pero no se como ayudarla. (She's scared, but I don't know how to help her.)"

"Estar allí para ella, como siempre lo haces. (Be there for her, like you always are.)"

"No creo que eso sera suficiente, Mamá. Ella piensa que el Diablo la persique. (I don't think that'll be enough, Mom. She thinks the Devil is after her.)"

"¿El Diablo? Por qué? (The Devil? Why?)"

"Ella dijo que un demonio vino por ella. Ángel protejela. (She said a demon came for her. Angel protected her.)"

"¿Ella vio a un ángel? (She saw an angel?)"

"No, el muchacho que ellos piensan mato a nuestros amigos. Mamá, Jason me dijo ellos tambien estan buscando a Santano. Pensamos que el hizo. (No, the guy they think killed our friends. Mom, Jason told me they are looking for Santano too. We think he did it.)"

Michael's aunt opened her mouth to speak but was cut off by her husband's shout, "¡Michael, ven aca! Pronto! (Michael, come here! Quick!)"

Michael leaped off his bed as his aunt stepped out of his way, following closely behind as he bolted through the house to the living room. "¿Que pasa? (What's wrong?)" Michael shouted as he entered the living room.

His uncle pointed at the television. "Tu novia, (Your girlfriend.)" he said.

Michael looked at the screen. A picture of Nicholas and Rebecca's senior pictures shared the screen. "Angel was found injured at Nicholas Rannulf's house and taken into custody," the reporter said. "The owner of the house, Nicholas, was pronounced dead at the scene. Rebecca Virtue, also found at the house, was unharmed and taken into protective custody."

"Nicholas?" Michael asked shocked. "Que estaba ella haciendo con el? (What was she doing with him?)" He ran his hands restlessly through his hair. "Tengo que ir hacia ella. ¡Tengo que encontrarla! (I have to go to her. I have to find her!)"

"¡Mijo, espera! (Son, wait!)" his uncle called as Michael ran to the closet for his jacket.

"¡No puedo esperar! (I can't wait!)" Michael shouted as he threw the closet door open and reached for his jacket. "¡Ella me necesita ahorita! (She needs me now!)" Jacket in hand, he threw the door shut. Behind it stood a man with his skin flayed from his face, the sinew dry and rough. Michael jumped back and his uncle pulled him farther back and stood between Michael and the intruder.

"There is no rush Michael," the intruder said.

Michael recognized the voice. "Santano?"

His fleshless lips curved into the resemblance of a smile. "Very good."

"My God, it's true. It's all true."

Santano pointed the Blood Sword at Michael. "Are you ready to come with me?"

"Who are you?" Michael's uncle shouted, his accent not carrying over to his English much. "Get out of my house."

Michael started to pull at his uncle's arm, trying to pull him back. "¡Corre! (Run!)" he shouted.

"¡Llama a la policía! (Call the police!)"

"Can't let you do that," Santano said as his sword began to pull in energy and glow. The pull was subtle, gently milling the hair of the three before him.

"¡No Papá! No es humano, es un demonio! (No Dad! He's not human, he's a demon!)"

Santano swung his sword and released a wave of dark energy across the room. Michael braced himself as the wave washed over him and his adoptive parents. He felt his body chill and tingle, but he stood his ground. His aunt and uncle were engulfed by the energy, whereas it only touched him. They were thrown across the room and slammed against the wall, causing the pictures to fall and the wall to crack.

"Mamá! Papá!" Michael cried.

"Don't worry," Santano said as the flesh returned to his face, "they're not dead. I couldn't risk killing you."

"You monster! You won't get away with this!"

"And just who is going to stop me?" Santano asked as his sword began to glow. Michael entered into a defensive stance. Santano laughed and took a lunging step forward with the sword poised for Michael's shoulder. Michael in turn moved forward and shifted his weight to the inside of the sword, allowing the blade to pass by harmlessly. Michael grabbed Santano's sword arm and slammed his open palm beneath Santano's chin. A grunt escaped Santano's lips as his head was forced up. Michael added his free hand to Santano's sword arm and threw his body into Santano, facing his attacker away from his unconscious aunt and uncle. In one fluid motion from his first strike, Michael threw Santano over his shoulder and onto the ground. With Santano prone, Michael threw a downward straight punch at Santano's face, but the avatar was quick and caught the blow. Santano threw his leg up and kicked Michael away, sending him onto his back and putting some distance between them. Michael kicked himself up off the ground quickly and returned to a defensive stance while Santano lay on the ground and watched.

"That was very impressive," the avatar said as he slowly returned to his feet.

"Glad you liked it," Michael said. "There's plenty more where that came from."

"Hmph. I'm well aware of your troubled past."

"I'm a black belt, so you'll have to work for this kill."

"Who said I was going to kill you here? No, no. You're far too special to be sacrificed like the common rabble so far."

"You killed our friends," Michael said as he started to round the room, keeping the display case behind Santano in his sights. "You went after Rebecca."

"Demonic Angel did, actually, but yes. She's important to me too." Santano let Michael circle him, spewing his monologue.

"I won't let you."

Santano's head cocked to the side as Michael reached behind him and fumbled with the door to the display case, keeping Santano in his sights. "And how exactly are you going to do that?"

Michael gripped the six foot staff with a blue center grip from the case. He spun it around quickly in his right hand as he brought it forward and into his waiting left hand. "I'll beat you into unconsciousness," Michael threatened.

"Peter stood against me too. He lost."

Michael ground his teeth and nearly growled. He forced his jaw lax and breathed. "Relax," he whispered. "Have to stay relaxed. Never let your opponent rile you. He'll win." Santano smiled. "I'll try sensei."

"I don't have time for this," Santano said as he raised his sword. Again it began to glow. "I have a very busy night ahead of me so we really must get going."

Santano moved forward with a downward slash. Michael stepped to his right as he hit the flat of the sword with his staff, knocking it away and unbalancing Santano. Michael continued his momentum into a one hundred eighty degree turn, looked behind him and thrust the staff backwards. He struck Santano's side and pushed him back, nearly making him fumble. Continuing his turn to face Santano, Michael twirled the staff behind his back before bringing it back to form.

Santano rubbed his side as he stood back at attention. "That was unexpected," he growled.

"I told you, I'm not going to let you hurt her," Michael said.

"Hm. Unquenchable resolve. Fierce in what you want to protect. I see why the fire will take you."

Shock flooded Michael's face as a familiar, but unknown, voice whispered into his ear, "She is going to lose you. You will die by fire." Michael tightened his grip. "I don't care," he told the voice, "as long as she's safe. I'll die for her, if that's what it takes."

"Who are you talking to?" Santano asked.

"Don't worry about it."

Michael went on the offensive, aiming a jab at Santano's knee. Santano parried and blocked with the edge of his sword, digging into the wood of the staff. Santano pulled the blade free and, still glowing, struck at Michael again. Michael manipulated the staff with ease, deflecting the two upper blows and lower blows with simple flips and twists of the staff. After deflecting the second of the lower assaults, Michael flicked the staff up and struck the tender part between Santano's legs. Santano's body stiffened as he started to fall to his knees. Michael pulled back and with a lunging thrust struck the blunt end of the staff into Santano's chest. Santano sprawled backwards and onto his back. The momentum of the fall rolled him back onto his feet where he was able to block Michael's overhead blow with the flat of his sword.

Santano pushed Michael back and with gritted teeth rose back to his feet. "I don't have time for this Michael," Santano growled. "I'm trying not to hurt you, now come along!"

"That makes one of us," Michael said, "because I'm trying real hard to hurt you."

"Fine."

Santano rushed forward with a violent downward blow. Michael raised his staff and caught the blade in the center. The sharp edge again dug into the wood. Michael twirled his staff into a three point strike, pulling the sword free and off balancing Santano. Blood flew from Santano's mouth as his head was jerked left and right by the first two blows. Flipping the staff up for the ending strike caught beneath Santano's chin. Blood flew up to the ceiling, sizzling and smoking, as his teeth cracked. Michael struck Santano once more as he returned the staff to the first strike position. Santano staggered backwards as Michael brought his staff over to his left side in second strike position and lunged forward with a thrust aimed at Santano's face.

Santano's face stripped of flesh as his motion suddenly stopped. Standing in a position he should have little balance in, he reached out and gripped the end of the staff in an iron grasp, bringing the thrust to a sudden halt. Michael struggled in the grip, trying to alternate between finishing the strike and pulling away. He watched as Santano found his feet and the rips in his face mended, his teeth realigned and the blood dried. Suddenly the head of the staff broke off in Santano's hand. Michael stumbled backwards with the sudden end of the struggle. Before he had a chance to take in what had happened, Santano dashed forward with his hand outstretched. Michael brought his staff forward and let Santano's fingers wrap around that instead of his throat. Michael tried to push his attacker back, but Santano refused to move. Their eyes locked. Santano's eyes were empty and devoid of emotion. His grip tightened until the staff snapped in his hand. Michael stumbled before falling back. Looking at his broken staff, his face filled with shock.

"That's impossible," Michael stuttered. "This is rattan. There's no way you could just snap it like that."

"I am no longer an ordinary man," Santano said with a smile.

Michael stared onwards, coming to terms with what he was seeing, what Rebecca had told him. "Just what are you?"

Santano's smile became wider, more sinister. "Not 'What am I?' What am I becoming? I am becoming one of the most feared beings in the world. A being of such immense power that it brings entire nations to their knees, but I can't achieve that power alone. I need help Michael; from you and your friends, whether you like it or not."

Blood Sword glowing, Santano attacked again in quick thrusts. With his staff broken and no training in two handed combat, Michael's instincts took over, incorporating his staff knowledge as much as he could into his motions. He was successful in deflecting the initial thrusts, but Santano's attacks became quicker and quicker. Michael was forced back as Santano advanced. Finally Santano broke through Michael's defenses and cut his arm. Michael winced as he jumped back. Santano's assault ceased. Michael held his bleeding arm as Santano examined the blood on his blade. He ran his fingers through it and felt the texture. Even though the blood was fresh, it wasn't wet, already drying on his fingers. Santano looked at Michael and said, "Bind."

The blood running down Michael's arm and through his fingers suddenly came to life. It coagulated into a sticky mass that lashed out and gripped his arm and hand. Michael pulled his hand free of the living blood's grip and tried to shake it off his hand, but pseudopods reached out and began to travel up his arm. The blood from his cut latched onto his body and pulled his arm against it tightly as it began to envelope him. Michael tried to pull it off but only found his arms pressed against his body. The living mass moved quickly and covered Michael's body from head-to-toe until he was simply a red squirming mass.

Michael, encased in his own blood, fell to the floor. He struggled trying to force himself free, but the bond was too strong. Angry muffled sounds escaped the mass as it had completely covered his head, preventing any form of speech. Santano approached and placed his foot on the writhing mass. He stared down at the cocooned Michael and said, "You certainly do have a fire about you. Don't worry, it'll be over soon." Santano pulled his hand across the flat of his sword, igniting it, and both he and Michael vanished in a veil of smoke.

***

Monica was home alone save for the large Doberman her parents kept. She sat on her bed with a small photo album in her lap. The dog with the studded collar slept peacefully on the floor at the side of her bed. Monica browsed the photos of her now deceased friends as she occasionally wiped the tears from her eyes. She hadn't seen Rebecca since the day before her outburst and wanted to apologize in person, but Rebecca hadn't been in school since. She wasn't answering her phone either. Monica wasn't sure what to make of that.

The Doberman's head suddenly shot up, instantly waking from his sleep. Monica didn't notice until he started to growl. She looked over the edge of the bed and watched in confusion as the dog rose to its haunches with fur bristled. "Taurus?" she asked the dog. "What is it? What's wrong boy?" She jumped when the dog began to bark. Suddenly it took off out of her room and down the stairs. "Taurus!" Monica called as she threw the book down to chase after it.

A black mist wafted in around the cracks in the front door and compressed into a solid form. Taurus stared down the demon as it took shape. The mist solidified into a grinning disease as the dog menacingly barked. Monica came to a stop at the base of the stairs just before entering the living room. She stared stunned at the nude, sickly looking man in front of her. Supporting himself on his crude, gnarled staff, the disease licked his dry lips with a chuckle. He offered his arm, currently unaware that his target was even in the same room. "Go ahead," he said. Taurus lunged forward and took the decrepit arm into his mouth. Monica frantically shouted his name, trying to call the dog off. Black blood sprayed from the withered arm. Disease's arm jerked in the dog's mouth for a few short seconds before Taurus released the arm in deep hacking gags.

Taurus' body started to quickly be covered in a worsening case of mange. Yellow mucus ran out of his eyes and ears and his nose dried. He stumbled away before falling to the ground in convulsions. Monica wanted to scream, but the mere sight of the disease turned her stomach. Coupled by the noxious smell wafting from his body, she held her mouth and nose as she gagged. She turned and ran back the way she came. The disease grinned as he slowly advanced, leaning each step into his staff. "Low constitution," he mocked. "You'll be easy to catch."

The disease followed Monica through the hall's threshold and found her heaving on the steps of the stairs. Disease watched in glee for a moment, enjoying the sight of Monica regurgitating her lunch. She wiped the spittle from her mouth as she tried to catch her breath. "Aw, do I make you sick?" the underling laughed. He reached out a withered hand. "Let me touch you and make it worse." Hand stretched out, the disease advanced. Fear and nausea hit Monica. She pulled herself to her feet and ran up the stairs. In her frightened haste she stumbled up the steps. The disease watched with glee. "Monica," he sang. He hacked up mucus and then spit the milky black green bile like a bullet. The bile hit Monica dead in the center of her back as she reached the landing. She tumbled over and tried to crawl away, the smell of the bile making her heave. Her limps quickly lost strength and her body ached. The disease chuckled as he slowly ascended the steps. Monica's body began to shake and quiver as her muscles spasm and her temperature dropped. She was in the fetal position when the disease set foot on the landing. "Don't worry," he said as he kneeled down beside her. "It'll pass soon. For the moment, we need you alive."

The disease's body began to lose its solidity and became a dark mist. The vapors moved about Monica's body, forming tightly around her, consuming her until she became one with it. The mist, now slightly larger in size, traveled across the floor and to the nearest door. It opened to Monica's room, where the mist stopped only momentarily. It traveled across the floor and over the bed. The pages of the photo album turned as the mist passed over it and through the cracks in the window. The final vapor trail left the album open to the last page, a picture of Monica overlooking the Grand Canyon from the previous summer.

***

A sparrow struggled flight into Heather's back yard. It landed on a bare branch and slouched. The cold mist that escaped its beak became dark. A thick accented chuckle began to fill the air. "Birdie birdie, how hungry are thee?" the voice of hunger sang. "Birdie birdie, what a tasty treat." The mist wafted to the ground and began to take on hunger's form. "Birdie birdie, sing to me a serenade." His dark hand reached up and plucked the bird from the branch as he fell to the ground. "Birdie birdie, what a treat bathed in vinegar and marmalade." His mouth opened wide as the bird's wings flapped frantically and it chirped in distress. The hunger placed the frightened sparrow into his mouth and closed his jaws around it. He swallowed and the bulge of the bird moved down his throat in frantic spasms. The hunger rubbed his stomach and sighed. "Good eats, but KFC it ain't."

The hunger moved across the backyard, up the patio and to the back door. He left his bare footprints in the unshoveled snow. A few inches had accumulated over the light flurries in the past week. He eyed the door knob quizzically. "I wonder," he thought to himself as he reached for the door knob. He touched it only with his fingers and turned it. It was unlocked. He pushed open the door that led into the kitchen. "That was easy," he said as he entered the room. "So careless humans are." He closed the door and took in the empty room. As kitchens go, it was nothing special. A sink full of dirty dishes, a still warm pan on the stove. A microwave cornered the refrigerator that rested beside the counter. The table in the center of the room was littered with text books and papers, as well as Heather's backpack. The hunger's eyes sparkled and his lips grinned when he realized where he was. He clapped his hands appreciatively together and said, "My favorite room."

The hunger skipped playfully over to the refrigerator and pulled it open. His eyes grew wider and his mouth began to water. "They're fully stocked." He smacked his chops as he eyed the contents. "Milk. Apples. Oranges. Eggs. Bacon." He shook with glee as he named the contents of the refrigerator to himself.

Heather walked in laughing to herself and shaking her head. "Haden, you goof," she said. "You don't have to come all the way back here because—" She stopped when she heard the hunger ecstatically naming off different foods. The refrigerator door was open and hid him from her. The hunger was so focused on the food that he hadn't noticed Heather's entrance. She reached for the pan on the stove and shouted, "Who are you?"

The hunger broke his attention from the refrigerator's contents and closed the door. He smiled at her, showing his dull white teeth. "I am your hunger," he said.

"How did you get in here?"

"Oh, your backdoor was open."

Heather was almost stunned by his frankness. "You can't just walk into people's houses! Get out!"

"But I came for dinner."

Heather swallowed. "Alright, I'll give you food, but then you have to—"

"Thanks!"

The hunger tilted the refrigerator forward and pried his jaws open. Like a snake his jaws wrapped around the refrigerator and in an almost cartoon-like fashion he swallowed it whole.

The hunger's body expanded to accommodate the huge item in his gut. He sighed gleefully and rubbed his engorged belly as his body slowly shrank back to its normal size. "Delicious," he said. Heather shook with fear. She found herself unable to move, barely able to hold the pan in her hand. She gripped the handle with both hands, trying to steady it. The hunger burped in satisfaction and a dinner knife flew from his maw and into the air. It fell into his hand and he said, "That was yummy." He grinned. "You're next."

With a flick of his wrist, the hunger threw the knife at Heather, almost carelessly and without aim. The knife struck Heather's side, burying the entire blade into her, but missing any vital organs. The pan crashed on the floor as Heather stumbled back and reeled over. The hunger laughed as she pulled the bloodied knife from her side. "Getting hungry yet?" the hunger asked. Heather dropped the knife and ran back the way she came, leaving bloodied hand marks as she supported and guided herself on the walls. "One, two, I'm coming for you," the hunger sang as he walked after Heather. "Three, four, can't open a door."

Knees weak and shaky, Heather's bloodied hands fumbled with the door knob. "Why won't you turn?!" she demanded.

"Five, six, my power packs a kick," the hunger sang as he entered into the living room.

Heather spun around quickly, nearly losing her balance and fell into the door. She found she was having trouble standing.

The hunger laughed. "The weakness hits before the hunger does,"

"What are you?" Heather asked. "What do you want?"

The hunger bowed in introduction. "I am hunger, servant of the Second…and the big, bloated—You know what, never mind. I serve the Horseman of Famine in all incarnations." Then he mumbled, "Unfortunately."

"What do you want with me?" Heather couldn't support her weight anymore and slid to the floor, leaving a trail of blood with each hand as she tried to support her weight.

The hunger frowned. "That is the sad part, I'm afraid. You've been chosen for a watery grave. I've been sent to fetch you." He patted his stomach with a smile. "Don't worry. I'll bring you first class."

Heather struggled to stand, to try and get away, but she was barely able to sit up. Her stomach started to churn and growl. She was starving.

"It'll be over soon," the hunger said. "You'll feel my power at full force any minute, then we can—Hey, is that China in there?" The hunger's attention shifted from Heather to a cabinet that held various China and knick knacks. "You mind if I have a snack first?" he asked. Heather slumped to her side and struggled to cry out for help, but barely spoke louder than a whisper.

The hunger skipped over to the cabinet singing, "Yummy yummy." He opened the cabinet doors and one-by-one plucked the various contents from the cabinet and placed them into his waiting mouth as he continued to sing. Each thing was chewed only a few times before he swallowed. The crunching and churning of glass filled the room as tears ran down Heather's face. She could no longer cry out for help. She was light headed and her vision was losing focus. The pain in her stomach was unbearable. Soon she blacked out.

The hunger looked in Heather's direction, popping a tea cup into his mouth. It crunched and crashed in his mouth before he swallowed. "My, you were a tough one," he said. "But I guess it's time to go." He walked to where Heather lay and studied her for a moment. "Yup, definitely tough. Water will accept you gladly." He shrugged and lifted her in his arms. "Oh well, in you go." He opened his mouth wide and placed Heather in head first. He pushed her further in with each chomp of his jaws. Heather's legs dangled lifelessly out of his mouth as he paused at her waist, catching his breath. After a moment he swallowed, slurping Heather the rest of the way into his mouth like a spaghetti noodle. His body expanded to accommodate her girth before returning to its normal size. The hunger patted his stomach. "Sweet and delicious." The hunger turned back into the room and advanced. He looked around and thought aloud, "I wonder if she has anything else to eat?"

"Time doesn't allow for it," Úna said.

The hunger spun around to find Úna standing behind him with arms crossed. "My Mistress!"

"How goes the preparations?"

"Everything is going according to plan. I took my time getting here, waiting for the others."

"Good. Rebecca is on her way to Angel. The sacrifices cannot begin until she arrives. The destruction and disease will not hold back against them. You will. Do not win your battles."

"I had no intention."

"Good. Your false Lord is far away. With some luck, he will stay far away. Make sure everything stays going according to plan."

"I will Mistress."

"Good." Úna approached the hunger and laid her hand on his stomach. "This one at least must live. Our hero must have something to fight for."

"Yes, Milady. I will do what I can. I shall not win my battles."

Úna nodded her head. "Then be off."

The hunger moved past Úna and placed his hands on the door. The door began to crack and erode. When the hunger opened it, it led to the interior of the school.

"One more thing," Úna said, causing the hunger to wince and sheepishly look back. "Cough up the bird."

The hunger chuckled. "Yes ma'am." He hacked and heaved until the bird, thick with mucus, flew from his gut and onto the floor. Úna picked it up into her hands and nodded. The hunger walked through the door and closed it behind him. The door returned to normal as quickly as it had changed.

Úna wiped the spittle from the frightened bird. "It's okay now," she said. "I won't let you be hungry for a few days, okay?" She opened the door and released the bird back into the wild.

***

Sirens blaring, Rebecca arrived at the police station safely. She turned the sirens and lights off as she approached the building. She took the waist strap from her trench coat and wrapped the blade of the dagger in it before hiding it in an inside pocket. She wouldn't get far in a building full of cops with a drawn weapon.

The interior of the station was in chaos. The phones were ringing endlessly as calls of some disruption came pouring in. Rebecca wondered if it had anything to do with Santano. She didn't know where the holding cells were and couldn't risk asking someone. She heard someone shouting at the frantic officers in the room. Rebecca guessed he was the Chief of Police.

"Have you heard anything back from Jeff?" he shouted at someone. Rebecca wasn't sure who as she tried to just stay out of sight and find where to go.

"His back-up should be there soon," someone called back.

"Keep me updated on his situation! I want to know if it's Santano!" He looked at the few people in handcuffs. "Get these guys out of here! Clear this place out!"

Several officers began to escort their prisoners towards the back of the building, presumably to the holding cells. Rebecca thought this was her chance. They weren't taken in large groups and she waited for the last group, joining them with her hands behind her back. Angel's coat was too big for her and the sleeves covered her hands. Even if she was wearing handcuffs, they would have been hidden by the sleeves.

Rebecca stayed towards the back of the group, but away from the rear guard. She was the only girl in the lineup of five. Angel's head shot up when Rebecca walked in. He was in a cell alone wearing a disposable scrub top for a shirt. Worry crept into him. If Rebecca had been arrested, she no longer held the Dagger of Power. Without it, he had little chance of escape. With Rebecca in a holding cell holding up the final sacrifices, it would only be a matter of time before Santano came to retrieve her. Then matters would only get worse.

The four men in the lineup, none looking especially dangerous in Rebecca's opinion, were put in a cell together. The officer behind Rebecca took her by the arm. She felt his fingers and thumb squeeze her arm. Jason had told her a pressure point was in the bicep which helps control anyone they are transporting. He had showed her where it was once, but with the loose jacket, the officer had missed it. Rebecca looked around the room. There were three officers standing guard, most likely for Angel. That was five armed officers.

"Don't worry," the officer holding her said. "We won't put you in a cell with the guys."

Rebecca took a deep breath. "I'm sorry."

Rebecca broke away from the officer's hold and spun around on a pivot. She sent a hard blow to his solar plexus and made him stumble. He bent forward holding his stomach and Rebecca continued forward, delivering a hard kick to the side of his head. She brought her elbow down on the back of his head and sent him down unconscious.

The cells came alive with cheers as the inmates cheered her on and rattled the cell doors. The second officer hastily locked the cell and ran to help his partner as the other guards dashed from their seats. Rebecca turned quick to face them. One down, four to go. The first officer threw himself to tackle her, but Rebecca dropped to the floor as he came close, kicking him over her and back first into the cell door. He groaned and tried to stand before blacking out. The other guards were practically on top of her. Rebecca rolled to her hands and knees and kicked out her leg, driving it into the nearest guard's stomach. She kicked his legs out from under him as she got to her feet. The third guard reached for her and she took a quick grip of his hand and twisted. The guard howled as Rebecca bent his hand. She pushed him down and used his body as leverage to kick up into the air and kick the fourth guard back into the fifth. She then dealt a hard blow to the back of the third guard's head and sent him down.

Angel gawked in awe as the guards went down one by one. The fourth guard reached for his gun. Rebecca reached out and grabbed his hand before he fully drew it from its holster. She kicked her leg straight up and caught her heel against his chin. She jumped into the air and wrapped her leg around his neck and pulled him hard to the ground in a twist. The fifth guard had fully drawn his gun as Rebecca quickly came back up. She grabbed his wrist where she knew there was a pressure point and lifted the gun away from her as she pressed another pressure point in his collar. The guard went down in a pained grunt. Rebecca held the points tightly until the guard dropped his gun, then she delivered a hard chop to both sides of his neck, knocking him out.

The cells roared with cheers as Angel stood in proud amazement. Shoulder hurting, Rebecca searched the unconscious officers for their keys and brought them all to Angel's cell.

"Where did you learn to do that?" Angel asked as Rebecca began to try the keys.

"You taught me," Rebecca answered.

"I taught you?"

"I've seen you in my dreams for as long as I can remember. Everything I know, especially about fighting, you taught me."

"I see." Angel smiled. "You've been prepared for this."

"I have no idea. All I know is something bad is happening. Something came for me and Jason. It wasn't human."

"I know. Use that key. The Collection has begun."

Rebecca pulled the door open. "What's the Collection?" Rebecca finally got a good look at Angel. He had aged. "Why do you look so old?"

"We need to get out of here first. Where's the dagger I gave you? Do you still have it?"

"Yes." Rebecca pulled it from the inner pocket and unwrapped it.

Angel held it with her. "Psionic Camouflage." From the dagger's hilt a green mist wafted and twirled around the two. Rebecca looked at the twirling mist panic stricken as she and Angel began to vanish. "Don't be afraid," Angel said. "I'm enshrouding us in its magic. It'll help us slink away." Angel completely disappeared for a moment before he reappeared in Rebecca's distorted sight. She looked around the green hazed room.

"What happened?" Rebecca asked over the wails of the inmates.

"We're invisible. When you release the dagger, it'll only last a few minutes. Use that time to get out and wait for me outside."

"What are you going to do?" Rebecca watched as an officer rushed into the room to see what had happened. After a quick look around he radioed for backup.

"I'm going to get my sword."

"But you're hurt."

Angel placed his hand over his bandaged body. "I'm alright. My job does come with some perks. Now go and wait for me."

Rebecca nodded and let the dagger go. "Quickstep," Angel said as he began to move. His already distorted form froze, his hazed body blurred and then he was gone. The inmates' shouts brought Rebecca's attention to them. They were begging, shouting, and demanding for their freedom. The guard that came in was checking on the officers she had beaten while relaying what he was seeing over his radio. "Sorry," Rebecca said as she made haste for the exit. "We have to save the world—or something."

Rebecca left their shouts behind her and left the station as quickly as she could, not sure when the cloaking magic would fade. She reached Jeff's squad car and rested on it, letting the adrenaline fade. As she watched the green haze fade she realized what she had done. "I just assaulted a bunch of cops," she said. "I'm so going to jail for this."

Rebecca didn't wait long for Angel. He pulled up in another squad car, scaring her.

"Where did you get this?" she asked through the open passenger window.

"Desperate times call for desperate measures," Angel answered. "Get in. We have to hurry."

Rebecca pointed at the car behind her. "I have a car they won't look for!"

Angel looked at her in shocked disbelief. "Wow, you're already good at this."

"My boyfriend's best friend's father is a cop! Now let's go! He's in trouble!"

"Alright, but I'm driving. I know where to go."

"Whatever! Just hurry!"

CHAPTER XIV

Sirens blaring, Angel rushed to their destination. Rebecca used this time to finally try and get some answers.

"Just who are you?" Rebecca asked.

"I've given a lot of thought to that over the centuries," Angel answered. "I had thought I was the last one."

"What are you talking about? What are you? The other day you looked my age, now you look thirty years older."

"That's because I'm aging. I was born in London in the eleventh century. I have been alive for over nine hundred years."

"No, that's not possible."

"I thought that too, once. That callousness is what destroyed my family. I couldn't protect them and my sins stunted my power."

"You're serious, aren't you?"

"You've seen what I can do. You've bared witness to my enemies. You've seen what the avatar is becoming. What else could it be? Please, don't make my mistake."

"Who are you? How could I do those things? How have I known you all my life, but we've never met?"

"You were being prepared for our encounter. My name is Angel Virtue. I am your ancestor."

Rebecca swallowed hard and remained silent for a moment. "You said you thought you were the last one. What happened?"

"My friend betrayed me. He introduced me to the occult and I followed him into Satanism to spite my parents. I was an atheist in a time when blasphemers were executed. I had a lover who was devout, as most of the populace. She didn't know about what I did. I wanted to wed her and tried leaving the cult. That's when I saw my first avatar and began to discover the truth of my lineage."

"What truth? If we're the same, what are we?"

"Demon hunters; God's mortal soldiers. My friend, the leader of the cult, was an avatar. He turned the true believers into demons and killed the rest. He tried to turn me, but I wouldn't. He succeeded in becoming the Third Horseman."

"Pestilence."

"Yes. He unleashed a plague on my blood. His plague hounds sniffed out anyone carrying Virtue blood and injected them with a plague that killed them in minutes. My lover was pregnant with my child. I thought she too dead, but he missed her. My son's blood was hidden from him."

"They survived? How?"

"I had hid them with the very cross you wear."

Rebecca touched her cross. "Our heirloom? This was yours?"

"I bought it and blessed it for her. I was atheist no longer. I had stared evil in the face and knew it was coming for her. I gave her that as a gift and sent her away, trying to protect her."

Rebecca stared at the ancient cross in her fingers. "The wearer of this cross is protected by an angel's love." She looked at Angel. "The saying isn't about an angel, is it? It's about you. The wearer of this cross is protected by Angel's love."

Angel nodded. "My love for Amanda and our child hid them and their descendants from Hell for nine centuries. But now they know there was a survivor and our bloodline grew."

Rebecca eyes grew wide with fear. "Wait, if they almost killed us once…what about my family now?"

Angel solemnly shook his head. "I'm sorry. Heaven is on high alert, but…"

Rebecca shook her head. She already knew the truth. "No. You're wrong. You have to be! My mom; my dad—They were just catching a cold!"

"I'm sorry." Angel reached between the seats and handed Rebecca the sheathed Sword of Might. "Expose the blade and ask it yourself. Ask it to show you the Virtues. It will show you what it showed me."

Rebecca took the sword and exposed the blade an inch or two. She was silent, afraid of what it might show her. She closed her eyes and took a deep breath. "Please, show me my family. Show me what's happened to them."

Rebecca's mind's eye opened for the first time. The images the sword showed her at first were of people she did not recognize. The images were quick. Gun shots and the sounds of wrecks echoed in her ears. She saw blood spill. A realization came to her that these were distant relatives whose blood was diluted. Their friends and lovers shared their violent deaths. She watched others fade away from starvation, or mauled and eaten by hungry animals. The sword showed her increasingly familiar faces. She watched as they coughed up blood and their organs failed and ruptured. She watched as the faces of close family began to fill her mind. Tears were rolling down her face and her lips were trembling. She watched her aunt pass out for the last time as her blood sugar fell drastically. She saw a cousin's concussion knock him into a coma and watched as his respiratory system failed. She saw her grandfather clench his chest as he went into cardiac arrest. Then she saw her father. He was slumped over in his wheel chair, trying to wheel it to the stair lift. He was slouched over so much that he fell from the chair and down the stairs. Her mother was in an emergency room. She was cut up and bleeding. Rebecca knew she had a wreck. The doctors were losing her.

"Enough," Rebecca cried as she sheathed the exposed blade, ending the visions. "Mom. Dad. Everyone. I can't believe it. They're really gone."

"I'm sorry. I know your feelings, I've suffered them too. There is nothing you can do for them now, but you can ensure it never happens again."

Rebecca opened her tear stained, rage filled eyes and growled, "How?"

"You must fight. You must take my place. You must become the next demon hunter."

Rebecca wiped her tears away. "How do I do that?"

"You'll know when the time comes."

Rebecca watched as Angel pulled up to her high school. He had cut the sirens and lights as they approached. "What are we doing here?" Rebecca asked as she followed Angel out of the car.

"This is where they are waiting for us," Angel answered.

"You mean Santano and that thing? This is where he took Jason?"

"This is the Collection, the ceremony that seals the avatar's powers. He cannot start the ceremony until all five of the sacrifices have been gathered. Rebecca, they wait only for you."

"I'm one of them? I'm supposed to be one of the sacrifices?"

"Yes. Once you pass the threshold, we will have little time. We have to find the avatar and his allies and stop them. For each sacrifice Santano is able to make, he becomes stronger. He becomes ever closer to Death."

"Then what are we waiting for? We have to stop them." Rebecca began to run towards the building, but Angel grabbed her arm and pulled her to a stop.

"Wait," he said. "Once you enter that field, there is no turning back."

"Field?" Rebecca looked at the school. "I don't see anything. Angel, we're wasting time."

"They'll wait for you. To begin without all the sacrifices would kill Santano. They will wait. Rebecca, there is so much I need to teach you, but I don't have the time." He took the Sword of Might from her and handed her the sheathed Dagger of Power. "Listen, this is nothing new. This is a war that has been raging long before written history."

"Written history?"

"Yes. We've been fighting that long, holding Hell's forces back the best we could, preventing Satan from bringing the Four Horsemen to life. Though we win battle after battle, we haven't won them all. We are losing this war. Three Horsemen have risen and now Santano means to be the Fourth."

"We can't let the Fourth rise. That's what you always said to me in my dreams. I never knew what that meant, until now. Can we stop him?"

"We have to. The more sacrifices he makes, the stronger he'll become. We can't let him make anymore. From this point on, we will fight together." Angel began to cough hard for a long minute. He spit out red tinted phlegm. "I am fading fast. I will not survive the night. I wish I had the time to teach you everything I know, but what I will share with you now will have to do." Angel held the Sword of Might before her. "This is the Sword of Might. It is, largely, an offensive weapon. What you hold is the

Dagger of Power; mostly a defensive weapon. These are the Heavenly Weapons, which feeds on our faith and life. You've seen some of what each weapon can do. They are feeding off you, drawing strength from you. In turn, I am recovering some power as well."

"How do I use these powers? When I fought that…thing…I'm not sure how I did it."

"My father once told me these heirlooms are at once tainted and blessed. Only mortal hands can hold them. Only the blood of a Virtue can harness their power. You'll learn how to unite with them. Their power is greatest when your mind is clear and your spirit is in line with theirs. Calling out the name of a power with the intent of use will unleash that ability to its fullest potential."

Rebecca exposed the dagger's rusted blade and examined it. "How will I know what they are? What was that mist thing you made it do?"

"Psionic Camouflage. The mist enshrouds you and bends the light around you. It's good for getting around undetected. Another useful ability is Whirlwind. The blade unleashes hurricane force winds. If it doesn't move your opponent, it will at least slow them down. Use Quickstep when you need to get away. The world around you will look like it's standing still, but in truth you're moving faster than the eye can follow. When you need to shield yourself from an attack, use Psionic Shield. It will create a field of holy energy in front of you that can stop bullets and many demonic attacks. Its integrity isn't infinite. The stronger the attack, the more it weakens. Enough bullets, especially armor piercing bullets, can break it."

Rebecca looked the dagger over. Holding it away from Angel she said, "Psionic Shield." An opaque white field of energy formed from the dagger's hilt in front of her, protecting the length of her body. Where she moved the dagger the shield followed. She touched the shield to find it warm and pleasant. It rippled under her touch and her fingers passed through it. "Cool," she smiled. "This will protect me?"

"It won't let any harm pass through it. The dagger has one attack I'm able to use, Cosmic Crush. It's a close quarter power, so it has to touch what you mean to destroy and it takes a moment to power up." Rebecca shook the dagger in her hand, causing the shield to dissipate. "It pulls in all the molecules around it, turning it into empty space. When you break contact, the implosion reverses, throwing everything it pulled in, out. It has strong recoil, so be careful."

"I will."

"Use Cosmic Crush only if you need to. They mean to capture you, so don't get drawn into a fight. Run if you can. Call out to me."

"I'll call you, but if my friends are there, I'm going to save them."

"Alright." Angel looked at the building. "I don't know where they'll be, so we'll split up and look for them. The building is empty so our voices will travel. Stay on the same floor."

"Alright."

"Let's not keep them waiting anymore."

They entered through the main entrance. Rebecca saw a flash of red as she crossed the threshold but saw nothing when she looked back. It must have been the field Angel had spoken of. Rebecca tied the dagger's sheath to the belt loop of her pants as she followed Angel. With him she felt safe and didn't feel the need to draw her weapon. She looked down the hall and then up the stairs as they passed. Angel had moved the Sword of Might to his side and held the handle, ready to draw it at a moment's notice.

"Angel, wait," Rebecca said.

Angel turned to her, not dropping his guard. "What is it? Do you see something?"

"I know you want us to stay close, but I know this building better than you. I think we should take different floors. From here there's only one way to go anyway."

"If you get in trouble and we are too far away—"

"You have to trust me. I'm prepared for this. I think I've been preparing for it all my life. I have your dagger and I know how to use it. I'll be safe. Take upstairs. We'll meet at the other end. If anything happens I'll use Quickstep and find you."

Angel coughed and cleared his throat. "Alright, but remember, don't let them lull you into a fight. Santano is not alone. He has three high ranking demons helping him."

"I know. I've met one."

"Be safe."

"You too."

Rebecca drew the dagger and began down the hall. Angel moved towards the stairs, keeping Rebecca in his sights for a moment. "Angels protect her," he said before climbing the stairs.

Angel stared down the quiet hall. He breathed out. He raised his hand and closed his eyes. He whispered, "Holy Father, be my light. Shine upon the way and direct me now. Wisdom eternal, scatter the darkness of my ignorance." Three bright flashes appeared against his closed eyes, illuminating the level's interior through the wood and steel. During the second flash, Angel caught a glimpse of a shadowy light. It was quick and he wasn't sure exactly where it was or what it was. He wasn't sure if what he saw was good or ill. "There is something here," Angel said as he took sword draw stance. "I wish I knew its number and intent."

Angel moved cautiously through the hall. His sword was silent. He was relieved to see the classroom doors staggered in the hall. It would prevent a direct back attack as he searched the rooms. He peered in through the glass from a safe distance. His sword remained quiet. No threat in the room, and upon peering inside, no victims either. This continued for the next three or four rooms, Angel zigzagging through the hall, until the Sword of Might began to emit a slight hum in Angel's ear. *They are trying to hide,* Angel thought. He continued down the hall, his head in constant motion. The sword's hum began to intensify and Angel tightened his grip. A demon was near.

Angel eyed his surroundings. For demons, there were plenty of hiding places. The lockers, the doors, the ceiling or floor, even the air itself. He did not know which demons Santano had at his side. A loud crash pulled Angel's attention. A classroom door flew at him. "Keen Edge!" Angel shouted as he drew his sword in a vertical slash. The door cleaved in two and passed around him. They crashed into the lockers behind him, rattling them as they shattered. The destruction charged behind the door, a glistening grin on his face. He was unarmed and put all his strength behind a punch. Angel faced the flat of his sword out and held his free hand against it. The sword clanged as the destruction's fist struck the flat of the blade. The force was so strong it pushed Angel back on unmoving feet. He lost his stance when he slammed against the lockers. The destruction continued his advance, drawing back for a second blow. Angel threw himself to the side and rolled back to his feet several paces from his attacker. The locker clanged and buckled under the destruction's strength. His hair flared up from his attack. He stayed still with a grin on his face until his hair fell back into place. He stood erect and faced Angel.

"I didn't take you to be so nimble," the destruction said.

Angel sheathed his sword to conserve its power and stood battle ready.

"You might be worth the effort after all. A good warm up at least. Yes, I think I'll have fun ripping you apart."

"You mean we'll have fun," the disease stated.

Angel looked about and saw a dark mist drift from the ventilation system. The mist drifted down behind Angel and formed into the minion of Pestilence. He struck the butt of his gnarled staff against the floor. The shaft became straight with a swirl carve. The head of the staff was tipped with a black steel, serrated spear point. Black feathered flesh tied spear to shaft. The disease stood from its hunch and gripped his newly acquired seven foot spear in both hands.

The destruction chuckled. "If you share my definition of fun."

"I think we can work something out."

The disease took a strong step forward while raising his spear over head. He brought the spear down where Angel stood. Angel took a step back and to the side as he drew his sword and deflected the spear point. The spear struck the ground and yellowed and cracked the surrounding tile. Black mold sprang from the cracks and uplifted the edges. The destruction pulled his fist back and charged. Angel spun towards the heavy steps but couldn't get his guard up. The destruction connected with Angel's jaw and sent the demon hunter sprawling across the floor. The disease thrust his spear in an arc as Angel flew past him. "Did I hit him?" the disease asked as he spun around. The destruction rushed past his partner and shouted, "Keep fighting!"

Angel left blood splatter where he struck the ground. His jaw hurt and he thought some of his teeth were broken. He was unprepared for the strength of the destruction. Angel heard the destruction rushing forward and threw himself away from the encroaching shadow. The force of the destruction's blow punched a hole in the floor several times the size of his fist. Angel moved back, trying to find his feet as the destruction moved in pursuit. He drew back a second punch. On unsteady legs Angel caught the blow on the flat of his sword. Again the force pushed him back, but it forced Angel to find his footing. The destruction moved in a quick step and thrust his leg out, slamming it into Angel's stomach and pushing the demon hunter back across the floor. The air was knocked out of his lungs but he stayed on his feet.

The disease rushed forward with a twirl of his spear in a downward slam. Angel drew back as the spear point eroded the ground. The disease moved forward, thrusting out the spear in quick motions. Angel did his best to deflect the quickening flurry of thrusts with his sword. He tried to keep the distance between them. The disease found an opening in Angel's guard and thrust the spear its full length. Angel threw his weight to the side as the tip cut into his chest. The cut was deep but didn't break past bone. Angel stumbled for his balance. His body became hot and he fell against the lockers. He heard the destruction charge again and rose to a kneel with his sword raised to block. The flat of the sword caught destruction's punch and it vibrated Angel's whole body. The ground beneath him buckled as the destruction added a second fist and pushed against the blade's flat. Angel could hear the cracking of the wood and tile beneath him, maybe even his own bones.

Through blurred vision, Angel could see the destruction's grinning face and smoke wafting from his hands.

"Look at you," the demon of destruction said. "Pathetic."

Angel pushed against the strength of the creature over him, but the destruction pushed with equal force. Angel's hands were beginning to burn as the sound of burning flesh filled his ears.

"I'm going to crush you."

"Lord," Angel prayed. "Give me strength."

Angel felt his arms fill with power. He pushed against the blade and as the destruction pushed back, Angel felt a second pair of hands on his that added to his strength. The destruction was pushed back. Angel swung the sword in a horizontal slash and shouted, "Eternal Fire!" A wave of flames erupted from the blade and halted the destruction's advance. The two demons moved back, their smiles not once leaving their faces.

The destruction flexed his fists. "So you still have a little fight left in you," he stated.

"This is the best he has?" the disease asked. "That's sickening, even by my standards."

"I guess nine hundred years has taken its toll."

Angel watched them through blurred vision. The cut on his chest ached and burned. Green puss was forming on it. Sweat beads poured down his face and he was burning up. *I can't believe how strong these two are*, Angel thought. *That cut...the second one infected me with something. How am I going to beat these two when I couldn't beat a single cut rate demon?* Angel sheathed his sword. *I may have one chance, if I can gather enough strength. It'll be tricky, but if I can pull it off...*

"What are you waiting for?" the destruction asked. "Your move."

"You're giving him the advantage?" the disease asked.

"Yes. He has a new fire in him. I want to see it."

"Let's just finish him and get on with the sacrifices!"

Angel coughed. Blood splattered from his bloody mouth. "Well, if you're going to give me a fighting chance," Angel grinned through bloody lips, "there is something I want to try. It's been awhile, so bear with me."

"Enough!" the disease shouted as he began to move forward. "This isn't a game!"

The destruction held out his hand, blocking the disease's advance. "On the contrary," he said. "War is nothing but a bloody, brutal game. The battles within are simply the rounds. Each player takes his turn. Now, it's Angel's turn. Show me."

Uri, Angel thought. *I pray you are with me. I cannot do this without you.* Angel released his sword long enough to draw the sign of the cross over himself with his right hand. He traced the silver cross around his neck with his fingers and lightly gripped it. "Lord God, I beseech Thee. This unworthy servant begs Thine aid. Release Thy angels unto me. Saint Uriel, Regent of the Sun, bring me salvation. Grant to me the fires of your fury and give me strength through this dark hour."

Panic appeared on the disease's face. The grin on the destruction's face widened until he broke into joyous laughter. Fired light appeared around Angel, strengthening his weak aura. "Uri," Angel whispered as he gripped his sword, "guide me."

Angel darted forward at an arc. He leaped from the ground and ran alongside the face of the lockers, running as fast and strong as his legs would carry, using his momentum to keep on the surface and parallel to the ground. The disease moved to attack, thrusting his spear forward. The destruction reached out and grasped the shaft of the spear. "No!" he shouted. "I want to see!"

"Sword of Might!" Angel cried out as he drew his sword and leaped off the lockers with a downward thrust. The destruction, thinking Angel was aiming for them, pivoted the disease to the side so Angel had a clear shot. He was almost disappointed when Angel's blade penetrated the floor. "Seismic Crush!" Angel finished. The ground rumbled and the tiles and dirt lifted off the ground. The area distorted with the energy Angel had gathered and was released through the sword. The area concaved and the energy was released in a violent wave of seismic energy. The ground split and erupted, throwing the underlings against the lockers as the energy released in a thunderous explosion.

Hand gripping the dagger's handle, Rebecca walked down the hall. Her fingers flexed on the handle and her eyes were constantly on the move. It felt like her stomach was doing flips and she realized she was holding her breath. She was cautious as she checked the locked classrooms. They were empty. "Alright," Rebecca whispered to herself. "This is going to get you nowhere. Think. Where would Santano go? His classroom? The teacher's lounge? What is secluded that he could hide a murder? No, they're not murders, not to him. They're sacrifices. Where could he prepare a ritual sacrifice? Does the place even matter?" The ceiling above rumbled. She could hear heavy footsteps. She instantly knew what was going on above her. "Angel…"

Rebecca pivoted on the spot to rush to the nearest set of stairs, but stopped cold when she saw the flesh stripped face of Santano. He tapped the Blood Sword against his leg with a grin on his face.

"Santano," Rebecca growled. She drew the Dagger of Power and held it horizontally before her. At chest level, it felt comfortable.

"Hello Rebecca," Santano said as the flesh returned to his face. "Found me out, I see."

"What is wrong with you?! Why are you doing this?!"

"Isn't that obvious?" a voice from behind Rebecca said. She turned to see the hunger. "He is doing it for what all humans crave. Power."

"Power?" Rebecca asked as her eyes began to fill with tears. "You killed my friends for the promise of power? We were your students. You were supposed to watch over us; to guide us. We trusted you!"

"Exactly why you all were chosen," Santano said. "You were all in my care and innocent in your own way. You gave me the means to my desire, so I took it."

"You're going to pay for what you did." The ceiling shook and rattled from the battle above. "Now where's Jason? If you hurt him—"

"You're more concerned about him than your boyfriend?"

"Michael? You have Michael too?"

"Among others."

"Who?!" Rebecca shouted as tears ran down her face.

"Let's see." Santano began to count them on his fingers. "We have Jason and Michael. Monica. Heather's waiting for you too."

"The flower was tasty," the hunger said as he patted his belly. "Not filling either."

"You—You ate her?" Rebecca exclaimed.

"I spit her back up."

"If you hurt any of them—"

"I haven't hurt any of them, I assure you," Santano said. "Now, if you'll please come with me."

"Let my friends go!"

"I'm afraid I can't do that. Don't worry, death isn't the end. It's only the beginning. I'm on the winning side, Rebecca. Now come along."

Rebecca held the dagger tight and wiped the tears from her eyes. In order to save her friends, she would have to fight someone who held her trust. Once she would not have questioned him, now she must kill him. "If you want me," she said calmly, "you'll have to take me."

"So you'll fight me, just like Michael?" Santano asked. "You shouldn't be as difficult. You're only a girl and none of you have been entirely challenging."

"I hope he gave you a good thrashing, and there's nothing wrong with being 'just a girl'."

"Question!" the hunger called out eagerly with a raised hand, pulling their attention to him as the ceiling shook again. "Are we going to fight now?"

Santano gritted his teeth as his face stripped of flesh and shouted, "Yes!"

"Yay!" The hunger opened his mouth wide, wider than should be possible, and stuck both hands deep down his throat. Slowly, he pulled his arms free and in each hand was a large mace. The shaft was the color of dried clay with brown spots decorating the length. The shaft of the mace was that of a snake, with the end of the shaft opening into the head of a snake. The head of the mace was shaped like an egg, with the smallest part being devoured by the snake. The mace's head was a dirty brown with light and dark tones. The hunger flicked them once and threw the mucus from his hands and weapons. "Let's go sweetness."

Santano's sword began to glow and with Rebecca's momentary distraction, he rushed to the attack. Santano thrust with the Blood Sword as Rebecca turned around. She raised the Dagger of Power and caught the Blood Sword edge to edge, pushing it above her shoulder and evading the attack as the crimson blade slid across the rusted dagger. Her shoulder began to throb as her wound was aggravated again. She wondered if it was bleeding yet. Santano's featureless face showed the shock that it could. He could not believe that she caught his attack. Her eyes didn't show fear or confusion. She knew what she was doing and she was angry.

Rebecca pushed the Blood Sword away and slashed at Santano's midsection. Santano moved back, but the dagger cut into his shirt and grazed his stomach. He could feel the burn of the dagger as its tip cut his flesh. Angel had come close to cutting him, but had not managed, not since he began to ascend as an avatar. Santano was shocked. Had he been so careless as to allow this girl a score that Angel could not? A trickle of blood seeped from the fine cut. She had drawn blood.

"My turn!" the hunger shouted. Rebecca spun around to find the hunger nearly on top of her. He swung his right mace in a wide arc. Rebecca's hand jerked painfully as she deflected the mace's blow. It twisted her body and left her vulnerable to the second blow, which struck her side. It didn't hit bone but buckled her. She grabbed the shaft with a grimace so he couldn't pull back for another strike. The hunger raised his other mace with gleeful laugher. Rebecca raised the dagger and hoarsely said, "Psionic Shield." The opaque white field appeared over her and caught the blow. Even though the field was not physically connected to her, Rebecca could feel the force that travelled through the shield and into her arm, causing her shoulder to throb more. The hunger tried to pull back, but Rebecca held his mace tightly and pulled him close as she thrust with the dagger, throwing out the shield. The hunger did not pass through and hit the field as if it were a solid object. She released the mace as the hunger stumbled back.

Rebecca tried to move back to offer some space between them, but ran against a body. One hand reached across her and gripped her armed hand as a crimson blade pressed against her neck. Her hand was pulled against her, holding her against her captor.

"That is quite enough," Santano said. "Lower your shield."

"Or what?" Rebecca asked. "You'll slit my throat? Like you did Adam and Melissa?"

"That certainly is an option."

Rebecca steeled herself, trying not to show her fear. She didn't know much about the Collection, but she hoped Santano knew even less. "No it's not. You can't kill me out of sequence."

"And what would you know about what I can and cannot do?"

"I'm an A student, remember? I pay attention. If you kill out of sequence, you die."

Santano was silent.

"The devil didn't tell you that; did he?"

"No, he didn't; but why should I believe you?"

"Because she's right," the hunger said. "You know the order. Earth, wind, fire, water. Then the final offering."

"I guess the elements are picky," Rebecca said. "Don't want to snub them."

"You think you're pretty smart, don't you?" Santano asked as he lowered the sword from her neck.

"You tell me. You grade my work." The shield dissipated as Rebecca released the dagger into her waiting hand. She drove it into Santano's leg. "Cosmic Crush!"

Santano remembered that attack. Angel used it to destroy the Blood Dagger and half his arm. His leg was already being sucked into the dagger's energy as it collapsed the space around it. Santano threw his arms off Rebecca and fell back. Pulling his leg away released the attack prematurely. The flesh of Santano's leg was blown away, searing the exposed bone. Rebecca stumbled forward from the shock wave, her coat singed from the explosion. The hunger rushed forward shouting, "Come on!" Rebecca, in a panic, threw both hands up and shouted, "Shield!" This shield was different than the last one. Its color was more solid, showing more of a shadow through it than the hunger itself. The shield was larger than the last, slightly longer than the length of her body and arching slightly around her. The bottom of the shield rested flush with the floor. The hunger beat mercilessly on the shield. "Little pig! Little pig! Let me in!"

"Crimson Tide!" Santano shouted.

Rebecca turned her head to see Santano guide his spilt blood to his blade. It circled the Blood Sword as Santano raised it high and slammed it into the ground. The blood lashed out as a wave across the floor. Rebecca turned her body and moved her hand with it. The shield moved with her hand, expanding its circle with the motion of her hand. Rebecca was almost completely enclosed by the circle now. The blood wave struck the shield with force enough to make Rebecca wince, but washed around it. A few splashes broke through the unprotected side of the shield and burned where it touched her. Between the hunger's beating and Santano's Crimson

Tide, the shield shattered. Rebecca spun around as the hunger moved in. She raised her dagger in defense and instinctively shouted, "Quickstep!"

The hunger suddenly moved at a snail's pace. She turned around to see that Santano was moving at an equally slow pace. She ran around the hunger and away from Santano. She didn't have the strength to finish the fight. Her side still throbbed from the mace hit. Suddenly, Santano ran past her and spun to a stop in front of her, forcing Rebecca to a halt.

Santano grinned. "Nice try, but I'm faster, even with this wound."

Rebecca looked at his leg. The bleeding had stopped and the bone was no longer exposed, but he still had a gaping wound. The entire ceiling shook, making them look at it for a moment.

"I'm sure that doesn't bode well for Angel," Santano said. "You've already seen destruction and what he can do. His partner, disease, won't make things any easier on him. He's done."

"Naw," the hunger said nonchalantly. "Knowing destruction, that last boom probably came from Angel. Thirst for war and all that."

"Even still, he's not walking away from them. Now, Rebecca, if you're out of tricks, please come quietly."

"Sorry," she said, "but I have one more. Whirlwind!" She trained the dagger's blade on Santano as a twirling vortex of hurricane winds ripped from it. Santano braced himself against the strong winds but could barely keep his feet on the ground. The hunger laughed as it vaulted into the air towards her. Rebecca turned and trained the vortex on him and without anything to brace against was blown down the hall. Santano's form blurred as Rebecca spun back around, her hair and coat flailing about in the winds. Santano blurred back into existence within the vortex barely within arm's reach of Rebecca. He couldn't brace against it, only managing to touch the floor with his finger tips as he was blown down the hall.

Finally, Rebecca was offered a moment's repose. The wind had died and Santano was at the other end of the hall. His Quickstep was faster, so Rebecca knew she couldn't out run him. She had to hide. "Psionic Camouflage!" Green smoke wafted from the dagger's hilt and encircled Rebecca. She didn't wait for its magic to completely enshroud her before she began to run. The hunger had been blown by the stairs. He couldn't see her now, enshrouded in the dagger's magic. The world was a green haze again. On the floor above Angel was fighting two demons of his own. Would her presence be more of a hindrance? Rebecca had to trust that Angel could take care of himself. Santano needed her to begin the sacrifices. She couldn't let herself be captured. She had to hide. Rebecca turned the corner and headed for the stairs that led into the basement. She just hoped no one saw her opening the door. She wasn't sure if there was another way out.

Smoke rose from Angel's body. He breathed heavily, leaning against his sword. Nearly all the windows on the floor had shattered. The nearby classroom doors had buckled and splintered as they were blown into the rooms. The lockers in Angel's vicinity had been pulled out of the walls and battered, their contents strewn about. The walls and ceiling had collapsed, making Angel stand in a pile of debris. Water poured out of the broken waterlines. Angel forced himself to stand, struggling against his own weight. The attack had taken everything he had. His chest was burning and the green puss slid down it. He looked around with blurred vision, his focus going in and out. He could not see the demons or sense them. Angel coughed and laughed weakly. "Did I...really beat them?" The smiled faded from his face when a pile of steel and paper began to move. Destruction's chuckle echoed in the empty hall. Painfully, Angel faced the debris pile and readied his weapon. A crash echoed behind him as the destruction leaped into the air shouting, "Guess again!"

Angel spun around and took a swing of his sword, but the destruction landed hard on him. The force of his landing was so great that the weakened floor gave way beneath them. Angel took the brunt of the fall as they fell through the second floor and the floor below. They landed with a loud crash in the basement, into the school's band and sport's equipment. Balls and bats rolled away as cymbals chimed as they struck the ground. The Sword of Might flew from Angel's hand and across the basement's floor. Rebecca's shroud was fading when the two came crashing down. She watched the disease tumble down the hole and into the basement. She knew what the destruction looked like so concluded that it was the third creature, disease. He and the destruction were fighting Angel so Rebecca knew he must be close by. She hid behind large boxes and broken desks to stay out of sight. She was still recovering from her fight with Santano and the hunger. She wasn't in a hurry to get into another fight, especially with something that might be stronger than what she'd already encountered.

The disease flexed his hand. "I think that actually hurt me," he said.

"That's because you're weak," the destruction said as he lifted Angel by his shirt collar. "But it was a good attack. I felt it, barely." He chuckled and tossed Angel to the side. "He's nothing. Let's go, Santano is calling. He must be starting." The destruction began to walk towards the stairs.

"What about him?" the disease asked. "Shouldn't we finish him off?"

"No need. Consider it a reward for his tenacity."

The disease groaned as he watched Angel lift himself from the ground. The disease took aim with his spear and the tip shot off it and impaled itself into Angel's side. "That will finish you off…in time."

Angel pulled the spearhead out as his opponents left to join Santano. "Rebecca," he groaned, worried that she had been captured.

"Angel!" Rebecca called as she ran to Angel's side.

"You're safe. That's good." Angel winced.

"You're hurt!"

"There were…ointments in the jacket. Are they still there?"

"Yes!"

"I need one that is bright yellow and the other that is a light pink."

Rebecca rummaged through the pockets, taking out the jars as she searched. "I'm glad I put all this back." She gave Angel the two jars with the ointments he asked for. He took a dap from both and rubbed them together in his fingers until it turned a light orange. He rubbed enough to cover the long cut on his chest and applied the rest to his impaled side. He applied pressure to his side to keep it from bleeding out. "Please give me a moment," Angel said.

"You used some of that on me, didn't you?" Rebecca asked. "What is it?"

"Special salves I have learned over the years. One to fight infection. The other to numb pain and stop bleeding. My journal says where to find what you need. Many of the plants are rare and hard to find."

Angel spied his sword and held his hand out. The sword jittered on the floor before flying into his hand.

"How did you do that?" Rebecca asked.

"The Heavenly Weapons will always return to the demon hunter. I can find them anywhere in the world if I lose them." Angel used the sword to help himself stand. "Just a few moments longer. We will have to hurry. I think they are about to start the sacrifices."

"Without me? I thought they needed me."

"They do, and now you're here. You're not first in the sequence."

"What am I? Whose first?"

"Earth is first."

"Earth?" A vision of Monica flashed in Rebecca's head. She was crying. "Monica? Monica's first? How—How do I even know that?"

"They're your friends. Rebecca, my power is divided. You are rejuvenating it, but you are also using it. The share is more in my favor, but we are sharing it."

"How am I doing that?"

"The demon hunter passes his power down to his eldest when he passes. I should have passed long ago, but was unaware of my son. I've held this power for far too long. It wants to move on."

"I think I understand. It wants to continue like it's supposed to. I'm the eldest child and now the last living Virtue. It's my turn now."

"Yes, but I need to hold onto this power a little longer. When this is done you will take over this power."

"How do I do that?"

"With prayer."

"I'm religious, but I've never been very big on prayers. I don't really know any."

"You will, when the time comes. It's a prayer of the heart. You will know what to do when the time comes to ask Him." Angel released the pressure from his side. "I'm ready. Let's go before it's too late. We haven't much time if they are starting."

Rebecca nodded as Angel raised his sword. "Sword of Might," Angel said. "Show me the way." The sword began to glow. Rebecca could hear

Monica struggle. She closed her eyes with Angel. The vision she saw was traversing the building, from the school's main entrance to the end of the west wing. She saw Monica bound with dark energy beneath the stairs. She cried and begged as Santano stood over her, sword drawn and speaking. She and Angel opened their eyes simultaneously and in unison said, "Follow me."

Angel and Rebecca ran up the stairs and through the path the sword had shown them.

"How did I see that?" Rebecca asked.

"As I said, we are sharing. You're connection to them is strong. It allows you to see what I see."

Rebecca looked down the hall as they turned the corner. "Hold on Monica. We're coming." She looked at the dagger at her side. She gripped the handle and shouted, "Quickstep!" Her form blurred and vanished.

"Rebecca, no!" Angel shouted.

A rumble filled the hall. A scream and loud crash followed. Rebecca appeared at the other end of the hall and fell to her knees. She fell forward, supporting herself on her hands and stared in disbelief. Angel knew she was too late. Santano must have already left to begin the next.

When Angel caught up to Rebecca tears were rolling down her face. The stairs had collapsed and blood seeped from beneath the ruble.

"Monica," Rebecca cried. "I'm so sorry."

Angel placed his hand on her shoulder. "I'm sorry Rebecca," he said.

"Santano was here." Her hands clawed into fists. "He smiled and said I was too slow. Then he disappeared." She struck the ground with her fist. "I'll kill him! You hear me you bastard? I'll kill you!"

"Rebecca, calm down. There are other lives to save as well as the spirits of his victims."

"Spirits? You're talking about their souls, aren't you?"

"Yes. If we can defeat Santano and stop his ascension, their souls will be freed from Hell."

"That's right," Rebecca said as she wiped her tears away. "You said they're in Hell." She stood up. "You're wrong about something though."

Angel looked confused. "What do you mean?"

Rebecca looked at him with fierce determination. "There is no if. I am going to kill him."

Angel smiled. "Right. There is no if, only when."

"Angel, why did he gather everyone first? Why did he do this to her? This isn't how he killed everyone else."

"It's been awhile since I've had to deal with this, and I've never dealt with an avatar at full power at this point. My knowledge is limited, but this is what is called The Collection. It's the final ceremony to seal an avatar's power. This is acted upon more like a ritualistic sacrifice. Santano must offer up Satan's Chosen Five to the elements, sacrificing each to their respected element. Then he sacrifices a token of innocence and humanity to the Horseman in order to become it. I don't really know more than that. I was always more concerned with stopping it than understanding it."

"What do you mean Santano is at full power?"

"Normally, a demon hunter can stunt the growth of an avatar early on. So if they do get to this point, they are much weaker. Their power doesn't grow. Santano was stronger than I thought. I wasn't able to stop his growth."

"How many avatars got to the Collection at full strength? What are we dealing with?"

Angel was silent and looked at the collapsed steps and pooling blood. Only three had gotten that far. None could be stopped. He couldn't tell her that. He needed her fire. If she ascended, with the help of the Four Angels, she might have a chance. She might. "Stay focused to the task at hand. We have to stop Santano. Air is next."

Rebecca's face filled with shock. "Michael," she whispered.

"What?"

"I heard Michael. They're in the boiler room!"

"How do you—"

"Michael's calling me! Come on!" Rebecca wasted no time and took off. Angel followed pursuit.

"How? How do you know that's where they are?"

"Michael's my boyfriend! They have him too! Oh God, what if he's next?"

"Do you know how to get to him?"

"Through the teacher's lounge! They made that the entrance and closed the one in the basement storage years ago!"

"The sixties?"

"How did you know?"

"I thought this place looked familiar. I came here to deal with a demon problem back then. I sealed the gate in the basement somewhere. This was a Catholic school back then."

"That explains a lot."

They reached the teacher's lounge and Angel pulled Rebecca to a stop before she could reach for and open the door. "Wait," he said. "The Sword of Might is giving me warning. There's a guard."

"Can we use the dagger to sneak by?" Rebecca asked.

"Its magic can hide us, but not our manipulation of the world around us. As soon as we open the door, it'll know. I'll draw it away instead, and then you can sneak in. I'll follow behind shortly, so wait as long as you can. Avoid a fight if possible."

"I can't promise you that. I will stop Santano from making another sacrifice."

"Just try to hold them back. Remember, you are not the demon hunter. Not yet."

Rebecca nodded.

"Now hide and wait for me to clear him." Rebecca gripped the dagger's handle. "Take cover. I don't know how violent this will get."

Rebecca hesitated before hiding behind the wooden panes that made a door for the washrooms. She hid between the two panes of the nearest one and gripped the dagger tight. "Psionic Camouflage," she whispered. The green smoke wafted from the hilt and encircled her.

"Don't worry Rebecca," Angel said to her through the panels. "You have an angel watching over you, just take care."

"Thank you," she replied.

Angel drew his sword and entered the lounge. The hunger sat reclined on one of the couches. His maces were resting reclined against the couch while the hunger tossed peanuts he had found into the air and caught them in his mouth. He smiled, "I don't want to play with you. Where's candy cane?"

"The girl is not a threat," Angel answered. "I am."

The hunger broke out in laughter. He popped the remaining peanuts into his mouth as he sat up. He took up his maces and rose to his feet.

"You're not a threat," the hunger said. "You're too old. You're weak."

"Care to test your claim?" Angel asked. He pointed the Sword of Might at the hunger. "As the demon hunter, I challenge you to mortal combat. I challenge you under the Banner of God. Do you accept?"

The hunger tapped a mace against his jaw in thought. He looked up and around him. "No," he said flatly.

Angel stood dumbfounded. "You—You can't do that. Demon's can't refuse that challenge."

"Yes they can, but they don't. Pride and all. Especially against a human." The hunger laughed. "Besides, I'm in a different category. I—" He heard Úna clear her throat. He saw her reflection in a door's window. She had her arms crossed and glared sternly at him. He sighed. "Yes ma'am."

Angel watched in confusion.

The hunger raised his maces. "It's your lucky day. I changed my mind. I accept! Let's go angel cake."

The hunger rushed forward with his right mace drawn back. Angel retreated through the door on the hunger's swing, drawing him out of the room. Angel side stepped hunger's second swing to position himself to push the hunger back and allow Rebecca the time she needed to sneak in. The hunger pivoted following the swing, taking an instant to recoup his steps to continue after Angel, swinging his mace. Angel caught the mace at the base of its head with the flat of his sword. The hunger followed through with his second mace. Angel focused for an instant between the blows and reached his hand out and grabbed the shaft of the mace. The hunger was stunned by Angel's sudden surge of vigor. Angel grinned. He pushed the hunger's right mace away with his sword as he pulled the mace he had gripped free of the hunger's grasp. Angel cut across the hunger's chest with a downward slash as he leaped back. Angel followed through with a strong focused kick to the underling's cut chest. The hunger stumbled back but kept his footing. Angel took aim and threw the hunger's own weapon at his face. The hunger opened his mouth wide and the weapon disappeared down his gullet, his body shifting as the mace found its way to his stomach.

The hunger shook his head; he began to hack and heave, spitting his mace back into his hand. He shook the spittle from it and smiled at Angel. "Ah," he mused, "she's giving you a little energy boost."

"That apparent, is it?" Angel smiled back. "Yes, I'm drawing power from her. Still think I'm not a threat?"

"Eh," the hunger shrugged. "I thought you'd be stronger."

"I admit I'm not as strong as I used to be, but the strength I have is enough to deal with you."

"Oh, you think so?"

Rebecca held the Dagger of Power tightly in her hands as the two bantered. Images of Jason cursing and threatening legal action flashed before her eyes. Santano was preparing the next sacrifice, but Angel and the hunger were still too close. "Angel," she whispered. "Hurry. We're running out of time."

The hunger's eyes darted to the side quickly and he grinned. "Let's get this over with. The sacrifice is starting."

"Then let us not waste any more time."

Angel reinforced his stance and concentrated, aligning his power with the Sword of Might and consciously drew power from Rebecca. He could feel a presence behind him adding to his strength. The hunger grinned. "Oh yeah," he said as the heads of his maces tripled in size. "I'm not holding back on you." Spikes the color of dried earth erupted from the enlarged heads. Angel rushed forward feeling the invigorated strength in his body. It wouldn't last long so he had to make full use of it. He rushed forward and attacked with a powerful blow. "Force Shock!" Angel shouted. The hunger braced himself and blocked with his maces spiked heads. The blow released a force that pushed the hunger back across the hall. Angel closed the distance fast with another strike. Again the hunger was pushed back. He struck the ground with a mace to anchor himself and stop his backward motion, tearing up the ground as he was pushed back. He rushed forward to meet Angel and their weapons collided.

Angel and the hunger were far enough away for Rebecca's purpose. She caught a glimpse of the two trading blows down the hall. Their attacks were strong and focused in a manner Rebecca did not know was possible. The visions permeating her mind did not allow her time to watch. She needed to move. She saw Jason positioned between two of the central cooling generators. His hair was waved against the increasing intensity of the winds. Not once did he stop shouting as Santano spoke. She could only make out a few words over Jason's shouts. Through quick flashes she watched it unfold. She ran through the lounge watching as time slipped away. The generators spun faster and faster. Rebecca threw open the door to the basement stairs. She needed Quickstep, but no matter how many times she called for it, nothing slowed. The green haze of the world continued to move at a constant. She waved her hand through the haze, trying to wave it away. "Damn it, break!" she cried. The haze finally broke as she reached the door at the end of the steps. She gripped the dagger's handle in its sheath and reached for the door's handle.

Jason had no time to scream, but his shouts suddenly ended. The generators exploded, sending the fan's blades and shrapnel into his body. The vision was gone and Rebecca had stopped. Her grip was tight around the door handle. "Jason," she cried. "I'm sorry. We were too slow." She rested her head against the door. "Jeff, I'm sorry. I couldn't save him." Through the door she could hear the faint sound of crying. "Rebecca!" Michael's voice called into her ears. She stepped away from the door. Michael and Heather were still alive. She could still save them.

Rebecca drew the Dagger of Power and coated herself in its light bending magic before slowly opening the door, trying not to make it creak. If she could catch them by surprise, she could use Whirlwind and rescue her friends. The door opened out. She peered into the darkened room beyond. She could hear Heather's crying echo off the concrete walls and steel pipes. She pushed the door open more to pass through, keeping her body close to it. A powerful hand gripped her wrist and pulled her through the threshold. The destruction came out of the shadows and punched Rebecca hard in the stomach. "I gauged your height when we first met," he said as he spun around and slammed her into the wall. The dagger fell from her hand and hit the floor. "I know your proportions." He gripped her neck and raised her off the ground. "I don't have to see you to hit you."

With the breath knocked out of her the destruction threw Rebecca hard onto the cement floor, breaking the cloaking magic. She tried to get up only to find the destruction's knee land hard on the center of her back. "By the way," the destruction grinned. "That was for stabbing me." He tore the trench coat from Rebecca's body and threw it aside. "No tricks from that." He pulled Rebecca's hands behind her back. He held her hands together at the wrist with one hand while dark bands of energy appeared in the other. He placed the bands against Rebecca's wrists and they bound around them tightly, burning her flesh and making her wince. The destruction lifted Rebecca to her feet by her hair. "I'm disappointed," he said. "You should have hid the dagger. I would have let you keep it. Now I'll not see your strength."

The destruction pulled Rebecca roughly through the cold dark maze of boilers and pipes by the hair. She fought against the bonds, but the more she struggled against them the tighter they became and the more they burned. She remembered what Angel had said about the Heavenly Weapons; that they would always return to the demon hunter. She knew she wasn't the demon hunter yet, but hoped her bond to them was strong enough that it didn't matter. Fighting against the destruction's strong hold she concentrated on the dagger, hoping and praying that it would come to her.

Rebecca didn't realize where the destruction was taking her until he threw her on the ground next to a sobbing Heather. "Stay," the destruction said as he pointed at Rebecca. He walked away and took his place beside the disease's withered form. Rebecca sat up and tucked her legs beneath her. She could see the destroyed generators and Jason's bloody and torn body. His death did not happen far away. Michael kneeled in front of a massive furnace bound by the same dark energy Rebecca was bound by. It crisscrossed his body, holding him still and anchored to the floor. The furnace's flames were turned up high and licking the sides of the metal grate. Michael was breathing heavily and seemed disoriented, as well as being a pale shade of green. Santano, with his human face, kneeled beside the furnace adjusting its force.

"Michael!" Rebecca cried.

Slowly Michael raised his head. When he saw Rebecca he smiled. "Rebecca," he said weakly. "I'm so glad…I got to see you again." Tears rolled down his face. "I just wish…"

"Just hang on Michael! Please! I'll save you!"

"You can't," the disease said. "It's over. Santano started his sacrifices. You'll never be strong enough." He chuckled. "Sorry about your boyfriend's state. He had to be…'subdued'."

"He had a lot of fight," the destruction grinned. "Much more entertaining than the other one."

"There," Santano said. "That should do it. We can begin the next sacrifice."

"Why are you doing this?" Heather cried. Her hands were bound behind her with the same dark energy.

"Why else do humans destroy one another?" the destruction asked. "The only real reason there is; Power."

"Come on, come on, come on," Rebecca said under her breath. "Please come to me." She was concentrating, trying to call the Dagger of Power to her. "Please, I need you."

Santano drew the Blood Sword and touched its tip to the ground. Thick red liquid poured from the blade's tip and circled Michael and the raging furnace behind him. Lines crisscrossed the circle forming a pentagram star. With the symbol drawn, Santano lifted his sword from the ground.

"Element of fire, hear my call," Santano said. "The Avatar of Death offers you a sacrifice. Open the third seal to the Fourth!"

The flames of the furnace burned stronger. Michael winced from the pain. The red circle began to glow. Michael glared at Santano. "You won't get away with this," he said.

Rebecca was crying. "Please, please," she begged. "Let me be strong enough." Suddenly, she felt the dagger's grip in her hands. She turned the dagger in her hand and began to cut at the energy bonds, hoping she could slice through it. "Just a little longer Michael," she pleaded in a whisper. "Please, just a little longer."

The disease noticed something come into Rebecca's hand. He moved to investigate, worried she might interfere, but the destruction outstretched his hand and shook his head. The disease sneered but kept his place.

"Fire," Santano continued, "accept this sacrifice, whose desire burns endlessly. Accept the fierce flame in the heart of his soul."

The flames burned stronger and ignited the liquid circle. A voice, distant, light and crackling with embers whispered, "I accept."

Santano raised his sword and placed his hand at the hilt. "Last words?" he asked.

Michael looked at Rebecca and smiled a weak smile. "Rebecca, I love you so much."

Tears ran down Rebecca's face as she pulled against her bonds. Her hands bled from the cuts she gave herself as she tried to cut through the energy bonds. Slowly her hands were gaining play. "I love—" she began.

Santano pulled his hand over the blade's flat and shouted, "Take him!"

The frame of the furnace ripped open and the flames lashed out at Michael. They consumed him quickly and his screams echoed against the pipes.

"Michael!" Rebecca cried. "No!"

Heather shut her eyes and looked away. Rebecca could not pull her eyes from him. Just a few feet from her, the love of her life was leaving her alone in the world. The flames died and retreated back into the furnace, leaving its front blown out. Michael's burned husk fell forward. Rebecca sat frozen. She watched the smoke rise from Michael's scorched body. He didn't even look human anymore.

"Michael?" Rebecca cried. "Michael? Please, get up. Please? Michael, don't leave me. Please. I love you."

Heather leaned into Rebecca, trying to comfort her friend, but they both were in tears. Rebecca could feel a warm presence around her, holding her, trying to sooth her pain. "I love you," Rebecca cried.

Santano walked to them. "It's almost over," he said. "You'll see him again soon." He grinned. "In Hell."

Rebecca gritted her teeth and breathed quickly and deeply. She pulled the dagger's blade hard against the dark energy band. She pulled her hands hard against them, trying to pull them apart. She remembered something Angel had said when he cut her free; Keen Edge. She screamed.

Heather moved away in fright. The dagger's blade shinned and finally cut through the bonds. Rebecca pulled her bloodied hands forward and lunged at a very surprised Santano. She struck hard with the Dagger of Power, Santano blocking against her blows with the Blood Sword. Rebecca struck fast and strong, pushing the avatar back. He used Quickstep to avoid her increasingly furious blows and put distance between them. Rebecca heard the thunderous steps of destruction echo off the walls. She gripped the dagger in both hands and trained the blade on the destruction and disease as they rushed forward. "Whirlwind!" The torrent of hurricane wind launched the disease almost immediately, but the destruction was barely able to hold his ground. "So strong!" he laughed. He tried to move against it, but was ultimately taken by it.

Heather watched in shock. She didn't know where Rebecca had gotten a dagger, or more importantly, how it was creating such a strong wind. The cone focused its force, but wind gusts still flew in all directions. Heather stared wide eyed as her hair flailed in the wind. Santano rushed forward with his blade glowing. Rebecca took a stepping pivot and focused the winds on him. Santano's motion was stopped and he drove the sword into the ground to anchor himself. The winds were stronger this time.

"Rebecca!" Heather exclaimed.

Rebecca turned her head and saw the destruction rushing forward with a grin on his face. The disease aimed his spear and the spear's head fired like a bullet. Rebecca broke the Whirlwind and turned to defend herself. She brought the dagger forward to deflect the spearhead. She felt hands on her arms to help position her defense. The spear head struck the dagger's blade with enough force to twist Rebecca's wrist. The destruction was on top of her with his fist drawn back. "Quickstep!" Rebecca shouted. The destruction's blow passed through Rebecca's blurred form and she appeared beside Heather in a blur. Rebecca grabbed Heather's arm and pulled her up off the floor. "Come on!" she shouted.

Hands still bound and Rebecca holding her arm, Heather ran. The door was in sight. Rebecca was certain they could find safety beyond it. They could find Angel. The two screeched to a halt when Santano's blurred form appeared before the doorway. "Where do you think you're going?" he asked. "There are still two more sacrifices to make."

The hunger crashed into Santano, entangling them and knocking them both to the ground. Angel stood in the threshold cut and bleeding. "Move!" he shouted. Rebecca pulled Heather forward and over Santano as he tried to untangle himself from the dazed hunger. The destruction advanced at a calm pace. "Angel," he grinned. Angel raised his sword and steadied his stance as Rebecca and Heather ran past him. "I'll meet you in the lounge," he said calmly.

The destruction reached for the pipes and pulled them free, hot steam whistling into the room. He threw them in a twirl at Angel. "Keen Edge!" Angel shouted as he followed through with two quick cuts to the spinning pipes. The halves flew and embedded themselves into the walls. The destruction charged as Santano got back to his feet. Angel raised his sword. "Sword of Might. Meteor Strike!" The blade was consumed in a flame. Angel struck with the Sword of Might in a downward slash. Several flaming rock cores erupted from the flaming blade. Two struck the destruction and halted his forward motion. Angel winced as some of the pain was redirected to him. Santano struck a rocky fireball, the resulting explosion dazing him. The rock flames struck the walls and pipes, making the walls shake under the released pressure. Angel drove the blade into the door's threshold above. "Holy Strike!" The glowing energy of the blade erupted around the frame and caused the already damaged structure to collapse. It would buy them some time. Angel grabbed his trench coat from the floor, forcibly pulling the tail free from the ruble and made his way to rejoin Rebecca and Heather.

The destruction pounded on the ruble barrier. His punches resounded against the brick and wood.

"Hurry!" Santano shouted. "They're getting away!"

"Relax," the destruction said. "Enjoy the chase."

"Besides," the disease added, "they have nowhere to run. There is only one way out."

"Through the grave!" the hunger chimed in gleefully. "I just hope Angel doesn't do it."

"What does he mean?" Santano asked.

"Don't worry about it," the destruction answered as his fist plowed through the debris. "He'll never do it."

Rebecca was cutting through Heather's bonds in the lounge.

"Rebecca, what's going on?" Heather asked. "What's wrong with Santano? How did you do all that?"

"It's hard to explain," Rebecca answered. "For now, just keep running!" The dark energy finally broke.

Heather rubbed her sore wrists. "To where? What are those things?"

"High ranking demons," Angel answered as he ran up to them and slipped his arms through the coat sleeves. Knowing only that Angel was wanted for murder, Heather shrank away from him. "That barricade will not last long."

"Angel!" the destruction's voice boomed.

"Run!" Angel shouted.

That was all the incentive Heather needed. She ran first, followed by Rebecca. Angel turned to block the way behind them. He held his sword parallel to the ground before him and shouted, "Sword of Might! Eternal Fire!" Flames spewed forth from the blade and ignited all it touched, setting the room ablaze. "Meteor Punch!" Angel shouted as he began to move, aiming his attack at the sprinkler system. Water gushed from the destroyed pipes and the roof fell. It would buy some time, especially once this was all over. Santano's field cut off all routes to the outside, so no signal would get to the fire department. Hopefully the fires would be out by the end of the ordeal so no one would find the devastation until Monday morning.

Angel took off running, running far behind Heather and Rebecca. His sword sheathed to give it time to recharge. Heather led the way.

"Heather!" Rebecca called. "Slow down! We have to stay together!"

"Rebecca!" Angel shouted. "I need a large area for a Haven! Head to one!"

"Heather! The gym!"

Heather didn't turn at the gym. She turned towards the main entrance. "We have to get out of here!" she cried.

"Stop her!" Angel called. He knew he could not reach her in time. He slammed his elbow into the trophy case as Rebecca's form blurred with Quickstep. She did not know what would happen if Heather reached the door and did not want to find out. Angel pulled a trophy from the case and hurled it down the hall as hard as he could past Heather as Rebecca blurred into existence in front of her. Heather slammed into her friend, unable to stop. She saw the trophy hit the glass door and become locked in chaotic red energy before it was thrown away from the door, battered and broken. Heather and Rebecca watched the smoking singed metal cup bounce across the floor.

"My God," Heather said. "That—That could have been me. Rebecca, what's going on?"

"Follow Angel right now," Rebecca said. "He's trying to help us, okay? Those things aren't far behind."

Heather nodded. "Okay."

"The gym. Go!"

Rebecca and Heather made their way through the gym doors across from the main entrance. Angel searched his trench coat for one of his vials of holy water. When he found it he poured a line in the hallway from wall to wall. Angel drew the sign of the cross over himself before laying a hand down on the wet floor. "Sanctum Murum!" Angel said. The holy water began to glow. "Elementum Aquarum!" The water sprang to life and blocked the hall, rising from floor to ceiling. "Duratus!" The sounds of freezing water rang in the hall. "Gelida Obice!" The water wall suddenly froze solid. "That'll buy some time."

Angel followed Rebecca and Heather into the gym after setting up his barrier.

"Will someone tell me what the Hell is going on?" Heather asked.

"Hell is exactly what's going on," Angel answered.

"What does that mean?"

Rebecca placed her hands on Heather's shoulders to try and calm her. She had stopped bleeding but hadn't wiped her blood off. "Heather," she said, "Santano sold his soul. We're the price he has to pay. Angel has been trying to stop him this whole time."

"What? How—"

"Do you believe in God?" Angel asked.

"Yes, but—"

"Then you must also believe in Satan. You cannot have good without evil. You are aware of the War in Heaven as well?"

"What war? I know Satan fell and all but—"

"He did not just fall. He waged a long and terrible war in Heaven. His fall was the consequence of his defeat. This is the subsequent war, the War for Heaven. Rebecca," Angel held his hand out. "I need the Dagger of Power for Haven."

Rebecca un-tethered the sheathed dagger and handed it to Angel. "What's Haven?"

"A place that bars entry to evil and sin. Inside you'll be safe."

"What does this war have to do with us?" Heather asked as Angel walked to the center of the gym, digging through his jacket. The two followed him. Heather stared in shocked awe as she watched Angel's hair visibly become grayer.

"Humans are everything to his war," Angel said. "Souls may be punished and tortured in Hell, but Hell is not a place of punishment. Souls not fit to enter Heaven have any goodness drained out of them. They are conditioned and trained to add to Hell's ranks. Eventually, all damned souls become demons, but humans do not have to die for this to happen. Santano is an example of that." Angel pulled a pouch from one of his pockets. The contents were a white powder, which he began to sprinkle on the floor in a large circle, large enough for the three of them to stand inside. "Please stay out until I finish," Angel said as he emptied the pouch's contents.

"I still don't understand," Heather said. "How do humans turn into demons? What's happening to Santano? Who are those people with him?"

"They are the embodiments of the risen Horsemen," Angel said. "Humans who sell their souls are damned to Hell. Keen Edge." The edge of his sword shined and he began to carve into the floor. They could hear pounding from the hall.

"They're coming," Rebecca said.

"The wall will hold long enough. Listen, Santano has sold his soul. For what, I don't know. Every avatar is different. Satan found him a worthy candidate and made him a better offer. Humans become some of Hell's greatest generals." Angel had carved a cross into the floor. "In order to rise in power, the avatar must offer ten blood sacrifices, innocent souls somehow connected to him. If an avatar can make all of his sacrifices, he rises as a Horseman. This is the final stage of their ascension." Angel placed the Heavenly Weapons on the floor across the carvings. He searched for another vial of holy water and poured it onto his crossed weapons through his fingers. After emptying the vial, Angel flicked the water at the powder at the cross's four points. "This is the Collection. Once begun there are only two ways to stop it. Kill the avatar or send the Chosen."

Heather swallowed hard. "What do you mean 'send'?"

Angel didn't look at them as he answered. "To kill and send to judgment."

Heather and Rebecca gasped.

"If the demon hunter kills the Chosen, it will break the sacrificial chain and kill the Avatar. The demon hunter only has to kill one to break the chain."

Heather moved behind Rebecca, hiding behind her friend. "He's your friend, right? Tell me he's not going to kill me."

"He's not," Rebecca replied. "Angel, how many Avatars made it this far?"

"Many, but like Santano? Only three. Their power was too great for the demon hunter to stop." Angel kneeled before his weapons at the base of the cross. "That's how my father died and I became demon hunter. Santano is the last. I can't let him rise."

They heard ice shatter. Angel folded his hands, closed his eyes, lowered his head and entered into silent prayer.

"If he rises?" Heather asked. "What happens if he rises?"

Angel did not answer, remaining in silent prayer. The holy water was spreading out towards the circle of powder.

"What happens?!"

"World's End," Rebecca answered. "He'll become Death and bring World's End."

Heather's lips trembled. "The End of the World? This is…the End of the World?"

"Yes," the destruction said as the gym door creaked open.

The disease walked in first, leaning on his gnarled staff. "You sit at the precipice of the world," he said. "The end is neigh."

The hunger walked in next, carrying his spiked maces. "It's going to be an all you can eat buffet."

Finally, Santano entered. "End of the line."

Heather moved behind Rebecca as she stood in defiance to Hell's forces. Rebecca's stomach twisted and knotted. She was unarmed. "Angel," she said. "A little help?"

Angel did not answer. His mouth lipped the words he prayed. The powder, now wet, had begun to glow.

"Are you ready?" the destruction said as he took a sprinting position.

"Angel?" Rebecca called as she and Heather took steps back.

"Three…"

Angel remained silent. Beads of sweat rolled down his face and his lips moved faster. The faint glow of the powder flashed slowly, brighter back to duller.

"Angel, we need you," Rebecca said.

"Two…" the destruction continued.

The disease and hunger took their place beside him. The hunger licked his lips as the disease struck the butt of his staff on the ground, turning it into a spear again.

The powder's flashing became faster and more intense. Still, Angel did not move. He couldn't. He had to get the Haven up.

"One."

The underlings charged forward as the glow of the powder flashed skywards into a force of light. "Run!" Angel shouted as he gripped his weapons and stood. Heather and Rebecca turned and ran toward Angel within the field of light with the underlings close behind. Angel gripped the Heavenly Weapons tightly and felt helpless as he watched the destruction quickly close the distance. The destruction roared in laughter as he reached out for Rebecca, who took up the rear. Heather braced herself as she ran into the light field, expecting to slam into it. Rebecca's hair caressed the destruction's fingers as he tried to grab it. Heather and Rebecca slammed into Angel's braced body and the destruction slammed to a sudden halt against the field. The hunger and disease, being slower than the destruction, stopped short.

The destruction stepped away from the field and twisted his head with his hands. There was an audible crack and pop and his smile never left his face. The hunger looked back and waved Santano away. Santano nodded and left the gym.

"Why didn't you help us?!" Rebecca cried as she hit Angel hard in the chest.

"I had to create Haven," Angel answered. "It's the only way to keep you safe."

"After it was up! You just stood there!"

Angel sighed. "Because I cannot enter Haven."

"What?"

Heather was trying to calm herself. "What does that mean? What is this?"

"This is Haven," Angel answered as he sheathed his weapons. "It protects anyone within from harm. Good souls can come and go as they please, but corrupted souls may not pass."

"But you're not bad," Rebecca said. "Your soul—"

"Is tainted. I have committed an unforgivable sin. It not only stunted my power, it prevents me from entering Haven once I have left." Angel looked at the underlings. They had backed away and were waiting. "Rebecca, this is where we part ways."

"What? What do you mean?"

Angel began to un-tether his sheathed weapons. He coughed hard. His eyes were wary, his skin pale and his hair almost completely gray. He looked to be nearing sixty now. "My remaining time is short. My time as demon hunter is coming to an end."

He handed Rebecca the Heavenly Weapons. "No," she said. "I—I can't do this without you. I don't know what to do!"

"I know and I'm sorry I can't be there to teach you." He removed his trench coat and gave it to her. "You found the journal? All I know is written within. When the demon hunter passes, the next can rise."

"No," Rebecca cried. She felt like she was watching an uncle die. "I need you Angel. I can't do this alone."

Angel tilted her head up. "And you will never be alone. You are stronger than I ever was. Everything I was denied you will have. You are the last now. You have the power to stop Santano. This I truly believe. Remember, you are not alone. You will never be alone."

"But...what will happen to you?"

Angel knew the answer but could not tell her. Only Hell awaited him. "I do not know. I have betrayed God as well as Satan. I have harmed many people. I will go to Judgment and await my fate. Whatever it is, I will accept it." Angel drew the cross on Rebecca, then on Heather. "Bless you both. I will deal with the underlings. Rebecca, I leave Santano to you. Ask and you shall receive."

Rebecca watched broken hearted as Angel left Haven. The light allowed him passage. Angel stood before his opponents with unyielding resolve, ready to face his fate. Rebecca cried, feeling as if she was watching a beloved relative slip away. She realized that was exactly what she was watching. Angel had helped raise her, at least in some sense. She had known him all her life. She trusted him. He was the same in the waking world as he was in her dreams. "Good-bye Angel," she whispered.

"Are you ready to give it your all?" the destruction asked. "If this is your last stand, make it worth my wile."

Angel breathed out and his body was outlined with a white energy. "Our Father on high," Angel said. "Grant me strength this time for this last act in Your name." The white energy around him grew and glowed brightly.

The color in his hair returned some. His muscles bulged as the strength he lost returned. The color of his flesh became bright again. For at least a short time, enough time, the hands of time reversed.

"What do you know," the destruction said with a smile. "He was answered."

Angel looked at his adversaries as the white energy faded and prepared for battle. With a wide grin the destruction charged. "Whatever happens," Angel said, "stay in Haven." The destruction pulled back his fist and almost leaped at Angel as he released his punch. Angel stood his ground. He shifted his weight to avoid a direct blow and grabbed the destruction's arm. Using the demon's own motion, Angel threw him over his shoulder and slammed him into Haven's field. The hunger made a large leap into the air with his maces held high. Angel twisted in a quick snap at the waist and slammed the destruction into the hunger as he came down. The disease lunged forward with a thrust of his spear. Angel threw himself to the side as the spearhead struck Haven's field with a clang. Angel pushed off his hands and twisted in the air to face the disease which followed in quick pursuit.

The disease swung his spear in a high arc. Angel bent back and let the spear tip fly over him. His hands touched the ground and continued into a hand stand as the disease swung his spear overhead and brought it down hard. Angel spring boarded away as the spear struck the ground, sending wood chips flying as the wood cracked and molded. The disease pulled his spear back as he rushed forward. He attacked with quick thrusts. Angel moved with suburb speed, faster than he had been able to move in a long time. He bent his body around every thrust, not letting the spearhead or shaft touch him. Angel knew he could not dodge forever. There were two other enemies to deal with and soon the disease would attack with something other than a thrust.

The disease was quickening his thrusts, but Angel had little trouble keeping up. He grabbed the spear and jerked it back, pulling the disease off balance momentarily. Placing his hands on the shaft of the spear, Angel used it as a guide and rushed the disease. He reached the demon and gripped the spear when the disease tried to disengage. Angel slammed his open palm into the disease's chin, pushing his head up. Angel released the spear and struck the disease in his solar plexus. The disease gasped as Angel twisted and struck him across the face with his elbow. The disease dropped the spear as Angel swept his legs from beneath him. Angel was fast and kicked the disease away before he hit the ground.

The destruction rushed forward and batted the disease out of his path. He leaped forward with a sadistic grin, his hands interlocked and pulled overhead. Angel leaped away and the destruction brought his locked fists into the ground. The floor buckled and broke. Shards of wood flew into the air as the destruction punched a hole into the floor. Angel knew he could not touch this demon directly. He had learned that painful lesson already.

The destruction moved forward with vicious punches. Rebecca and Heather watched in amazement as Angel instantly took what they assumed to be a martial arts stance and began to deflect the destruction's blows with open handed blocks and parries. Angel fell back as the destruction pressed forward.

"Just who is he?" Heather asked. "How does he fight like this?"

Rebecca looked at the sheathed weapons in her hands. "Because it's what he was trained to do," she said. "It's what he spent his entire life doing; protecting the world from Hell. He's the demon hunter."

"That's…hard to take in. Hell and demons."

"I know, but that's what it is. Come on Angel, you can beat them."

The destruction punched at a downward arc. Angel jumped straight up in a crouch as the destruction punched another hole in the floor. Angel landed with both feet on the destruction's arm. The war demon reached with his other hand to grab Angel's leg, but Angel stepped on his wrist as he leaned forward with a hand on the destruction's shoulder. Angel pulled himself into a one handed handstand as the destruction began to rise. Angel twisted as he brought his body down, placing his feet on the destruction's shoulders. Angel pushed off while the destruction was still rising, pushing him forward and stumbling into the hole. The destruction fell forward as Angel leaped through the air.

The hunger rushed forward in an attempt to take advantage of Angel's airborne vulnerability. He swung with his spiked mace, but Angel caught it between the spikes with his hand. He continued over the hunger, pulling the mace with him. The hunger jerked as his mace was pulled back over his head. Angel spun around as soon as he landed. He gripped the hunger's maces by the creature's hands, preventing him from releasing them.

The destruction rushed forward and Angel kicked out one of the hunger's legs to break his balance. As Angel manipulated hunger's arms and pulled one back the hunger uttered, "Uh-oh." Angel caught the destruction's blow with the hunger's mace. The hunger screamed as his mace connected. Angel kept the hunger's legs from finding ground as he struck the destruction with the hunger's maces. The hunger's body buckled and bled with each blow the destruction took, his body taking the damage instead.

Heather and Rebecca watched the unfolding fight in amazement.

"He's amazing," Heather said.

"Yeah," Rebecca replied.

"I didn't think fighting like that was possible outside of movies."

Rebecca was worried. This wasn't strength Angel had been fighting with. How long would it last? Would Angel be able to defeat them before it did? If not, would she be able to? She was scared. Soon she would have to fight against these monsters, and she would be alone. Angel would not be there to help her. At the same time, however, she wanted to. Rebecca was a mix of fear, anger, and anticipation. Soon, it would be her turn.

The hunger threw his feet up and pressed them against the destruction. He pushed against the destruction's solid body, which had weakened and slowed with the effect of the hunger's powers. The destruction fell back and the hunger kicked off the ground before Angel could kick out his legs again. He flipped over Angel, causing him to lose his grip on the demon. The hunger slammed his feet into Angel's back and kicked him forward, the hunger itself falling flat on his back. Angel stumbled forward into the destruction. The destruction backhanded him across the face. The blow wasn't devastating, but it was strong. Angel stumbled away and caught himself on his hands as he tried to stay on his feet. The hunger flung his maces forward and the spikes that coated the heads burst free and flew towards Angel. He twisted his body and twirled in the air as the spikes rained down on him. The ground was awash with spikes. Angel landed in a defensive stance and faltered. A spike had impaled his side. Painfully, he pulled it out and watched as the underlings gathered.

"I guess now is as good a time as any," Angel said to himself.

"In a few minutes he'll be done," the hunger said.

"Angel!" Rebecca cried out.

"Stay there!" Angel shouted back.

"Looks to me like you need all the help you can get," the destruction laughed.

"My move though, right?"

The destruction nodded, holding his strong arm out to halt the disease from moving forward.

"Good. I have one trick left." A white glow surrounded Angel as he let out a deep breath. The glow grew slowly into a mist like aura around his body. "Every demon hunter has a special attack. A sort of miracle, I suppose, to use when there is nothing left. Mine I can use but once."

The disease stepped back. "Not this time," he whispered. He raised his spear and threw it at Angel. The destruction reached out for it, but it slipped through his fingers. The spear pierced through Angel's stomach, exiting through his back. Heather and Rebecca's breath caught in their throats. The color in Angel's hair began to fade. The mass in his muscles began to shrink. The hands of time moved forward again. Angel spattered blood.

"Disease!" the destruction shouted as he reached for his sickened ally.

"He is to die!" the disease shouted back as they locked hands. "Now he will!"

The hunger watched them for a moment. Then he looked to Angel with a smile. "All according to plan Mistress," he whispered. "Your move."

Angel fell to his knees as blood poured from his mouth. The sounds around him became muffled. He could barely hear Rebecca and Heather calling out to him. His wounds burned and his vision blurred. His body became numb and his brow filled with sweat. His focus began to wane and his bright mist of light began to dim. "I'm…sorry," he choked as he began to fall forward.

Loving arms wrapped around him and kept him from tumbling over. "I have you," a woman's voice said. "I've always had you, my sweet Angel."

Angel recognized the voice. He knew the embrace as it pulled him close. "Uri…"

"Yes my boy. I am here for you." She caressed his face. "I have always been here."

"I don't deserve…your grace." The burning pain began to subside. "I did not before. I do not now."

"But my grace you have always had." Her hand gripped the spear. "You could not feel it, but you were never without it." Angel winced as she pulled the spear from his body. The hunger smiled as he watched. The destruction and disease were too busy arguing to notice. Heather could only see a bright and warm light surrounding Angel. Rebecca could see a person come in and out of focus within the light. It was holding Angel.

Uriel placed her hand on Angel's wound. "When you were lost, it was I that guided you. When you were thirsty, it was I who gave you water. When you were hungry, it was I who fed you. When you were alone and tired it was my bed you shared. It was my touch that drove away the loneliness. I could not abandon you, I could not. Alas, I had to stay so far away. I am truly sorry."

Angel's light began to grow again. "The woman at the police station," Angel smiled. "The guard at the hospital, they were you, weren't they?"

"From the smallest child to the oldest woman, I have watched you every step of the way." Angel rose to his feet, his light strong and bright again. The destruction and disease finally noticed. "I have been with you throughout all the years. You have done well and done Heaven proud. You have made me proud, but it is time to let go Angel."

Angel focused his power, drawing the light inward. "Yes," he said. "It is time."

"I will see you on the other side," Uriel said.

Angel was silent for a moment. A tear ran down his cheek. "No, you won't."

Tears poured down Uriel's face. "No, I won't." She kissed his cheek. "Good-bye, dearest Angel."

Uriel released Angel and tearfully left him to his fate. Angel had drawn the light into him, making his body glow. "We probably want to get him now," the hunger said.

The destruction gritted his teeth angrily, realizing he had made a mistake. "Go!"

The three underlings rushed forward and Angel released the energy in a shout. "Redemption!" The energy exploded from within, filling the room with a blinding light. The screams of the underlings echoed as Heather and Rebecca were blinded by the light. A powerful force shook Haven and knocked them to the ground. A loud hum rang in their ears, followed by a fierce boom. Waves of energy washed over them as the screams faded away. The bright light faded. Slowly their eyes adjusted. The smoking bodies of the underlings lay on the floor. The ground where Angel had stood was scorched and smoking. He was gone. Heather almost panicked when she saw that Haven was gone as well, including the cross that Angel had carved in the floor. Rebecca looked at the smoldering bodies of the underlings as they flaked away. Defeated, they left the world of Man. Rebecca looked about for Angel, but he was nowhere to be found. Tears formed in her eyes. The last member of her family, of her entire bloodline, was gone. Now she was the last. Now she was alone. "Angel!" Rebecca cried out, hoping that he would call back. "Angel!" she cried again. "Angel, answer me!" Tears rolled down her face.

Heather put her arms around Rebecca and pulled her close. "I'm sorry," she said. "He's gone. He sacrificed himself to save us."

They heard a door open. "How anti-climatic," Santano said. "All that fuss and he still lost."

Rebecca glared at her teacher, her temperature rising. Looking at him and knowing all he's done drowned any bit of fear Rebecca had with anger. Her life, her future, everything she had and had ever known were taken away from her by him.

"You…" Rebecca growled. Tears rolled down her face. "This is…" She made tight fists. "This is all…" She glared at Santano and shouted, "All because of you!" She tried to lash out at him, but Heather threw her arms around her and held her back. "This is all because of you! My family; my friends! They're all gone because of you!"

Santano laughed. "What exactly are you going to do about it?"

"I'm going to kill you!"

"Rebecca, calm down!" Heather cried. "Please!"

"Kill me?" Santano asked. "How exactly? With the rusted sword at your feet?"

Rebecca started to calm as she looked at the Heavenly Weapons. "Yes."

Santano laughed again. He raised the Blood Sword and it began to glow. "I'll shatter them in one blow. They're old, weak, and brittle. Face it, you've lost."

Rebecca pulled Heather's hands away from her. "I can heal them."

"Why do you think that? Did Angel tell you?" He laughed again.

Rebecca picked up the Heavenly Weapons and Angel's trench coat. "No," she said as she stared at the last remnants of Angel, "but I know it's true."

"Fine. Go ahead and try. No matter what you do, you'll die anyway. Didn't Angel tell you? I'm too strong now. By ascending, you'll only leave your friend to die alone. Satan already told me that Virtues who find themselves in the Collection forfeit their place without harm to me if they ascend. I can kill you without consequence. A new pure soul will be chosen. If I don't kill you outright, I might sacrifice you anyway. Either way, I kill you."

"Rebecca..." Heather cried. Haven was gone. Angel was gone. She had seen Santano's monstrous face. How would they survive?

Rebecca approached Heather. "I need you to do something for me," she said. Heather saw a fierce determination in her blue eyes. Rebecca gave Heather Angel's coat. "Hold this for me and stay back."

Heather took the coat. "But—"

"Please Heather," Rebecca interrupted. "I have to do this or everything—it will all be for nothing. Please, do as I ask."

Reluctantly, Heather nodded and moved away. Santano looked towards the door behind the two girls. He pierced the ground with the Blood Sword. Red waves of light crossed the floor, walls, and ceiling. "I hope you're not thinking of leaving us Heather," Santano asked with a smile. "Don't worry. I'll take you swimming one last time."

"Shut up," Rebecca said as she let the sheaths fall to the floor. "You're not taking her anywhere. I'm going to kill you, send you to Hell, and save my friends. In that order."

"Then please hurry before I get bored with you."

Rebecca stood between Heather and Santano. She looked exhausted and angry. Her hair was tangled, her face red with tears she had been crying, but her gaze stern and unforgiving. Her hands were cut and bleeding only slightly, the blood trickling down the blades of the weapons she held. Red showed through her shirt where the wound she had gotten from Demonic Angel had reopened and bled anew. She was a mess, but she was defiant. Rebecca closed her eyes and took a deep breath to calm her storm of emotions. "God," she began, nearly a whisper at first. "Please hear my prayer. I'm ready—" She opened her eyes and spoke confidently, "to accept my destiny."

Heather was gripped with fear. Santano smiled smugly. Then they heard the rumble of distant thunder. Rebecca crossed the Heavenly Weapons and raised them skyward. She broke her stare on Santano's smug smile and raised her eyes towards the heavens. "Though I walk through the darkest valley with the shadow of death, I fear no evil for You are with me."

"Psalm of David," Santano said unimpressed. "Everyone knows that part. Can't you be more original?"

Rebecca didn't acknowledge him. "The world is entrenched in darkness. Let me be its light; its beacon of hope in the night." The rumble of thunder grew closer. Heather held the trench coat tight. Was the thunder from a coming storm; the one they had been expecting all week, or something else? "Give me the strength to protect those that need protecting," Rebecca continued. "Let me save those that need saving." The rumble had grown to a roar. Santano's smile was slipping. This was no ordinary storm. "Let me bring justice to the fallen and honor to the sacrificed. Strengthen me with Your power to free the Earth from his unholy grip." The thunder crashed. Heather covered her ears, it was so loud. "I give myself unto You! I will be Your vessel, the extension of Your justice and wrath! Lord God, make me as I was always destined to be! Your last demon hunter!"

Thunder boomed and the room flooded with light. Lightning crashed through the ceiling and struck the Heavenly Weapons. Santano and Heather shielded their eyes as Rebecca was bathed in light, becoming a pillar of pure white light. Thunder roared and wind howled as sparks of lightning danced around the surface of the pillar. The building began to shake as the pillar hummed with energy. It began to collapse on itself. Heather had no idea what was happening. "Rebecca!" she cried out, barely audible over the roar and howl of power. Santano slid across the floor inch by inch. Suddenly the energy exploded out. Santano braced against the shockwave and stood his ground but was blown back several yards. Heather was thrown to the ground and she covered her head. When the violent storm had subsided all she could hear was the hum of energy. She looked up to see Rebecca bathed in light and hovering off the ground by wings made of that same light. Slowly, her friend descended back to Earth. When she touched the ground, the light flaked off her body, from toe to head. Rebecca had changed.

Smoke rose from Rebecca's body and sparks of energy danced around her. Her fair skin had a glow to it, the cuts on her hands gone, the blood washed away. Her long blonde hair appeared light and soft and shinned as brightly as pure gold, no longer the tangled mess that it was. Her blue eyes were deep and bright, shinning like sapphires. A blue band with a small red ruby hugged her head. The redness from her tears gone, the exhaustion vanished. The clothes she wore were different now. A pink undershirt shown around a strange purple jacket. It buttoned down to her midriff then tapered off into a split tail. Down the arms of the jacket and the sides of her purple pant legs were a band of green trim. The green trimmed the jacket's tail as well. An orange belt wrapped around her waist and held a dual sheath to it, one long and curved; the other short. Her shoes, which fit snuggly on her feet, were blue and laceless.

In Rebecca's left hand she held a very different Dagger of Power. The blade was large and straight. One side of the blade's base was serrated, while the other had a blade shard protruding from it, like a second hand guard. The blade was pure steel with no hint of rust ever having touched it. The hilt was golden with emeralds at the ends of the hand guard and base of the handle. A blue stripe lined the center of the blade. In her left, where the Sword of Might had been, the rusted scimitar was no more. The scimitar had been re-forged into a mighty katana. The hilt was forged of two pairs of half folded wings encircled with a golden halo. The white handle was wrapped in yellow. The long blade of platinum hue was lined with a streak of purple. The hilt, where the blade forged together, was set with a red ruby. The wings of light flapped and faded, placing Rebecca firmly on the ground and revealing angel wings stitched to the back of her jacket. The lightning storm around her dissipated and the smoking ceased.

Four formless lights hovered near Rebecca. Santano stared on in shocked surprise. He swallowed and whispered, "Uh-oh."

Sitting on the ground, Heather gawked in awe at her friend. Rebecca was so different now. She seemed so much stronger. "Wow," was all Heather could say.

Rebecca could feel the divine energy flowing throughout her entire being. She could feel the presence of powerful entities at her side, but she never broke sight with Santano. "You're not laughing," she said.

Santano struggled to control his trembling body. What happened to Rebecca? She was totally changed. The Heavenly Weapons were totally changed. This transformation was not what he had been expecting. "You—You got some new clothes!" Santano stuttered. "So what? You're still the same girl! Nothing's changed!"

"No," Rebecca responded calmly. "You're wrong. I am justice."

"I don't care what you think you are or what you look like! I'm still going to kill you!" His face stripped of flesh, leaving only bare eyes in his sockets and a tongue in his mouth. His form blurred out of existence.

Rebecca's sword arm moved slowly and calmly. Its motion left after images that moved slightly behind its predecessor movement until it caught up. The katana's blade stood fast before her when Santano blurred into existence in front of her. The Blood Sword came down and clashed edge to edge with the Sword of Might. A force escaped the blades, rocking

Rebecca's hair back, each strand moving in unison before falling back into place. Santano stared at Rebecca in disbelief. *Impossible!* he thought. *I was in Quickstep and barely saw her move!*

Rebecca pulled her sword out into a slash, pushing Santano away. He stumbled back, her push so strong it forced him to open the distance between them. His left arm stung. He was bleeding. *When did she cut me?* He waved his sword arm by the blood and guided it with the blade. "Crimson Tide!" he shouted. He slammed the sword into the ground. The blood raced across the floor as a wave. Heather gasped as she held Angel's coat tightly. That wave would wash both her and Rebecca away.

Rebecca bared her sword before her, arched towards the wave. The Crimson Tide slammed into the sword's tip and split around it. Heather was unmoving with fear and amazement as the tide split at Rebecca's sword and washed harmlessly at their sides. The Sword of Might's blade began to glow. Light was surrounding it. Slowly, Rebecca raised it overhead. "This is for Adam," she said. "Lunar Radiance." The blade glowed like moonlight. Rebecca swung the sword, releasing the light in an expansive tide. The light ripped into Santano, pulling darkness from his body. The light pulled him back and slammed him into the doors. Santano pulled himself forward. The attack was pure moonlight. "Lunar Halo," Rebecca continued with another wave of her sword. The lunar light, before it had completely faded, drew over Santano in a ring. "Sting." The halo broke into several sharp shards and rained down on Santano, piercing his body. Blood poured from his puncture wounds as the light shards faded. "For Melissa," Rebecca added. Santano fell to a knee. Rebecca was defiantly stronger than Angel, but Santano was determined to not let that stop him. He began to laugh. "You think any of this matters?" he asked as he stood. "Look, I'm already healing. You can't stop me!"

Rebecca looked at Santano's body. It was true, his wounds were closing, but she was unimpressed. She readjusted the weapons in her hands. "Your power may be light," Santano said, "but mine is blood and you gave me a lot of it." He waved his sword over the floor, pulling the blood from it and his body. "Normally my blood disappears if it touches the ground, unless I will it not to. Now try that trick again with this." He held his sword overhead, gripping it with both hands. The blood from the floor and his body pooled around it. "Crimson Deluge!"

Santano slammed the blade into the ground. The amassed blood drove into the floor and surged up as a massive wave that reached at least ten feet high and five or six feet across. "Oh God," Heather said as she watched the wave rise up. Rebecca took one leap backwards to stand near her friend. She cut her sword across the floor as she said, "Earth Tide." The ground reeled up into its own wave and slammed into Santano's Crimson Deluge. The giant wave crashed onto the ground and shattered through. Now greatly reduced in scope the tide continued forward. Rebecca raised the Dagger of Power. "Earth Ward." The shattered ground pieces rose up and encircled the two in a number of rings. The tide slammed into the rings and finally fell. Heather and Rebecca remained unharmed.

Santano's skulled face stared in utter disbelief. Rebecca had stopped the attack completely. Suddenly she was gone. Before Santano could react, her sword sliced through his body, releasing a massive spurt of darkened blood. Santano screamed in agony as Rebecca appeared behind him, her body extended in attack. "That one was for Nicole," she said.

Santano stumbled away holding his bleeding chest. The cut was deep and clean. *She attacked me in Quickstep?* Santano thought. *How? I've always had to come out of it.* Santano could not understand how Rebecca was besting him so easily. A sharp pain pierced into Santano's back. The platinum hued blade of the katana burst from Santano's stomach. "Peter," Rebecca said. "This one's yours."

Santano pulled himself from Rebecca's blade. He raised his hand in a commanding gesture, willing his blood back into his body and speeding his healing. "I told you it's useless," Santano croaked. "I control blood. I will heal from everything you do to me."

"Then you won't die before I'm finished," Rebecca said coldly.

Santano knew if this kept up he would lose. He had to gain the upper hand. He had to start fighting, really fighting. He had become lax dealing with Angel. He could always hold back and Angel could still barely land a blow, but now it seemed his role was reversed. He spied Heather across the gym. She watched the fight in fear and awe and hadn't moved from that spot. She could give Santano the advantage. He smiled. He knew his Quickstep was faster than Rebecca's and this time he would go at full speed.

The world around Santano hushed and stagnated. Heather saw only Santano blur out of sight and then Rebecca with him. Santano ran as fast as he could, the space around him frozen in time, unmoving. He looked over his shoulder. Rebecca moved slowly as she went into Quickstep. Santano looked back towards Heather and a blur raced past him.

Heather gasped as Rebecca simply appeared in front of her, her sword bared. An instant later Santano's form blurred into existence, his neck an inch or two from the blade's point. Santano leaped back as fast as he could. He stumbled as the world spun slightly around him. He still wasn't used to that kind of speed.

"How did you—?" Santano shouted.

"You're not faster than me anymore," Rebecca replied. "What do you have to say for yourself, Mr. Santano?"

Santano quivered in rage. She was making a fool out of him. "Do you think this is funny?!" he shouted. "Making a mockery out of me?"

"You killed my friends. I find nothing funny in that."

"You little bitch! I know the angels are helping you! I know that's what that light is!"

"Angels?" Heather whispered. She looked at Rebecca's glow. "Those are...angels?"

"You know as well as I do that that power is not yours! Demon hunters aren't that strong!"

Rebecca didn't answer, but she felt that Santano was right. She could feel the angels around her; feel their hands on her, guiding her strikes. She could hear their whispers, their encouragement and guidance in the use of her powers. She could feel something else too, the knowledge of the past. It flowed out of her mind and into her limbs. The whispers told her what it was. The power of the past; the accumulated knowledge of past demon hunters surging through her. All her moves were at once foreign and familiar. It was as Angel had told her. She would never be alone, not truly. The past would be there to guide her.

"Since I don't expect them to bow down and leave you to your fate," Santano continued, "I'll bring my own help."

The voices whispered to Rebecca. "You can't," she said. "Your circle's points have been extinguished."

"I don't need a circle for this."

The voices whispered again. "Minions."

"Servants of death and decay!" Santano shouted. "Your master beckons you! Servants of the dead, come forth!"

A rumble echoed in the room. Heather quivered as she looked around, afraid something would burst out from anywhere. Rebecca's calm demeanor helped to keep her from panicking, but she was still afraid. No matter what Rebecca did to Santano, he kept getting back up. Now he was calling some kind of warriors of death to aid him. Could Rebecca stop an army?

"Rebecca," Heather said. "What's going on?"

"Don't move," Rebecca responded. "Stay exactly where you are."

Though stricken with fear, Heather nodded. "Okay."

A decrepit hand burst through the floor in front of Santano and he began to laugh. "Yes, come forth my army!" A second hand burst forth and began to pull its body free. It was male in old worn clothes. He wore a blue tattered jacket and black slacks. Dirt and dust fell from his maggot filled body and his black loafers were grimy and dirty. He stretched his stiff body, standing about five and a half feet tall. His head was nearly bare, his skin pale. His veins with cold blood in them appeared a dark blue through his skin. His eyes were stark white, lacking a pupil and his teeth were decayed. He looked as if he was a man going through Riga mortis and dug up from his grave. Santano continued to laugh as the decaying man squatted on the ground. His laughter slowly ceased as he realized nothing else was coming.

"What's going on?" Santano asked. "Where's the rest of my army?"

The decaying man looked over his shoulder and scoffed at Santano. In a weak, scrapping voice he said, "You are not our Master yet."

"What?" Santano shouted. "I am Death! I control you!"

"The true Death still commands us. You can command but one and I am here…for now."

Rebecca laughed. "What's the matter Santano? Already facing a mutiny?"

"I order you to destroy her!"

The creature looked at Rebecca. "I don't feel like it."

Heather could not help but giggle a little herself. "I guess they're on strike," she said.

"Yeah," Rebecca replied. "I guess they don't like their aspiring boss."

Santano moved his hand in a commanding gesture. "I command you to destroy Rebecca!"

The creature dropped to his knees and held his head in pain. "I will obey…for now."

Santano smiled. "That's better."

The creature stood up. Rebecca readied her sword. Heather's fear returned and she took a step back.

"It doesn't look that strong," Heather said. "Right?"

"Don't move," Rebecca said. "I'm not sure what this thing is."

The creature chuckled as it began its slow advance. "We are what happens to all beings. We are decay."

Rebecca noticed that with each slow step he took, the floor beneath him began to rot. "Heather, get back," Rebecca said.

"But you said—"

"Look at the floor. Stay far away from this thing. Don't let it touch you."

Heather watched as the wood beneath the creature's feet rotted. She nodded and ran across the room. Rebecca darted forward with great speed and swung the Sword of Might in a horizontal slash. She wanted to end this fight quickly and continue with Santano. The decay reached out with his hands and caught the blade. Blood seeped from his hands. Rebecca stared at him in shock.

The decay smiled. "So, your weapons are immune to my touch." His hands began to smoke and his blood to boil. "It seems I am not immune to its. Let's see if the same is true for you." The decay pulled a hand away and reached for Rebecca. She didn't know if she was immune to his touch or not, but she had no interest in finding out. She pulled back, pulling her sword free of his grip and cutting his hand deeper. His blood spurted out and drops hit her hand. Rebecca winced. The joints in her hand hurt and she found it troubling to hold her sword. The decay's blood splattered on her hand and jacket arm. The color around the blood faded from the jacket and the glow of her skin dimmed.

"I guess not," the decay said. He flexed his cut hands. "Impressive of you to draw blood though."

Rebecca raised her blood splattered arm to her mouth and blew on it. A cold mist escaped her lips and froze the blood. With the jeweled pommel of the dagger she smashed the frozen blood from her. The faded color and glow from the blood spots returned.

"You see?" Santano laughed. "Your angels can't protect you from everything. I told you, you can't win."

Grinning, the decay raised his hands. The cut on both were visibly mending. Rebecca readied her sword. "Make her rot," Santano said. The decay reached forward and Rebecca leaped back. She was unsure what would happen with a direct touch. How long would his power linger? The decay continued forward, closing the distance between them quickly. His speed may not have been superhuman, but it was certainly faster than his rigid body would imply. Rebecca raised her dagger and willed Psionic Shield into being. Her will alone was enough. The opaque white shield appeared in front of her and the decay slammed his hands into it. The opaque white became milky and cracked. His touch was destroying it. Rebecca could feel the force he pushed against the shield, but she did not budge.

The shield shattered and the decay moved forward. Rebecca pointed her dagger at him and a vortex of powerful winds ripped free. The decay was quickly whisked away by the vortex and slammed high into the wall. The area around him rotted and pieces of decayed wood and drywall fell to the ground with him. Upon hitting the ground, it too rotted. The decay rose to his feet and shook his head.

"Don't just stand there!" Santano wailed. "Destroy her!"

"Don't push your luck," the decay said. "I'll fight her, but I refuse to kill her. My touch is not meant to be in her immediate future."

"I don't care! Just keep pressing!"

THE LAST DEMON HUNTER

The decay rushed forward. The Sword of Might ignited as Rebecca raised it. Without a verbal command, she unleashed Eternal Fire. The flames sprang forth from the blade and created an intense wave in front of her. The decay shielded itself and barreled through the flames. The little hair he had burned and patches of fire dotted his suit and pants. He reached for Rebecca, but she evaded his touch. He continued forward, reaching out. Not trying to grab or hit her; just lay a finger on her. Rebecca weaved about his reaches and backed away in small leaps, but the decay kept the distance close. Rebecca knew she was getting close to Heather. Being so close to her friend, it would give the decay the advantage. She had to increase the distance between them. She couldn't attack it directly. The whispers guided her. Rebecca willed the ability's activation; Force Shock. She struck the decay with the Sword of Might. It did not cut him, but there was a bright flash and he was thrown back. He couldn't stay on his feet and tumbled.

The decay tumbled across the floor, leaving a trail of rot behind him. He used the tumble's momentum to spring back to his feet. He rushed forward. Rebecca nodded to the whispers. "The Meteor Strike? Okay," she whispered back. Her katana's blade once again ignited. She swung it out before her, the flames leaving a trail of fire that threw forth rock core fireballs. The decay braced itself, the fireballs striking around him and rocking him with the force of their detonations. Sword still blazing, Rebecca thrust it forward. Several more fireballs ripped free, surrounding the decay in explosive flames. The fireballs struck him and threw him yards across the room. He groaned as he slowly stood; his suit and skin burning.

The light of the moon surrounded the katana's blade as Rebecca raised it overhead. "Lunar Radiance," she said. Rebecca released the light in a swing, the moonlight washing over the floor. The decay braced himself against the wave which ripped gray matter from his body. "Lunar Halo," Rebecca continued as she waved her sword. The light collected itself over the decay in a glowing ring. "Sting." The halo broke into shards of light and rained down on the decay. He screamed as his body was pierced by nearly a dozen large shards. He fell forward onto all four, blood dripping onto the floor.

405

"I don't have to touch you directly," Rebecca said. "And I won't let you get close again."

The decay chuckled. "You are stronger than could be imagined." His body began to sink into the ground.

"Where are you going?" Santano shouted. "You're not beaten!"

"You are not my master. I will not die for you. Our bond is severed and I leave."

"Stop! Get back here!" Santano's commands were ignored and the decay returned from whence it came.

Rebecca's eyes locked onto Santano. "Where were we?" she asked. Santano looked towards Rebecca. The eyes in his sockets showed fear. She spun the Sword of Might in her hand and faced the blade downward. "Stone Spikes," she said as she drove the blade into the ground. A trail of up heaved ground darted from the sword across the floor to Santano. He took several steps back, but the trail reached him. The ground around him erupted with stone spikes that pierced his body and held him trapped. "Monica," Rebecca said.

Santano's blackened blood seeped down the stone spikes. He groaned in agony. Blood seeped from the confines of his mouth. His body twitched on the spikes. "You little bitch," he groaned. His blood boiled and sizzled on the surface of the spikes and floor. "I am...a fully realized avatar. You...are nothing." A dark mist began to form around Santano's body. "You are...a pathetic little girl. An insect." The mist grew in size and became darker. The spikes began to crack as the mist surrounded them. "You cannot...best me. You...will not...best me!" The spikes shattered and the mist enveloped Santano. "I am the end of all things!" Santano shouted; his voice was becoming deeper and hollow. "I am what all things fear!" Santano's body was consumed by the growing mist, his very being vanishing into the darkness, including the Blood Sword. "I! Am! Death!"

The mist, grown to a large mass, split open. A large skull with only brown eyes and a tongue burst from the swirling mist. It wailed as it darted across the floor. It was wrapped by a shadowy shroud that draped over its body. It floated over the ground with no legs. A pair of large skeletal hands reached from the shroud, its right holding a large crimson scimitar with two white spots etched along the sides. It swung its massive blade at Rebecca. The massive thing before her took her by surprise. She raised the Sword of Might to catch the enlarged Blood Sword edge to edge. She pressed the Dagger of Power against her sword to strengthen her hold, but she was still pushed back across the floor.

Rebecca stared at the creature before her. It was no longer Santano. It was literally the Shadow of Death. Perhaps Santano had been dead for a long time. The Shadow of Death reared back and struck a powerful blow with the Blood Sword. There was a bright flash and Rebecca's hand stung as she was pushed across the floor. She stumbled but kept her footing. *He's so strong now*, Rebecca thought. *What happened to him?* The Shadow of Death raised its sword as it glowed with dark energy. With a wail it released the energy in a wave across the floor. Rebecca quickly retaliated with Lunar Radiance. The two waves of energy slammed into each other and fought to press forward. Rebecca found herself locked in her release position. She could feel the pressure against her and she pushed back. She didn't quite understand what was going on. Little by little her feet slid across the floor. The voices urged her to concentrate. Santano had released all his power. She must do the same.

Rebecca realized how weak her previous attacks had been. She knew the words and the motions, but there was no conviction behind them. It was the bare minimum of power. Now Santano wasn't holding back. He had accepted she was stronger and released all his power. Rebecca knew she had more strength, but she wasn't sure of her limits. Putting more conviction into the attack, her latest Lunar Radiance was stronger than its predecessors, but Santano was still winning. She was afraid to go at him any harder. Her power was already hard to control. What was the point in defeating Santano if her own power killed Heather in the process? Heather had to live. If she didn't, what was the point of Angel's sacrifice? What was the point of her fighting?

In her moment of weakness, the Shadow of Death's attack broke through. The darkness washed over Rebecca. She screamed as it pulled the light from her body and threw her to the ground. "You see girl?" the specter spoke in a deep eerie tone. "Darkness will always consume the light."

Rebecca calmly rose to her feet, though her body ached. "And from within the light will always chase away the darkness," she said. She stumbled a bit on her feet as her glow returned. "I won't let you win." Rebecca disappeared. The Shadow of Death moved its sword and caught Rebecca's strike, forcing her out of Quickstep. The Shadow of Death drew its blade back, as did Rebecca. Their weapons clashed with a loud clang and bright flash. They were pushed back and pressed forward again, repeating their force shock attacks over and over again.

Heather twisted Angel's jacket in her hands as she anxiously watched the battle. Her life, the very existence of the world, hung in the balance. Whether she lived or died, if life itself would continue to exist, would be determined by the victor. Santano had become a frightening aberration towering over Rebecca. Just looking at it, Heather could feel the dread of death. She watched as the two traded blows back and forth, being pushed back and rushing forward again. The lights surrounding Rebecca weaved back and forth with her. "Come on," Heather whispered. "You can beat him. I have faith in you."

The Shadow of Death flew back, opening the distance between itself and Rebecca. Her swing hit nothing as the specter retreated, its sword swirling with dark energy. Rebecca leaped back but the specter released it too quickly. Rebecca caught the dark wave with her sword and struggled against it, but it was too strong. It knocked her off her feet and threw her high into the wall. Rebecca's body cracked the surface and pieces fell with her to the floor.

"You're not worth my time," the Shadow of Death groaned. "I will finish the sacrifices."

The specter sped towards Heather, its boney hand reaching out for her. Paralyzed with fear, Heather could only scream. Rebecca's form blurred and she was gone. She blurred back into existence between Heather and the cold hand of death. She caught the skeletal hand with the Heavenly Weapons. Though pushed back, Rebecca did hold her ground. Rebecca pushed back, forcing the Shadow of Death to give ground. Rebecca continued forward, attacking the shadow relentlessly, pushing it back. Their swords clashed again and again as the shadow drew back.

"I won't let you hurt her!" Rebecca exclaimed.

"You can't stop me!" the specter boomed.

The Shadow of Death thrust its hand forward as it withdrew. A force escaped from it and halted Rebecca's advance. It held the Blood Sword out and placed its hand to the blade. "Crown of Sins!" Rebecca started to advance again but was stopped when a dark thorny ring appeared around her. "Binding!" The thorns shot out and pierced all over Rebecca's body. She screamed as the ring closed tightly around her, binding her in its thorny embrace. "Break free!" the voices whispered. Rebecca struggled against the dark bindings. All of her body burned, everywhere the ring and thorns touched.

"You will not escape it," the specter assured. "The sacrifices will continue as planned."

The ruby on Rebecca's forehead began to glow. She pulled hard against the bindings. Her eyes shined and with a shout of "No!" she broke free of her confines.

The Shadow of Death's blade began to swirl with an immense energy. "It doesn't matter if you die now or later," it said. "You're not necessary!"

Battle wary and hurt, Rebecca held the Sword of Might forward as it began to glow with swirling moonlight. She concentrated. It had to be stronger. They both raised their swords overhead as their energy and light swirled about their weapons. They verbally released their attack in unison.

"Black Wind!"

"Lunar Radiance!"

The moonlight and dark wind raced across the ground and slammed into each other. They pushed against each other, trying to break through. The whispers urged concentration and focus. The ruby jewel on Rebecca's blue headband glowed brightly. Rebecca poured her strength into her attack. The moonlight beat back the dark wind only to be overtaken again. Shards of energy ripped off as they struggled, ripping holes in the room. The Shadow of Death grew as it shouted. The Black Wind grew against the Lunar Radiance and finally overtook it. Overtaking the Lunar Radiance ripped the Black Wind in half and caused it to sprawl erratically forward. It had lost much of its power as it broke through Rebecca's attack. Rebecca slashed into the first wave and shattered it completely. The second arched over her as it deflected off the ground. Rebecca had thrown her weight behind her sword, trying to hit the second wave, but with its last minute arch, she missed.

Rebecca watched helplessly as the second half of the Black Wind barreled towards Heather. "No!" the Shadow of Death shouted. Heather screamed as she braced herself. Rebecca was too off balance to shift into Quickstep. She could do nothing to protect her friend. By holding back she had allowed an opening. Now she could do nothing but watch Heather die, and in turn watch the Shadow of Death die without its sacrifice. Rebecca had failed.

An Irish accented giggle echoed in Rebecca's ears. The world slowed, including herself. She could not stop the remnant of the Black Wind.

"Shall I save her?" a familiar voice asked.

"Yes," Rebecca answered.

"Will you do what you must?"

"Yes."

"Very well. Do not disappoint sweetness."

Life returned to the world. The Shadow of Death moved forward as Rebecca caught herself and spun around. The Black Wind was upon Heather. Suddenly, the Black Wind struck something and came to an abrupt halt. It was thrown away, across the room and slammed into the wall. Deep gashes etched the impact zone. Úna stood with a defiant grin and one arm outstretch toward the gashed wall.

"Don't worry sweetness," Úna said. "I'll protect the little sun flower." She pointed towards the specter. "You deal with that."

Knowing what she must do, Rebecca nodded and faced the skulled shadow.

Heather stared at Úna, almost as if she recognized her. Úna looked over her shoulder with a childish grin. "Úna?" Heather mumbled.

"Who are you?" the Shadow of Death shouted.

"Don't worry about her," Rebecca said. "Worry about me."

"You? What are you going to do?"

"Not hold back."

Rebecca's blue headband and ruby began to glow in unison. Its glow resonated a glowing halo above her as energy erupted around her. The etched wings on the back of her jacket grew and expanded into real feathered wings with over a fourteen foot wingspan. Her entire body began to glow as she released all her power. The Shadow of Death in turn did the same, howling as its form darkened and mist rose from it. The building shook with their rising power. Heather quivered. It was about to get more intense? Úna laughed gleefully. She looked back to Heather. "Now we'll see some real action!"

The Shadow of Death moved and found Rebecca's hand instantly on his face. She threw him across the room with one thrust and slammed him into the wall. It crumbled beneath him, his red field the only thing stopping any further decent. Heather stared on in awe. Rebecca was flying. Rebecca flapped her wings once towards the specter. Dozens of feathers flew free and shot towards the shadow and rained down upon him. They pierced his body as if they were sharp as steel. Smoke and debris rose from the destruction as the shadow was punctured towards the ground.

"That was for Jason you monster," Rebecca said.

Screaming, the Shadow of Death rushed forward. It swung its sword with all its might, but Rebecca deflected it away with a single counter cut. The shadow drew back and began to stab wildly. Rebecca weaved around each thrust of the sword, the blade not once touching her. The shadow drew back again and gathered swirling darkness around its blade. Rebecca blew, a cold cone traveling the distance between them and freezing the shadow, making its movements rigid. Rebecca held the Sword of Might to the side and it ignited in a blaze. "This one is for Michael." She dashed forward, afterimages trailing behind her. She attacked the shadow from all sides, Rebecca invisible to the naked eye, flames bursting from the shadow's frozen form. Seven strikes.

The ice shattered and the shadow fell to the floor. Rebecca landed on her feet before it. It dragged its sword across the floor slowly and in agony. Rebecca walked up to the sword and slammed her foot down on the blade.

"For my mom and my dad." Moonlight swirled around the Sword of Might. With a commanding shout Rebecca released her Lunar Radiance with such concentrated force that the shadow broke through its crimson field. Rebecca looked down at the massive blade beneath her foot. The Sword of Might began to glow a bright white. "This is for all the members of my family, both known and unknown." She touched her glowing sword to the crimson blade. "Purify." The large blade began to crack. The shadow wailed in pain and stumbled back into the gym. "Get away from that!" it echoed. The light spread away from the Sword of Might and onto the Blood Sword. Rebecca backed away as the Shadow of Death reached for his sword. "Shatter." Rebecca said. The Blood Sword exploded into countless pieces and with it so did the specter's right hand.

The Shadow of Death wailed and reached for Rebecca. With one swing of her sword his left hand was gone, shattered into countless pieces. The shadow screeched and drew back. "That was for Angel, and everyone else you hurt."

The Shadow of Death began to grow as it wailed. The building shook. The weakened walls gave way to the ceiling and pieces began to fall. Heather covered her head as boards and beams began to tumble. Úna raised her hand and each piece deflected and shattered on an invisible shield. "Don't look away," she said. "You'll miss the best part."

Rebecca raised her dagger and it began to glow. "It is time to end this," she said calmly. With a quick motion, Rebecca threw the dagger at the Shadow of Death. It struck true and the glow became a bright light that bound itself around the shadow and anchored it to the ground.

"What is this?" it screamed. "What are you doing to me?"

"Angel said every demon hunter has a unique attack," Rebecca said as the Sword of Might began to glow. "This is mine." She held the sword overhead and the light glowed ever brighter. The sword began to shake and hum with power. Rebecca slowly reached her free hand up and gripped the handle with both. "This is the end, Samuel Santano." The sword shook in her hands.

"It's not fair!" the shadow wailed. "It's not fair!"

"You're right," Rebecca agreed. "It's not fair. You killed my friends and destroyed our families. You tried to kill Heather and me. You destroyed our lives. It'll never be the same. That's what's not fair. Good-bye, Samuel Santano."

Rebecca's wings flapped and took her off the ground. "Final Judgment!" The glow shot straight up and solidified into a blade of pure light. With a shout Rebecca brought it down on the wailing shadow. The ground beneath it buckled as the blade of light came down his center. The binds shattered and the light drew inside of him. When Rebecca pulled her hands apart, the Dagger of Power was back where it belonged.

A bright white line divided the dark creature in half. Cracks of seeping light appeared throughout its being. Its form bloated as the light within expanded and tried to escape. The shadow finally broke, revealing a skull-faced Santano. His screams filled the halls as his face cracked with light. His skull shattered, leaving behind only a mortal man. His body cracked and filled with light. "I was so close!" he screamed before the light escaped. His body was destroyed, blown to oblivion. The energy of the light condensed and then blew out again. A massive gnarled hand had burst from the floor. Light escaped around it as it pulled the floor open. Tendrils slithered around the opening and began to pull. Rebecca stood her ground, holding the Heavenly Weapons tightly.

"What's happening?" Heather asked. "What is that?"

"Hell's gate keeper is prying open the jaws of Hell," Úna answered. "You are witnessing a Salvation of Souls."

Rebecca relaxed her grip. She had heard Úna. The voices whispered the same. Abaddon was opening Hell's Gate.

The gate was pulled open. Smoke wafted from the sides and the tendrils held it open as the hands withdrew. Light ascended to the heavens. "Rebecca," a lost voice said. "Thank you."

Surprise filled Rebecca's face. "Melissa?"

"You saved us," Melissa said. "Thank you."

Melissa, robed in white, emerged first. Her throat never slit. Her body never hurt. Her face was peaceful, serene and grateful.

"We always had faith in you," Peter said as he rose after.

Monica followed. "Thank you Rebecca," she said. "I'm so sorry for what I said."

Rebecca's eyes filled with tears. "Don't be."

Monica smiled. "Thank you. Good-bye Rebecca. Heather."

Heather dropped to her knees. Tears flowed down her face. She couldn't believe her eyes. "Our…friends," she said.

Úna looked at her and smiled. She placed a hand on her shoulder. "Yes, they are free." She looked back to Rebecca. "Good job cup cake," she whispered. She turned and walked away, simply disappearing.

Heather and Rebecca watched as their friends slowly rose out of Hell. First Adam, then Nicole, each saying their thanks and final good-byes. They reached for each other and pulled each other close. Michael followed.

"Michael," Rebecca gasped.

"Wait," he pleaded. His ascent stopped. He floated from the rising light and touched the ground. As he approached Rebecca, his spirit solidified. The Heavenly Weapons clanged on the ground when Rebecca dropped them. Tears ran down her face as she stared at him. Tentatively, she touched his face, trying to prove to herself that he was really there. She had watched him die. She was sobbing when he took her hand and kissed it. "Thank you Rebecca, for everything." Rebecca threw her arms around him and hugged him tightly. She cried into his shoulder.

"I love you," she said.

Michael returned her embrace. "I love you too Becca, so very much. I'll miss you."

She held him tighter. "No, don't go!"

"I'm sorry Becca. I have to. Be strong, okay?"

"I don't want to."

"Please? For me?"

Rebecca fought to control her sobs. "Okay. I will."

Michael slipped through her arms, his body reverting to an insubstantial spirit. He lingered, holding her hands. The afterlife called to him. Jason had already risen and answered that call. "Come on," Jason said. "It's time to go. Thanks Rebecca. It was good to know you. Good-bye Heather."

Rebecca tried to hold Michel's hands, but his spirit slipped through. "I don't want you to go."

"I want to stay with you too, but I can't. You know that. Be strong sweetheart." He had been pulled back into the light and continued his ascent. "We all have faith in you. You can win this. Just believe in yourself. I do. We all do." He blew her a kiss. "Good-bye Rebecca. I'll love you always."

Rebecca took a few steps forward. "I love you too."

Then Michael was gone. The tendrils withdrew, allowing the jaws of Hell to close and with it the ascending light of Heaven. All that remained were Heather and Rebecca. The dead had gone and the battle was over. Rebecca fell to her knees. The glow of her body faded, her clothes glowed and pulled away as she fell, leaving behind what she wore before her ascension. The Heavenly Weapons glowed and changed. The large bladed dagger changed to a thin pointed dagger with a single steel strip for a hand guard. The handle's grip was black steel. The katana's blade straightened and the hilt changed. The Sword of Might had become a straight sword. The hand guard was silver with a slight upward curl and blue hand wrap and tail at the handle. Rebecca felt the power of the angels pull away and Heather could no longer see the light. Rebecca wiped away her tears and looked at Heather. She tried to smile. Heather could do nothing but return the bittersweet smile with tears in her eyes. The battle was won. The nightmare was finally over.

EPILOGUE

The sun was just beginning to break through the horizon that Sunday morning before Heather and Rebecca had the strength to brave the outside world. They sat on the steps of the school. Both were quiet. Heather looked out at the sleeping world; at the houses that lined the street. Heather found herself envious of them all. No one knew of the intense battle for life that took place across the street from them. No one knew how close the world came to ending.

Rebecca stared out blankly at the world. Her face was red with fresh tears she had cried. She had strapped the Heavenly Weapons at either side of her. Angel's coat, which was a little too big, kept them from sight. It wasn't necessary. Somehow, Rebecca knew that. She didn't have to hide the Heavenly Weapons. Angel's jacket was heavy with his articles, but Rebecca didn't mind. It kept her savior, and a piece of her family, close to her. It was hard to believe that she was truly the last of her family. She was the sole remaining Virtue, the last of a bloodline. It hurt, but she was unable to cry. Perhaps it hurt too much, or because she didn't have the time to mourn. The Sword of Might was warning her of a new avatar.

"Is it...over?" Heather asked after long moments of silence.

"Yes," Rebecca answered as she lowered her eyes to the ground. Her hands were lined with light scars from the cuts she had given herself with the Dagger of Power. "This nightmare is over."

"What do we do now?"

"You continue living," Rebecca answered as she stood and descended the steps. "Never forget our family and friends."

"Yeah. Our parents will be glad to know we're alright."

Rebecca shook her head. "I don't have a family anymore."

"Rebecca, that's not true."

416

Rebecca turned to face her friend. "Yes, it is. Everyone I know, every relation I had, is dead. I am the last one. I'm all alone."

"No, you're not. You still have me."

Rebecca smiled. Her eyes began to finally swell with tears. "Thank you Heather. That means a lot to me, but…"

"But what?"

Slowly, the tears began to run down Rebecca's face. "This is where we have to say good-bye."

"Good-bye? Why? Where are you going?"

Rebecca's tears flowed freely now. "I'm the demon hunter now. This is my fight. I'm the only one that can hold them back. I'm the last."

"That can't be true."

"It is. Hell made sure of it. And I could never carry a baby while doing this. I'm the last of my blood. There will be no more demon hunters after me." She turned and began to walk away.

Heather ran down the stairs and grabbed Rebecca's arm. "Wait!" she called. "There has to be something I can do to help."

"Remember," Rebecca said. "No one else will. Our friends are dead and their case will go cold. For the world, Angel and Santano will have both just disappeared. My family has been killed and it will be blamed on a disease. They will all be mourned. But me?" She shook her head. "No one will remember me. I'll just be forgotten and at the end, no one will mourn my death." Rebecca gently pulled Heather's hand away and smiled. "So just remember me, okay?" A green mist began to seep from the sheathed dagger at her side. "Do that for me. Good-bye Heather. I'll miss you."

The smoke enveloped Rebecca and she was gone. Heather reached for her but could not find her. "Rebecca!" Heather called into the wind. "Remember, I'll always be there for you!" She sighed and whispered, "I'll always be your friend. Good-bye, Rebecca Virtue."

***

Úna sat atop the school roof, kicking her legs playfully over the edge. She watched as Heather braved the winter's cold without a coat on her return home. She was lucky. An angel tailed her, helping to keep her warm in the cold. Úna looked towards the east with a mischievous grin across her lips. "Run, run little demon hunter," she said. "Hell is on your heels."